Chained!

Chained!

Lauren Henderson

HUTCHINSON
LONDON

First published in the United Kingdom in 2000 by Hutchinson

The Random House Group Limited
20 Vauxhall Bridge Road, London SW1V 2SA

Random House Australia (Pty) Limited
20 Alfred Street, Milsons Point, Sydney,
New South Wales 2061, Australia

Random House New Zealand Limited
18 Poland Road, Glenfield
Auckland 10, New Zealand

Random House (Pty) Limited
Endulini, 5a Jubilee Road, Parktown 2193, South Africa

The Random House Group Limited Reg. No. 954009
www.randomhouse.co.uk

A CIP catalogue record for this book is available
from the British Library

Papers used by Random House are natural,
recyclable products made from wood grown in sustainable forests.
The manufacturing processes conform to the environmental
regulations of the country of origin

ISBN 009 1800501 Trade paperback
ISBN 009 1800455 Hardback

Typeset by Deltatype Ltd, Birkenhead, Merseyside
Printed and bound in Great Britain by
Mackays of Chatham plc, Chatham, Kent

Acknowledgements

Much gratitude to Margot Gavan Duffy and everyone I met on 'How Do You Want Me 2 – The Second Coming' for sharing with me the fast-paced, action-packed world of a BBC shoot. Except the caterers. I ate so much I thought I was going to explode. Thanks too to Lars Macfarlane, who answered lots of inane questions about TV productions, and to the friend – who wants to remain nameless – who gave me all the hunt sab information. As usual, any factual errors are not due to my own shoddy research techniques or inability to read my own notes, but are entirely the fault of my interviewees.

CHAPTER ONE

Someone had been using my head for staple gun practice. If I shut my eyes and concentrated I could even make out the cluster formation they had used. But consciousness was filtering back in fits and starts. It took a little longer to realise that I was handcuffed.

Neither of these scenarios was unusual enough to cause me to panic. Yet. I tried lifting my head a fraction to see if any of the staples had gone right through. That was when the real pain kicked in. Impossible to tell which was worse: the red throbbing shock-waves of agony as my head came up, or the nasty thud as it hit the ground again.

Normally – if I could use that word in this context – when I woke up badly hungover, I had a violent thirst and my head hurt all over. This time the thirst was noticeable only by its absence, and the pain was much more localised, as if I had been kicked in the back of the skull by a donkey with world-class hoof action. And despite my rather louche lifestyle, I did not make a habit of passing out on cold paving stones.

The handcuffs were less puzzling. Though it did seem odd that I had fallen asleep in them.

Great waves of pain were radiating from the back of my head like the diagrams in a headache advertisement, bands of red and purple and yellow clamping around my skull, each one pulsating evilly on a different frequency. Where was my Solpadeine? Desperation finally prised open my eyes. The lids rasped up like metal screens, grinding as they went. At least the scene before me caused me to forget my physical discomfort for a few moments. My jaw would have dropped if I hadn't been lying on my side.

I

I had vaguely imagined that I would find myself on a patio in someone's back garden after some sex game had taken a turn for the bizarre. That would have been bad enough. Instead I was in some sort of cellar, long and narrow. Stone flags stretched away from me to a door I could dimly make out at the far end of the room. It was dark, but a faint pale light was filtering in dimly from above my head. Turning painfully onto my back, I made out two horizontal slits of window, set high up in the stone walls and probably too narrow for an anorexic nine-year-old to climb through. The question was moot. An anorexic nine-year-old could have stepped up on one of the stone troughs conveniently positioned in front of the windows, but would then barely manage to pass his or her arm through the bars directly in front of the glass.

And yes, thoughts of escape had begun to percolate through my brain. This was probably because, as I turned over, I had heard the unmistakable sound of a heavy chain slithering across the floor behind me. I raised my hands and shook them experimentally. The chain rattled. How Gothic. I tugged at it. Above me, something creaked. I squinted up into the gloom. The chain was looped round a beam overhead, running down on either side to meet the handcuffs. Twisting one hand round, I fingered the join. It was soldered quite smoothly, probably a better job than I could have done myself. My soldering had never been that hot.

What the hell was going on? If this were meant as a practical joke I found it about as funny as a case of the clap. But I didn't really think it was a joke. Something about the way that chain was soldered to the handcuffs had had a sobering effect. Besides, it wasn't April Fool's Day. As far as I remembered, we were in October. Lucky for me it wasn't winter yet. It was already so cold in the cellar my teeth were chattering.

I tugged at the chain once more, grabbing it above the handcuffs and pulling as hard as I could, again and again, putting all my weight on it till my sore muscles screamed in protest. Though I made the beam creak like an old oak staircase with the jitters, that was all; the chain didn't give. I collapsed back on the floor, already exhausted, the adrenaline ebbing fast. Reaching my hands to my skull, I explored the sorest area. There was a lump on the back of my head the size of a squashed orange.

One of my feet bumped against something soft, and for a moment I thought there was someone else in the cellar with me. Poking it further, I realised with disbelief that it was a pillow. I scrabbled it up and manoeuvred it under my head. It smelt of damp and floral air freshener, in that order, but I was too punch-drunk to care.

My eyes were closing. The effort of rattling my chain had sent me into the twilight zone again. I let my head sink into the pillow and passed out almost immediately. I was good at that.

It was much brighter in the cellar when I woke up for the second time. The sunlight glittered off the flagstones to great effect. I was particularly struck by the twin parallelograms of shadow stripes cast by the window bars, one on each side of the room.

What the hell I was doing here was as much of a mystery as it had been the last time I regained consciousness. Still, my head was hurting less, which meant I could sit up without screaming. Result, as Lurch would have said.

Then I practically did scream, at my own idiocy. About four feet away from me, just far enough so I hadn't rolled onto it in my sleep, was a pallet with a couple of blankets trailing over it. And I had spent all night on the stone floor. My bones felt so infused with damp I could have filled a bucket with what I wrung out of the marrow. The pillow hadn't helped much. I had a crick in my neck which could only have been sorted out by an osteopath who specialised in twenty-stone wrestlers.

I heaved myself to my feet, wincing with pain, and looked around the room. On the other side was a drainage channel cut into the floor with a large metal grille set at the far end. Directly above the grille was a tap in the wall, and on the edge of the channel were propped a few rolls of toilet paper and an air freshener spray. Thoughtfully, I stared at the latter object for a while. The whole scenario was certainly preferable to a brimming bucket. And Turkish-style squat-over-a-hole-in-the-floor toilets were supposed to be more hygienic than the sit-down version. As long as nothing got stuck to the grille.

I transferred my gaze to the other side of what I supposed I would have to call my cell. With a surge of excitement I suddenly spotted a small pile of Tupperware and what looked like a Thermos beyond the pallet. I was across it in a single bound. Dragging my chain with me in a triumph of impromptu choreography, I ripped open the largest box.

In it was a stack of sandwiches. I lifted the top slice of bread to check out the filling. Vegemite. So was the one below it, and the one below that, and the one below that . . . I sagged back on my heels, disappointed. I hadn't been expecting smoked salmon and cream cheese bagels, but some egg and cress, or tuna, would have been nice to break the monotony. Ah well, food was food. I snarfed down two of the sandwiches, saving the others. Best to pace myself. The other Tupperware container was filled with chunks of carrot. I stared at it in disbelief. Maybe this was some kind of diet prison camp for which I had signed up in a particularly drunken moment. We'll chain you up and feed you raw vegetables and loads of vitamin B12 for a week! Purify those clogged-up intestines, and fast!

By this time I was not expecting the Thermos to hold lobster bisque with herb croutons and a swirl of heavy cream. Thus I was not disappointed when I unscrewed the top to find it full of black coffee. I took a cautious sip. Sweetened. Damn. And Nescafé into the bargain. There was no mistaking instant coffee, the way it promised richness and then melted immediately on your tongue, leaving a flat, bitter aftertaste. I took a longer pull at it anyway.

The fools! Didn't they realise how dangerous it was to give me caffeine? Already my headache was fading and the blood was racing faster. Forget your beaker full of the warm South, this was the business if you found yourself chained to the ceiling of someone's back basement. I screwed the cap of the Thermos back on, resisting temptation to drink deeply. Who knew when I would have a refill? Then I took another long surveyal of my surroundings. My bladder was bursting. I could put off squatting over that grille no longer. Gloomily I approached it, my chain rattling behind me. At least the sanitary arrangements were cleaner than my own toilet. White showed the dirt so badly. Next time I installed a bathroom I would make sure I bought a chocolate-coloured suite.

Pretty much everything hurt, but squatting was the worst. Not to mention wiping myself with my hands cuffed together. I was fuelled with caffeine and getting angrier by the minute. When I got hold of whoever had done this to me I would kick the living daylights out of them. And that was a promise.

'Kick the shit out of him! Nah, not like that! For fuck's sake, Chaz, put some sodding effort into it, why don't you?'

'Like this, Gav?'

Chaz redoubled his efforts. Gav gave a long, slow sigh and took another pull on his cigar.

'Jesus, Chaz, you – are – fucking – *crap* at this,' he said wearily. 'Look.'

With a single leisurely movement, he swung himself up from the battered old kitchen chair on which he had been sprawling. Slowly he strolled across the room to Chaz and the huddled body at his feet. It whimpered at his approach.

'You're just going at it with no science,' Gav continued. 'Couldn't you hear him still bloody whining when you were giving it to him? He shouldn't be making a fucking sound, Chaz. Not a sound. He should be too fucking scared to open his tiny mouth. Right?' He aimed one precision kick at the foetally curled-up body. 'Watch that. Did'ja see? Get it in the right place, he'll open up like a flower. Just for that moment. It's a work of art if you do it right.'

Chaz nodded eagerly. A few beads of sweat ran down his forehead, gleaming like glycerine against the darkness of his skin. He took a step forward.

'Wait a minute,' Gav said impatiently. 'We got all day. Might as well take this window of opportunity to give you a training session. Here, hold this.'

He passed Chaz his cigar. Chaz took it as solemnly as if it were a communion wafer.

'Now, watch where I'm putting them. Check it out.'

Circling his victim's body, he placed three kicks, spacing them out with deliberate sadism. In contrast to Chaz and the man on the ground, Gav was white, very light-skinned, with fair hair and a long, thin, haughty nose. He was tall and would have been handsome if not for the twist of his mouth and the coldness in his grey eyes. Pounding his foot into the unresisting flesh beneath him, he breathed evenly with the effort, as if he were working out, and when he came to a halt he stretched his arms back behind him and smiled at Chaz, a peculiarly unpleasant smile, his lips hardly moving.

'Your turn,' he said. 'And Chaz?' He left a little pause. 'Get it right this time.'

There was a pause. Then:

'Cut!' came the director's voice. 'Good. Print and check.'

The slump of relief from cast and crew was felt rather than heard.

'Printing and checking,' the first AD responded.

'If the gate's clear we've done that one,' said the director, leaning back in his chair. 'Nice work, everyone.'

Movement whirred around the actors as people who had been standing still, watching the scene, or moving slowly with the camera, came to life. Gav promptly turned to squint around the wall o'lights.

'Is there a glass of water anywhere around?' he said plaintively.

A girl in layers of fleecy jackets bustled towards him with a brimming paper cup. He swigged down its contents.

'Thank God for that,' he said, relaxing. 'Those cigars are *foul*. Hard to believe the BBC budget couldn't run to something slightly better. They taste like they were rolled on the withered old thighs of Panamanian mule-herders. Excuse me while I spit.'

'Don't worry about me, you cunt,' said the kickee, slowly unwinding himself and standing up. 'Don't bloody ask me how I am.'

'You're always fine, Tony,' Gav said dismissively. 'You have *padding*. Whereas I have already stubbed my toe twice in these over-tight, ridiculous boots.'

'I'll stub you, you cunt.' Tony faked a punch at Gav's face.

'Such paucity of vocabulary,' the latter lamented. He dropped the banter for a moment. 'You're all right, aren't you? I got you square where the X marks the spot.'

'Yeah, fine, mate. Your aim's getting better with practice.'

'Tell me we've made perfect,' Gav pleaded, looking out beyond the lights. 'Tell me that's it.'

'Yeah, the gate's clear,' said the camera operator. 'At ease, men.'

'OK, setting up for the next scene,' said the first AD in the over-loud, officious voice which seemed to be the main requirement for assistant directors. 'Let's not waste any time, please.'

'Thank fuck for that,' the actor playing Chaz said fervently. 'I'm sweating like a pig. Time for a shower.' He flashed a smile at Gav. 'Hey, Hugo, fancy coming to rub my back?'

'Not even if you drop the soap, Keith.'

'Can't blame a boy for trying.'

One of the costume assistants appeared, camera in hand, and took photographs of each actor in turn for the files. This procedure was so automatic that they just stood still for a split second as the Polaroid flashed and whirred then kept on with whatever they had been doing before, like a freeze-frame.

'I need some more revolting tea,' Hugo announced. 'And a good cleanse.'

Another girl wandered up, bearing two polystyrene cups. In her battered leather trousers and baggy sweater she looked at first glance like any of the other crew members busy around the set. Until you noticed her face, matt with foundation and powder, highlighted so that its planes caught and held the attention even more than they did naturally. She was the only woman present wearing make-up and its careful detailing gave her a half-mask, half-human appearance, striking but alien.

'Hugo? Tea, darling,' she said with the slightly exaggerated enunciation that immediately marked her out as an actress.

'A ministering angel thou,' Hugo said gratefully, accepting the cup. 'Thank you, my little junkie lovebird. I need it desperately. Being Gav is so exhausting. All that thrusting the jaw forward menacingly – very hard on the mandibles,' he complained, in his normal Brideshead intonation.

This was just as fake as Gav's East End accent – Hugo had been brought up in relative poverty in Surbiton – but he had been drawling in Oxbridge for so long that it was second nature to him now. Still, he knew perfectly well that second nature wasn't first.

7

Hugo was acutely aware of the difference between pose and reality. It made him a very good actor, if a bloody annoying boyfriend.

'Well, I'll be off,' Keith announced with what seemed like unnecessary emphasis. 'See you guys tomorrow, I'm done for the day.'

'Lucky you,' Hugo sighed. The little junkie lovebird ignored Keith's exit a shade too pointedly.

'Long day,' she commented to Hugo, sipping at her own cup. She fiddled absently with the scrunchie holding back her dark ponytail. 'At least they've kept *you* busy.'

'I'm always busy,' Hugo retorted. 'I am the Anti-Hero. What have you been up to?'

'Oh, messing around with power tools as usual. Practising. It really kills the time.'

'Have you got any better?'

'I don't think so. But at least I look as if I know what I'm doing. Lurch was quite impressed for about ten minutes this morning.'

I nudged Lurch. He was sitting next to me on a folding chair tilted precariously back against the wall.

'Were you impressed, you bastard?' I muttered.

'Nah,' he said loyally. 'But she kept rabbiting on so I just said somefing to shut her up.'

I grunted. It was bad enough training up someone to be me without my sidekick going over to the enemy camp.

'What does Sam think?' Hugo was asking the enemy camp. 'Is she around? Sam?' he called round the corner of the set. 'Where are you?'

'You gonna answer him or what?' Lurch said to me, rocking back and forth on his chair as if he were imitating the dead mother in *Psycho*. His skin was at the apex of its regular breakout cycle at the moment; that, together with his general state of extreme emaciation, would have made him an ideal stand-in for a rotting corpse of either sex.

'Yeah. I'm just not going to jump up when he calls my name straight away, OK? I have my dignity.'

'Got a chip on your shoulder, more like,' Lurch muttered. I stuck my nose in the air and pretended not to hear.

'Sam!' Hugo sounded petulant. It was time. I stood up and strolled over to him and Sarah.

'Darling!' he said with gratifying enthusiasm. 'How was I?'

Lurch and I always got the giggles when we watched Hugo doing Gav.

'It was really good,' I said, suppressing a grin. 'Um, very convincing.'

Hugo looked at me narrowly.

'What?' he said, his tone suspicious.

'No, nothing . . .' I was choking back the laughter. 'You were great . . . especially when you were kicking him . . .'

I would have managed to keep my cool if Hugo hadn't chosen precisely that moment to flick a pastel Sobranie out of his cigarette case. It was so not Gav. I started sniggering.

'Always so supportive, my sweet,' Hugo said coldly. 'I feel so lucky to have you.'

'It must be funny for Sam, though,' Sarah said sympathetically. 'It's hard for non-actors.'

I resented this. 'I met Hugo when he was playing Oberon,' I pointed out.

'Yes, but that wasn't so much of a stretch, was it?' Sarah observed. 'I mean, the king of the fairies . . .'

'Probably my career high point,' Hugo said, taking a long drag on his cigarette. 'Never will I be that perfectly type-cast again. I was pretty good,' he added complacently, the memory of his reviews having restored his mood.

Just then Joanne, the make-up girl responsible for Sarah, came towards our little group. She and her sidekick Julie were the only ones, apart from the actors, to wear make-up on set, and Joanne favoured a bright lipstick lurid enough to make me crave sunglasses the occasional horrible morning I had had an early call. Everyone had made jokes about it in the early weeks but seemed to have settled down to it now. Oddly enough, considering her job, the colour didn't do anything for her. Or maybe that wasn't so unusual. I'd known fashion stylists who couldn't dress themselves to save their lives.

'Sarah, could you come back to the trailer?' she said. 'I need to have a go at you again while they're setting up.'

She looked at Hugo. 'Your skin looks *great*, Hugo,' she observed, with more coquetry in her tone than professional comment. 'Are you still having those facials?'

'Religiously. I bow down before the altar of Elizabeth Arden twice a week.'

'Mmn.' Joanne reached up to stroke his cheek. 'Lovely and soft.'

Sarah rolled her eyes at me. I appreciated the solidarity. Joanne was famously flirtatious; film sets were usually male-dominated, and Joanne made the most of the imbalance. The girls who worked as crew members dressed in the shapeless utility gear most suitable for humping stuff around or getting covered in paint. Joanne, with her lipstick and mascara and bottom-hugging jeans, was a fashion-plate by contrast, and she made it clear that she knew it. Any remotely attractive actor she considered her rightful prey. Hugo, however, would never succumb. He wouldn't have dreamed of going to bed with a girl whose lipstick didn't suit her complexion.

With a last pat on his cheek, she flashed him a come-hither smile and turned back to Sarah.

'God, why can't I be Sam,' Sarah sighed. 'Wearing a nice welding mask that covers my face. No muss, no fuss. All right, Joanne, off we go.'

She followed the latter out of the studio. I watched Sarah disappear through the door with my usual mixed feelings. She was perfectly amicable with me; I liked her, but there was something about her that kept me from being more than moderately friendly. It was understandable enough. Not only did she have a series of almost clinically explicit sex scenes with Hugo, but part of the character she played was based on me. Either would have been enough to set anyone's teeth on edge.

'Those trousers look much better on you,' Hugo said, sensing my ill humour.

'They hang better on Sarah,' I said crossly.

'She's thin, darling, that's why. She is an ACT-ress. ACT-resses are contractually obliged to remove their bottoms by whatever means necessary. Come here and let me pinch yours to remind myself of what I'm missing whenever I have to get naked with her.'

I scowled to pretend I wasn't flattered.

'God, you've been working out,' Hugo said respectfully. 'Hard as the Rock of Gibraltar, though much more scenic . . .'

'Hugo?' called the director. 'Can we have a rehearsal?'

'Coming, coming.' He stubbed out his cigarette. 'Later,' he said, giving my bottom one last grope. 'I have to go and practise snarling ruthlessly.'

Hugo was playing the leader of a gang of criminals who stole luxury cars for shipment abroad; we had just witnessed him putting the boot into a contact at a dealer's who had failed to come through with the dodgy documents in time for the latest containerful of Mercs and BMWs to make the boat for Pakistan. Gav ran a tight ship. Until he was rear-ended at a service station (note the dramatic irony) by Sarah, playing a bohemian sculptor with a smack habit. Naturally, he promptly fell madly in love with her, and his well-organised life started to unravel before his eyes. It was more sophisticated than it sounded. And it was a six-part prime-time drama series for BBC1, called *Driven*, with Hugo as the anti-hero. His ego was the size of a barrage balloon at the moment. Bad analogy. Any minute now he'd decide he really could fly.

'Don't you 'ave to go and make some sparks fly?' Lurch said, appearing next to me.

'I hate when they make me do that,' I complained. 'It's so fake. Not to mention unsafe.'

Lurch shrugged. 'TV, innit,' he said, summing up the whole situation in a masterly couple of words. Lurch was sometimes capable of great profundity.

I was Sarah's stunt double. Not in the Tony sense: I didn't need to pad myself up and get kicked by Hugo, fortunately. It would have sent the whole complex equilibrium of our relationship fatally off-kilter. Instead my role was confined to the tricky bits with the power tools. Lurch was giving Sarah a crash course in basic use so she knew how to hold them properly, but anything beyond that and, as Sarah had commented, it was me in the welding mask. Or with my back to the camera. We were roughly the same build, though I went in and out considerably more than she did; but you could hide a lot beneath baggy sweaters. And our hair was nearly identical.

Though it was a coincidence that she happened to resemble me superficially, her character's profession was my fault, if by proxy. Hugo had been cast early on in script development, and at that stage his paramour had been a painter. The writer and producer had taken him out to dinner, cocked up their ears on hearing his girlfriend was a metal sculptor, and promptly altered the script accordingly. They thought it sounded more glamorous. Hah. I had never pointed out to them how much damage a junkie could do to herself with even a small selection of my equipment; burning yourself alive when your jeans caught on fire was presumably their idea of high style. Painting was a hell of a lot safer. You couldn't even get high on the fumes nowadays.

Lurch and I went to get some more tea. We did this on average about eight hundred times a day, as did everyone else. The BBC might as well have issued us with portable drips and saved a lot of wasted time spent hanging round the urns.

It was drizzling outside, and a group of people was huddled under the wing of the studio entrance, making forays out to the hot drinks trolley. Tony was just dispensing himself a cup of Workman's Special.

'All right,' he said, always friendly.

'Could you move about two feet to the left, Tony?' I said, reaching for a polystyrene cup. 'You're blocking the light.'

It was only half a joke. Tony had the build of a rugby player, but fortunately the good humour of the Jolly Green Giant. He reminded me a little of Wesley Snipes: he had the same extreme darkness of skin, long jaw and lavishly full mouth. But Tony's eyes were narrow slits, perfect for a stuntman, ideally suited to all the punches he was required to take in the face. And they were perpetually amused, lacking the menace Wesley could project by holding his breath and making them bug out like ping-pong balls.

'When'm I taking you to the gym, then, Lurchie?' Tony said, slapping the latter on the back. 'Build up a bit of muscle on them bones, eh?'

Lurch ducked his head and shuffled his feet.

'Ladies like a bit of muscle,' Tony continued, 'don't they, Sam?'

'Too right,' I agreed.

'Yeah, well,' Lurch muttered. 'It's not my thing, is it?'

He looked at me imploringly, wanting to be saved. But I'm not that nice.

'I mean, I'm a bit of a spaz,' he went on. 'Everyone'd take the mickey.'

'Not if you're with me they won't,' Tony pointed out.

'S'pose not,' Lurch said gloomily.

'No pressure, mate. But the offer's open any time you want to take it up, all right?' He looked around, checking, and then lowered his voice. 'You see that article on Sarah in the *Indie* this morning?'

I shook my head.

'Siobhan's got it if you want a look. God, she ain't half stirred up enough trouble for herself.'

'Any publicity's good publicity . . .' I offered.

Tony wobbled his hand from side to side. 'Yes and no, you know what I'm saying? You got to be so careful these days. Politically correct's the name of the game, innit? Red's really pissed off with her.'

The name of our producer was enough to sober us all. Woe betide us if Red caught us gossiping. Tony, having delivered the latest snippet of information, strolled away. Lurch looked after him rather longingly.

'Why don't you go to the gym with him?' I suggested. 'It might be a laugh.'

'Yeah, for everyone else but me,' Lurch said snappishly.

I shrugged.

'D'you want to go and watch them setting up for your bit?' he said.

'Why should I? They'll call me when they're ready.'

'Suit yourself,' Lurch said rather sulkily, and slouched back inside the studio.

I stared after him, sipping my tea. He had a nerve telling me I had a chip on my shoulder. Today he was sporting one the size of

Bournemouth. Well, fine for him if he didn't want to catch up on the latest instalment in the Sarah saga. As soon as I had a spare moment I was off to find Siobhan and sneak a look at the *Independent*.

CHAPTER TWO

I spent the rest of the morning making sparks fly in a way that was completely alien to all normal safety procedures, with Phil, the director, urging me on to ever-increasing acts of lunacy. Clearly he was a closet pyromaniac. I made a mental note never to ask him to organise a Guy Fawkes party. Finally, after a solid hour, I was allowed to put down my tools and stagger off the set, leaving Sarah to take over for the close-ups. Nearly lunchtime, thank God. I hadn't got to the elevenses biscuit tin till only the nasty dry ones at the bottom were left.

'Thought you'd never stop,' Lurch said as I slumped into my folding chair.

'I didn't think Phil'd let me till I'd set myself on fire for the grand finale.' I yawned. 'Only a few more days to go, anyway.'

Lurch's face fell. 'Why d'you have to go and remind me?'

I looked at him. 'You're really enjoying this, aren't you?'

'I dunno. It's a laugh, innit? Makes a change from the theatre.'

I had met Lurch a year ago, when I was building mobiles for a stage production of *Midsummer Night's Dream* at the Cross Theatre. He had been the master carpenter's charge hand, detailed to help me with routine tasks, but had turned out to be much more enthusiastic and creative than anyone, including himself, had bargained for. Not to mention having a much steadier hand than me with the soldering iron. Ever since then I had been longing to buy his indentures from the theatre. When the producer suggested I work as Sarah's stand-in, I had managed to blag Lurch onto the shoot as well. It had been surprisingly easy; they were hiring all my power tools for authenticity and I had insisted that Lurch was the only one I would trust to look after them.

'Developed a taste for the high-octane world of BBC drama?' I said, gesturing around the cold, grimy stone barn. We were over at the far corner now, which had been set up as the interior of the East End warehouse Sarah's character used as a studio.

Lurch was looking plaintive.

'It's only you what's finished,' he pointed out. 'Sarah's still got scenes to shoot here. They'll need me around to keep an eye on the tools, won't they?'

'God, that's true. I'm not letting those out of your or my sight. I must have been out of my head to agree to it. Why the hell did I? Oh yes. Lots and lots of money.'

'Good enough reason, innit?'

The BBC offer had caught me at a low fiscal ebb. I had had a group show in New York at the end of last year which had been a very minor success critically and a less minor disaster financially, and since then I hadn't done a stroke of work. It wasn't New York's fault. I was just burnt out. Every time I thought about making another mobile, my heart sank. Welding a chain on a hunk of metal, hauling it over a beam ... I had the feeling that not only was I currently over mobiles, but that I would be for the rest of my life. Which left me, creatively speaking, halfway through vanishing down a big black hole. I had absolutely nothing to do but lie in bed and fiddle with myself while watching daytime TV. I could mock this production as much as I wanted but the bitter truth was that I would have agreed to stand in for Meg Ryan, wig and all, if they paid me enough and threw in distraction from the gaping void of my life.

Lurch was rocking in his folding chair again, a sure sign of unease. Not to mention imminent precipitation.

'You all right, Lurchie?' I said.

'Yeah. Nah. Well.'

'Try again,' I suggested, 'this time with a bit of focus.'

He shrugged. This was not easily combined with the rocking. I grabbed at the back of the chair to steady him.

'I dunno,' he said, sticking out his long spidery legs and bringing himself to a halt. 'I just don't want to go back to the Cross, y'know? I need to do somefing else. Have a change, like.'

'D'you want to go into TV? You know enough about it by now,' I suggested. 'I bet all the boys on props'd put in a word. You're always giving them a hand.'

When I wasn't forcing him to listen to my whinges, Lurch spent most of his time hanging round with the crew, making himself useful. Everyone liked him, particularly when they realised how handy he was. He had a real mechanical knack and he was a fast learner. Moreover, he was very willing to help out, especially when sworn at. It was his little motivational quirk.

'Yeah.' Lurch shrugged again. 'But, y'know, I fink I want more of a change than that. I can't build sets all me life, can I? I'd go bonkers.'

I looked at him with respect. Lurch was a youth of hidden depths.

'Be a lot easier,' I suggested.

'Yeah, well, that's not for me.'

'Maybe you could be a stuntman. Train up with Tony.'

'Yeah, right. And you could be a bleedin' actress.'

'Oi, watch it with the sarcasm. Get us another cuppa, go on. Make yourself useful for once.'

'Yes, boss!' Lurch dragged himself to his feet, saluted, and ambled out the door. I stared after his skinny figure, a wave of depression enveloping me. What were things coming to when a teenager whose idea of skincare was rubbing his face down every night with a Brillo pad had a better idea of career priorities than I did?

'Psst!' Someone tapped me on the shoulder. I swung around.

'Wanna see a copy of today's *Indie*?' muttered Siobhan, the assistant to the costume designer.

'Great! I was going to come and find you,' I said, eager for some distraction. 'Where is it?'

'Not on me! You mad? Red'd rip my head off if she caught me handing it round. Come back to our den.'

Our boots rang as we went up the metal steps of the costume trailer. Cosy and brightly lit, it smelt of fabric softener and hash, two fragrances which actually worked together better than one would think. A corner at the end even boasted two tatty built-in padded couches in front of the mini-fridge, making it something of a Mecca for people whose time hung heavy on their hands. The trailer rocked gently on its wheels as I crossed the floor to the formica countertop on which lay a much-thumbed copy of the *Independent*, open to the relevant page. Siobhan started rolling up a joint. She had a clear set of priorities.

'The New Amorality,' I read out loud. 'Not much cop as a headline . . .' I scanned the article. It was illustrated with several photographs: the central, largest one was of Sarah, in costume as Anne Boleyn for a film she had made last year. She wore a heavy brocade dress with a wide strip of ermine round her shoulders, from which her bosoms rose in approved Tudor Wench style. Her hair was secured under a lavish gold headdress studded with pearls and diamonds. The contrast between it and the smaller photograph to its right, in which she was walking along a street, her head ducked, could not have been greater. In this she looked anything but regal; her expression was rather cross, and the image was blurred, as if she were turning her head to avoid the camera. She was wearing a tailored duffel coat with a big fur-trimmed hood pulled up to frame her face, and her hair was scraped back. No make-up or jewellery: her only accessory was the actor with whom she was arm-in-arm, another rising star who I had met a couple of years ago. Good-looking, if you liked them ginger, but no brains to speak of.

'Paul's come out well,' I observed.

'He always comes out well,' Siobhan commented. 'Can't take a bad shot of him. Can't act for shit, either,' she added, plugging in an iron.

'But hey, who cares? Certainly not Britain's best-loved TV vet,' I said.

The article had made the most of this dramatic irony, in a dry, understated, *Independent* way. The tabloids hadn't been so restrained. A few days ago it had been 'TV Vet And Bunny-Girl Sarah: The Oddest Couple'. That one had been passed round the set like samizdat too.

'God, how that man fancies himself,' Siobhan said. 'I worked on the last series of *Country Vets*. You couldn't straighten his Barbour without him thinking you were coming on to him. Worked his way through loads of girls on the crew.'

'You too?'

'Must be joking. Though I hear he's got a nice willy. Still couldn't be as big as his ego, though.'

'That was before he started seeing Sarah, right?' I said.

'Yeah. Bet he's still up to his old tricks, though. You don't just change like that, do you?'

She spat on the iron to see if it was hot enough.

'Sarah's getting loads of hate mail,' Siobhan said, changing the subject. 'Red's trying to keep it quiet but it's coming in in sackfuls.'

'What does she expect?' I said unsympathetically. 'Sarah, I mean, not Red.'

'Mmn.' Siobhan was ironing a pale green jacket with considerable care. 'She really pissed everyone off. I mean, she said a load of bollocks. Not just defending wearing fur – what was it – oh yeah, that it's totally natural to wear it and people who don't are just a bunch of hypocrites? Nice one, eh? I mean, don't just get the animal rights lot against you, piss off everyone else as well while you're about it.'

I looked again at the photographs of Sarah. The Anne Boleyn ermine might not be real, but the fur she was wearing in mufti certainly was. If nothing else, she had provided a rich source of gossip for the jaded set of *Driven*. Sarah had put her foot in the middle of a big no-no and then trampled it all over everyone's nice, clean, politically correct carpets.

'Red's been on at her again,' Siobhan continued. She lifted the jacket and slipped it over a hanger. 'Telling her to keep her mouth shut. But there's loads of journos ringing up for interviews, and what actor can resist that?'

We exchanged knowing glances. Siobhan was a kindred spirit, despite being the posh daughter of a filthy rich Irish brewing family with a surname so famous it was like meeting someone called Laura Budweiser or Magda Holsten Pils. My cod-Irish friend Tom was dying to meet her, even though she was scarcely the type of skinny neurotic blonde he usually lost his head about. But he was so fixated on the trust fund and endless supply of beer he presumed came with the package that he had declared himself willing to ignore the fact that Siobhan was what they used to call black Irish, with masses of sooty hair, pale eyes and a very square jaw.

Naturally dark-skinned, she was currently the same colour as practically everyone else on the production, the curse of TV work; her cheeks the same grey as the combat gear she wore, a cigarette perpetually between her fingers. Only Red, our producer, was constantly smart and fresh, not having to hang around the set twelve hours a day. The crew, after two months of shooting, would have made perfect extras for a post-nuclear holocaust movie.

'You're done for the day, aren't you?' she was saying to me.

'Sticking around for lunch.' I checked my watch. 'Ooh, it's five to one. I'm off to queue. You coming?'

'Just got to finish this.' She nodded to the pearl-grey fabric she was now pressing. 'Hugo's suit for the set-up after lunch.'

'Amazing, really,' I commented, swinging myself to my feet. 'Watching someone iron his suits for him. Maybe we should have a ménage à trois.'

'You must be joking! Both of you together? One would be bad enough!' Siobhan grinned at me. 'I can't decide which of you two would be more annoying to have sex with,' she said thoughtfully.

'You're right,' I admitted. 'It'd be a really hard call.'

We were on set in Windsor, not California. Lunch, as breakfast had been, was ninety per cent stodge to ten per cent health. And that was a conservative estimate. Even the salads were coated in emulsified low-quality gunk. I wasn't sure about the technical difference between mayonnaise and salad cream, but I was pretty sure that the latter was worse for you. The vegetable pie looked like two well-cooked slabs of suet with a few sorry carrot and broccoli peelings peeping out forlornly from between the crevices, like meagre strands of grass growing through paving stones. I took the skate wings instead, wondering whether this was the cheapest cut of fish known to humanity. They came swimming in butter, or possibly margarine, which chimed in nicely with the congealing fish fat.

It was still drizzling, and the queue of people for the catering trailer curled in tightly under its awning. The ground underfoot was scratchy with gravel slipping on the muddy concrete. I might mock everyone's survivalist gear but I had to admit its rationale. These were primitive living conditions. I was held up for a while by Joanne, who was in front of me in the queue, flirting with the cooks. As befitted their cuisine, these were all beefy short-order types, lardy and cheerful in their dirty striped aprons, slapping the food onto plastic plates with gusto and bewailing loudly the fact that most of the girls were in baggy jeans.

'Off you go, darlin',' one of them finally said to Joanne. 'Give us a watch of you climbing into that trailer, then.'

'You get worse and worse,' she said, batting her eyelashes and turning away towards the dining trailer, giving them a little wiggle as she clambered up the stairs into the bus.

'God, she never stops,' muttered Tony, at my elbow. 'Pathetic, with this lot. Stuck behind that counter all day. They'd whistle at a dead granny with her ankles showing.'

I snuffled with amusement and started heaping a second plate with cheese from the salad table. Garnishing this with a couple of grapes and a few green leaves, more for effect than their negligible nutritional value, I scooted out from the awning, through the drizzle, and climbed up into the dining trailer. This was a bus which had been partially converted into a diner; instead of plastic booths we had bus seats, but the tables were the authentic chipped formica of your neighbourhood greasy spoon, even down to the plastic bottles of ketchup and brown sauce sitting in puddles of their own excrement by every window. It took a while to get used to the surreal experience of eating bad diner food on a poorly modified stationary bus in the middle of nowhere.

'God, girl, you eating for two?' Tony said, sliding in opposite me. It was always a wonder to me how he manoeuvred his huge frame so effortlessly in and out of narrow spaces – like watching someone back a tanker into a parking space barely adequate for a Mazda coupé.

'If I stuff at lunch I can roll home without worrying about dinner,' I explained.

''S always the ones who drop in occasionally who eat like pigs,' Tony said, forking some skate delicately to his mouth. 'They don't have time to get used to it.'

'The constant food or the grinding boredom?'

'Both, girl. Both.'

I didn't know how they could do this for a living. I started craving antidepressants if I had a twenty-minute wait for someone at Camden tube station. The thought of spending months on end hanging on for other people to sort themselves out – mostly the lighting crew: God, the time they could spend up stepladders fiddling with things was phenomenal – chilled my blood.

The stand-in came past us, heading for a booth at the far end, his anorak rustling like wet leaves underfoot. At first I hadn't realised how humiliating his job was. Then I saw him come through a door on set three times, no one actually looking at him, just his contours, the light on his face, which might as well be featureless for all they cared, while the real actor slumped in a chair, picking his fingernails. The rest of the time the stand-in, whose name hardly anyone remembered, just hung around, and I had noticed that nobody liked to look him directly in the face. It was too embarrassing, perhaps, to acknowledge his humanity off-set, when on he was simply a body to be lit, an anonymous slab of living flesh.

'You done for the day, yeah?' Tony said to me.

'Far as I know.'

'Heya!' Lurch slid in next to me. He looked much more cheerful than when I had last seen him. 'Shepherd's pie!' he announced, the plastic plate he carried sagging under the weight and heat of its load. 'My favourite!'

With great satisfaction he blanketed his chips in enough ketchup to drown a small animal. The bus was filling up now; we had been the early shift, but clearly they had broken now for lunch, and the crew was streaming in.

'There's free seats down there,' came the unmistakable tones of our producer from the doorway of the bus. Red was always around; she came to the studios early in the morning and stayed in the office till they had wrapped for the day. Some producers would have been off by now setting up a new project, dropping in every now and then just to remind the director of their existence. But Red was more hands-on than a Swedish masseuse.

She made her way down the aisle, greeting everyone as she went with exactly the right mixture of camaraderie and detachment: the crew wanted to feel that the producer liked them but would be uncomfortable if she were over-friendly. Behind her was Phil Green, the director, a lumbering bear of a man in a back-to-front baseball cap, effortlessly filling out his extra-large T-shirt. They took the pseudo-booth opposite us. Red said hello, but she was rather abstracted, her attention not fully in the moment, as if she were watching out for someone. She and Phil plunged into a discussion about yesterday's rushes, but my instinct had been right. A few minutes later she rose from her seat, calling:

'Sarah! Hi! Come and sit with us!'

The trailerful of people hushed for a moment. Then conversations sprung up again with renewed, exaggerated intensity, as if a volume knob had been turned down and up in the space of a couple of seconds. Sarah came down the aisle, her plate loaded with fruit and cold cuts. Sliding in opposite Red, she gave the latter a wary, almost hostile, nod, then ducked her head to her lunch.

'Nice one,' Tony leant across the table and said to me quietly under the hubbub. 'Red knew Sarah wouldn't have lunch in her trailer cos that way Red could buttonhole her in privacy. So she staked out here instead.'

Red and Sarah reminded me of two dogs stalking warily around each other, growling, lips slightly raised to show the tips of their canines – as much as a producer and an actress eating bad food in a lunch bus can. Though Phil knew exactly what was going on, it wasn't his fight. Phil had a long and solid career at his back and this series was going fine; the buzz on the set was excellent. Nothing that happened with Sarah would make or break him. He could even joke about it.

That was his mistake.

'Hey, Sarah, why didn't you have the shepherd's pie!' he suggested through a mouthful of his own. 'Top-quality stuff! Need some hot food on a miserable day like this.'

'No thanks,' Sarah said rather coldly. 'I don't eat meat when I can't see how it's been cooked.'

'Oh, for God's sake—' Phil became even more jovial. 'Didn't know you were that fussy! Thought you were one of us!'

Keith came down the bus, moving so lightly I hardly heard his approach, and slipped in next to Tony.

'One of us?' Sarah repeated frigidly.

'Yeah, you know. None of this politically correct stuff about you, right?' Phil dolloped another large mouthful of shepherd's pie onto his fork and looked at it with a satisfied gaze. 'Bollocks to the health Nazis!'

'Old-school director,' Tony muttered to me. 'Dying breed.'

Red went on eating. What else could she do? Her hands were tied; Phil was the director, and she couldn't tell him to stop teasing the talent. Maybe she had kicked him under the table, though, because his voice became more appeasing.

'OK, I got the message. No shepherd's pie for you,' he said, putting the forkful with which he had been gesticulating into his own mouth. 'Just the ham, right?' He nodded at her plate.

'I bring this in myself,' Sarah said. 'It's not processed, like that reconstituted mince you're eating.' She pushed her hair back from her excellent cheekbones and cut off a small slice of ham, which she sandwiched on her fork with a piece of green apple.

'It's not muck, Sarah,' Phil said mildly. 'It's good old shepherd's pie, like your mum used to make.'

'It's *reconstituted meat*!' Sarah said with surprising venom. 'Do you know how they make that? *Get* that? They take the bones and the leftovers and the fucking eyeballs and they strip them down with power hoses and they sweep all the crap they get in one horrible mucky pile and make it into fucking hamburgers! Eyelashes and all!'

Phil's fork clattered onto the table.

'You,' he said, leaning towards her, 'are really up yourself right now. OK? I know you're not having an easy time of it—'

Sarah's laugh was shrill.

'—but get a grip, Sarah. There was no need for all of that. You've completely ruined my effing lunch. Completely effing ruined it. I was enjoying that pie.'

'God, I'm sorry,' Sarah exclaimed, pushing back her own plate. It is impossible to leap dramatically to your feet when you are sitting in a sagging bus seat with a formica table abutting closely onto your bellybutton, but she managed a sort of sideways jump that conveyed

24

the idea, if not the action. 'I'm sorry that I messed up your *lunch*. I expect it doesn't matter that my entire life is being messed up by psychos persecuting me, does it? Just as long as you get your *fucking lunch* down your throat.'

Again, it is extremely hard to make a dramatic exit down the crowded aisle at the centre of a dining trailer. But she did her best. Almost every head turned to watch her go, which added to the effect.

The only non-spectators to Sarah's rush across the concrete forecourt in the direction of her own trailer suite were Red and Phil. Red raised her head from her plate and gave Phil a long glance. Her eyes were large and seemed clear, until you looked closely and noticed that they were faintly bloodshot. They had that over-shininess which denotes the recent use of eyedrops. Red was more stressed than her calm manner conveyed.

CHAPTER THREE

'Nice work, Phil,' Red snapped, once the hubbub caused by Sarah's storm-out had settled down.

Phil shrugged. I noticed that, despite his reproof to Sarah about her ruining his appetite, he had gone on eating the shepherd's pie.

'What can you do?' he said. 'And, you know, I've seen so much worse in my time. Jesus, I could tell you stories. The Yanks are the worst. Or the Germans. That one –' he nodded in the direction that Sarah had gone – 'thinks she's thrown a tantrum. To me it's like a bat squeaking. I can't even hear it.'

Red went silent again. She looked as if she were grinding her teeth in frustration. To give her jaw something to work on, she shoved her fork into her food at random; whatever came up on the tines went into her mouth. The time taken to chew and digest had calmed her voice down a little when she next spoke.

'Still,' she continued, more evenly. 'We didn't need it.'

'Oh, she'll be fine for work,' Phil assured her. 'That one's ambitious. Wouldn't have shot her mouth off to a journo if she hadn't wanted the press. She'll come on set after lunch, we'll have a moment –' he put this last word in inverted commas with a twitch of his upheld index and middle fingers – 'and she'll be OK. You'll see.'

'If you're sure.' Red sounded unconvinced. But Phil was a veteran, and she was relying on his experience. Her next question showed this clearly enough.

'Should I go and see her?' she asked.

'Nah,' Phil said, unconcerned. 'Leave her to sweat.'

'But I wanted to talk to her about ... you know ...' Red lowered her voice slightly.

'Hate mail,' Keith mouthed to me. He was sitting across the aisle from her.

'Leave it for now,' Phil repeated. 'She'll calm down and decide she's gone too far. Which she has. Right little madam.'

The last three words came out with a certain emphasis. Red glanced over at us and saw at once that we were all eating too industriously, too silently, to be doing anything but listening.

'Let's get some coffee,' she said to Phil. 'In my office.'

'Fine by me,' he said, pushing his plate away from him and burping lightly. 'You got any chocolate digestives in today?'

'Don't we always?'

'That's her karma coming round really fast,' Keith said smugly as soon as they had gone.

'Red's?' Lurch said, confused. 'What, you mean somefing to do with the choccie biscuits?'

Keith sighed theatrically.

'No, Sarah's, you idiot,' he said. 'That's one director and producer who won't want to work with her again.'

'Come on, Keith, they must be used to bad behaviour from actors by now. No offence,' I added hurriedly, having temporarily forgotten that Keith was one.

'That together with the hate mail?' Keith smiled in satisfaction. 'The great wheel turns with surprising speed. Bad acts will rebound upon you faster than you think.'

'Fuck's sake, Keith, pack it in. You sound like Neil out of *The Young Ones*,' Tony said. 'I'm going to get some blueberry cheesecake. Anyone else want some?'

'Please sir, me, sir,' I said, putting my hand up.

'I'll come too,' Lurch said, sliding out from beside me. Keith had to get up to let Tony out, and I wondered if he would take the opportunity to leave; but instead he sat back down, scooting over to sit opposite me by the window.

'No cheesecake?' I said. 'Weight watching?' I was very used to this with Hugo, who was obsessive about gaining a pound.

'Animal fat,' Keith corrected me.

'God, you're really strict,' I said respectfully. I had already clocked his austere plateful of broccoli (a watery death) and baked potato;

27

now I noticed that the single sachet of emulsified fat he had allowed himself was sunflower margarine.

'I'm a vegan,' he explained. He looked good on it, I had to admit; even the whites of his eyes gleamed with a healthy shine, making Red's Optrex-aided gleam seem even more artificially enhanced. And he always seemed energetic and centred, probably a result of the Buddhist meditation he did every lunchtime.

Which made me wonder.

'Keith?' I said suddenly. 'What are you doing in here? You never join us peons at lunch, you're always in your trailer standing on your head or something.'

His smile deepened, creasing the darker lines around his eyes. Keith was not handsome, but he had made the absolute best of his assets, and he had a smile that could charm birds off trees at a hundred paces. Not that Keith was remotely interested in charming birds.

'*Well*,' he said confidentially, leaning towards me, 'I knew something was brewing, and I wanted to see the fun. I worked out that Sarah would eat in here, and I thought Red would have the same idea. So I popped in. And I was right.'

'That's very devious of you, Keith.' I was impressed.

'Besides,' he added, 'even if Red's changed her mind and dropped in on Sarah to give her a piece of it – which is more than possible, I didn't think Phil totally convinced her to back off – I wouldn't be able to hear a thing.' He paused for a moment, then said faux-casually: 'Hugo's much better placed.'

Hugo and Sarah, as the two principals, shared a trailer divided into only two sections, giving them larger accommodation than the rest of the cast. The latter had to content themselves with a third of a trailer each, and fewer status symbols: a smaller bathroom and no freezer to their fridge. Life was tough on the lower rungs of the ladder.

'Not really,' I said, thinking this over. 'Because his and Sarah's bathrooms back onto each other. Even if you were squashing your ear against the wall of his, you wouldn't hear a thing if Sarah were in the main room with the bathroom door closed.'

'You could if she was shouting,' Keith pointed out.

'Then you'd hear it just as much outside, through the window.'

'Well, but you couldn't hang around outside, it would look much too obvious. Oh, I'm just tying my shoelace, I much prefer doing it in the open air with a little light rain coming down, it's *so* much healthier, you know,' he said with exquisite scorn.

I looked at my watch.

'Maybe I'll go and see how Hugo's doing,' I suggested. 'He'll have had his lunch by now.'

Hugo always brought his own and ate it in his suite, resisting the temptation to join the rest of us in Saturated Fat World down at the catering trailer.

'I'll come too,' said Keith with alacrity. 'I wanted to talk to Hugo about – well, something.'

'Blueberry cheesecake!' announced Tony, plopping down a slice in front of me. I took a mouthful. It was gluey and sweet, the biscuit base pleasantly crunchy. A blueberry burst between my teeth, deliciously synthetic. As different from a real blueberry as tinned vegetables are from fresh, it had, like them, its own distinctive pleasures.

'When I've finished my cheesecake,' I said to Keith firmly. 'No sense rushing, is there?'

Keith had produced a granola bar and was still chewing on it as we wound our way around the honey wagon and round the corner of the star trailer. It looked like coconut matting and was so thick and sticky that he had to clamp his teeth down when he took a bite and wiggle his head from side to side to tear the piece off. Yet again I was glad I wasn't a vegan.

Ascending the three steps that led up to Hugo's door, I rapped on it imperiously.

'It's me and Keith. Can we come in?'

'Be my guests,' Hugo called. He was stretched full-length on his sofa bed, smoking a post-prandial cigarette, head tilted back, looking very content. The cigarette was not one of his pastel Sobranies; he tended, thriftily, to keep those for public display. I found these small economies of his quite touching.

'Our cover story,' I announced, as Keith closed the door behind us, 'is that we've come to hang out with you. But actually we wanted to see if we could hear anything going on next door.'

'Sarah?' Hugo sat up, swinging his legs onto the ground to give us room on the sofa. 'Has she been having a dust-up with someone? I haven't heard anything bouncing off the walls.'

'She and Phil had a tiff over lunch,' Keith explained. We both sat down. We had to. Even though Hugo's suite was the deluxe version, being in it with two other people felt like we were playing a variation of Sardines. At least when you were seated there was the sensation of space overhead.

'Oh, dammit.' Hugo took a long drag on his cigarette. Usually he was the keenest of gossip-mongers, but this series was his big break almost as much as it was Red's. If it turned out as good as the buzz predicted, he would be a TV star. It was that simple. Shooting was going well: the last thing he needed was a bust-up between the director and the leading actress which would make her difficult to work with.

'Tell me,' he said resignedly. 'I might as well know the worst.'
Keith filled him in with gusto.

'You've really got your knife into Sarah,' Hugo observed rather irritably. 'To hear you talk you'd think she was a cross between a vivisectionist and Cruella De Vil.'

'To see her is to feel a sudden chill,' I chipped in, which didn't help much.

'Did you *read* that interview?' Keith snapped back, caught on the raw. 'I mean, no one's perfect, I don't expect everyone to be a vegan, but *really*. She was so *blatant*. And she was very rude to me when we were rehearsing yesterday,' he added.

'For God's sake, Keith, she's under a lot of stress! Can't you try to cut her some slack?'

'Oh right. She tries to cut my lines and I have to cut her some slack. Very fair, I don't think.'

'She wasn't trying to cut your line,' Hugo said wearily. 'That was Phil.'

'Egged on by her.'

'And it was only a few fucks. I mean, you have enough of those.

Dear God, an unintentional double entendre. How embarrassing. I must be more wound up by this than I thought.'

Hugo slumped back against the flowery padded headboard, lighting another cigarette from the butt of his first.

'I know,' he said, catching my eye. 'Too many cancer sticks and not enough exercise. The deadly spiral of filming. Do you think I should get a treadmill at home?'

But I was only half-listening. A row had suddenly broken out in the adjacent suite. Keith and I exchanged glances and made for the bathroom, bumping into each other as we both tried to be first through the door.

'Crude physical comedy,' Hugo said sourly. He hated being ignored. 'How I loathe it.'

'No, I won't!' Sarah was yelling. I had been wrong about the acoustic penetration. Her voice came through nice and clearly. That was the great thing about actors. They did know how to project.

'Don't you realise how stressed out I am right now?' she went on passionately. 'I can't believe you're pestering me like this! You're so insensitive!'

No matter how much we strained, we couldn't hear the person she was talking to. I assumed they were trying to calm her down by speaking quietly. Which made it probable that it was Red next door with her.

'I've said no! How many times do you need to hear it before you get the message?' Sarah shouted. 'I've made my decision! I'm not going back on what I've already said!'

Another pause.

'It's finished, OK? It's over! I'm not— No, listen to me— OK, I admit I was an idiot, I should never have got drunk and said all those things, but— How dare you tell me how to run my life! How dare you!'

Through the wall we heard her come into the bathroom and slam the door behind her. No chance now of hearing who she was talking to.

'Fuck off!' she yelled. 'Just leave me alone, OK! Get out of my face! How many times do I have to tell you?'

'If that's Red in there Sarah's a dead woman,' Keith hissed to me.

'No, don't come round! I need to be alone, OK? Can't you see what a difficult time I'm having?' Sarah was howling by now. 'And all you think about is your bloody—'

There was a knock on Hugo's door. Keith and I jumped as guiltily as a pair of kids caught halfway through playing I'll Show You Mine If You Show Me Yours.

'Hugo?' It was Phil. He opened the door as Keith and I bumped into each other once more trying to get out of the bathroom simultaneously.

'Jesus,' Phil said, 'it's like a motorway pile-up in here. What were you two doing in the bog?'

'Sam keeps trying to convert me,' Keith said airily. 'No joy so far.'

'You OK about that, Hugo?' Phil said, his stomach filling the room like a bulkhead.

'As long as I can watch them at it,' Hugo said languidly. 'It's all I have the energy for, the way you're slave-driving me. The poor girl needs to get her satisfaction somewhere.'

'I'm sublimating in food,' I added. 'Skate wings and blueberry pie.'

'God. Not simultaneously, I hope. Right, Terrible Twins, leave me in peace,' Hugo said. 'I have a gentleman caller.' He fixed us with a beady eye. 'I hope you got what you came for.'

'Yes and no,' I said pertly as we left. It was true enough. The distraction caused by Phil's advent had thrown a spanner in the works: passing Sarah's end of the trailer, I listened so hard I could almost feel my ears pinning back, but there was a deathly silence in there.

'No one in there with her now,' Keith confirmed. 'We'd hear *something*.'

'But no one came out, either,' I observed. 'We'd have heard that too.'

Keith looked thoughtful.

'She must've been talking on the mobile,' he said.

'Siobhan? Siobhan!' a voice called behind us, sounding out of breath. Footsteps pounded up and a hand caught my shoulder. I swung around. It was Jimmy, the runner, living up to his job title. He was panting as if he'd just done ten laps of the studios.

'Oh, shit, it's you, Sam. Sorry, thought you were Siobhan.'

'You need to give up the fags,' I said sternly. 'Or do more cardio.'

'Next life, OK? Got no time in this one. You seen her?'

'Try round the back of Stage Two,' Keith suggested.

'Thanks, mate.' Jimmy took off, winded but game.

'What's the attraction of Stage Two?' I asked curiously. The individual studio buildings were called stages, for some arcane reason. Battered and blackened, poorly soundproofed and draughty, they squatted in a rough ellipse round the central office buildings, five in total. In Stage Two they were currently shooting a First World War film: the floor had been dug up to make trenches. It was bizarre to see the ground ripped open as if a couple of giant worms from *Dune* had just burst out of it moments before, contemptuously shredding it in their passage. The camera equipment and lights – not to mention their human operators – were huddled alongside these great eruptions of earth, dwarfed by the comparison.

It was definitely not the cosiest of sets. As far as I knew its only attraction was for guys who got off watching the large selection of earthmovers do their stuff. There were always a few of them hanging around eyeballing the latest excavations.

'She's got a mate on sound over there,' Keith explained. 'Boyfriend, maybe. She always comes back a bit spliffed out, know what I mean? It's like the back of the bike sheds round Stage Two. Sex, drugs—'

'And big diggers. You know everything, Keith,' I said respectfully. 'You are God.'

'Be cool if God was a black gay vegan, wouldn't it?' Keith said cheerfully. 'And, you know –' he grinned at me – 'it'd suit me, too. I look *great* in white.'

'People like you are the polluting scum of the earth. You are not worth the death of one animal. But you are guilty of the death of uncountable numbers. You wear dead animals on your back like a trophy and eat their maltreated flesh for pleasure. The Animal Rights Action Group has pledged itself to avenge these acts of murder. Be very careful not to make yourself the spokeswoman for the slaughterers. Back down now and no harm will come to you. We are at war. And you are a torturer.'

'Jesus.' Hugo looked shaken.

'I know,' Sarah said, crumpling up the note. 'Bastards, aren't they?'

'Actually it was the abattoir details from that other one you read,' Hugo said. He shivered. 'Maybe I should stop eating meat. Jesus, look at this.' Gingerly, he picked up a sheet of paper with a black and white photo of cows hanging upside down from meat hooks; the miracles of modern technology had allowed its creators to scan in a dead human in place of one of the cows.

'Clumsily done, but it makes its point,' he said, dropping it with a grimace. 'Turns your stomach over nicely.'

'What's that?' Karen called from the office next door.

'Bloke hanging on a meat hook,' I said.

'Oh yeah, I've seen that one. Not a high score on the yuck-ometer.'

We were in the production offices of *Driven*. Red had insisted that Sarah come in to sort through the post that was still arriving for her every day, and Sarah, reluctantly agreeing, had asked Hugo to add moral support. On the principle, as he charmingly put it, that cutting people down to size was my main interest in life, he had co-opted me too, hoping that I would add some healthy scepticism to the proceedings. So far it wasn't working. Some of the facts related in the animal activists' letters I knew already; others were new to me, and all of them were horrendous. I was feeling distinctly queasy. Not that I would let on. It was all very well for Hugo to admit to his stomach being turned; he was a guy. I had my female machismo to maintain.

So, clearly, did Karen. She was the production coordinator, a tall, rangy, Amazonian girl in the regulation grey and black layers of clothing favoured by the crew. However, working in a warm office rather than on a draughty set, instead of jeans she preferred an A-line mini-skirt which I had seen her in almost every day. It was an odd garment for someone to be so attached to; it had enormous side pockets and was made of bobbly charcoal fleece whose insulating properties were completely wasted on a skirt which came only to mid-thigh. With it she wore clumpy knee-length boots which made her rather thick legs look as if they were of equal circumference all the way down. Still, Karen didn't seem to give a damn whether people thought she had ankles or not. I doubted the Amazons did either.

'God, it's true that women have stronger stomachs than men,' Hugo called back. 'You and Sam are so blasé you make me look like Little Bo Peep.'

'I read James Herbert,' Karen said, pushing her chair back from her desk and coming through to join us. 'I like all that gruesome stuff. Blood and gore and people having their guts ripped out.'

'Oh, *gruesome*,' Hugo said dismissively. 'That would cover most modern literature. No novel complete without one evisceration, three back passage rapes and a few obscure Aztec tortures. Terribly wearing after a while. I'm going to read nothing but Somerset Maugham for a couple of years till this latest craze passes.'

Karen propped herself against Red's desk, around which we were all sitting, and started rifling through the pile of letters with the air of a connoisseur.

'You know what we were saying, when these started coming in?' Karen said, letting a couple fall from her hand back onto the desk. After the first hate letter, Sarah had asked the production office to screen the post for her. Karen seemed to have enjoyed this task immoderately. I expected it was a pleasant change from trouble-shooting endless crises on only a BBC budget. 'That the ones from your supporters are scarier than the death threats. Know what I mean?'

She gave Sarah a friendly grin. Karen had pale red hair and a round, stolid face with a permanent high colour. A casting director would have marked her down instantly as a dairymaid in a rural costume drama. The almost bovine calm of her face belied not only her efficiency, however, but also her reputation for sexual excess. I knew a few crew members who had had flings with her and could only whistle devoutly when her name was mentioned.

'Worse than *death threats*?' Sarah said snappishly.

'But look at all these ones from retired majors who want you to

join the Countryside League and come on pro-fox-hunting demos!'
Karen protested, laughing. 'Jesus!'

'Why, Sarah,' Hugo said gleefully, 'you've become the poster girl
for the *Telegraph* letters page.'

'That *is* scary,' I agreed.

'Actually, the *Sunday Telegraph* want me to do a shoot for them
wearing fur,' Sarah admitted. 'Do you think I should?'

She leant back in Red's chair, arms behind her head. The frown
she had been sporting most of the morning faded. Sarah had the kind
of face it was difficult to stop looking at; not because of its intrinsic
beauty, but a fascination, an intensity of feature, which the best
actors possess. Her clear pale eyes were misty and reflective. She was
like the actress in the Agatha Christie short story whose best dreamy
gaze was conjured up by thinking of peppermint creams; even
though I knew Sarah was merely contemplating a pageful of colour
photographs heading up whatever the *Sunday Telegraph* called their
lifestyle section, she was still mesmeric.

She fiddled absently with one long dark curl.

'What does Naseem say?' Hugo asked. Naseem was Sarah's agent.

'Oh, I don't know,' she said dismissively. This meant that Naseem
had advised against it. 'I'm kind of tempted to take the bull by the
horns, you know? I mean, if this thing's happening, maybe I should
use the momentum. Just go for it. I mean, I wear fur, I don't give a
shit, and there are lots of other people who feel the same! Why
shouldn't I model some coats? Who does it hurt?'

'Apart from the dead animals?' I suggested. 'Hey, I've got a good
idea. Why don't you say you'll only model stuff from domestic
animals? Cat and dog fur, or rabbit? That would be really radical. Get
the *Telegraph* readers' hypocrisies right where they hurt.'

'What a brilliant idea!' Karen said fervently. 'But could they get
enough?'

'Well, there are all those Made in China hair scrunchies and glove
trims, for a start,' I said. 'Don't know about actual doggie *coats*—'

'You're both joking, right?' Sarah said flatly. 'I mean, I'm
assuming you're joking.'

Karen and I exchanged an amused glance.

'After all,' Karen said, 'do you actually know for sure what fur it is on your coat?'

'Ah, the designer duffel. I do love these pleasant little culturally constructed oxymorons,' Hugo observed.

This whole crisis had started when Sarah, out drinking at a seedy little after-hours club in Soho, had bumped into a journalist who had admired her duffel coat. Since it was by a hugely expensive and fashionable Italian designer, and so much the latest cutting-edge trend that there were waiting lists for it as long as your arm at the relevant Bond Street shop, Sarah had naturally been flattered to have it recognised. The duffel not only had a fur trim to the hood, but was fur-lined as well, and, after several oohs and aahs, the journalist had apparently said idly how interesting it was to see that Sarah had no problem wearing fur.

Sarah insisted, in retrospect, that the woman had been stirring, to see if she could be provoked, and if that were true the journalist's efforts had paid off in spades. Sarah, her insides sloshing with various cocktails, had launched into a tirade which had caught the attention of a singer further down the bar, well known as a proselytising vegetarian, who had promptly taken issue with everything she was saying. Before long it was a full-blown row. The journalist, seeing her opportunity, and having a mini tape recorder in her bag, had switched it on and let it roll.

Neither of the participants had been at their most articulate, but the singer had come out of it much better, managing to sound socially concerned without being off-puttingly smug. Sarah, easily riled at the best of times, had made a fool of herself.

'That coat was incredibly bloody expensive!' she protested now. 'You don't even want to *know* how much it cost! Of course it's not rabbit fur!'

She pronounced the word 'rabbit' with such disdain that any members of that species present would have crawled away to slit their throats in shame at being fit only to provide hair scrunchies for the Chinese.

'Price of a country cottage, was it, sweetie? Didn't know you had that kind of money,' Hugo drawled. 'Lucky you.'

'It was a present, actually. And I was very grateful,' Sarah said defiantly, 'and I'm going to keep on wearing it.'

'It's very well cut,' I commented. Despite being fully lined with fur, the coat was darted and waisted so neatly that it didn't make its wearer look bulky. I could see why she didn't want to give it up; modern actresses might get designer duffels from Prada, or Dolce and Gabbana, instead of diamond necklaces and mink, but they were equally reluctant to part with their trophies.

'Shall we change the subject?' Hugo suggested. 'I feel we may have gone as far as we can with the now-legendary coat. Sarah, these little love notes.' He poked them with one long finger. 'What are the police doing about them?'

'They don't know who most of them are from,' Sarah said. 'They said there're so many animal rights groups now they can't keep track.'

'Surely they have infiltrators everywhere?' Hugo said. 'It's all MI5 have left to do nowadays, I imagine, dress up in faux-combat outfits bought at Laurence Corner and memorise Twenty Best Ways With Soy Mince.'

'That's MI5, though,' Sarah said.

'Oh come on, the police must be at it too. They probably pick out the most pasty-faced specimens at training college and earmark them as undercover animal activists. Oi, Spotty! You! Over here! Try this donkey jacket on for size!'

'Hugo, you are so unfair,' I said.

'Darling, rich vegans may be the healthiest people ever – look at Keith – but poor vegans have bad skin. And all activists are poor. Ergo—'

'All right. Shut up.'

'And don't talk about Keith,' Sarah said crossly. 'He's being such a bastard to me.'

Hugo sighed. 'Come on, Sarah. I heard you making some deeply tasteless comments about vivisection to him just the other day.'

'He was getting on my nerves,' Sarah said sullenly. 'Bloody vegetarians. They're just doing it to make themselves feel interesting and superior to the rest of us. It's pathetic, really.'

'Oi, watch it,' Karen said, pleasantly enough. 'I'm a vegetarian.'

It didn't need to go any further; Karen wasn't asking for an apology. All Sarah had to do was leave it alone. But she couldn't.

'*God!*' she exclaimed, staring rudely at Karen. 'I can't believe Red got a *veggie* to sort through my post! How insensitive! Have you been egging her on to give me a hard time?'

'No, Sarah, I haven't.' Karen slid off the desk and stood up, all amiability wiped from her face. 'I'm just doing my job, OK? Which is trying to make sure this shoot runs smoothly. And people like you arsing round and stirring up trouble, getting us the wrong sort of publicity – *hate mail*, for God's sake – and then refusing to do anything about it aren't helping me much. Not that you seem to give a damn what effect your behaviour has on anybody else.'

And with that Karen stalked out of Red's office. We heard her go through her own and into the kitchen. Shortly afterwards came the hiss of a kettle set to boil.

'Maybe you should go and have a word,' Hugo suggested to Sarah. 'Say you flew off the handle a bit.'

'Are you crazy?' Sarah snapped. 'You mean I should apologise to her? Did you hear what she just said to me?'

'Uh, *yes*,' Hugo said with a certain emphasis which completely passed Sarah by. He caught my eye and flicked me a comprehensive glance.

'How's it going?' came Red's voice from the door.

Sarah swung round to face her. I could see Hugo trying to catch Sarah's attention, signalling her to shut up and be nice: but Sarah would or could not take the hint.

'Karen's just been rude to me!' she said, her voice rising. 'I really don't need this kind of upset right now!'

'Right, that's it. I'm wending my merry way,' Hugo said, rising to his feet. I got up too. We passed Red, standing in the doorway and looking ominously calm at this latest development.

'I don't know why you asked me to come along and hold your hand, Sarah,' he added as we left. 'As far as I can see the only conceivable way I could have helped would have been to stuff it into your mouth. That way at least you couldn't deliberately piss off

39

people whose lives you're making even more difficult than they are already.'

And he stalked off down the corridor. Hugo had an actor's sense of a good exit line.

CHAPTER FOUR

'Yes . . . yes . . . Oh *God* yes . . .'
  'Like that? Mmmn . . . Or that?'
  'Both, damn you, both—'
  'Can't do both at once—'
  '. . . Incompetent tart . . .'
  'Oi, watch it . . . Like that?'
  'OH GOD YES—'
  'Do you know . . .' I was gasping myself now – 'what atheists yell
. . . when they come?'
  But Hugo was over the edge and falling down the other side.
'Jesus—'
He grabbed my hips so tightly he might have been drowning and
I a lifebelt. I closed my eyes and ground myself into him. My
universe contracted sharply down into a few very precise areas of
extreme physical sensation. It was like being sucked down through a
boiling-hot air vent into a tumble dryer on spin cycle. Dark as pitch
and just as intense. Finally I was whooshed out the other side and
washed up, panting for breath, on the far shore. My poet friend Tom
would have been beating his head against a wall by now at the
promiscuous mixture of my metaphors, but it was the best I could do
at the time.
  It was the best either of us could do. Beneath me Hugo was
another shipwreck victim, his arms flung back against the padded
backboard of his sofa bed, his head slumped to one side like a puppet
with a string that needed tightening. Nor was I in any hurry to
move. When someone started banging on the door they were about
as welcome as a fag hag at a gay orgy.

We let them pound for a while, hoping that they would become discouraged and leave us in peace. I knew the door was locked because I'd done that myself. But Hugo's visitor showed no sign of giving up.

'Leave me!' Hugo yelled at last, still motionless apart from the rise and fall of his chest beneath my head. 'I must never be disturbed when I'm reading Spinoza!'

The best technique with Hugo is to ignore most of what he says, and Sarah knew him well enough by now to employ it.

'Hugo!' she called urgently. 'You're there! Please let me in, *please!*'

'Oh, *bugger*,' Hugo sighed, bringing his head upright and opening his eyes. 'So much for sodding afterglow.'

'At least we did it,' I said consolingly.

'There is that, of course. You're so brutally practical, darling. Sarah?' he yelled. 'This had better be urgent!'

'It is! Really! Let me in!'

She rattled desperately at the door handle. I swung myself uncomfortably to the floor and we both made the necessary adjustments. My hair was sticking up as if someone had just electrified me, which on reflection was not a bad comparison. I tidied it as much as I could in the long strip of mirror running over the sofa – these suites couldn't help reminding one of train carriages – and opened the door to Sarah.

'Hugo's just in the loo,' I explained. 'Come in.'

'I'm really, really sorry to disturb you,' she said in heartfelt tones as I shut the door behind her. I warmed to Sarah. She might be a stubborn idiot but she meant well – as long as you weren't a battery chicken, or a foie gras goose with a funnel down its neck, or a baby calf, throat slit, bleeding slowly to death . . . Nor was she one of those actresses who considered it crucial to have an affair with their leading man. I never thought I was a jealous person till I met Hugo. You live and learn.

Except for the ritual appearances at TV awards and film premieres, when she dressed up in Voyage and Chloé with the best of them, Sarah was a real urban survivalist: in her combat trousers, heavy cotton sweater and padded gilet she looked exactly like a member of the crew. She must just have come on set. I knew she wasn't called till this afternoon.

'Sarah,' Hugo said resignedly, coming out of the toilet. 'What is it now?'

'I know you're pissed off with me about that scene I threw in Red's office,' she said straight away. 'I don't blame you. Honestly.'

She had sunk onto the sofa bed we had so recently vacated. It would be nice and warm for her.

'I got here five minutes ago,' she said. 'I went into my suite to dump my bag and then go over to make-up.'

'And?' Hugo still sounded impatient. 'What?'

'Oh, Hugo, please . . . I know the trouble I'm causing, I really do. It's all got out of control. Everything.' She sighed. 'I've been having some personal problems which I'm not going to go on about,' she said, turning her head to look at me, so I wouldn't feel excluded from the conversation. It wasn't a tactical decision not to piss me off; she really meant it. And then I thought of how rude she had been to Karen. Sarah was a mass of contradictions. 'I've been really on edge,' she was continuing. 'It's made me do stupid things, OK? But from now on enough is enough. I promise.'

'What's brought on this change of heart?' Hugo enquired, in a slightly more neutral tone of voice. He had brushed his hair so rigorously in the bathroom that it shot straight back from his widow's peak, gleaming almost platinum, emphasising the shape of his skull; with the high bridge of his nose, it made him look even more haughty than usual.

'Next door,' Sarah sighed again. 'You'd better come and see. But I don't want the word getting round, OK? It's bad enough as it is.'

Outside the wind was whipping down the narrow alley between Hugo and Sarah's trailer and the windowless back of the honey wagon. Sarah paused on the threshold of her suite.

'The work hasn't suffered, has it?' she said to Hugo intently. 'That's been OK, hasn't it? I haven't been buggering that up?'

'No,' he said almost gently. 'It's been fine. You haven't.'

Sarah turned and led us inside. Her suite was a mirror-image of Hugo's, but so cluttered with clothes, pinned-up postcards, pot plants and general junk that it was hard to make out its contours at first.

She gestured into the bathroom. We filed past her as she switched on the light. This too had every surface, not just the sink surround, but the top of the toilet, the tiny windowsill, the shower base, crammed with jars and bottles: more lotions and creams and Oxygen-Rich Anti-Cellulite AHA Toner Exfoliators than I had ever seen gathered together in one place. It's always the girls with scrubbed-bare faces who spend the most on skin creams. The bathroom, small and peach, smelt pleasantly of this blend of a hundred different unguents. The rather Arabian Nights effect was marred only by the dead animal pinned by its tail above the mirror, its head pointing down into the sink.

Beside it were some words scrawled in lipstick. They should really have been red, but Sarah had clearly not been able to provide that, being a skincare girl rather than a make-up one. I had never seen her in anything stronger than matt pink. The graffiti artist must have been very frustrated by having to write their slogan in Blush Rose. It undercut the effect considerably. Perhaps that was why the words were slapped on so heavily that they left stubs of lipstick at the end of most of the letters. The writer had not been in a good mood.

'You Callous Animal-Hating Bitch,' Hugo read out. 'Just Pray You Have A Better Death.'

He leant over and flicked the dead animal. Its glass eyes caught the light for a moment, glinting eerily, and then subsided.

'It's a stuffed fox fur,' I said over my shoulder to Sarah. 'Did you see? They'll have bought it from some market stall for a fiver.'

'That's what I thought,' she said, edging into the bathroom. 'But I was scared to look too closely in case it wasn't.'

'We're not dealing with someone prepared to go out and knock a stray cat on the head just so they could nail it up over your mirror,' Hugo said reassuringly.

'Be against their principles, anyway,' I said. 'Do you think this was the *Telegraph* thing?'

'Naseem was right.' Sarah shoved her hands through her hair, pulling it back, flat to her scalp. The curls sprang straight up as soon as she released them. 'He told me not to.'

'I don't like him,' Hugo observed, 'but he's got good instincts.'
Sarah let out a small, unamused laugh.

'Unlike me,' she said bitterly. 'I can pick a good part, but that's about it. I shoot my mouth off to tabloid journalists when I'm pissed, I do stupid photoshoots everyone tells me not to and as far as men go I'm a bloody disaster.'

'What about Paul?' I said.

'He's not exactly being a tower of strength.' She sighed. 'But when I get a tower of strength, I go and overdo that too. I can't even get that right. You know the funny thing?' she said ironically. 'I used to have this ex who was a bit of a villain. Really dodgy. If I found out who did this and told Vince about it, he'd do stuff to them they couldn't even imagine. Then they'd really have a reason to call me a callous bitch.'

I cleared my throat and said, as delicately as I could:

'How was your break-up with this guy? I mean, would he have a reason to do something like this?'

Sarah's laugh this time was genuinely humorous.

'You must be joking!' she said. 'It's the other way round. I'm still Vince's princess. Like I said, he'd sort out anyone who messed me around. He's done it before.' She looked at the dead fox. 'Besides, if Vince wanted to send someone a warning, he wouldn't buy a dead animal to do it.'

'What would he do?' Hugo enquired. 'Nail their family pet to the wall while still alive?'

'Something like that.'

'Charming,' I observed. 'I see why you broke up with him.'

But Sarah was still staring at the dead fox, and didn't answer. The conversation tailed off, and without it the bathroom immediately became claustrophobic. Sarah, standing in the doorway, looking into the mirror where her striking features were reflected back at her through smears of her own lipstick, seemed transfixed by the sight. She could not tear her eyes away from it. It was like the beginning of a slasher movie. Maybe, like *Candyman,* a hook would suddenly smash through the mirror.

Hugo cleared his throat.

'Sarah? Fascinating as your bathroom is, I feel we've exhausted its entertainment possibilities for now.'

She didn't move. I reached out and touched her lightly on the arm.

'Come on,' I said. 'Let's go and get a cup of tea.'

'So what *do* atheists yell when they come?'

'I thought you weren't listening.'

'I was listening,' Hugo corrected, 'it just wasn't top of my priority list. Answer, please.'

'Oh, Darwin! Darwin!'

'Mmn. A dry smile rather than a belly laugh.'

'What do you call it when a blonde dyes her hair dark?' Sarah said unexpectedly. She had been lost in a reverie for the last few minutes, sipping her tea. I had thought her attention miles away from our banter.

'Artifical intelligence,' she said, cheerfully, when neither of us hazarded a guess. 'What do you say to a blonde who's got a job?'

Hugo raised his eyebrows in silent query.

'I'll have chips with that, please.'

'Actually,' he observed, 'technically *I* am a blond. Though without an e.'

'I know a geezer who'll sort you out,' Lurch offered, joining our little group. We were standing round the tea trolley, and he arrived bearing the afternoon biscuit tin with quiet pride.

'Sort me out?' Hugo was genuinely baffled.

I was giggling. 'For an e, he means,' I explained.

'Yeah. No worries, mate,' Lurch said earnestly. How he loved to make other people happy. 'You want me to give him a call?'

'Maybe, Lurch. Maybe. Not right now, though. Hand me the biscuits.'

We foraged through the tin for our particular favourites.

'So do you think I should tell Red?' Sarah said finally. This question had been the point at which she had left us, in spirit, some minutes ago, and clearly she had been meditating on it ever since without reaching a conclusion.

'Lurch, why don't you take the biscuits off to Props?' I suggested. 'I don't think they've had any yet.'

'OK.' Lurch ambled off.

'Just being a bit discreet,' I said. 'I trust Lurch to keep his mouth shut, but there's no point pushing things.'

'Actually,' Hugo said slowly, 'no, I don't think you should tell Red. Why don't we just keep this among the three of us?'

Sarah turned a transfigured face to him. Her pale eyes glowed like white sapphires, almost clear, but with a light blue cast to them. Without a setting of dark mascara to ground it, their colour in her pale face was almost eerie.

'Oh, God, I was so hoping you'd say that,' she exclaimed. 'I don't want to tell *anyone*. I just want this thing over and done with. I've got no interest at all in playing the victim.'

'Good.' Hugo let out a long breath. 'Good.'

'Sarah! God! What the hell are you doing here!' Joanne, the make-up designer, exploded behind us. 'I've been looking for you everywhere! You should have been over half an hour ago!'

Joanne was wearing her brightest flame-red lipstick today. She only avoided looking clownish because of the care with which it had been applied. I thought suddenly that it hadn't been Joanne who had written on Sarah's bathroom mirror. She would have known Sarah's tastes enough to take for granted that there wouldn't have been a red lipstick there. And besides, she would have had some on her. The make-up girls were always lugging big canvas shoulder bags around with them, as if in perpetual expectation of setting off on a weekend break.

Did that mean it had been a man who had done it? Someone who would just blindly presume that all girls had red lipstick in their bathrooms? A straight man, then. Keith wouldn't have made that assumption. Keith . . . I thought about him for a moment.

'I'm so sorry,' Sarah was saying devoutly to Joanne. 'It won't happen again, I promise.'

'Well, come on then! You know I hate being rushed. If they weren't spending all this time setting up we'd be in real trouble.'

'Seems to have had the right effect on Sarah, anyway,' I observed as they vanished round the corner of the studio.

'I know,' Hugo said. 'I was just wondering in my Machiavellian little way whether that was exactly the kind of result whoever did it had in mind. Scare her into stopping these antics.'

'Very twisted,' I commented appreciatively, looking round us to make sure there was no one in eavesdropping distance. 'But you don't really think – I mean, who? Red? Karen? What if it hadn't worked?'

Hugo shrugged.

'Better that than Scenario B,' he said. 'Because if someone did it to get a reaction, and Sarah doesn't give them that satisfaction – very commendable of her, by the way – they might start upping the ante.'

'Oh, *shit.*'

'My thoughts exactly.'

It was as dark in the studio as if we were playing a game of paintball, stalking each other round the flats. Though a basic complement of working lights was on in the far set, they percolated only faintly through the fake walls and backdrops between me and them. A rehearsal was going on. If I concentrated hard I could hear the muffled voices of actors and director. It was part of Phil's work process to insist on run-throughs before each scene from which all the crew were rigidly excluded. When the bell rang everyone was supposed to leave the studio; but it was raining outside, yet again, and the late-afternoon sandwich platters had arrived only a few minutes ago . . .

I rounded the corner of the set I had seen the art department grunts painting late last night, their grey faces, worn down by exhaustion, hardly even relieved by the flattering peach they were slapping onto the walls. Now, with its swags of curtains, thick carpet and bed piled high with pillows, it was the battlefield for Gav's fights with Lorraine, his long-suffering wife. Ahead of me was my target, and I was closing in fast. In a darkened corner a group of people crouched round something on the floor. Their huddled bodies blocked any view, but one of them was shining a powerful torch down on it like an amateurish play about international spies, and they were whispering conspiratorially to one another. As I approached the hissing became clearer:

'Is that cheese and onion?'

'No, that's the egg and cress – I think—'

'Here, give us the torch a second, Tone—'

'Shit, where's that ham one gone—'

Crew whispers were an exquisite thing; to hear these big bulky guys murmuring to each other so carefully, half-eliding any sibilants, was a fascination in itself. They looked like they were having a midnight feast out of an Enid Blyton boarding-school book: sardines and ginger cake a special delicacy. This had always baffled me, particularly since she never specified whether they were eaten together or apart.

'Squash up,' I muttered, sliding in next to Jimmy the runner. 'Where's the cheese and onion?'

'Careful,' he hissed, pointing them out to me. 'They make your breath stink. Tony's been stuffing them down and he don't half reek.'

'Sod off,' Tony retorted.

'I'll score a mint off someone after,' I reassured them.

Loaded with sandwiches, I retired to the back door, followed shortly by Jimmy. It was his job to stand outside it, pointing to the red studio light flashing off and on above our heads, indicating that a rehearsal was taking place. Technically he was supposed to stop people going in, but when they knew there were sandwiches in there it was hopeless. The best he could do was plead for quiet.

'Brr,' I shivered, wrapping my coat closer round me as the cold afternoon air, thick with damp, began to permeate through it.

'Nice coat,' Jimmy said through a mouthful of sandwich.

I stroked the lapel lovingly. It was second-hand fake leopardskin, a Seventies original, bought years ago when I was very skint but still unable to resist the temptation. It had served me faithfully and well.

'Spent fifty pounds on it years back and went hungry for a week,' I said. 'Worth every penny, though.'

'You look like the entrance to a brothel,' said the focus puller, who was getting himself some tea. 'Red light over you and Sam in that leopardskin. You look like a tart on a break. And Jimmy'd be the bouncer. Bit skinny, mind you.'

'Charming,' Jimmy said dismissively. The focus puller was old guard; perpetually lugubrious, he either made salacious sexual comments or told everyone darkly that they were wasting their time when they made the slightest variant from The Way Things Had Always Been Done. His huge, dirty old sweatshirt was randomly striped with pieces of coloured gaffer tape – red, yellow, blue, green, black and white – lending a bizarre note of whimsy to his lumpen appearance.

'Oi,' he said now, coming over to take advantage of the slight shelter provided by the studio entrance. He smelt musty and unwashed, but this was standard by now. I was used to the odours of dirty hair, bad breath, stale cigarette smoke and general poor hygiene. Most of the crew worked twelve-hour days, with another couple of hours travel time to and from the studios. Usually all they did when they got home was neck down some beers and fall asleep in what they'd been wearing that day. I was glad I'd be out of here before the end of the shoot, when the clothes and hair could confidently be expected to have reached their nadir.

'You see that dirty horoscope fax?' he was saying. 'I think sound's got it. Sexual positions for each sign. With drawings.'

He leered at us. I stuffed another sandwich into my mouth, not bothering to answer. Jimmy just shrugged.

The focus puller looked aggrieved. Propping his polystyrene cup of tea precariously on a ledge, he started to roll a cigarette.

'All right then,' he said, taking our indifference as a challenge, 'what about the latest with our diva? Heard someone put a dead cat in her dressing room.'

'Who told you that?' I asked as casually as I could.

'Little bird,' he said, tapping his nose. 'Bit of a laugh, eh? Cut her down to size.'

'It's not funny,' Jimmy said, reacting with surprising vigour. He was a nice, sensible boy, barely out of his teens but with a good head on his shoulders. He would also have been very pretty, scrubbed up, shaved and wearing a pair of trousers that fitted him properly: but I was mature enough to make my character assessments quite irrespective of the physical attractiveness of the subject in question. I hoped.

'Sarah could have been really upset,' Jimmy was continuing. 'It might have fucked things up badly. She's been going off the handle enough as it is. Did you see that scene she pulled in the lunch trailer?'

The focus puller shrugged, a nasty gleam in his eye.

'If you'd seen as much as I have, boy,' he said, poking Jimmy in the chest with one stubby finger, 'you wouldn't get so worked up. 'S all par for the course, innit, bit of trouble on set.'

'Jimmy!' The first AD put her head through the door behind us. 'Rehearsal's over, we're setting up, let's get going!'

Jimmy jumped to attention, shooting inside. Seconds later the light stopped flashing, signalling the end of rehearsal, and the bell rang twice, ditto. I hated that bell. It was metallic and insistent and sounded just like the one that rang at school for the end of break.

Everyone piled back inside. The wall o'lights and kenoflows were all switched on, flooding the set with what always seemed a disproportionate amount of white light. It would be as bright in there by now as if it were about to spontaneously combust. As everyone threw themselves into activity, the sandwich tray was left to its own devices, and now that we could see properly Lurch and I took our time making a further snack selection as the art department clunked into action around us. Riggers and stagehands, their hair tied back, drills in their hands, rolls of tape hanging off their black Velcroed work belts, piled back and forth. In the distance we could hear them moving furniture. Sometimes it seemed to me that all they ever said to each other was an endless round of:

'Is this staying?'

'No, that's going, mate, is that going too?'

'No, it's staying, mate, is that going?'

'Dunno . . . Is that staying?'

'Right, we've decided we're moving the set round a hundred and eighty degrees, let's move it, we want to do this BEFORE THE END OF THE DAY please and it's a complicated set-up,' the voice of the first AD came loudly over the din. She was abrasive but very efficient. She hadn't been Phil's choice for first AD: Hugo had told me that Phil had wanted someone he had worked with before, who'd already signed up for a film.

'One of those nice public school boys who can't quite make it in the professions,' Hugo had drawled. 'Loads of them doing first AD work. They're solid and they know their place.'

But this one had higher ambitions of which she made no secret.

'In too much of a hurry,' Hugo said. 'She's getting so far up Phil's nose she'd better worry he doesn't explode one day and sneeze her out.'

I wandered past a couple of riggers heaving a large and expensive sofa through a passageway too narrow for it, hugging the wall to round the set. I hadn't seen this one yet. It was Gav's living room, and was very well thought-out. The art director had resisted the temptation to give Gav and his wife the classic gangster Essex mansion, all gold finish and artistic black shiny sculptures from expensive department stores; instead he had gone for a comparatively minimalist look. The floor was a dull parquet, the colours muted. They had found a great kitchen to shoot those scenes in, granite and marble, but the rest of the house hadn't been what they wanted so they had decided to build a set instead.

Maria, who played the wife Gav was neglecting for Sarah's character, was smoking a cigarette by the open back door. She was a striking blonde, painfully thin in real life, her arms so etiolated you could see the bones through them when she had her back to a wall o'light; but on camera she looked no more than slender. And she wore the clothes wonderfully.

'Fab, isn't it,' she said to me, indicating her pale mint trouser suit.

'You read my mind. I was just thinking about your outfits.'

'Armani, darling,' she said. 'Nothing but the best for me. Even if my hubby isn't giving it to me where it counts.'

'He's too busy giving it to Sam,' Keith said, joining us by the door. 'Oh, lovely, a breath of fresh air. I *don't* think,' he observed, looking out into the wet grey air. 'Heard you two were at it like rabbits in Hugo's suite yesterday. Lucky, lucky you. That boy is a mystery to me. He's such a homo. And yet he isn't.'

'I don't think rabbits do it in that position,' I said. 'How the hell do you know—'

'Ssh!' Keith said, raising a finger to his lips. 'Can't reveal sources, darling. You know my methods.'

'You are out of control, Keith,' I said crossly.

'Should have seen him in rehearsal just now,' Maria said. 'Thought he was going to rape me on the sideboard.'

'Wait for the real thing, darling,' Keith said, waggling his eyebrows. 'So,' he added, lowering his voice. 'The latest on the Sarah front. Is it true someone put a dead cat in her bathroom? Do tell.'

I closed my eyes for a moment. 'It wasn't a dead cat. As far as I've heard,' I hastily qualified. '*I* heard it was a stuffed animal.'

'A teddy bear?' Keith said disbelievingly. 'Surely not.'

'No, a real animal. But dead a while back.'

'Oh, I see.'

'Who told you that, Keith?'

Keith widened his already large eyes so that the whites were visible all around the dark irises. It was meant to express theatrical innocence but the effect was more witch-doctor about to cast a particularly nasty spell.

'Ugh, stop it,' I said, shuddering. 'You look like a voodoo priest.'

'It was supposed to be my Laurence Olivier blacked-up for Othello impression,' Keith said. 'Those rolling eyes! Those quivering lips!'

'He could be a real old ham, our Larry,' Maria said, stubbing out her cigarette. 'So what's this about a dead animal?'

She sounded totally indifferent. It was obvious she was asking only to keep some kind of conversation going. Keith pounced on her at once.

'I can't believe you don't care about our big scandal!' he said reprovingly.

'Keith.' Maria looked tired. 'I have a three-year-old and a small baby at home, I'm having trouble expressing my milk, my bloody husband's being as useless as always and I'm going straight onto a three-month shoot in Glasgow after this. I'm just doing my job and getting out of here, OK?'

'Well, put things in perspective if you must,' Keith said tartly.

'Apology accepted,' she said, softening a little. She lit another cigarette. 'God, it's lucky we don't have scratch'n'sniff TV. I must reek like an ashtray by now. Go on, bring me up to date, I know you're dying to.'

Keith filled her in. 'But the latest is an outrage actually committed on set,' he finished. 'Talk about bringing things close to home.'

'But how did someone get into her trailer?' Maria said. 'Is there a master key or something?' She frowned. 'You mean it was someone on production?'

I shrugged. 'I'll bet you most keys fit most locks on those trailers,' I said. 'Like old hotel keys. And if not you could get in with a credit card in a minute, just flick back the latch. They're not built for high security, those things.'

'God, that's not exactly reassuring,' Maria said. 'I've always left all my stuff in my trailer. My bag's sitting there right now with my phone and all my cards in it.'

'This isn't a thief,' Keith said dismissively. 'It's an activist. Someone putting their money where their mouth is.'

'Yeah, well, they didn't have to do it on set,' Maria said firmly. 'This was going OK. I wish they'd keep their consciences to themselves. We've all got jobs to do.'

'Just because you're a mother doesn't automatically entitle you to sound superior,' Keith retorted, stung.

Maria, sensibly, ignored him. She stared outside instead, dragging on the cigarette as if its oral satisfaction somehow compensated for having a baby pulling on her breasts as soon as she walked in the door each evening. But I looked at Keith, feeling worried. I didn't like the way he had jumped to the defence of whoever had left that dead fox in Sarah's suite.

He read my mind at once.

'Relax, sweetie. It wasn't me,' he said reassuringly. Then he flashed a big smile. 'Or was it? Can you be quite sure? I do lie for a living, you know. I tell you what.'

'What?' I said reluctantly.

'If it *was* me . . .' Keith said tantalisingly. Maria and I waited for him to finish. 'They'll never find out,' he concluded. 'Don't worry. I'm too clever to get myself into trouble.'

'Oh God,' she said wearily. 'I don't even care. I just want all of this to go away.' She waved a huge, comprehensive arc with her cigarette. 'Too much to bloody ask, isn't it? Just make it all go away?'

'Sorry,' I said regretfully. 'Left my magic wand at home.'

'Even if my tits would stop leaking,' Maria said, hardly listening to me. 'That would be a real result.'

'Ugh.' I shuddered. How did she bear it? That was putting things into perspective with a vengeance.

CHAPTER FIVE

'Maria? Oh, there you are. Let's be having a look at you, then.'

Maria automatically pushed herself off the doorjamb to allow Siobhan full access to her body. Siobhan adjusted Maria's necklace, smoothed down her lapels and swivelled her round by the shoulders to check out the back view much as if she were a store dresser putting the last touches to a fibreglass mannequin.

'Are you *sure* I don't have VPL?' Maria said fretfully. 'I'm always worried about this suit. The jacket's so short.'

'I swear. It's fine. You look fine. I'm more worried about your nipple pads. How're they doing?'

Maria prodded her breasts with the hand that wasn't holding the cigarette.

'Seem OK so far,' she reported. 'They don't even feel damp.'

'Great. I really don't want to have to be holding a hairdryer to your bosoms between shots. And the milk'll mark the suit.'

Siobhan flashed a smile at me. 'The things we have to think of,' she said. 'First time I dress a nursing mother. Always something new, eh?'

'I think it'll be OK,' Maria repeated like an automaton, her face drawn with exhaustion. She looked as if the cigarette were the only thing holding her together.

'No offence,' Siobhan said cheerfully, 'but I look at how knackered you are and all I can think is, Am I using enough contraception?'

'No,' Maria said fervently. 'Believe me. Whatever you've got is not enough.'

'Pill and condom,' Siobhan said.

'Get a cap too,' I suggested. 'Make them fight their way through two layers of rubber instead of one.'

'And if they manage that there's all those hormones lying in wait,' Siobhan said.

'Or just don't have sex,' Maria said wearily. 'It's not worth it. I'm totally off it right now.'

'Not *possible!*' Siobhan exclaimed happily.

'You're rich enough to get someone to look after them for you, though,' Maria said, stung by Siobhan's seemingly limitless bonhomie. 'Nannies help.'

Siobhan wasn't that keen on having her family money mentioned, but she handled it well, I thought. Besides, with a surname as famous as hers, comments must be inevitable.

'Can't pay someone to have 'em for you, though,' she said pleasantly enough. 'Well, you can, but look at how complicated it gets. Nope, I'm never having babies. Not if it puts you off sex. I just started shagging this new guy, and it's fucking brilliant. Literally.'

'Oh, I get it. No wonder you can't stop talking about sex,' I said.

'I think I forgot how good it could be,' Siobhan said smugly. 'My ex and I did so much E together he could never get it up anyway, and I was too out of it to mind. I'm never making that mistake again.'

'Some guys have that problem on blow,' I pointed out, having hardly ever seen Siobhan without a joint in her hand.

'Not Sanjay!' she smirked.

'Is he the bloke from Stage Two? You can't hide anything from Keith,' I added before she could ask how I knew.

'Yeah. He's a real sweetie.'

Siobhan gave Maria one last assessing, professional look, then pulled the relevant Polaroid off her belt, where it hung with several others all pierced through at the corner with snap-on rings. Carefully she checked Maria up and down against it, and finally returned it to its place with the others.

Joanne, her lipstick flaming through the gloom, her eyelashes heavy with mascara, had already appeared to check out Maria's make-up and hair. The cut, loose and unstructured, needed plenty of attention. Joanne fluffed and backcombed and played around with individual strands as showily as a camp TV hairdresser for the benefit of the cameras. Like many make-up girls – the politically correct term was actually 'make-up designer', but it was hardly ever used except on the credits – Joanne had been to drama school but failed to make it as an actress. Plenty of people managed the transition without bitterness, but Joanne wasn't one of them. She liked to go out with actors because she thought it raised her status and one-upped the actresses they might otherwise have been dating. And plenty of actors dated make-up girls. Hard not to be attracted to a pretty chick whose job it was to make you look good.

The first AD came over to call Maria on set. Keith was already there, talking to Phil.

'Hang on a sec,' Joanne said, quickly touching up a few tiny spots on Maria's face with a colour she had already blended on the back of her own hand. 'And more powder . . . there . . . Now don't touch your hair!' she warned Maria. 'There's not that much of it as it is!'

Julie, Joanne's sidekick, was waiting close to the set with her powder and sponge ready. She would have to be ready to dash in and powder Keith just before the shot.

'He's got such a shine problem,' Siobhan muttered to me. 'It's a bloody nightmare.'

'Poor Julie.'

Siobhan snorted. 'Look, when someone shines, they're like, *shining* all over, right? Know what I mean? He's so sweaty I have to wash everything he wears at the end of every day. It's a right bore.'

She stretched her arms out to each side, narrowly avoiding about sixteen polystyrene cups stacked precariously on an old cupboard to her right.

'I'm dying for a spliff,' she said confidentially. 'You smoke?'

'Not really.'

'Don't know what I'd do without it on set to pass the long weary hours.'

Joanne, standing beside us, clicked her tongue disapprovingly. Siobhan bridled.

'Hey,' she said, 'we've both got our ways of making the time go quicker, right? You flirt with everything in trousers, I smoke spliff. Each to their own.'

'I'll ignore that,' Joanne snapped.

Siobhan shrugged and lit a cigarette.

'Maria looks good,' I said to cut the tension.

'Thin hair,' Joanne said dismissively, walking away to the other side of the set to stand next to Julie instead.

Siobhan rolled her eyes.

'That thin hair thing! God, she gets up my nose. We were on *Country Vets* together and we were both doing Natasha Daniels.' This was a very pretty young actress who had just broken free from *EastEnders*. 'Joanne kept saying to her every morning, in this fake-concerned voice: "Oh dear, what *are* we going to do about this thin hair?" Poor Nat was a nervous wreck by the end of the shoot.'

'Can we have a bit of quiet, *please*?' the first AD said loudly in our general direction. Siobhan pulled a face at me.

'OK. Now, you're sure about when you hit that mark?' Phil was saying to Maria.

'The first line – "Do you really think that's any of your business?" – I've finished that by the time I come through the door, yeah?' she said.

'Continuity?' Phil turned around, looking for an answer.

'As she comes through the door . . .' Continuity rifled through the sheets of paper on her clipboard. 'No, she's still speaking. Last two or three words as she actually comes in.'

'OK. Got that, Maria?'

'Yeah.'

'Great. OK, we're as ready as we'll ever be. Let's run it. Red light, please.'

'OK!' the first AD called. 'Let's do it!'

The bell rang fiercely once. Outside Jimmy would be stationed under the red light, now on continuously, barring the door even to sandwich-seekers.

'Settle down please, nice and quiet,' the first AD said loudly to everyone assembled to watch the shot. 'Checks, please. Is sound ready?'

'Yes,' came a distant voice.

'Backing clear . . . Shooting!'

'Turn over.'

The camera trainee darted in with the clapperboard. This and carrying around the many rolls of coloured gaffer tape seemed her two main tasks in life. The tapes were slung on a cord over her shoulder, six giant beads of primary colours adding a welcome touch of brightness to her drab grey sweater.

'Four-eight-seven take one,' she said loudly, clicking the top down.

'And . . . action,' said Phil, his attention not on the live actors but their images on the little monitor in front of him.

'Don't you care what Gav's getting up to behind your back?' Keith called to Maria through the open door. He was lounging against the fireplace, legs crossed.

'Do you really think that's any of your business?' Maria came through the door, carrying a glass of wine. The tired nursing mother was gone, her body now inhabited by a provocative, self-assured gangster's wife looking for some payback.

'You need to watch that,' Keith said, nodding at the glass. 'Classic bored housewife stuff. You don't want to go the dipso route, do you? Why don't you take up a hobby or something?'

'And what exactly did you have in mind?' Maria said challengingly.

Keith crossed the room to her in one swift movement, taking the glass from her hand.

'You know exactly what I've got in mind. Sort yourself out with a bit of what Gav's not giving you.' He tossed down the rest of the wine and put the glass down on the sideboard behind her, reaching around her to do it, his hand caressing her arm as it returned.

'I've been wanting to get into your knickers ever since I saw you,' he said, his voice low now, husky with sex. He took another step forward till he was standing so close to her that from my angle she was almost hidden from view. The sexual charge between them was suddenly palpable. Ah, the miracle of good acting.

'Well?' Maria said, sounding nervous but titillated. She leant back to look up at him. 'Let's see you do it, then. Or haven't you got the bottle to fuck the boss's wife?'

'I'm not stupid. I know you're just using me to get back at him,' Keith said, starting to unbutton her jacket. 'But guess what? It don't matter. I really don't give a toss why you're doing it just as long as I get to have you.'

He pushed her back against the sideboard, kissing her hard. Maria's arms came up behind his head, cradling it, then pulling it down to her breasts. After a few moments, Keith sank to his knees. The spectators were absolutely silent, like peeping Toms who had finally hit paydirt. The zip of Maria's trousers going down was loud and clear. Keith buried his head between her legs. Maria grabbed onto the sideboard with one hand, stuffing the other into her mouth, moaning behind it.

'And . . . cut! Good!' Phil said. 'Hot stuff, you two!'

'We got a problem with the sound,' the recordist called. 'It's that sodding lorry reversing again.'

'Oh, fuck,' Phil said with surprising mildness. 'Fuck these bloody unsoundproofed stages.'

'*Jimmy!*' yelled the first AD. He came running from the far side of the studio. 'That *fucking lorry was reversing again*! Sound's picked up the beeps! Why aren't you doing your job?'

'I told them, honestly,' Jimmy said desperately. 'I told him we were shooting, but he wouldn't stop!'

'Right, that's it, I'm going to deal with this myself.'

She shot off like a human cannonball. Her anger levels seemed to rise in direct proportion to Phil's ability to maintain his calm.

'Damn, damn, damn,' Keith said, rising to his feet.

Maria zipped up her trousers and sank wearily onto the sofa. Keith flopped onto it beside her. She lit a cigarette and resumed staring blankly ahead of her, all in one practised gesture. Keith wound his fingers together and started twiddling his thumbs idly. From illicit oral sex to existential boredom in twenty seconds. I watched him thoughtfully as Julie, perched on the arm of the sofa, dabbed his forehead with an absorbent sponge and then applied another dusting of powder. His expression never altered.

'He's good, isn't he?' said Siobhan, echoing my own opinion. 'That was well sexy. You'd never know he was a bum-bandit. I'll just give him another de-lint,' she added meditatively. 'That black sweater he's wearing shows up everything.'

She picked her way through the camera tracks and waited until

Julie had finished with him. How odd it must be to have this supply of people hovering around you, your appearance their only task at that moment. It must make you feel omnipotent. I watched Keith again submitting to Siobhan's de-linter, hardly moving a muscle, and thought that he must be in particular danger of it going to his head. In Keith's eyes, Keith himself was by far the most important person in the world, and always would be; he constantly lamented his inability to find a steady boyfriend, but what he really wanted, or needed, was a worshipper rather than a partner. Someone to fuss round him at the end of a long day's shooting, listen appreciatively to his stories, and – maybe – give gasps of appreciation at his cleverness in putting that stuffed fox in Sarah's trailer?

Well, if Keith had done it, one thing was for sure: I believed his own words on the subject. It would never be traced back to him.

CHAPTER SIX

Red always gave me the impression of someone who would have been happiest dressed as the crew did, in baggy jeans and layers of comfortable sweaters. The smart suits, the power earrings, the careful make-up seemed incongruous, as if she wore them only because she felt they were required of a producer. There was something sketchy about her accessorising, as if she had bought a job lot from an expensive shop without looking at it too closely, and then pulled on the first thing that came to hand in the morning from the cupboard marked Work Clothes.

'Well,' she said, leaning slightly back in her chair. We were in her office, a long, irregular room in what had once been the attics of the old house around which the studios had been built. The production team on *Driven* occupied most of the top floor; there was a large central office for Karen, the coordinator, and the two secretaries, with a kitchen and editing suite beyond it. Red and the line producer shared this office, which, with its sloping ceilings, timbered beams and view over the green fields beyond, was a world away from the cold stage below. The old boiler fizzed and clanked in a reassuringly noisy way through the wall and the carpets were worn-down at the edges. It was like the headmistress's office at an old-fashioned girls' boarding school.

I waited to see what Red had to say. She had asked me to come in to talk about Sarah's progress with the soldering iron, but that had obviously been a pretext and her questions on the subject had borne that out, being perfunctory in the extreme.

'So,' she said, as if summing it all up. 'You think Sarah's getting on fine?'

'Enough for what she has to do,' I said patiently. 'It's not much. Just to look right from a distance.'

'You're pretty much finished, aren't you?' Red asked.

'Just a couple more days here and there.'

'I imagine you'll be relieved. Filming can be very tedious.'

I was beginning to get some inkling of her drift.

'It's been quite interesting, actually,' I said, thrown onto the defensive. I had been coming in more than I was needed, and this emphasis on the tedium of filming made me look like Nancy No-Mates, prepared to put up with any amount of boredom just to have people to hang out with. 'I work on my own. Apart from that theatre project I did. It's nice to have a chance to be part of a team.'

'That's how you met Hugo, wasn't it?' she said. 'Working in the theatre.'

'That's right.'

'The Cross. Where they found that dead body.'

I nodded cautiously.

'And didn't one of your mobiles once fall on someone? Oh, don't get me wrong.'

She held her hand up quickly. I had already started to bristle.

'I'm not saying it was your fault. Just that you seem – well, would trouble-prone be a fair way to put it? You have a rather chequered past.'

The headmistress analogy was seeming more and more apt.

'What's your point?' I said coldly. 'You had plenty of time to check me out before you hired me. And since you actually based Sarah's character on me – well, the metal-sculpting part – it seems rather weird to be coming down on me now.'

'I'm not coming down on you, Sam.'

'Could have fooled me,' I muttered.

Red leant forward over her desk, steepling her hands together and resting her chin on the top of the fingers.

'You were with Hugo when he went into Sarah's suite, weren't you? You saw the dead fox and the writing on her mirror.'

I bit my tongue hard, wondering whether she was trying to weasel information out of me by pretending that she knew it already.

Chained!

Silence seemed my best course. It was annoying, though. I felt like a sulky kid forced into a corner.

'I know what happened,' she said. 'There's not much happens on this set without my finding out about it.'

'It's not exactly my story to tell,' I said, sounding prissy. 'I felt it was up to Sarah.'

'Do you have any idea who would do something like that?'

And now she was trying to make me into the school sneak. I hesitated a moment too long.

'Look,' I said finally, 'it's none of my business. Obviously I want the production to go well, mainly for Hugo's sake. But beyond that . . .' I tailed off.

'Hmm.' She was still staring at me hard. 'Sarah seems to have settled down a lot. She's not giving any more interviews except ones approved by her agent, or the BBC publicity department. But all these rumours and gossip on set . . . it can lead to a terrible atmosphere. I don't like it. I won't put up with it.'

'Not to mention the worry that this might not be the last we've heard of the phantom fox-fixer,' I said smartly, meaning to needle her.

Her eyes narrowed. 'Exactly. Well, I think we understand each other.'

'Clear as mud. Do you want to spell out exactly what we understand?' I said icily. By now I was buried up to the neck in her drift and beginning to catch cold.

'Maybe after you'd finished the scenes you have still to do, you could limit your visits here to the strictly – well, conjugal,' she said. 'Obviously I can't tell you not to come in and see Hugo. But I think outside presences on set don't really help the atmosphere. Not to mention all this trouble with Sarah.'

She might have been a football referee handing me the red card. I couldn't have had a clearer warning-off. Red thought that I was the one who had put the fox in Sarah's trailer. For all I knew that meant she also assumed that I had been behind the sending of the hate mail. Forget Nancy No-Mates; Red had cast me as Sam Scapegoat. Maybe because I was an outsider; maybe because she thought I might be

65

jealous of Sarah's sex scenes with Hugo. Whatever her reasons were, there was no way to prove her wrong.

I didn't try to deny Red's suspicions: any attempt to protest would just have made me look guiltier. And then there was my chequered past. I snorted. Why exactly was the expression 'chequered'? Squares made no sense at all.

Red had taken the calculated risk that I wouldn't mention this talk to Hugo. Maybe, in her assumption that I was the culprit, she would think that I wouldn't be brazen enough to bring the possibility of my guilt to his attention. I was so lost in speculation that I nearly walked straight into Karen, who was coming out of the kitchen with a cup of tea.

'God! Sorry!' I said, jumping back just in time.

'What's with you?' she said, staring at me. 'You're a million miles away. On a not very happy planet.'

'I'm only gradually coming back,' I said, slapping my cheek lightly. 'Ow. OK, neural reflexes still working . . .'

'Want a fag?' she said. 'You look like you could do with one.'

'What a good idea.'

'We'd better smoke in there,' she said, nodding to the kitchen. 'The packet's on my desk. Why don't you get it and I'll put the kettle on?'

Along the wall of the main office were pinned the black and white, eight by ten publicity photographs of the featured actors in *Driven*. There was something unbearably poignant about this massed rank of super-public faces, each with their head tilted to their best angle, trying to look both confident yet malleable enough to suit any role that might be on offer. And the subtext screamed: Pick me! Pick *me*! so loudly that it might as well have been printed below their heads. Even Hugo wasn't immune. Looking at his handsome face, I felt an odd stab of fear and tenderness at the vulnerability the context conferred on him. Joanne might envy actresses, but she was wrong. Better a secure niche doing make-up than the perpetual insecurity of an actor's life.

The sound of movement in Red's office made me start. I grabbed the cigarettes and scarpered into the kitchen.

'Did you want a tea?' Karen said. The kettle was just coming to the boil.

'No, thanks. A fag'll do nicely.'

I lit one and drew the smoke in deeply. It was tremendously calming. Karen lit up too, shoving the pack into the large pocket on her fleecy miniskirt, where it sat on her thigh like a rectangular growth.

'Did Red just do you over?' she asked companionably, her squarish pink face expressing nothing but friendliness. If Red had confided her suspicions of me to Karen, the latter was keeping an open mind on the subject. Or she was a very good dissembler.

'It was like she knew every single button to press,' I said reflectively, beginning to recover. 'And she did them one by one, in order.'

'She's terrible for that,' Karen agreed. 'What was it, budgets?'

'Budgets?' I said blankly.

'It's not her job, but with Grania off sick . . .' Grania was the line producer, who had a bad case of flu. 'I know she was saying something about you being around a lot and hoping you wouldn't be expecting to be paid for more than what you'd agreed.'

'Of course not. I mean, of course I wasn't expecting it. I'm just at a, um, a quiet point work-wise and it's a nice opportunity to see a bit of Hugo.'

God, I hated having to justify myself, even if Karen didn't expect it of me.

'Well, sure,' she said, as if it were the most obvious thing in the world. 'It's really great for him, I bet. It's so difficult for most actors not being able to see their boyfriends or girlfriends for months on end – because you know what it's like, even when you do have a day off, or they come down to see you on location or whatever, they're so distracted they can't really snap out of work mode. The other person's expecting quality time and ends up feeling like they're being a nuisance instead. Or excluded because they're completely out of the loop – you know, all the in-jokes and stuff.'

'You sound like you've got lots of experience,' I commented.

'Oh, I've seen both sides. Done loads of location work and had my fair share of actors,' Karen said cheerfully. She named a few of them. 'And I was seeing Paul Hinks for a while a couple of years ago. First series of *Country Vets*, before he got really big.'

She caught my eye.

'Oh, that was well before he started seeing Sarah,' she assured me. 'No complications there. Besides, Paul sleeps with everyone he works with sooner or later. We went out for a couple of months. Actually,' she said meditatively, 'Paul wasn't so bad. He's so self-obsessed it was the same all the time. I mean, I didn't exactly get any sense of disillusionment when he was working hard and didn't have much time to see me. He always just talked about himself anyway.'

'Yes, that's how I remember Paul,' I said.

'You know him?'

'Just a bit. He was in the play I did the sets for. *The Dream.*'

'He's got a nice cock, I'll give him that,' Karen said reflectively. 'And have you ever noticed how redheaded guys taste different?'

'God! You too? I thought that was just a one-off.'

'No, it's definitely true.'

'More delicate.'

'Sweeter.'

'Do you have a big thing about redheads?' I asked curiously. 'Like to like and all that?'

Karen's hand rose automatically to her pale ginger hair. Naturally curly, it was scraped back from her forehead in the current fashion, which only worked if you had poker-straight hair: little fuzzy twists had escaped at intervals around her face and there were odd kinks running along her scalp, like stunted cornrows. She used brown mascara on her lashes but didn't dye her eyebrows. The effect was schizophrenic: my eyes kept flicking from one to the other, trying to integrate them, and failing.

'I used to,' she said meditatively. 'I got really put off by one guy, though. This one – you won't believe this, but he used to look down at us and yell: "Red pubes! Red pubes!" when he was coming. Yuck.'

I started giggling. If nothing else, Karen had completely distracted me from my recent experience as number-one suspect for the dead fox incident.

'One for the record books,' she observed.

'That wasn't Paul?'

'Britain's best-loved TV vet? No, no. Very into looking at himself, though. Mirrors everywhere. You can imagine. *So,*' she added, her tone signalling the introduction of a new topic, 'did you hear about Sarah's little incident?'

'Everyone seems to have by now.'

'Oh dear. Anyway, it seems to have given Sarah the shock she needed,' she said. 'It's an ill wind. She actually came and apologised to me for that scene in Red's office.'

'Oh, really? That's good.'

'I know.' Karen started rinsing out her mug. 'I was really pissed off with her.'

'You handled it very well. I mean, you just said your piece and walked out. You didn't seem too worked up.'

'You can't lose your temper easily doing a job like this,' Karen said. 'That's production – keep your head while all around you are losing theirs. It gives you much more power that way. Besides, things always work out in the end,' she added, stacking her mug in the drying rack. 'Sarah calmed down and came back to say sorry. End of story.'

Her face was so expressionless as she said these last words that it looked positively stolid.

'Still waters run the deepest,' I observed.

She gave me a very nice smile. '*Oh* yes,' she said, as cheerfully as ever. 'You bet they do.'

CHAPTER SEVEN

I was walking across the studio parking lot. It was well after sundown, and the only illumination down at the end of the lot was a couple of pale neon lights by the security guard's booth, far over by the entrance. The lights seemed washed-out, too weak to cast more than a faint glimmer. People were always complaining how difficult it was to find their cars in the virtual darkness.

I was going home; I'd finished for the day. Hugo had a couple of hours to go and I was too tired to wait for him. In my hand were the keys to my minivan. I stopped for a moment to put on my jacket. It was colder than I'd thought. Not for the first time I envied Hugo, who, like all the other actors, had a unit driver to ferry him to and from the studio. No such privileges for a lowly stand-in.

There was no one around. The lot was totally deserted. Crew who had finished shot off as fast as they could. The caterers had packed up hours ago. Besides, it was dark, the weather nasty and damp. People were either on set, pushing to get done for the day, or in their trailers working on their budgets and sorting out things for the next day's shooting schedule. Stage One, opposite the lot, was empty for the week, its doors shuttered. The earthmovers of Stage Two stood silently to my left, their shapes silhouetted against the dark sky, faint neon gleaming on their dirty paintwork.

The rounded-pumpkin shape of my Golf van was unmistakable. I had coveted one for years and when finally a few decent sales had allowed me to buy it I had said goodbye to the Escort without a backward glance. Still, the minivan was rather put in its place by Siobhan's Rav4 jeep just beyond it, with its sleek lines and cutely stubby backside. I sighed. A Rav4, a flat in Notting Hill, and she didn't even seem spoilt by her riches. Life could be very unfair.

I didn't hear their approach, but they wouldn't have needed to be particularly stealthy. It was a blustery night. A couple of empty cans and bottles were bowling down the alleyways between the stages as if the wind were playing a game with them. Besides, footsteps on the tarmac of the parking lot scarcely triggered any warning signal in my brain. Just some other lucky sods, done for the evening, heading for the warmth of their cars, their own music on the stereo, the comforting familiar pattern of red and green lights flashing on the dashboard.

So when the bag dropped over my head I was taken completely by surprise. For a split second, idiotically, I thought that the wind had somehow blown my jacket over my head. Then the bag tightened over my face, pulled harder than any gust of wind could manage, and I knew something was badly wrong. Smacking both my hands into the side of the car for extra leverage, I brought up my right knee and kicked back as hard as I could. The edge of my boot sole whacked satisfyingly into my attacker's upper thigh, propelling him backwards. A grunt of surprise and pain, and the hands on the bag slackened. He was probably fighting the impulse to grab the wounded leg. Always a bad distraction.

I swung round, stiffening my right arm and bringing it round in a long swooping trajectory that connected with his shoulder and probably hurt me more than it did the shoulder in question. I had meant to stab him with the car keys, but I had judged the distance all wrong and instead the keys went flying out of my hand, jarred by the impact. Picking your targets was so hard with a bag over your face. At least it was fabric, I could breathe easily enough—

I had it half off when the second one grabbed me from behind, his hands closing over mine, forcing the bag down again. If I'd assumed the first attacker was a guy, I knew for sure this one was. The smell of stale beer, together with the damp, urinous stench of clothes that have been wet with sweat, dried off and then sweated into again, was unmistakable. It was then, for the first time, that it occurred to me to scream. I let out a yell which resounded off the concrete like a series of ricochets. The one behind me cursed and slapped a hand over my mouth. Every time he moved another wash of foul smell surged from his pores. I slammed my elbow back and up, into his face. I heard his wail of pain and used the moment to twist free and start running. Only, still blind, trying to wrestle the bag off as I went, I crashed into the guy who had grabbed me first, rebounded off him and, as I was catching my balance, the one with the hygiene problem grabbed me, swung me round and threw me against a car. I tripped again, my head smashing backwards into the door handle.

What an ignominious way to get yourself knocked out. So much for being kicked by a mule.

Thinking about it now, I realised that I must have slid down the side of the car and hit my head on the ground as well. A mere door handle couldn't have done that much damage. The back of my skull was throbbing like a jackhammer.

I took another long sip of coffee and assessed my situation. Neither of the kidnappers had said a word that could give me some sort of clue to what they wanted from me. Well, it could scarcely be money. I didn't have a penny; nor did anyone who might want me back. If there were such a person. But if they didn't want money, what were they after? People were usually kidnapped for one of two reasons: hard unmarked cash, or publicity. I could scarcely see myself providing much excitement on either front. Maybe they were radical art terrorists from the Pottery Protection Front and wanted to exchange me for a ceramicist who was being held hostage by a breakaway pro-sculpture group in the Midlands . . .

I cursed. This was getting me nowhere. I needed to concentrate on what I knew. Swinging round, I made a long, slow survey of my cell. Something scuttled across the floor behind me, but my back hurt too much to turn a hundred and eighty degrees to check it out. Not a rodent. Mice sounded like balls of feathers on tiny greased wheels, and rats were heavier, their claws clicking much more loudly.

The blanket had slipped off my shoulders, and I had to put down the Thermos top and go through an exhausting procedure of shrugging and pulling the blanket back up again, half with my teeth and half with the tips of my fingers, stretched awkwardly over one shoulder. It was so hard to do even the most basic things with your hands cuffed together.

Right, that was it. I was fuelled up with coffee and sandwiches – not to mention the carrot wedges – and I wanted to know what the hell was going on. I started shouting. My chain was fixed across a beam towards the back of the cellar and didn't allow me to reach the door. Very sensible of them. I wouldn't fancy opening it directly onto an enraged metal sculptor armed with a Rose Glade dispenser wand and a couple of Tupperware containers.

At least I was assured of a look at them, whoever they were, if they deigned to show up. Whichever medieval property developer had designed this cellar had not allowed sufficiently for the requirements of anyone wishing to keep prisoners in it. There was no handy grille on the door for easy captive-viewing. They would have to open it to check on me, and give me at least a quick glance at them in the process.

Pretty soon I got bored with shouting. I refused on principle to yell 'Help!'; it seemed pointless, as no kidnapper who had taken the trouble to solder me this solidly into my chains would have put me anywhere with a chance of my screams reaching an outside audience. Calling out 'Help!' to the very people who had put me here could only be humiliating, if not positively degrading. So I went for a more generic 'Oi!', which became monotonous after a while.

Then I had a stroke of genius. I started belting out Depeche Mode albums. The sound of my own voice singing always cheered me up, even though it rarely had that effect on anyone else. I yodelled happily, if not always with total accuracy, every so often punctuating the latest offering with a few coyote-like howls. All my energy was going into putting out the lyrics with as much force as I could. I refused to let myself think about what would happen if my voice gave out, or I came to the end of my repertoire and still no one had shown up. It was a very lonely prospect. Alone in this cellar with nothing but a dwindling sandwich supply and my own croaks to keep me company. Not to mention total ignorance of why I was here, which was somehow the worst thing of all. I shivered.

Think about something else, and keep singing . . . They hadn't drugged the coffee; it had been a couple of hours since I'd drunk it, and I was still firing on all cylinders. I had been wondering about that. But if they'd wanted to kill me they'd had plenty of time to do it already, and frankly, if the coffee contained some sort of soporific that was fine with me. Knock me out and keep me under for the duration.

I was concentrating very hard on seeing this incarceration in short-lived terms.

I didn't have a watch, so I had no way of timing how long it took before I heard someone at the door. For a moment I thought I had hallucinated the shuffling outside, and I broke off to check. Then I thought that if I stopped they might go away again, since it was the noise I was making that had brought them here, and I snapped back into the second chorus of 'It's No Good'. By the time it was finished, there was still no sound of the door opening. Maybe they had blocked their ears and were squinting at me through a crack. Or the keyhole. The frustration boiled up in me like stomach acid.

'The fuck are you doing!' I heard myself shouting. 'I can bloody hear you out there! Get your arses in here, you pathetic fucking cowards!'

Furiously I reached up and rattled my chains, whipping and crashing them against the beam, the links smashing into each other. Maybe that was what did it. Despite this racket, my ears were so attuned to any noise not of my own making that through it I heard a key turning in the lock of the door. Cautious of them. I couldn't even reach the bloody door but they had locked it anyway. Did they think I was particularly sneaky, or dangerous, or were they just careful by nature?

The door swung open. It was made of heavy wood and now I could see how thick it was, a solid slab. I was surprised they'd heard anything through that. Maybe that was why it had taken them so long to show up.

Someone came through the door and stood just inside the room, out of distance of the length of my chain. They must have measured it beforehand. Following them was another person. They stood and stared at me and I, frozen in mid-rattle like a ghost interrupted halfway through a meaty bit of haunting, stared back at them. There was total silence.

Then the first person spoke. And my jaw dropped. Whatever I had been expecting – threats, intimidation, stagey German accents that would indicate an elaborate practical joke – it wasn't this.

'Fuck!' said the first kidnapper. 'Fuck! Fuck! Fuck!'

'Wha'?' said the second one nervously.

'Fuck!' repeated the first one. 'Fuck, fuck, fuck!'

Both of the kidnappers were wearing balaclavas, so their facial expressions were a mystery to me. In fact they were covered from head to toe in oversized anoraks, combat trousers and hiking boots. At a superficial glance they could have been anyone, from off-duty bankers to dole boys hanging round the shopping centre. It was the Nineties uniform for men. Though on a closer glance, the second one's trousers were a faded black, worn almost threadbare, too snug to be combats: they clung tightly to his skinny flanks, stopping short just above his ankles. And his boots were DMs – no, not DMs, I should know what those looked like by now, but they were still familiar—

The first one's head was jutting forward like a prehistoric reptile. He took a few steps towards me, looking me up and down. I stayed very still, hoping he would come far enough for me to grab him. This was a bad plan; I had nothing worked out and no weapons to hand. But the element of surprise would count heavily in my favour. And by the looks of things I had that in spades.

No joy. He didn't come within my range. Finally he said, his voice hushed:

'I don't bloody *believe* this.'

'What?' I said crossly.

'Who the hell – no, scrub that, *what* the hell – oh, shit. Shit on a fucking stick.'

The second kidnapper had come up behind him.

'Wha' is it?' he said, even more nervously than before.

'We're dead. We're fucking dead men,' said the first one. He turned and walked towards the open door. Grasping it in both hands, he nutted his head on it with considerable force. Leaning back, he took a breath and then did it again. 'All right?' he said to the second one. 'All right? We Are Fucking Dead Men. Got it?'

'But *why*?' pleaded the second one.

The first one beckoned him to come nearer and whispered something in his ear. Though I strained to catch it, I could make out nothing at all.

'*What!*' the second one exclaimed, the final 't' coming clear now under the stress of the moment.

'Yeah. Exactly. Got it? *Fuck.*'

'What the hell is going on?' I demanded.

They both swivelled to face me.

'Are you sure?' the second one said despondently.

'Course I'm bloody sure, you turd.'

'What am I doing here?' I said furiously. 'Do either of you have any fucking idea?'

'Oi, watch your mouth, slag!' said the first one with automatic menace. But he was too distracted to deliver the threat with full force.

'What are we gunna do?' the second one asked him *sotto voce*.

'Get out of here for a start. Can't talk about it in front of her, can we?'

'Wait a minute!' I said desperately as they started to go. 'How long am I going to be here? What's going on?'

The first one let out his breath on a long slow whistle.

'Your guess is as good as mine, darlin'.'

'You all right?' the second one asked diffidently.

'No, I'm bloody not!' I shouted. 'I'm chained to the bloody ceiling!'

He wriggled nervously.

'Can we get you anything?'

'HOW LONG AM I GOING TO BE DOWN HERE?'

'I dunno . . .' he said wretchedly, shooting a glance at the first kidnapper, who shrugged in a way that did not give him confidence, let alone me.

'Then get me something to read, OK?' I demanded. 'And food. More sandwiches. And coffee. Can I drink the water?'

'Yeah. I mean, we are.'

How much of a recommendation this was I didn't know. Still, it was too late to stunt my growth.

'Come on, Mother Teresa,' said the first, impatient with this exchange. 'We've got a fucking crisis on our hands and you're talking about the sodding water.'

Grabbing him by the hood of his anorak, he swivelled the second one round and gave him an unceremonious shove through the door, following him without as much as a word to me. The door shut. After a second it opened again and the first one's balaclava poked through the gap.

'And you, shut it, all right?' he said warningly. 'We got enough to think about without you making a racket. Come to think of it—'

He walked slowly towards me. As he approached I realised that he stank like a pub toilet. Anyone who had ever cleaned up a bar floor at the end of a long evening would recognise that smell at once: fresh piss and beer mingling unpleasantly with the old vomit and stale piss which no amount of rinsing would ever get out of the mop.

'You gave me a black eye, you fucking slag,' he said, almost conversationally. 'Have one on me.'

And he punched me in the face.

Without a mirror, I couldn't tell whether I had a black eye. My whole face felt bruised, but it could have been even worse; half-prepared for a blow, I had managed to get my forearms up to block it. Only partially, but at least it had taken the edge off. I had reeled back and could have caught my balance, but instinct told me that if I stayed standing he would hit me again. So I fell back, twisting so I landed sprawling over the pallet. I had misjudged it, though, and the back of my head took another nasty crack.

He kicked me in the back. Hard enough to hurt, but not enough science. I didn't open up like a flower.

'That'll teach you, bitch,' he said. 'Don't you go trying nothin' on. Or there's more where that came from. I got nothin' else to do right now.'

I heard him cross the room, his heavy boots ringing on the stone flags. Pulling the door closed, he locked it behind him. I stayed down for a couple of minutes in case he was listening. It wouldn't do any harm for him to think he had hurt me so badly I couldn't move. Then I got to my feet and promptly tripped over the sodding chain. I nearly went flying again. The twist I had to do to stay on my feet caught right where he'd kicked me in the back. I shrieked with the pain.

When I'd caught my breath, I unwound the chain from my ankles, cursing horribly, and limped over to the tap. The water was icy. I stuck my face under it, wincing at the agony, and kept it flowing, cooling down the bruising. He hadn't broken my nose; bringing my arms up had deflected his fist. Thank God for that. I didn't see them doling me out painkillers on demand.

At least there was some coffee. If not, I would have lost it completely. I was gritting my teeth so hard in an effort not to scream out loud with the pain that I'd be down to the nerves in days.

I sat down on the pallet, wrapping a blanket round my shoulders, and poured myself a trickle of coffee. How easy that all sounds. The sitting down was difficult enough, with the burning ache in my back half-crippling me. And unscrewing a Thermos lid, taking off the cup and managing to direct the hot coffee into it when your hands are linked three inches apart is not an easy procedure, requiring a considerable amount of patience. Which is not my primary virtue. My head was ringing like a carillon, however, which perversely helped by slowing me down. One step at a time, execute each task with painstaking precision . . . maybe this wasn't a diet farm at all. Maybe it was an extreme Buddhist retreat, designed to teach me inner quietness in adversity.

This lunatic idea triggered another one, inchoate but definitely floating in the back of my brain. I didn't try to force it out. Experience had taught me that the more you let things go, the faster they come back of their own free will. Instead I sipped the coffee. The warm flood of caffeine shot reassuringly through my blood-stream, invigorating my brain cells, neutralising my headache.

I wondered about having another sandwich, and decided it was too soon. Who knew when they would bring me more? Especially after the recent debacle of our first face-to-balaclava meeting – OK,

Sam, work that one out. What the hell was going on there? Why did they seem so surprised to see you?

I collected all the pieces I had and put them slowly into place. The Vegemite sandwiches . . . Second Kidnapper's leather-substitute boots . . . radical terrorism . . . Buddhist principles . . . and their incredulity the first time they saw me in daylight . . .

Realisation hit me like another punch in the face. Goddamn it, this was all Sarah's fault. I was never standing in for anyone else as long as I lived. They'd kidnapped me in mistake for her.

CHAPTER EIGHT

I dozed for a while, as much as the pain in my back and head would let me. It felt like a fireworks display, a regular series of explosions punctuated by the nasty afterburn. Maybe this was what contractions felt like. Yet another reason never to have children.

Thank God at least I had been wearing my work clothes. They kept me relatively warm, right down to my very solid boots. Ever since I had met Hugo I had been in heels; he was six foot and I hated to be towered over. The extra couple of inches lessened my tetchiness considerably, but would have been an escaping disaster.

Escape. Definitely on the agenda, but not quite yet. I needed to let my back recover for a while. I wouldn't get far hobbling along bent double, like a chimpanzee without the superhuman strength. And then there was the small matter of getting out of the handcuffs. It was going to take some careful planning. I was calculating that I could afford to take a little time to get it right; I didn't see myself in much danger of Stockholm Syndrome just yet. So far I was bonding with my captors about as successfully as the various parts of an Italian coalition government.

A nasty thought struck me. All very well for my own psychological stability, but what if they wanted to bond with me? Or had they already? It was the first time it occurred to me to wonder if either of them had played doctor with me while I was unconscious.

My instinctive reaction was that they hadn't. It wasn't just wishful thinking. When I'd come to I was all buttoned up. And I wasn't sore. I twitched my internal muscles reflexively to check. Nope, no bruising. And it hadn't hurt when I had a pee. Either I'd been interfered with by the smallest penis in the universe, or it hadn't happened at all.

Besides, if First Kidnapper had been fiddling around with me, I'd have smelt him on myself as soon as I woke up. Yech. I wriggled in automatic revulsion, remembering his stench. The only other person I'd ever known who'd stunk that bad had been Devo, a friend at art college; and, come to think of it, a wearer of leather-substitute boots. Devo had refused to use deodorant for motives both political (the global capitalist conspiracy trying to up its bloated profits still further by selling us totally unnecessary products) and personal (perfumes alienated us from our bodies' natural odours which were in any case self-cleansing). He actually had a much more varied sex life than one would have expected with a philosophy like that. But he was a very nice guy and apparently extremely considerate in bed.

Well, well. The highly particular smell of damp unwashed armpit penetrating through seismic layers of its own previous dried-off secretions had brought memories flooding back to whatever parts of my brain were still reasonably intact. Not quite Proust's madeleine, but when you were chained to the ceiling of a cellar with no chocolate in sight, you took whatever moments of distraction you could grab. I decided that the comparison with Devo was not particularly useful. First Kidnapper didn't strike me as the type to refuse to use deodorant on ethical principles, not even animal-tested ones. He was just a filthy bastard. Second Kidnapper seemed nicer, but that probably meant he was the one to watch, the nasty furtive type who'd pretend to be your friend and then go through the laundry basket while you were out in search of your used knickers.

Ick. This line of speculation wasn't helping me much. But it did thoroughly concentrate my mind on the area of self-defence. So far, my instincts had been to put up and shut up until I was in a position to hit back properly. If I'd slugged First Kidnapper back he'd have taken me to pieces. It wasn't just the black eye that had caused him to knock me down; it was the frustration at their having fucked up so comprehensively in kidnapping me by mistake for Sarah. I didn't fancy any more broken bones. The painkillers they doled out at the time might be world-class, but the ache in cold weather lasted a hell of a lot longer.

Still, there were exceptions to my no-hitting-back rule, and the prime one would be if either of them got to thinking that some bondage and discipline in the basement would while away an idle hour. It was more likely now they knew that I wasn't the person I was supposed to be; not a notorious TV actress, merely her stand-in. I might be a sculptor but that scarcely accorded me celebrity status, not until I started stealing human body parts from dissecting labs and pickling them.

I looked around me for anything I could use as a weapon in case of emergency. That was about as much as my brain could cope with at the moment: one simple short-term task. My chain extended far enough so that I had the range of the back half of the cellar, and I managed, with considerable cursing and yelps of pain, to clamber up onto the back of one of the stone troughs and tug at the window bars. They were solid in their sockets and the view through them was so overgrown I could see nothing but a thick tangle of straggling bushes. No joy there.

I climbed down again and stood in the centre of the room, turning slowly, letting my eyes linger a long time on each object, processing it for its possibilities. They hadn't given me a camp bed, or I could have tried to take that apart and use a folding leg to hit them with. Maybe I could suffocate them with the pillow. Or shove the air freshener wand down one of their throats till they choked.

But the cellar was as completely bare as only a cellar can be. The only other feature of any interest was a door set in the back wall, but this I had already tried, many times, and given up all hope of opening. It looked as if it had been closed for at least a century. I didn't know whether it led to another cellar, or a smaller storage room, or a flight of stairs leading up to a door onto the outside world with a Porsche waiting for me at the top with the keys in the ignition and a full tank of petrol. It was all moot. The door was barred with two long slabs of metal, each bolted with no less than four extremely rusty padlocks.

I had spent hours already rattling the bars and bolts, in the hope that some jointure, more fragile than it seemed, might crumble in my hands. But no such luck. Even if I had anything to use as a lockpick – and I hadn't, not even a hairpin – I doubted their wards were capable of moving, even fractionally. The rust was as thick as mould. The colours were beautiful in their way; the heavy iron padlocks, dully gleaming, encrusted with a patina of red dust, half-blended into the rotting door against which they hung. The door itself, painted a dark brown, was peeling away under the coating of cobwebs which glittered in the sunlight. It would make a lovely cover photograph for a coffee-table book. Picturesque rustic decay.

A couple of cockroaches scuttled out from underneath it as I watched, their carapaces gleaming black as if freshly polished. This was the true black, with no tinge of green or blue: if you shone a torch on them all you would see was black light, shining like fresh tar. I thought wistfully of my friends in New York, the corners of whose apartments were liberally studded with Roach Motels. Still, the advantage to country, as opposed to town, cockroaches was that in small numbers they were terrified of humans. Clearly I wasn't one in a long line of captives strung up in the cellar: the cockroaches had by no means accustomed themselves to their new cohabitant. I lunged out with my foot and watched them whizz under the door again like little motorised toys, back to their little cockroach home to put their feet up with a cup of tea and wipe their brows in relief at having escaped the monster once more.

I sighed in resignation. There was nothing for it. I was going to have to prise up a flagstone.

Twenty-four hours is a long time to spend chipping away at the concrete surround of a flagstone with a pair of handcuffs. I couldn't make an exact estimate of the time that had passed, but night had fallen and dawn was already a distant memory when I heard the door being unlocked once more. I had slept for what felt like long stretches, though not that deeply. The pain in my back was subsiding, but because of the handcuffs it was hard to get into a position that eased it enough. I kept trying to turn onto my stomach, half-asleep, and being woken by the metal bracelets digging into me. My shoulders were stiff from digging with my wrists bound together, even though I had spent a while doing exercises to loosen them up. Not to mention endless series of sit-ups, leg raises and stretches.

When this was over I could write a book called *Chained But Fit*. I bet I could sell it on the title alone.

By that time I would have the flattest stomach in the Western world. I had found that keeping physically occupied helped to stop my brain screaming, and had tired me out enough to let me sleep. As long as I didn't do any jumping jacks. I had tried some in a moment of respite from flagstone excavation, and automatically pulled my arms apart, yanking on my sore wrists. Yet another source of pain to add to my already extensive list.

Unsurprisingly I was in a foul temper by the time my gentleman caller showed up. It was lucky he was Second Kidnapper. I might have been unable to resist talking back to First, in an excess of frustration and bad spirits, and got another kicking for my pains.

Perhaps I should make up new nicknames for them. I wasn't that keen on this cod-Shakespearean thing I had going. First could be Urine-Breath, and Second . . . It seemed unfair to call him Knicker-Sniffer without any hard evidence. I would have to think about it.

I just had time to throw myself back from my flagstone of choice and onto the mattress before the door swung open. This hurt considerably, which in the short term was no bad thing. My groans were entirely authentic. Ah, the joys of Method acting.

'Are you OK?' said Second Kidnapper nervously, instantly earning for himself the sobriquet of Thick Boy. There was something odd about his voice: it sounded as if he were slurring his words, but he didn't seem drunk. He crossed the cellar towards me. I scrabbled myself up to a sitting position, gasping with pain.

'It's my back,' I said. 'Where he kicked me. It really hurts. I think he might have done some serious damage.'

'He kicked you?' said Thick Boy incredulously. 'Oh, shit, I don't believe it.'

'Here,' I said, trying to let my lower lip wobble in a holding-back-the-tears kind of way. This damsel in distress thing was much more difficult than one would think. Either you were born to it or you weren't. I reached my arms round as best I could, wincing, and indicated the small of my back.

'It feels all bruised,' I said pitifully. I had forgotten temporarily about the damage to my face. He was staring at me, but naturally I was unable to read his expression through the balaclava, so it wasn't until he said guiltily:

'I bet that doesn't 'alf 'urt and all,' stubbing one gloved finger towards my nose, that I realised what he was focusing on.

'Oh, yeah!' I said at once. 'Really badly! I think my nose might be broken.'

'Oh, *fuck*. Fuck, fuck, *fuck*,' he said. Tim Roth or Harvey Keitel, directed by Tarantino, could have done wonders with those few words, making them into a catchphrase *Loaded* readers would quote to each other for years to come. Thick Boy's delivery wasn't quite up there with the greats, but, for a raw amateur, he packed in plenty of pathos and distress.

'What about you?' I said acutely. I had noticed, as he walked across the room, that he was moving more stiffly than before, as if someone had been swinging a large boot in his direction as well as mine. And when he squatted down beside me, there had been a definite soreness in his movements, as if everything needed to be carefully studied to avoid straining bruised muscles more than was necessary.

'What d'you mean?' he said warily.

It was so annoying not to be able to read the expression of the person I was talking to, especially when so much hung upon it. Apart from the more primitive dating mores, my body language skills were negligible.

'Someone's been having a go at you too, haven't they?' I observed. 'Was it him?'

'You – I – nah – Look, I shouldn't be talking to you at all,' he said helplessly.

'But it'll just get worse,' I persisted. 'What if he starts on me again? I could die here with a punctured lung or something.'

'Nah,' he said. 'You'll be all right. It'll just – we just need to – there's stuff needs working out . . .'

His voice tailed off.

'I brought you some more food,' he said hopefully, as if this would distract me. 'Like you asked for.'

'I'm not supposed to be here, am I?' I said, ignoring this. I had already noticed the pile of clingfilm-wrapped sandwiches he had set down next to me. 'You got the wrong person, didn't you?'

'Well, *that*'s no secret,' he said with so much bitterness I was taken aback. Even allowing for their natural disappointment at having cocked up and got the wrong target, it seemed excessive.

'You wanted Sarah Fossett, right?' I pushed. I wanted to get him talking, to say as little as possible myself, but it was hard to resist when I couldn't see his face and judge how much prompting he needed.

'Yeah,' he said slowly. 'Yeah.'

'You sure about that?'

'Course I'm sure,' he said gloomily.

'Was it – you're not after a ransom, right?' I said helplessly. 'I mean, I was assuming it was to make some sort of statement.'

He subsided onto the ground till he was sitting next to me. Bending forward, he extracted a pack of cigarettes from the big knee pocket on his trousers.

'You want a fag?' he said, sounding almost friendly.

'No, thanks.' Though I felt the pull of a cigarette more strongly than I had ever done, that was exactly why I refused. Under these circumstances I could see myself getting hooked immediately. Then I'd be pleading with them for fags, too. It was bad enough having to ration out the coffee.

'She was really out of order,' he said, lighting his and drawing on it deeply. As he put it to his mouth I saw him wince, and, through the slit in the balaclava, it looked as if his lips were swollen. Someone had hit him in the mouth. That explained why his voice sounded thick. 'All that crap she spouted in the paper about battery chickens being too stupid to know what was happening to them. I mean, fuck it. Being in here'd have been too good for her. We should've shoved her in a box, see how she liked it.'

'Maybe you could have cut off her nails as well,' I suggested sarcastically. 'And taken out her teeth, in case she started turning on herself.'

'You what? Oh yeah. They cut off chickens' beaks and claws, don't they? Cos they all go mad in those cages. But, y'know, they're too daft to know what's happening to them, according to her. She was asking for it.'

'But *I wasn't.*' I thought it imperative to make this point loud and often.

He shrugged uncomfortably.

'You owe it to me to tell me a bit about what's going on,' I insisted. My voice was trying to rise into a scream of frustration, but I clamped it down again.

'I know,' Thick Boy muttered unhappily. 'That's the problem, innit? I mean, you're a wossit, an innocent victim.'

I was just preening myself when he added:

'Though, mind you, what about your boots?'

'My boots?' I looked down at them.

'That's animal skin, innit? And your belt.'

'HOW DO YOU KNOW WHAT MY BELT'S MADE OF?' I blasted, having an instant flashback to my earlier speculations about him and Urine-Breath playing doctor with my comatose body.

'I can see it!' he said nervously, pointing at my waist.

I looked down. My sweater had ridden up over the waistband of my jeans.

'Oh,' I said, relaxing slightly. 'OK. Fine.'

'So, y'know, you've got blood on your hands too,' he said more cheerfully.

'Bollocks,' I retorted. 'These are by-products of the meat industry. They're caused by meat eaters, not me.'

'Yeah, I've 'eard that before,' he said aggressively, 'and it don't stand up, all right? I mean, it's less bad, but it's still, y'know, *bad.*'

'What about your mate?' I snapped. 'I don't think his boots came from the Clumping Without Cruelty catalogue. They looked like fourteen-holer DMs to me. You want to check the print they made in my back?'

He shuffled his feet and didn't say anything.

'Why don't you just let me out before anything else happens?' I suggested.

'Can't do that,' he muttered to his leather-substitute boots. 'It's not down to me. Anyway, we've gotta make our point,' he added more feebly.

I sighed. I could have punched the little fucker in the face then and there, wrestled him to the ground and threatened to set him on fire with his own lighter, but what good would it do me? It was Urine-Breath I needed to get to. No way would he have allowed Thick Boy to walk around with the keys to my handcuffs in any of his seventeen hanging trouser pockets.

'I'm really hurting,' I whined, reverting to the pathetic-little-me strategy. It seemed the most successful. 'I need some painkillers. I feel worse and worse. It's very damp in here. Couldn't you move me somewhere drier?' I added without much optimism of this ploy succeeding. 'It would hurt my back less.'

'I dunno,' he said, standing up clumsily. 'See what I can do, OK? We can't move ya. But we probably got some aspirin or something.'

I would have sneered if I hadn't been trying to be nice. Aspirin, indeed! I wanted super-strength Solpadeine or Benylin Extra at the very least.

'And can I have a pen and paper?' I asked. 'I could do some sketching. It'd keep me busy.'

'See what I can do,' he said unpromisingly.

'How long am I going to be in here?' I said rather desperately as he started for the door.

'Have to see. Dunno. We got to have a think, don't we? Decide what to do. Make plans.'

'What plans?'

But he was already at the door. He'd had enough of me, and I couldn't say I blamed him. I had been showering him with questions he couldn't answer, and men notoriously dislike that kind of treatment. Despondently I watched it close behind him. Alone again with only my own resources to fall back on. For a moment I actually found myself hoping they were still planning to carry out Plan A and kidnap Sarah. If they strung her up to the beam alongside me, at least it'd be better company than the cockroaches.

CHAPTER NINE

I was finding it harder and harder to sleep for any length of time. My brain kept racing, as if to compensate for the limitations of my chain, pulling old memories out of drawers I had long thought closed for good. I resisted the childhood reminiscences, though. I was determined to avoid doing the classic captive routine where you keep having flashbacks to that traumatic incident that happened when you were six and which the experience of being kidnapped, extraordinarily enough, helps to exorcise.

This kind of thing was always happening in detective fiction. I was saved from banality by not having had a formative traumatic incident in the first place. Instead I was the kind of person other people had nightmare flashbacks about. My Aunt Louise was probably still screaming, poor woman. I contemplated the image of Aunt Louise, shrieking in horror at the latest atrocity I had committed. It was by far the strongest memory I had of her. Poor Aunt Louise. No one – teachers, boyfriends, Social Services, arresting officers – had ever been as glad to see the back of me as she had been, and I was willing to bet that no one ever would.

A couple of cockroaches scuttled across the far end of the room. How I wished I had stuff to throw at them. They were getting more used to me; even rattling my chain didn't scare them off like it did initially. The faint distracting clickety-click of tiny cockroach feet on the stone floor could always be guaranteed to wake me from my sleep, fitful at the best of times. I had a horror of them tip-tapping over me when I had dozed off.

I wrenched my thoughts onto a more positive track. Maybe Thick Boy would bring me pen and paper. I didn't really want to sketch anything: my draughtswomanship had always been atrocious. No one seeing my drawings would ever think I was a working artist. But a pen is a good weapon. The friend who trained me up in self-defence had done some kind of shadowy Mossad course, as well as all his other martial arts. He had shown me the various points on the body where you could kill someone by stabbing them with a Biro. Not just the ear and the nose, or the eye, though those were the most obvious. I still hadn't managed to prise up the flagstone, and a Biro would be a much more convenient weapon.

I had already killed one man in my life, though not completely on purpose. The inquest had called it self-defence, and who was I to argue with an official verdict? Still, I felt enough was enough. You had to worry that murder – or let's say killing people – got easier every time you did it. That was what Hercule Poirot always said, and he should know. And the way I had done it wasn't exactly comparable to sticking a Biro into someone's unwashed neck and having his blood fountain all over you as he choked to death on it.

Like John Cusack killing the other hitman in *Grosse Pointe Blank*. I loved that film. I just hoped I wasn't going to have to use it as a How-To guide.

Sitting back on my haunches, I looked at the flagstone. My wrists were to my mouth, licking away the blood in a gesture that was so automatic now I did it without conscious thought, the taste of salt and metal as familiar to me as the Vegemite sandwiches that were my rations. At least they were giving me plenty of food and coffee. I wasn't wasting away.

The edges of my handcuffs were so blunted now with scratching away at the concrete surround to the flagstone that it would be a challenge for them to cut through butter: dented into weird flanges, the wrists beneath them chafed to bracelets of bright blood around the bone. I was lucky that my captors seemed so unobservant. The damage to my wrists might be explained by constant dragging at the chain in a vain effort to break the solder, but the state of the handcuffs would be a total giveaway. The stone I had picked was smallish and already slightly loose, but it had still taken a day and a half to prise it free. I was lucky the handcuffs had lasted out.

Leaning forward, I nudged the stone. It shifted. Definitely loose. I tried again, this time harder. The stone rocked back and forth in its setting. I had a strong impulse to leave it there, pull the mattress back over it, lie down and go to sleep. I was exhausted from hard cramped labour, and it was a strangely anticlimactic moment. I had thrown all my energies into working on this and now I had prised it free, I felt oddly depressed. Perhaps because it seemed such a minimal achievement, after all, just digging up a flagstone; or perhaps because it reminded me how far I had to go, how many things could still go wrong before I was out of here.

But I couldn't rest till I had finished the job. Bending over, I picked up the stone, its weight pulling my wrists against the cuffs and setting them bleeding again. I carried it over to a far corner of the cellar, which was always partly in shadow, and dropped it onto the stone floor.

It didn't shatter. I picked it up and tried again, this time lifting it higher and throwing it down. Satisfyingly, it broke into three solid fragments. Two I restored to the hole the stone had come from, now concealed under my mattress. The third and sharpest I slipped under the top of my mattress, so I could reach it if I needed to. It would be a clumsy manoeuvre, as anything is when your hands are cuffed, but at least I had a weapon.

The depression hadn't left me. I knew that people would be looking for me by now, a mass of police and worried friends and those hypothetical undercover animal rights activists. I even had an old friend – well, ex-lover – who I had met when someone had been murdered (not by me – honestly) at a gym where I was working, and he had been the detective sergeant on the investigative team. Hawkins had now risen to the dizzy heights of detective inspector and if he had heard about my being kidnapped he would be doing all he could to make sure I was found in one piece and still breathing, if only so he could shout at me about having got myself into yet another scrape.

Even that familiar thought failed to console me, or even to touch me in any way. It all seemed infinitely distant from the cellar which was currently the limits of my world. I felt very alone. There was no point thinking about theoretical resources out there searching for me. The only help I could look to was my own. And that, strangely enough, was a much more comforting notion.

Urine-Breath and Thick Boy had clearly come to some sort of agreement. Or maybe Urine-Breath had just delegated the task of checking on me to his sidekick. Whatever had happened, the result was that it was Thick Boy and Thick Boy alone who brought me sandwiches and coffee and stammered out nervous questions about my general welfare before hurrying out of the cellar again. No longer was he up for a chat; now he wanted to spend the least possible time in my company. It was plain to see that they had put me on hold while they decided what to do about me.

I did not find this particularly encouraging. It implied that what they might eventually decide to do might not simply be to release me back into the community, like throwing back an old boot which had ended up on their line when they'd been fishing for trout. They could have done that days ago: put a bag over my head, shoved me into the trunk of a car, driven me round for hours to confuse me, and finally dumped me somewhere with no connection to themselves. I had tried to suggest this to Thick Boy but all he did was start like a jittery foal and hotleg it through the door. They could even feed me a couple of sleeping pills and carry me out so I didn't remember anything about the house they were taking me through. But so far neither the Vegemite sandwiches nor the coffee had had any narcotic effects. I wouldn't have minded. I wasn't sleeping well. It would have been nice to get a few solid hours' kip.

And the longer my imprisonment went on, the worse it boded. I guessed that they were trying to work out a way to exploit my presence, despite my essential non-Sarah-ness: and if they couldn't, logic suggested that they would turn on me in pique. Rack my brains as I might, I was completely unable to imagine any possible use I could be to them. Which did not augur well when it came to payback time. Urine-Breath had a pretty short fuse. Sooner or later he'd have a few too many beers, say, 'Ah, fuck it,' and stagger down here to shove me around a bit. Or worse.

So it was time for me to make my bid for freedom. That sounded jaunty enough, but I was looking forward to it less than my upbeat tone implied. If it went wrong I would be in serious trouble. Still, if I didn't try now, I might begin to lose my edge. It's extraordinary what you can get used to. These four walls, the beams overhead and the flags below, were coming to seem like the natural boundaries of my world. Alaskans called anything beyond their own state Outside, with a capital O; I had better get going before I started thinking that way about whatever was beyond the locked door of my cell.

I had a sort of plan. It wasn't much, but then I didn't have much to work with; just a few pieces of flagstone and the kind of attitude that means when I start a fight it isn't finished till one of us is bleeding on the floor. In that respect, and, Hugo would have immediately said, many others, I have all the sophistication of a wild boar on steroids.

Better not to think about Hugo. It weakened me.

The key was scratching in the lock. I wondered with a small, almost-totally detached part of my brain whether they had had to oil it or if it was new. Would that mean the building had been done up? But then there was the old door behind me, crumbling away, though unfortunately not quite enough. Maybe if I spent another twenty years in here I'd be able to kick my way through it.

Perhaps the key only scratched that way because of Thick Boy's poor hand-to-eye coordination. He was walking as awkwardly as ever, his muscles seeming strained, though it had been three days now since he had been given that going-over. That was the way with bruises; they stiffened up nastily if you didn't work liniment and Deep Heat into them and put yourself through the temporary pain of stretching exercises.

'I've brought you some more sandwiches. Are you asleep?' he said, coming a little closer to me.

Well, if I had been I wasn't now. Fool. I was lying on the pallet, slightly on one side, my cuffed hands up on the pillow beside me so I could rest one cheek on them. It was the best Lady of the Camellias impression I could do in handcuffs. Not to mention jeans, workboots and a great big chain running over my stomach.

'I don't feel hungry,' I said faintly. 'My back's really hurting. I think I need a doctor.'

I had been harping on this line ever since we had had our initial chat, but it was the first time I had mentioned a doctor.

'I think I've got a fever,' I continued, still feebly. 'I told you something was ruptured. I'm really ill.'

As soon as I had heard the key in the lock I had been rubbing my face frantically with my hands and by now it felt hot and red from the friction.

'You do look flushed,' he said reluctantly.

'I've got a fever,' I repeated. 'I need to see a doctor. Please. I'm really ill.'

I looked up at him beseechingly.

'You wouldn't leave an animal in pain this way,' I said, playing my trump card. 'Please. I feel terrible.'

I was hoping he wouldn't check the Tupperware container and see that it was completely empty. That would rather give the lie to my feverish lack of appetite. But he wasn't that clever. I closed my eyes, keeping a chink open so that I could peer at him through the lashes. He looked deeply worried. I let out a moan of pain.

'Shit,' he said. 'Look, 'old on, all right? Just 'old on.'

Which, considering my handcuffed state, was a pretty stupid remark. Like 'Will you be all right?' as you say goodnight to someone. Duh, I don't know. Two animal rights maniacs might shove a bag over my head in the car park and beat my head on the tarmac before chaining me up in their back basement for an indefinite stay. I mean, who can tell?

I held on nevertheless. It was only a few minutes before the door opened again and another set of footsteps crossed the room towards me. That unmistakable smell came right along with them. Urine-Breath was paying me a personal visit.

CHAPTER TEN

Urine-Breath cleared his throat. It was a long, rasping hack, punctuated by a couple of gurgly spits which splattered off the stone floor. He hadn't bothered to aim for the toilet grille. It was more than time spittoons made a comeback.

'What's up with you, then?' he said finally, his voice hoarse.

I gave a faint moan. It didn't have the same effect on him as it had on Thick Boy. He just said impatiently:

'You what?'

'I think I've got a fever,' I said weakly. 'I'm all hot.'

I had been doing another emergency face-rubbing session while Thick Boy had been gone, and it seemed to have paid off. Urine-Breath bent over to look at me closely and I heard him click his tongue.

'Yeah, you're red all right.'

He put one big damp hand on my forehead. The stench of his armpit was almost rancid. He couldn't have washed for weeks. For God's sake, if I had running water down here there must be some in the rest of the house, surely?

'Hot,' he said, as if confirming something to himself. There was a long, long pause. Then he said slowly:

'You've got a temperature, right? Feverish. Yeah. You're prob'ly pretty out of it, aren't ya? Bet you ain't got much of an idea what's going on right now. Eh?'

He wasn't talking to me. He was doing his best to convince himself.

'Yeah,' he continued. 'Even if you said somefin' – well, you had a fever, didn't ya? Could've been a dream or, I dunno –' he sniggered

– 'bit of a fantasy. Make you look a right slag telling people about that.'

His hand had slid down from my forehead. It felt like a damp, rank dishcloth which had never been rinsed out and hung up to dry. The smell it left on me would take several washes to remove completely. I could almost feel my skin breaking out in pimples in the wake of his touch. The dishcloth slipped along my neck, pausing for a moment.

He expelled a long and noxious puff of air, the sound of someone who has made his mind up. And the dishcloth stirred, wiggled itself underneath the neck of my sweater, started reaching down inside my T-shirt. Urine-Breath fell heavily to his knees beside me, breathing thickly, his other hand coming to my waist, fumbling to pull my sweater and T-shirt free from my jeans.

'You just lie there like a good girl,' he muttered. 'Just pretend you're sleepin'. I like that.'

I bit my lip, clenching my teeth down on it to stop me moving a muscle. I didn't want to scare him off. This was perfect. Just let him get his hands right up inside my sweater – God, when I got out of here I was going to scrub myself down with disinfectant from head to toe. There were probably fifty diseases I could catch just being this close to him.

His stench was everywhere now, hanging over us like a miasma. It was compounded by his breath: stale curry and beer on top of endless strata of general decay. He must have weeks of old dinners in there, stuck between his teeth, rotting away.

He was at my bra now, clumsy as a teenager, plucking at the lace trim. There was something particularly gut-wrenching about his black balaclava, the facelessness of this assault. Urine-Breath was pulling one of the cups away from my breast, getting impatient at his own ineptness. The cold wet sausage fingers closed around me. His other hand, meanwhile, was busy popping the buttons on my jeans.

This was one of the most disgusting things that had ever happened to me. I registered that quite clearly. But at the same time I was miles away, observing him coldly, able to control my revulsion, to wait until precisely this moment was reached. This was what I had wanted, the moment of maximum distraction. So much blood would have drained from his revolting head that it would take him minutes to work out what was happening—

He was panting like a dog. The mouth slit in his balaclava was wet with spittle and I could see his tongue through it, his lips parted with excitement. No better time to do it than now, while he was shuddering from the first sorry thrill of grabbing my breast, and his damp-dishcloth hand was beginning to scrabble at the top of my knickers. My hands were still by my cheek. I shifted a fraction, raising my elbows to give me extra leverage, and brought my fists up, backhand, aiming right for his Adam's apple. The piece of flagstone was grasped between them. Gradually I had been easing it down so that the point stuck out a good two inches from the edge of my fingers, sharp as a flint.

I smashed into his neck sideways. The stone landed soft in his Adam's apple; the blow was hardly audible. It was Urine-Breath who made the noise, a terrible strangled choking. His hands were stuffed so far inside my clothing that he couldn't use them to defend himself, or even to catch at his throat to cradle it. The one on my breast actually closed tighter, on a weird displaced reflex. A huge shudder of revulsion ran all down my body like a powerful electric shock. It was like a delayed reaction. I hadn't been able to allow myself to feel this disgust when he was actually groping me: but now it was surging up inside me. I literally saw red.

'You *bastard*!' I yelled, and brought my hands back to hit him again, this time on the side of the head. He was still gurgling frantically from the blow to his throat. I felt the flagstone shake within my fists as it juddered against the bone. He stumbled backwards, still grotesquely half-anchored by his hands, one of them tangled up in the underwires of my bra.

Suddenly, getting them out was my only thought. I shoved myself awkwardly backwards on the pallet, wriggling as if I had ants down inside my clothes, desperate to have him stop touching me. For a bizarre few moments he and I had the same immediate goal, and we almost hampered one another, my frantic writhings impeding him from getting the second hand free. As it finally slid out from my jeans, resting for a second on my stomach in a parody of a caress, I retched. Cramped from lying in one position so long, wrestling with the handcuffs as if they were the real enemy, I shuffled to my knees.

Urine-Breath had both hands pressed to his throat, his head ducked over them. The Adam's apple is one of the worst places to hit someone. I could have killed him if I hadn't been in handcuffs. And in that moment, still feeling his disgusting slimy hands on me, I wished I had. I reached up and brought my fists down again, driving the flagstone into the top of his head. At the last moment a tiny little voice reminded me with extreme clarity that I didn't want another death-in-self-defence on my conscience, and I felt the blow slackening off, the point of the stone slipping back slightly between my hands.

It wasn't lethal. But he slumped sideways, falling in a crumpled, ungainly mess, still unable to make any sound but a half-strangled choking as he struggled to draw in air. A flash of memory hit, of the time someone tried to strangle me. I remembered it vividly: my windpipe closing off, the bruising to my throat, the terrible, concentrated effort of taking the next breath, and the next, and the next, forcing in the air when each inhalation hurt so badly it was like taking burning petrol into my lungs.

Urine-Breath's terrible rasps didn't prompt any feeling of solidarity in suffering.

'Fuck you,' I said, clambering to my feet.

After the strangling attempt I had been able to hear well enough, even if it seemed like people's voices were coming down a wind tunnel. I knew my words were reaching Urine-Breath.

'You hear me? I said, fuck you, you fucking dirty bastard.'

The calmness of my tone was unnerving even me. God knew what effect it was having on him.

I grabbed the back of his balaclava and pulled it off, throwing it to the ground. Twining my fingers in his hair, I almost gagged. It was like the pelt of an animal caught in an oil slick. Only animals don't have dandruff.

'I could kill you right now,' I said, wrenching his head back in a way designed to strain his throat still further. He was still clutching it with both hands and now he made agonised, straining noises, splitting up into two registers at once, grunts and squeaks like a boy whose voice is breaking. 'You hear me?'

I kicked him in the stomach. He couldn't double over because I was still pulling his head back. And he couldn't even raise his voice or beg me to stop.

'You put your filthy disgusting hands on me. You smell like a beer mat in a cesspit and you put your disgusting –' I kicked him – 'filthy –' I kicked him again – 'hands on my *fucking tit.*'

I let his head fall and shoved him away. He crumpled.

'Give me the keys to my cuffs. Right now. Or I'll start kicking your face in.'

He made what sounded like it would have been a moan.

'I don't want to touch you again. I don't want to have to put my hand in your stinking clothes. And if I have to I'll jump up and down on one of your fat wet disgusting hands till I break some bones.'

Urine-Breath was gesturing frantically, his palms held up, wiggling them back and forth. His head was shaking back and forth as well.

'What?' I said impatiently.

'Don' – don'—'

'You don't have them?'

He shook his head even more frenziedly. Hard to believe he would be stupid enough to bluff me, with the damage I had already done him. The black eye I had inadvertently caused had developed to the chartreuse stage: psychedelic swirls of green and yellow, bloodshot-streaked with purple. But that wasn't the only mark on his face. The other eye was swollen up too and there was a big scabby cut on his cheekbone, for neither of which I had been responsible. No wonder he had resorted to trying to feel me up. Looking like that he wouldn't even have managed to score with a sheep famed for its lack of discrimination.

'If you're lying,' I said furiously, 'I'll—'

But he was spared the next round of threats. There was movement at the open door. I looked up.

Thick Boy was standing just inside the cellar, staring at the scene in front of him. God, how I hated balaclavas. I would have paid a lot of money to see the expression on his face at that moment.

There was a long pause. Thick Boy broke it. I had never heard such naked sincerity in all my life.

'Oh, *fuck*,' he said.

Thick Boy was poised on the balls of his feet – as much as that was possible in chunky fourteen-hole imitation-leather boots. His head darted from side to side, snatching glimpses of whatever lay beyond the cellar and the tableau inside it, as if wondering whether he had the nerve just to run away and abandon his partner. A flash of fear hit me. If he ran off now—

Taking a couple of steps towards Urine Breath, I dropped my cuffed hands over his head and pulled it back. He half-screamed raspingly in protest, his hands rising to his neck to pull at the lock of the cuffs.

'Get the key to my handcuffs. Now. Or I'll break your friend's neck,' I said conversationally. 'Don't think I won't.'

For an awful moment, it looked as if Thick Boy would turn and run for it.

'*Tell him!*' I yelled at Urine-Breath, panicking at the thought of seeing my escape route disappear out the door.

Urine-Breath's rasping rose to an agonised scrape along his windpipe which must have been excruciatingly painful. His hands frantically gestured Thick Boy towards him.

'See?' I said, giving Urine-Breath's neck another jerk. 'He wants you to do what I say. Don't worry,' I added. 'I won't hurt you. *You* didn't just try to rape me because you thought I had a fever and wouldn't be able to tell anyone about it.'

Thick Boy's shoulders sagged. He turned and walked out of the cellar. I swear my heart stopped. Panicked scenarios ran through my head: Thick Boy going to ring for reinforcements; Thick Boy starving me out till I was too weak to make good my threats to Urine-Breath; Thick Boy—

I was dragging in a long slow breath of relief. My heart started pounding again. Thick Boy had been reaching to the side of the door for the handcuff key. It must have been hanging there in case of need. He came back into the cellar, the tiny key dangling from his fingers, looking much too insignificant to be of the supreme importance that it was to me.

'Great.' I was pleased to hear how level my voice was. 'Now lock the cellar door and slide the key over to me. *Do* it.'

Once someone starts obeying they are much less likely to resist the second command, let alone the third. It gets to be a habit surprisingly fast. Every line of Thick Boy's body expressed his absolute unwillingness to carry out what I had just told him; but he did it anyway, bending down and skimming the key along the flagstones to finish almost in front of me. I stretched out one foot, meaning to hook it over so I could stand on it.

A hand closed around my ankle, wrenching me off-balance. Urine-Breath was making an unexpected comeback. It took me completely by surprise. I staggered, feeling his other hand coming round, trying to grab at my other ankle and tip me backwards. He was almost there. I tried to kick out at his spine and missed, disoriented, my thoughts so fixed on the key that it took me a few almost-fatal seconds to react. He nearly had me. He was lunging back now, trying to knock me over, strong and very angry. Instinctively I grabbed at the one thing I had to stabilise me: my hands around his neck. The cuffs jerked at his throat, catching under his Adam's apple, cutting off his breath as I leant precariously backwards, stumbling desperately to stay upright.

I didn't save myself. He did. As the handcuffs bit into his throat he doubled forwards to save himself from being strangled and this involuntary reflex brought me forward too, back onto my feet. His hands had come away from my ankles and were grabbing at the cuffs again, scrabbling for relief. I righted myself, widening my feet for balance, feeling the comforting scrape of the door key under the sole of my boot.

I was in a cold sweat of delayed reaction. I had fucked up big-time, underestimating Urine-Breath like that. But he had fucked up even worse; if he'd just held on for another moment he would have had me. I would have been knocked onto the ground. In a few seconds Urine-Breath would have been out of the stranglehold of the cuffs and taking his revenge. Jesus. First he would have raped me and then broken most of my bones. Or perhaps, with my new-found knowledge of his partiality for necrophilia, it would have happened the other way round.

'You're killing him!' Thick Boy blurted out. 'His eyes're popping out!'

I looked down at Urine-Breath's head, tilted back with the force with which I was pulling on the cuffs. It did look very flushed.

'OK,' I said, unlooping them from around his neck. He gurgled. I kicked him in the back.

'No more tricks. Or I'll break your arm for starters,' I said to him. 'I mean it. Now lie flat. Do it!'

Slowly he stretched out on the floor. I put one foot on the back of his neck.

I held out my wrists to Thick Boy.

'Come on, then,' I said. 'Unlock me. Or I'll break his neck.'

I jabbed my heel into Urine-Breath's neck to show I meant it. A stifled groan of pain from him helped with the effect. Thick Boy's hands were trembling so much it took him a disproportionate amount of time to fiddle the tiny little key into the lock. I think it was the sight of my wrists, too, slick with blood. With my hands raised, it was trickling down my forearms, soaking into my sweater.

'I shouldn't of left him to come down by himself,' Thick Boy said in a shaky voice. 'I'm sorry. But I wanted to watch the telly. I shouldn't of let him, though. I know I shouldn't.'

'Water under the bridge,' I said as the lock snapped open. 'Oh, *shit.*'

It was the shock of air on my wrists that had made me swear involuntarily. They hurt even more without the handcuffs cutting into them.

I had one of the cuffs clicking round Thick Boy's wrist before he knew it, the key itself dropping neatly into my open hand.

'Now you,' I said, wrenching Urine-Breath's right arm up behind his back and pulling him to his feet. The other cuff went round his right hand before I let him out of the grip. Grabbing the top of Thick Boy's balaclava, I pulled it off and stepped back from them in one movement, kicking the cellar key with me. All my movements felt choreographed. My brain was firing on all cylinders, generating so much energy it felt as if white light were exploding constantly inside my skull.

I bent to retrieve the key. The split-second as my hand closed round it was one of the best moments I will probably ever have in my life. Out of the cuffs and with the key to the door in my hand. I felt as if I could do anything: fly, walk on water, strike people down with one bolt of force from my eyes. I stepped back and heard a heavy crunching sound as my foot landed on something with a hard carapace. It cracked under my weight and my heel slid slightly as its contents squished out beneath it. I didn't need to look down to tell me I had just killed a cockroach. It was the final touch to a perfect moment.

Urine-Breath and Thick Boy were staring at me in silence, their two battered faces expressing fear and disbelief. I wished there had been some way to get the chain free. It would have been an excellent weapon, if a bit long. Chain's always good. It scares the shit out of people and it makes a great noise as it whistles down. Still, that one was firmly soldered to the boys' handcuffs. You win some, you lose some.

Thick Boy's mouth opened. He looked as if he was about to scream for help. Stepping forwards, I shoved his balaclava between his open lips. Then I turned and ran for the door.

Stone steps outside, leading up to a short tiled passage. I darted along it and found myself in a sort of storeroom, probably an old larder, because beyond it was a kitchen – through the open door it looked like something out of a show home on a new suburban estate, all light wood fitted cupboards and yellow walls. The table was piled high with detritus: empty boxes of frozen Sara Lee cheesecakes, Pop Tarts, Choc-o-Loop cereal, crisp packets scattered everywhere . . . I took this in with a single flash, my brain flicking through images like a super-fast camera.

Forget the kitchen. On my right, above a large old stone sink, was a big sash window. I didn't even hesitate. I wanted very much to explore the house but every single nerve-ending in my body was telling me to get the hell out of there, right now. In a moment I was scrambling onto the sink. From below came a bellow of rage and then a long series of yells. Thick Boy, true to his name, had taken a little time to work out that he had a hand free with which to pull the balaclava out of his mouth: but he had managed it in the end.

The window had a simple catch. It stuck, and I had to wrench at it, standing in the sink, which made unnerving cracking noises as I put all my weight on it to heave at the window. But finally the sash juddered upwards. I had a foot on the sill at once, levering myself through before the window was even fully open. My back screamed with pain, but that was in a parallel universe. The other foot followed. I wriggled through and jumped to the ground.

There was a brief glimpse of grass beneath my feet, fresh country air, a dull grey sky, trees in front of me across a muddy lawn. Then something hit me in the face and the grass came up to meet me like a foldaway bed snapping shut against the wall.

I didn't even feel the impact. I was out like a light.

CHAPTER ELEVEN

'Could we just leave it alone, Gary, OK? I was after a blow job tonight, not a rescue mission.'

'There's something wrong,' another voice insisted. 'I can feel it. You know how good my instincts are.'

A long sigh. 'Why can't you just let it be! Did you *see* that arse that just strutted by? Why do you always have to do the bleeding heart number?'

'It's not that—'

'They ask for it, you know! We're talking about people who willingly get their dicks nailed to boards!'

'Please, Lewis! You know I hate that kind of talk!'

Lewis lowered his voice. 'OK. But they come here on purpose to get the crap beaten out of them. I mean, sorry for spelling out the obvious. God, we've seen guys crawling out of here before in pieces enough times!'

'Lewis, I tell you there was something funny about the whole set-up,' Gary said defiantly. 'Those guys who dumped him didn't look like your classic rough trade to me. And what about him?'

'What *about* him?'

'I think he's just a boy. He was pretty small, didn't you see? Oh, for God's sake, Lewis, let me put this in a way you'll understand. Boy Beaten To Death In Notorious Queer Playground. If they don't try to close the park down, it'll be patrolled for years by legions of saggy-buttocked undercover policemen. Am I penetrating your selfish little skull?'

Lewis muttered something about penetration that had Gary giggling.

'All right, Florence Nightingale,' Lewis said eventually. 'Just to check he's breathing, OK?'

I heard the thump of feet and what seemed like an endless rustling and crackling of branches.

'My God, this bush is tearing me to pieces,' Gary complained. 'It's like something out of *Sleeping Beauty*.'

The voices were closer now. Dimly I wondered if I was paralysed: I seemed unable to move. I couldn't even open my eyes. I felt warm breath on my cheek, and then someone turning me over gently. It hurt like hell.

'Oh, fuck. Fuck a fucking duck. Lewis. Look.'

More footsteps. Someone else bending over me.

'Oh Jesus. What the fuck – No! Am I seeing things?'

'It's a girl, Lewis.'

'It can't be—'

'Lewis. Breasts. Remember those?'

A long pause, broken by Gary.

'I told you there was something wrong!' He sounded panicked, but also triumphant. 'I sensed it in my bones!'

'Look at her *nose*.' Lewis sounded repulsed. I couldn't blame him.

'We're going to have to take her to hospital. Thank God the Royal Free's nearby.' Gary was determined.

'We'll never get a taxi. Not with her looking like *that*.' Lewis's revulsion was, if anything, intensifying.

'Then we'll ring for an ambulance. Do you have your phone on you?'

'Oh, for God's sake, Gary,' Lewis said, all the pent-up frustration of having his night out completely ruined surging into his voice, 'as if I'd bring my phone out *cruising*.'

'Well, there's a phone box at the entrance. Come on, let's get her up. Poor thing. Talk about Sleeping Beauty for the Nineties. Beaten up and dumped in a bush.'

He bent over me.

'Can you hear me? You're going to be fine. We're going to take you to hospital and get you all patched up. God knows what happened to her,' he added as an aside to Lewis. 'Probably Prince Charming. I wouldn't be surprised.'

He put an arm under me and tried to get me to my feet. They hauled me up like a sack of coals, one arm over each shoulder.

'Can you stand?' Gary said to me.

I tried to speak, but my lips wouldn't obey me.

'Jesus, Gary, don't make her talk! Look at the state of her mouth!'

Lewis pulled my arm closer into his shoulder and grabbed hold of my hand to keep me steady.

'Hold on – Gary, get a grip on her, she's barely conscious – Oh, Jesus, her wrists, there's blood everywhere—'

My head slumped forward. The effort of standing was too much for me. Their voices seemed to be whirling around me like a spiral spinning faster and faster and faster. My last thought was the hope that I wasn't too heavy for them. They were being so nice. Well, I had probably lost a few pounds on my vegetarian retreat. Raw carrots and black coffee . . . My head was spinning as if I were tied to a giant top. I would have thrown up if there were anything in my stomach; but there wasn't. So I passed out instead.

There was a bright light shining in my eyes. It hurt. But that was scarcely a novelty; of late my life had taken a very pain-filled turn. I had enough material for a whole album of country and western songs.

I vaguely remembered passing out yet again. Nowadays I seemed to spend most of the time losing consciousness. When I got my *Who's Who* entry I could put it down in the 'Hobbies' section.

'Oh look, her eyes are opening!' exclaimed a familiar voice.

I tried to raise my head. Big mistake.

'Don't move,' Gary said anxiously. 'Here, I'll prop up a pillow for you.'

''ello, Gary,' I mumbled.

'You know him then, miss?' said a suspicious voice.

A face loomed over me. It was a policewoman, looking stern.

'Do you know this man?' she repeated, nodding to one side. 'You used his name.'

'Gary?' I said faintly. My lips felt like giant swollen pieces of rubber. ''e found me. Fank oo, Gary.'

I couldn't see him; my line of vision was too narrow. I was lying on a rather wobbly trolley in what looked like a hospital corridor. Welcome to the NHS emergency services.

'Not at all, sweetie,' he said with an edge to his voice, directed, I presumed, at the policewoman.

'So he's not involved in your disappearance, Ms Jones?' she persisted.

'No! 'e foun' me and go' me 'ere. 'e was grea'.'

'I *told* you,' Gary said crossly to the policewoman. 'Can I go now, DC Paranoid? I mean, if I'd been her kidnapper, I would scarcely have brought her in, would I? And frankly I could have got away from you seventeen times. I was staying to see if she was all right.'

'I suppose that's all right,' she said grudgingly. 'Since Ms Jones has confirmed you're not responsible for the attack on her. We'll be in touch with you about the identification of the men you saw dump her in the park.'

'You've got my number,' Gary said flippantly. 'Give me a call.'

He bent over me. For the first time I saw his face properly: blond, delicate, slightly acne-scarred. He was younger than I had thought, only in his early twenties.

'They say you'll be fine,' he assured me, pressing my hand. 'You'll probably be out of here before they manage to find you a bed. Whoops! *Do* you mind. That was my ankle.'

An orderly pushing another trolley past mine had banged into him.

'Sorry, mate,' the demoralised orderly muttered. The patient on the trolley exchanged a speaking glance with me as he went by. Solidarity in suffering. Lost souls together, wandering the nether regions, looking for the nirvana of a bed.

'Fank you,' I managed to say to Gary through my inflated lips. It wasn't just my lips: my entire face felt as if it had been inflated with a pump. 'Sorry for ruinin' your nigh' ou'.'

'One of many, sweetie. Don't you worry. Look after yourself.'

He bent down to kiss me on the cheek and stopped just before consummation. Clearly my face wasn't looking too kissable. I raised a hand to wave him goodbye and blinked as it came into view, the middle finger grotesquely swollen and a raw chafed ring of flesh around the wrist. It looked as if I'd been wearing the plastic handcuffs the police once used, now outlawed because of the damage they had caused. The cuff of my sweater had slipped back down my forearm. It was thick with dried blood. I must remember to suggest the effect to an avant-garde knitwear designer when I recovered: it was very striking.

'Never mind,' Gary said hurriedly as my hand fell back to the blanket. 'I'll just blow you a kiss, how's that?'

'Do you feel up to giving a statement, Ms Jones?' the DC asked after he had gone.

'My mouf 'ur's,' I said rather sulkily. I had barely woken up and the woman was pestering me already.

Besides, I knew how this went. If I gave her a statement I'd just have to go over it all again with the investigating officer. I might as well hold my fire for the bigger fish. Mmn, nicely expressed, Sam. Maybe you should go back to sleep for a while.

'We've contacted DI Hawkins,' the DC said encouragingly. 'He's on his way.'

''Aw'ins?' I said incredulously.

'He's a friend of yours, isn't he? He's been very concerned about your disappearance.'

'Wa'e me up when 'e ge's 'ere,' I said, closing my eyes. Ah, bliss. Sleep beckoned again with surprising force. They must have given me some high-quality painkillers, bless them.

' "She moves, she stirs, she seems to feel/The breath of life beneath her keel . . ." ' commented a familiar voice. 'Sam?'

''ugo?' I said feebly. My throat was as dry as if someone had been filing down the lining of my oesophagus while I slept. I tried to clear it and made an awful, chainsaw-starting-up, Urine-Breath-with-Adam's-apple-damage kind of noise. 'I wan' a drin',' I said, trying to sit up. 'Can I 'ave a drin'?'

Hugo sighed. 'Back to normal, eh? It was always too much to hope that she'd be brain dead,' he said conversationally. 'One knows that the perfect woman doesn't exist. But a tiny bit of collateral damage – just enough to disorient – I had this little image of a docile, biddable Sam, helpless and grateful for the smallest attention—'

'I wan' a drin'!' I said loudly.

'For God's sake, man! She's badly hurt! Look at her!'

''Aw'ins?' I said, trying to turn my head to see him. He was standing by the bedside table. Which meant that they had found me a bed. What luxury. I heard the beautiful sound of liquid being poured out and then he handed me a glass of water. I bolted it. Hawkins rounded the bed and propped himself on the end, leaning over the back rails, staring at me with what anyone who didn't know him would have interpreted as anger. It was: but there was plenty of concern and frustration in there too. Hawkins loathed my propensity for getting into scrapes.

'I' wasn' my faul',' I said defensively. 'Fis 'ime i' was comple'ely no' my faul'.'

'Jesus, listen to her,' Hugo said affectionately. 'Dropping her T's like they were her knickers.'

Hawkins swivelled around to give Hugo a furious glance. The latter was managing to lounge with reasonable success in an orange plastic chair with wood-effect arms. The upholstery clashed about as badly as it could with his pale pink turtleneck, a fact which was no doubt distressing him.

'How can you be so bloody flippant?' Hawking demanded. 'Look at her! Don't you care about the state she's in?'

'She's got two broken fingers, a sprained wrist, a couple of broken ribs and a broken nose,' Hugo retorted, looking down his nose at Hawkins. It would seem impossible for someone to do this while they are lounging in an armchair and the other person is standing up, but Hugo managed it effortlessly. This was the kind of thing that had won my heart. 'In Sam terms that's the equivalent of having a bad headache.'

'Bro'en nose?' I said excitedly, sitting up and reaching up one hand. It wasn't much good to me; my two middle fingers were strapped together and braced by a long metal splint which reached all the way to my elbow. Cautiously I tapped the splint to my nose. It seemed to be completely covered in bandages. I could feel sticky plaster holding them onto my cheeks. Already it was starting to itch.

'Will i' be s'raigh' now?' I demanded. 'Did fey s'rai'en i'?'

'I rest my case,' Hugo said to Hawkins. 'No, darling,' he added to me. 'They just put the pieces back together. They didn't file down your bump.'

'Oh, fu',' I said crossly, relapsing back onto the pillows. 'A' leas' fey coul' 'ave s'raigh'ene' i'. Fu'.'

'She's obsessed with this tiny little bump she has on her nose,' Hugo explained to Hawkins. 'A photographer once told her it was a problem and ever since then she's been a total bore on the subject.'

I hadn't even met Hugo when that bastard Tony Muldoon gave me a hard time about my nose. However, I was perfectly aware that Hugo was taking this uxorious tone to make it clear to Hawkins that the latter no longer had any claims on me. Hugo and Hawkins had never got on.

Though I had known Hawkins for years, he and I were fundamentally incompatible: apart from being a policeman – in itself, given most aspects of my lifestyle, an insuperable block – he was also genuinely nice, which alone would have ruled him out from serious-boyfriend consideration. Anyway, he had had a girlfriend at the time, whom he had subsequently married, and ever since the nuptials his admirable sense of morality had prevented him from coming round for our usual snatched afternoons of passion.

I could see the wedding ring quite clearly; his hands were grasping the top rail of the bed and the gold band caught the light. Hugo must have spotted it too. He was as sharp as a whip. Still, that wasn't stopping him from trying to mark his territory.

'Forget the nose for a moment. If we can,' Hawkins said in what was supposed to be a biting tone. 'I need to know what happened to Sam. Are you OK?' His voice lowered. 'I mean – did anything happen to you? Are you – did they – you know . . .'

'One of fem 'ad a go,' I said.

'Oh, Jesus – Sam! What happened?'

'I assume your concern is for the would-be rapist,' Hugo drawled. 'She probably cut off the offending organ and nailed it to his forehead with a staple gun.'

I thought for a moment that Hawkins was going to hit Hugo. His knuckles went white on the bedrail and his normally good-humoured, craggy face broke into an impressive scowl.

'I 'it 'im in the ne' with a bi' of flags'one,' I said quickly, by way of distraction. 'And 'en I 'i'ed 'im in the s'omac'.'

'You did what?' Hawkins stared at me.

'I 'i'ed 'im –' I raised one of my feet to demonstrate – 'in the s'omac'.' I pointed to my tummy. Then I subsided against the pillows. My back still hurt when I moved. I wondered if that was from Urine-Breath's original kick or whether somone had given me another going-over when I was unconscious the time before the time before last.

'You see?' Hugo spread his hands wide. The demands of shooting *Driven* were not allowing him to wear the nail polish he usually affected, which was a small mercy. At that moment seeing Hugo's Hard Candy-varnished nails might have pushed Hawkins over the edge into gibbering lunacy.

'Bu' 'e did feel me up,' I added, feeling that Hugo was being insufficiently sympathetic. I knew that it was partly a pose – Hawkins had cornered the market in emotional distress, forcing Hugo into a parody of his usual blasé self in order not to compete with him – but I felt that Hugo was taking it a little too far.

'He did *what?*' Hugo sat up in the armchair, momentarily forgetting to be an Oscar Wilde hero. 'Where? What did he do?'

''e grabbe' my 'i'.'

'Your what?'

I gestured to my right breast, frustrated with my limited ability to pronounce entire words. Sometimes, if I concentrated, I could get out more consonants: but it hurt more, so I didn't always try that hard.

'An' 'e un'i' my jeans an' pu' 'is 'an' 'own my 'ic'ers.'

I looked from Hugo to Hawkins. They were frozen, staring at me in horror. While I was gone they must have been imagining the worst. Well, this might be minor-league stuff as far as the average kidnap went, let alone the imaginings of those thriller writers forced by the demands of the market to invent ever-worse tortures for their (usually female) victims: but it had been real. And I hadn't enjoyed it. I was damned if I was going to minimise the worst aspects for the sake of Hawkins and Hugo. Besides, telling them about it and seeing their appalled reactions was causing my spirits to rise tremendously. A trouble dumped on someone else is a trouble halved.

''e'd 'ave rape' me, if I 'ad'n' 'i' 'im wif fe flags'one,' I went on. ''e 'ad my jeans 'alf-off.'

'Fucking bastard!' Hawkins said between gritted teeth. 'When I get my hands on him I'll smash his bloody balls to pieces.'

Hugo just sat there in dead silence, unmoving, his hands closed tightly around the arms of the chair. It was entirely uncharacteristic. I was not unsatisfied with the effect I was producing.

'Do you want to talk to someone?' Hawkins said tentatively.

It wasn't the first time Hawkins had had cause to suggest that I might want to see a counsellor. I shook my head.

'I go' i' all ou' a' fe 'ime,' I boasted. 'Prac'ical ferapy.'

Hugo muttered something about my inability to resist the worst kind of macho posturing, which earned him hostile glances from both Hawkins and me. Mine was because Hugo was dead on the money; he knew me too well. Not completely, though. I might be posturing, but there was some truth behind it. I still felt a surge of revulsion every time I thought of Urine-Breath's soggy fingers on my naked skin; not only what he had done, but what might have happened if I hadn't been able to fight him off. If I called up the image of that stone going into his throat, or my foot landing in his stomach, it seemed to neutralise the nausea well enough. But if he'd raped me? I really would have had to cut off his dick and staple it to his forehead just to be able to sleep at night.

The trick would be to try not to think about Urine-Breath at all. I wondered how long that would take, and realised that I was shivering.

'Well, thank God you're still alive,' Hawkins said.

I stared at him in surprise, unpleasant memories swept away. 'You fough' fey were going 'o 'ill me? Fey were animal righ's, no' the Re' Briga'e.'

It had been a consolation to me: who ever heard of animal rights activists killing anyone who wasn't directly involved in stapling open cats' eyes and squirting lighter fluid into the pupils? I had never actually thought that Thick Boy and Urine-Breath had any fatal intentions towards me. Not until I tried to rip the latter's Adam's apple out with a piece of flagstone. But Hawkins obviously thought it had been a real possibility. He must know something I didn't. I shivered again. Delayed reaction kicking in with hobnailed boots.

'She hasn't heard yet,' Hugo said to Hawkins. 'You'd better tell her.'

Hawkins fixed his gaze on me. His blue eyes were his one beauty; his face was too square and chunky to be remotely handsome, though it was reassuring in a rugged kind of way, like a rock, or a battered old statue. Seeing him stare at me so seriously brought back memories of some of those afternoons in my studio. That expression of intense concentration was very similar to the one he wore just before he started ripping his clothes off. I felt my face twisting into a reminiscent smirk. That was a mistake. Smirking hurt.

'Sam,' he said. 'Those people who kidnapped you – at least, we can't be sure it was them—'

'Is i' Sarah?' I said, suddenly struck by an odd kind of premonition. ''As somefing 'appene' 'o 'er?'

'Not Sarah. Her boyfriend.'

''er boyfrien',' I repeated. 'Oh, shi'. You mean Paw?'

Hawkins nodded slowly. 'He's been killed. In her flat. It was really nasty. He was cut right open. Practically disembowelled.'

Hugo wriggled uncomfortably in his chair.

'Wha' wif?' I said.

'Carving knife. One of hers. We think whoever did it was waiting in the flat for her, and Paul took him by surprise.'

''im?'

'Jesus, Sam. Maybe you could have done it – you're pretty strong for your size – only you've got an alibi. But this guy was gutted. Ripped open. Someone stuck a knife in his stomach and just kept going up. You need a lot of strength for that.'

He looked at me.

'I brought the crime scene photos, if you want to see,' he added, sounding doubtful.

'You did *what*?' Hugo said, half rising from his chair.

'I dunno. It seemed like a good idea at the time. I knew she'd want to see them. Might, you know, be a distraction.' He gestured at the bed.

Hawkins knew me pretty well, too. I didn't mind that so much. But then, I wasn't going out with him.

'But they're – well, you can imagine. It might not be such a good idea after all.'

My right wrist was strapped so tight I could hardly move it. I stuck out the left hand and waved it back and forth. The splint made it look as if I was giving Hawkins the finger.

'Come on, 'and fem over,' I said impatiently. 'Don' be a 'ease.'

'God,' Hugo muttered, sounding frighteningly sincere. 'I can't *tell* you how badly I need a cigarette.'

CHAPTER TWELVE

Hawkins dropped a brown envelope on my stomach. I turned it upside down with my splinted hand, grasping clumsily with thumb and little finger, and shook. Black and white photographs, heavy and glossy as actors' publicity shots, tumbled out. I picked through them, using the tip of the splint as a kind of probe.

It was as bad as Hawkins had said. Paul was unrecognisable, his handsome face so contorted by agony he looked like a gargoyle. Hard to believe the human face could distort itself that much, unless you had the evidence right there in front of you. And it was harder to go on looking at one shot after another of someone you had known, literally disembowelled, his mouth twisted in a terrible rictus of pain.

The worst part was the hands pressed to his belly as if he had been trying to hold in its contents. Or push them back in, because his intestines were spilling out, just like they did in the films. It was a constant effort of will to remind myself that what I was seeing was a real person, slashed open like an animal in a slaughterhouse. From *The Texas Chainsaw Massacre* when I could barely walk, I had trained myself all my life not only to take for granted the most powerful of special effects, but to mock them too. And now those reflexes were kicking in as I stared at these photographs of Paul. I felt sick and guilty.

''Aw'ins?' I said, pointing to the picture lying on my chest. 'Was i' jus' fa'? Fe one cu'? I mean—'

I was trying to limit myself to simple, short statements, to spare my swollen mouth. This time I could have slapped myself with frustration at my inability to convey my meaning. Luckily Hawkins knew what I was driving at.

'Yeah, whoever did it didn't just disembowel him,' he said wearily. 'They left him to die like that. Alone. Trying to hold in his own guts. Poor bastard couldn't even scream for help. Look.'

He reached over and tapped the central photograph, pointing at Paul's head.

'He had a scarf shoved right down his throat so he couldn't make a noise. Doctor says he choked on it. Better than bleeding to death, I suppose.'

His hand touched mine for a moment.

'You were lucky, Sam. You were bloody lucky,' he said. 'I can't bear to think what that bastard might've done to you.'

His eyes were as red as if a drop of blood were infusing through each one, and he was blinking hard. I stared at him, awed. I had never seen Hawkins cry before.

'An' you 'ink i' was 'e same guys oo 'i'nappe' me?' I said, my gaze inexorably drawn back to the photographs of Paul, screaming in silence.

'We haven't got much to go on,' Hawkins admitted. 'Well, I say we – it's not my patch. I'm sorry for the poor sods who have to deal with it. Talk about high profile.'

'Is Sarah all ri'?'

'Technically yes,' Hugo said. 'When you disappeared, there were these press releases left behind announcing that she'd been kidnapped by the Animal Rights Freedom Fighters. We didn't even realise then that they'd taken you by mistake, not until the next morning when I saw your van just down the road from the parking lot. We just thought it was another attempt to scare her. But as soon as we put the pieces together and worked out that they'd got you instead, she was under police surveillance.'

'Bu' if Paul was 'ille' a' 'er fla'—'

'No one was watching her flat when she wasn't in it,' Hawkins said. 'And she was staying with Paul. He went round to pick something up for her and never came back. She found him the next day.'

'Oh, fu',' I said devoutly.

'It was like something out of a butcher's shop, apparently,' Hugo said.

''ow is she?'

'Actually, much better than you'd think. The doctor's given her a load of tranquillisers, but she won't take much. Says they'd interfere with the performance.' Hugo looked down at his lap. 'She said the worst thing was the smell,' he said. 'The blood. And there were some flies.'

A long pause ensued.

'If you still need a cigarette, there's a smoking room on the ground floor,' Hawkins suggested to Hugo.

Hugo shot him a nasty look. Clearly he had no intention of leaving the two of us alone. We fell silent once more. When there came a scrape and rustle as the curtains surrounding my bed were pulled back, I think we were all more than grateful for the distraction. A doctor appeared, looking from Hugo to Hawkins with a certain amount of disapproval.

'I think that's enough for now,' she said. 'This young lady's taken quite a beating. Time for her to have a rest.'

'We do need to get a statement from her as soon as possible,' Hawkins said. 'My colleagues will be turning up here in an hour or so.'

The doctor tutted. 'Well, you two should clear out. Give her a bit of peace and quiet till then. And I'll tell them not to exhaust her.' She looked at me. 'How are you feeling, Ms Jones? In a lot of pain?'

Everyone turned to stare at me.

'Ac'ually,' I said, seizing my opportunity, 'I'm really 'ungry. I 'aven' ea'en in days. Could I 'ave a san'wi'?'

I overruled the doctor; I wouldn't let her send Hawkins and Hugo away. After the days spent in the cellar with only cockroaches for company, I found myself extremely reluctant to be on my own. It was a very odd sensation. I don't think I had ever said the words 'Don't go' before in my life.

This was partly pride, and partly my near-pathological need for my own space. Spending my formative years in Aunt Louise and Uncle Harold's bungalow, hemmed in by endless display shelves of crystal animals, ornamental plates and china figurines of dancing nymphs, had produced a powerful negative effect on me. My Aunt Louise couldn't open a Sunday colour supplement without ordering everything in it. Her monthly direct debits for those plates alone were astronomical. The front room was claustrophobia city.

So it was unprecedented for me to insist on both Hugo and Hawkins remaining in my tiny curtained-off cubicle for the infinite treat of watching me slurp my way through a plate of rice pudding with custard. It was the most liquid food the canteen could provide. A few days of this regime and I'd put back on all the weight I'd lost on the Vegemite diet.

'I'll bring you in some designer baby food tomorrow,' Hugo offered sarcastically. 'Though I expect that stains just as badly as the ordinary stuff. Could you be a little more careful with my pyjamas?'

I looked down guiltily at the striped silk lapels, already dotted with a wide range of rice and custard splodges.

'I's very diffi'ul' wif only one fumb an' finger, and a dodgy wris',' I said defensively. 'You bloody 'ry i'.'

Another dollop of rice landed on my, or rather his, pyjamas. Hugo winced. To distract him, I said quickly:

'Wha' 'appene' 'o my clofes?'

'The ones the hospital gave me?' Hugo raised his eyebrows. 'Well, since my local dry-cleaners didn't have its Fumigation Special Offer on this week—'

'You 'i'n' frow fem away!' I wailed. 'Fose were my favouri' jeans!'

'—I boil-washed them myself,' Hugo concluded. 'I was too embarrassed to take them into Sketchley's.'

'Fank you,' I said gratefully.

'You owe me big-time,' Hugo said. 'It was one of the most revolting experiences of my life. If I wanted to date a bag-lady I'd be down at Charing Cross picking some lucky *Big Issue* seller out of a shop doorway.'

'For God's sake,' Hawkins said, his sensibilities outraged. 'The girl was chained in a cellar for nearly a week! What do you *expect*?'

That was precisely the problem with Hawkins. He was too fundamentally nice for me.

The curtains rattled back again. I looked up and, fatally distracted, splodged a spoonful of rice onto my chin instead of into my mouth. I was beginning to feel like that very unsound joke about the differently abled boy and the ice-cream cone.

Hawkins turned his head to see who it was and promptly froze in that position, a stare of star-struck admiration on his face. Though this made me sulky, I had to admit that Sarah was in much better looks than I was at the moment. Besides, hers were set off by the gigantic bouquet of flowers she was carrying. Aunt Louise always said that white next to the face was flattering. Why on earth I kept remembering Aunt Louise all of a sudden was a mystery; maybe that when-you're-kidnapped flashback effect was factoring in after all.

Sarah did her best not to look too appalled at my appearance. An actor's training stood her in good stead. Her eyes widened a little and her mouth drew down at the corners in an automatic grimace, but she covered it up fast enough by holding out the bouquet to me, drawing all eyes to the mass of white roses. It was almost bridal. Maybe when I got out of here I could throw it to the next patient in line.

'I'm so, so sorry, Sam,' she said, coming forward. 'I feel like the biggest piece of shit in the world.'

She stood at the foot of the bed, looking at me earnestly. 'It was because you were coming out of my trailer, wasn't it? They thought you were me. I worked that much out.'

In the dark, coming down the steps of her trailer with my hair pinned back and my work clothes on, anyone would have assumed I was Sarah. My bad luck that I had dropped in to pick up a tape I had lent her. Or maybe it wasn't bad luck, but a punishment for breaking my own rule: never lend tapes to people. The cosmos moves in mysterious ways.

''Scuse me?' A nurse appeared through the curtains. It looked as if he was blushing slightly, but on Asian skin it's often hard to be sure. His large dark eyes were fixed on Sarah.

'I couldn't help notice you coming in with those,' he said, indicating the flowers with a diffident little bob of his head. 'D'you want me to find you a vase or something?'

'Yeah, that'd be great, thanks,' Sarah said distractedly, handing the flowers to him. He vanished. She turned back to me.

'I'm really sorry,' she said again.

'It wasn' your faul',' I said reassuringly.

'Yeah, but maybe if I'd taken those threats more seriously – apologised earlier – well, what am I saying, there's no maybe about it. No one would have tried to kidnap me if I'd retracted. I just couldn't back down, I was too stubborn. I didn't even *mean* half the things I said, it's just when my motormouth gets going—'

'I's all righ'. Really.'

'God.' Sarah collapsed on the arm of Hugo's chair and buried her face in her hands for a moment, her dark hair tumbling forward so thickly that all I could see was her wrists. 'I just – there's nothing I can say to make it any better – and when I think about what you must have gone through . . .' she said helplessly, her words muffled by the hair.

'Miss Fossett?' the nurse said shyly. 'I've done the flowers for you. Here they are.'

As if pulling a rabbit out of a hat, he produced the bouquet, now shoved rather inexpertly into a white china vase. Above it his face beamed hopefully at Sarah. He didn't favour Hugo with so much as a glance; he probably didn't even recognise him. *Driven* was Hugo's big TV break, but Sarah had been a jobbing TV actress for years, coming up through stage school and an apprenticeship on a minor soap, and her face was familiar to a large section of the public by now.

'Oh, that looks great,' she said, raising her head. 'Thanks.'

'I'll just put it by the bed,' he said. 'Um – I just wanted to say . . .'

Sarah's face took on a polite, almost over-attentive expression. She must have heard this preliminary a hundred times before.

'I loved you in *Getting Burnt*,' he stammered nervously. 'And *Park Lane*. You were really good.'

'Thanks. Thanks very much,' Sarah said, favouring him with a bright actressy smile. Even her voice had gone onto automatic pilot. 'That's great to hear.'

'Oh, well, I just wanted to – I'll put these down then – anyway, I'll be around if you need anything – I mean, if Ms Jones needs anything . . .'

He backed out through the curtains, the blush now so evident there was no mistaking it.

'Well, exactly,' Sarah said. 'I mean, I'm not the bloody patient, am I? It's all very well doing the star-struck bit, but really. I mean, we're in a hospital.'

I made a humphing noise of agreement.

'Won'ere' 'ow long it woul' 'a'e for 'im 'o remember me,' I said crossly. 'Oh, 'ello? Si' perso' 'ere! In fe be'!' I waved my splint towards the gap in the curtains.

'Do you want something?' Sarah asked immediately.

'Maybe jelly,' I said thoughtfully. 'Or pu'in'. I'm s'ill 'ungry.'

'I'll go and get it. No, let me,' she said, as Hugo and Hawkins both made signs of rising. 'At least it'll be something I can do.'

I had to admit that Sarah was behaving impeccably. No traces of luvvieness at all.

'Nice, isn't she?' Hawkins said, managing not to blush in his turn by a heroic effort of will.

'Mmn, very,' Hugo agreed. 'Actually, I think your being kidnapped helped a lot with Paul being killed, Sam, if you see what I mean. She was already so cut up with guilt about you being mistaken for her that it rather distracted from the shock. When she found him, she was even more worried about what they might do to you. Cried for hours, apparently, when she heard you'd turned up.'

He grinned.

'Dumping you in Golders Hill Park does display a peculiar sense of humour,' he said. 'And very clever, too. One of the few places in London where no one would bat an eyelid at two guys dumping a third one in a bush.'

'I'll ma'e a no'e for nex' 'ime I kill someone,' I said sarcastically.

'I should be going,' Hawkins said, looking at his watch. But he showed no signs of moving, and I bet he wouldn't till Sarah returned.

''ow long 'o I 'ave 'o s'ay in 'ere?' I said. It was the first time it had occurred to me to wonder about this. I was really not myself yet.

'At least a couple of days, they think,' Hugo said.

'Oh, *bugger.*'

'It's the best place for you,' he said persuasively. 'I mean, I thought you could come and stay at mine, while you're recovering, but I'll be out practically all the time for the next few weeks. We've got a really tough schedule. Here at least there's people to look after you—'

'When fey're no' ogli' my visi'ors,' I said sourly.

Hugo sighed.

'Anyway, I wan' 'o go 'ome,' I said.

'You can't go back to yours on your own!' Hawkins and Hugo said practically in unison. I was about to tell them both what they could do with their protective concern when Sarah reappeared, bearing a plate in each hand.

'Jelly *and* chocolate pudding,' she said triumphantly, 'as ordered.'

She took in the state of my pyjama lapels with one swift glance.

'Why don't I feed them to you?' she suggested. 'Would you mind? It'd make me feel useful.'

I appreciated her tact.

'Go a'ead,' I said. She sat down next to me on the bed and started ladling blackcurrant jelly through my swollen lips.

'You look as if you've been having collagen injections,' she said, grinning at me.

'Wis' I'd 'ad a nose job 'oo,' I said wistfully.

Her eyes dropped to my lap, as if she couldn't ask the next question while looking me in the face.

'Are you OK?' she said, her voice lowered too. 'I mean – oh, you know – shit, this is so hard – but did they – oh, shit—'

'I'm fine,' I said.

'Really?' Those extraordinary light eyes fixed on me again. I suddenly felt very tired, and not remotely in the mood for reassuring anyone else about my state of mind.

'Sarah?' said a voice from outside the curtains.

'Can I help you?' the voice of Sarah's lovestruck nurse cut in officiously.

'Yeah, thanks, mate. I'm looking for Sarah Fossett. She's visiting a girl called Jones, right? Should be somewhere round 'ere.'

'It's this bed,' the nurse said. He sounded distinctly unfriendly. The curtains rustled. 'But Ms Jones has plenty of visitors right now. Maybe it'd be better to wait.'

'Nah, don't you worry about that. More the merrier when you're in 'ospital. Bit of distraction, innit?'

The curtains were drawn back with a single sharp pull. From my vantage point I was getting more clumsy entrances and exits than at a Coarse Acting production. But there was nothing coarse about the man who appeared in the gap; at least, not visually. He was tall, wearing a sharply cut, three-button pale grey suit with a tight black V-neck sweater underneath. His fair hair was cropped short to his head and his merry grey-green eyes slanted slightly upwards, almost parallel to his cheekbones. I blinked in admiration.

'All right,' he said in a friendly greeting to everyone. 'I'm Vince Greene. Friend of Sarah's. Hugo.' He nodded at this latter. 'How's it going, mate?'

'Day off,' Hugo said. 'I insisted.'

'I wouldn't be Grania for anything,' Sarah said, spooning more jelly into my mouth.

'That's the line producer,' Hugo said kindly to Hawkins, who was staring at Vince, as hostile as the nurse had been to any good-looking men who announced themselves as friends of Sarah's. How immature. 'The poor thing has had to tinker with the shooting schedule seventeen times already because the lead actress's stand-in's been kidnapped, the lead actress has found her boyfriend slaughtered and the lead actor is throwing a strop because his girlfriend has just turned up with her face pulped unrecognisably in a well-known gay playground and he wants to fly to her side—'

'Yeah, that's right. Dumped you into a load of poofs on heat, I heard,' Vince said to me jovially. 'Still, you'd be safe enough there, eh?'

Sarah turned her head to shoot him a reproving glance.

'*Vince*,' she said, with the weary tones of someone who has said the same name with the same reproach hundreds of times before.

'Yeah, yeah, I know,' Vince said, raising his hands in mock-apology. 'But there's no poofs around here, know what I'm saying? Neither of these two look like uphill gardeners to me! Am I right, lads?'

He grinned at Hawkins and Hugo. His smile was enchanting. It's always such a disappointment when a drop-dead gorgeous man opens his mouth and toads start hopping out.

Hugo's eyes met mine over the last spoonful of jelly. He gives great speaking glance.

'Vince,' he said politely, 'this is DI Hawkins, an old friend of Sam's.'

Vince burst out laughing.

'No need for introductions, Hugo! The DI and me are old mates too. We go back a long, long way. Isn't that right?' he said genially to Hawkins.

'Vince,' Hawkins said calmly, acknowledging him with a brief, unfriendly nod.

I had been unfair to Hawkins. His antagonism to Vince hadn't been personal – males jostling for territory around an attractive female – but professional. I looked back at Vince, suddenly remembering his name. Sarah had mentioned him before, the dodgy ex-boyfriend who put contracts out on people. He was just the type. Below his easy manner and his striking good looks was the hard core of a man who didn't like to be messed with. I remembered, too, Sarah laughing at the idea of Vince being the kind of person to nail up a dead fox in her trailer. Now I realised why it had been so funny.

Vince and Hawkins were staring at each other, neither willing to be the first to look away. It was an impressive stand-off – if you went in for that kind of macho bullshit.

'Vince really tried to help when you were missing,' Sarah said quickly to me, trying to defuse the tension between the two men.

It worked. Vince looked over at me, while Hawkins stretched his arms behind him and yawned ostentatiously to demonstrate his indifference to Vince.

'Yeah, I put the word out,' the latter was saying. 'If you'd been snatched by anyone but a group of animal rights nutters, I'd've heard something soon enough. But that lot're a law unto themselves, know what I'm saying? Mouths shut tighter than a virgin's arse. Didn't get so much as a whisper, did we, Inspector?'

'Leave it, Vince,' Hawkins said, his voice still calm, but his manner indicating how little he was warming to Vince's friendly camaraderie.

'See? Not a whisper,' Vince said to me. 'Sorry, love. Did all I could. 'Specially knowing that lot might be coming after Sarah. Lucky you knew how to handle yourself, eh?'

Hawkins didn't like this comment any better than the previous ones. Even Hugo bridled. He considered it was his exclusive right to make sarcastic remarks about my capacity for violence.

'There,' Sarah said brightly by way of distraction, putting the empty jelly plate onto the bedside table, next to the bouquet. 'Do you want the pudding now?'

I shook my head. 'Have 'i for la'er,' I said. Wow, my first H. The jelly had helped tremendously.

'They did a job and an 'alf on you, didn't they?' Vince said to me sympathetically. 'How's it going?'

'No' 'oo bad.'

He shoved his hands in his pockets and rocked back on his heels. The jacket came open, revealing the flatness of his stomach under the tight sweater. He must work out a lot. He looked the type to hit the gym on a regular basis.

'Broke a couple of fingers?' he went on, nodding at my hand. 'Nasty one. I broke a couple myself in my time. Ain't no joke. Still, you're pretty tough, ain't you?' He stared at me assessingly. 'Been reading all the articles. You can look after yourself all right.'

'Fe ar'icles?' I didn't know what he was talking about.

'There's been a lot of press,' Hugo said. 'They pulled out, um, everything.'

'*Everyfing?*' I said unhappily.

'Self-defence, eh?' Vince winked at me. 'Say no more.'

Vince, eye candy though he might be, was beginning to get on my nerves. I was sure he meant well, but somehow that seemed not quite enough of an excuse.

'I think we ought to be making a move,' Sarah said, not before time. She stood up and zipped up her jacket. 'Can I come back and see you tomorrow?' she said to me.

'Sure,' I said. I was still reluctant to let anyone go. Even Vince was better company than my own.

'What can I bring?'

I brightened up at once. 'Ice cream,' I said eagerly. 'Häagen-Dazs Cookies and Cream. Ben & Jerry's Phish Food. Wall's Viennetta vanilla. Or chocolate. Not the mint.'

'Ms Jones?' The curtains were drawn back still further. It was as crowded in here as a bit-part actor's trailer. The nurse was in front, his eyes fixed dewily on Sarah, and behind him, like a couple of wingers, hovered two uniformed policemen.

'We've come to take your statement,' one of them said.

'Your timing is perfect, officers,' Hugo said, rising to his feet. 'Her powers of speech have just this moment been miraculously restored. I don't suppose you've brought any Ben & Jerry's? It seems to work wonders.'

I gave him the splinted finger.

CHAPTER THIRTEEN

'I am not sleeping on that bloody sofa!' Tom's voice rose alarmingly. 'I'd rather doss down on the floor in a sleeping bag!'

'Be my guest,' I said sulkily.

'Your guest? That's a joke. Your idea of being a good host means getting some poor sod so drunk he's easy prey.'

'That is so not true.'

Tom gave me a significant stare.

'Well,' I amended, 'not always. Lately people have been going to bed with me when they're relatively sober. I'm moving up in the world.'

Tom snorted. 'Anyway,' he said, kicking the sofa again. 'This thing is dead, Sammy. You should have thrown it away years ago.'

'And then what would I do? Sit on the concrete floor?'

'You would Go Out And Buy Another One,' Tom suggested.

'Don't be stupid,' I said dismissively. 'I don't buy soft furnishings. I'm not that kind of person.'

'Sooner or later we're all that kind of person.'

'Ooh, hark at Mr Bourgeois,' I mocked. 'Just because you've got a microwave in your house.'

'The microwave is great. The endless discussion meetings we have about whose turn it is to pick the crumbs out are slightly less so, OK? Sometimes I actually miss squatting. Never thought I'd say that, but I do. I mean, it was Scumsville, but we never had to have bi-weekly meetings about the microwave cleaning rota.'

'Castle Road was a co-op,' I pointed out. 'You didn't have rota meetings there.' This was the house Tom had lived in years back; a friend of mine had been killed at a wild party there. Hers had been the first dead body I had ever found. Since then it had been one long haul of corpses.

'Castle Road was even more of a filth pit than this studio,' Tom said. 'Do you remember the rats in the kitchen? They demolished it, you know,' he added, suddenly becoming nostalgic. 'The council.'

'Probably burnt it to the ground and called in the biological warfare people from Porton Down to make sure there weren't any more Black Death spores floating in the remains,' I said unsympathetically. 'Did you know a scientist from Porton Down actually died of the Black Death, in the Sixties?'

'What happens exactly with that one?'

'I dunno. Lots of buboes, I imagine, and exploding blistery things, and then you go black from blood congestion and die.'

Tom considered this. 'Nope. I don't remember anyone at Castle Road complaining about all of those put together. Though I think some of them may have had the early stages.'

'Most boys in Camden pubs have the early stages.'

'Ah, well,' Tom said complacently, 'I too have moved up in the world. No more rats. A large fitted kitchen instead, in the best part of Stoke Newington, with all the mod cons, and two – count 'em – *two* bathrooms. And of course I have my new career.'

Tom was a penniless, if published, poet who was currently training as a primary school teacher on the grounds that (a) they were always keen to have men in the profession and (b) it would provide the perfect opportunity to meet endless streams of single mothers desperate for a shag.

'No chat-up lines needed,' he had said cheerfully once, 'you just make some small-talk about how great it is that little Tiffany hasn't beaten anyone up all week, and look sensitive and caring. Then the mother asks you to dinner because she can't afford a babysitter. In the house and on the sofa on the first date. I can't imagine why I didn't think of this years ago.'

'Seriously, though,' I said now, 'the whole sleeping question. If this is some clumsy effort to share the futon with me you've got another think coming.'

'You're not my type,' Tom said coldly. 'You know I like them blonde and slender.'

'Skinny.'

'Delicately boned.'

'Urh, sounds like a chicken.'

'I think you should get a fucking sofa bed,' Tom said with an air of finality. 'It's time. You have the money, too, don't you?'

'Oh my God. I can't believe you're talking to me like this.'

'Sammy. A sofa bed costs three hundred pounds at IKEA. You can afford that. You spend loads on clothes.' He was gearing up for the final assault. '*You have a Marks and Spencer's charge card.*'

'You *bastard*! How do you know?'

'Noticed it in your wallet last time we went out for a drink.'

'You are scum.'

Maybe he was right, though. I had had that sofa for years, ever since I liberated it from the squat in Hackney Tom and I had shared, longer ago than I cared to recall. The velveteen on the arms was worn right through the nap, so that puffs of stuffing wheezed out at the slightest pressure; I had turned the cushions so many times to hide the latest set of stains that they were full-blown schizophrenics; and the single spring sticking through the seat had been going forth and multiplying when my back was turned. It was like sitting on a bed of nails.

'All right,' I sighed. 'I'll get a sofa.'

'Wey-hey! Can I come and help you choose it?'

'I can't get anything too posh,' I warned him. 'It'd show the rest of the place up.'

I lived in a studio backing onto a series of warehouses in a nondescript back street behind the Holloway Road. Since it was my work space, it was usually in considerable disorder; though, to be frank, that was something of an excuse. A couple of my mobiles were currently hanging from the ceiling, but the place was unusually empty of clutter, the BBC having denuded it of most of my stuff to give authenticity to their set of Sarah's workshop. Hugo had been hinting that it would be a good time to do a clean-out. I chortled to myself happily.

'What?' Tom said.

I held up my splinted and bandaged hands.

'Hugo's going to have to stop banging on about me tidying the place up now I'm out of commission,' I said cheerfully. 'Always a silver lining, eh?'

'I might have a go at the kitchen,' Tom said, nodding over to the far corner of my studio. It was all open-plan, apart from the bathroom: what he was referring to was an area with fridge, ancient gas cooker and large table, all ringed with the proud, hardened turmeric-yellow grease which denoted years of Indian takeaways. 'You couldn't boil an egg in there at the moment.'

'Since when did you know how to boil an egg?' I demanded.

'We cook for each other on a rota system,' Tom said rather shamefacedly. 'I've been doing some Delia Smith recipes. She's really good for morons. Practically tells you how to pour a glass of water. You can't go too badly wrong.'

'You're looking pretty good on it,' I admitted. 'That beer belly's almost gone.'

Tom patted his stomach with satisfaction. He had one of those big Irish frames that can pile on the pounds without too many ill-effects, and he used to work as a labourer, which kept his taste for fry-ups and Guinness under control; but ever since he had given that up in favour of the occasional shift doing telesales, he had been looking more and more as if he were wearing a lard overcoat. Till the new health regime started.

'We're a veggie household,' he said proudly. 'I can eat meat, but not at home. So I've cut down on the bacon butties. And I've been doing the garden as my work task. That's why I've lost the weight.'

'Doing the garden?' I echoed. 'What garden? You mean the rust heap?'

'Exactly. I've been getting rid of all those old bikes and stuff. Heavy-duty exercise. My biceps are like slabs of meat now.'

'Less of the meat references when Devo gets here, please,' I said. 'Emphasise the veggie household, OK? I want us to seem purer than pure.'

'Who is this Devo bloke, anyway?' Tom said, settling into the armchair. I arranged myself carefully on the section of the sofa it was still safe to sit on without getting a spike in a sensitive area. Maybe I could sell the sofa to an S&M master or mistress. They were always looking for new gimmicks.

'I knew him at art college. He used to play me tapes of abattoir workers' reminiscences. You know they hang these chickens on a belt and stun them with electric shocks? Well, they'd go wrong, or get stuck, and the chickens would all dangle there frying away, having ECT treatment for hours. Plus the mutilated calves running round screaming. Apparently it's the worst sound in the world. Made *Silence of the Lambs* look like *Winnie-the-Pooh*. There was one story about this cow—'

'All right! Enough! I'll stay off the bacon!' Tom held up his hands defensively.

'Anyway, Devo was a radical vegan activist. Obviously. He did all these rotting-meat installations which stank to high heaven.'

'Ahead of his time, eh? Or did Damien Hirst nick the idea off him?'

'Oh, lots of people were doing meat, but Damien Hirst had the brilliant idea of putting it in a big glass case so you wouldn't have to smell it. Much less in-yer-face. He was always very good at the marketing side of things.'

'Gotcha.'

'Anyway, Devo dropped out. He went hunt sabbing at the weekends and he decided to dedicate himself full-time to the cause. He was the legal officer when I last heard of him.'

'Legal officer?' Tom said in disbelief.

'Travelling round the country lecturing all the sabbing groups on what they could and couldn't do to avoid being nicked. And then how to sue for false arrest. But I lost touch with him years ago. It took me ages to track down his number.'

'So – let me see if my mighty brain has worked this one out – he's supposed to be your inside info on tracking down the Animal Liberation Front people who kidnapped you?'

'Not ALF,' I corrected. 'Animal Rights Freedom Fighters.'

'Bloody splinter groups.'

'You should know.'

Tom had sold advertising for *Marxism Today* some years ago and had always been piqued by people confusing it with *Living Marxism*. If I'd heard him give the pitch about being the European social democratic wing of the movement rather than the hard-line retrogressive Trot side, I'd heard it a hundred times. Anyway, we were all New Labour now. Or biding our time.

'There's some beer in the fridge,' I said. 'Why don't we sink a couple?'

'Great idea! I take back the hospitality crack earlier.' Tom bounded across the studio with the eagerness of a St Bernard which needed its neck keg refilled.

I sank back into the sofa and hunched my shoulders against the inevitable cry of dismay. The movement hurt, but then everything did. My entire body felt like one big yellowing bruise. The fridge opened, and a long ominous pause ensued.

'What the fuck – *Sammy*?' Tom held up a bottle. ' "Cruelty-Free Organic Lager"? "*Cruelty-Free Organic Lager*"?' His voice was rising again. 'What does that mean, all the hops volunteered individually to be picked?'

The doorbell rang.

'Could you get that?' I said. 'And try to behave as if we always drink that stuff, OK? This is important.'

Casting me a glance of loathing, Tom crossed the room, squinted through the newly installed spyhole, unbolted the door and flung it open with such force it thwacked back against the wall.

'I'm looking for Sam Jones,' came a voice that was so familiar it brought memories of years ago flooding back.

'Yeah, well, you've found her,' Tom said sourly. 'For better or worse. Come in. We've just been having a Save The Whales meeting, but I think we've passed all the resolutions unanimously. Right, Sammy?'

I glared at him. Sometimes his sense of humour was as heavy as a ten-ton truck.

'Devo!' I said. 'Sorry if I don't get up, but it's a bit hard with these.'

I waved my bandaged stumps. Behind him Tom was mouthing 'Sorry if I don't get up' in a way that was supposed to be pointed and sarcastic, but I hardly noticed. I was too stunned by Devo's appearance.

At art college, in the teeth of stiff competition, Devo had been the undisputed king of the crusties, the grungiest, filthiest student the faculty could boast. His dreadlocks were as frayed and tattered as the fringes on an ancient blanket, his skin as explosive with breakouts as a minefield in occupied territory, his cheeks and stomach of a concavity about which most young fashion models could only dream. He refused to wear anything which didn't come with a personally hand-signed certificate from the British Union for the Abolition of Vivisection; what he did for underpants I preferred not to think about. I doubted there was an approved stockist. Because of his hunt sabbing he lived in khaki and camouflage gear which was thick with the mud and blood stains garnered on the weekends he spent jumping out of the way of homicidal hunters trying to run him down with horses or Range Rovers, or police officers ready to whack him over the head so they could get him for resisting arrest. In short, he had done the survivalist look years before it became fashionable.

And now that it was sweeping the streets of every First World urban metropolis, Devo had moved on. He was unrecognisable. His hair was a short buzz-cut, he must have put on at least three stone, and he was wearing round gold-framed John Lennon glasses.

This wasn't the biggest shock, though. That was the suit.

In my astonishment, I had forgotten that my own appearance left something to be desired. I hoped I didn't look as appalled as Devo did, staring at me. At least my lips, under the constant application of arnica cream, had returned to something resembling their normal size, and I could talk properly. Well, I could talk.

'Christ! You look like you were in a train wreck!' Devo said incredulously. 'What happened? Car accident?'

'I got beaten up,' I said cheerfully.

'You *what*?' He swivelled round to stare at Tom.

'Not me, mate!' Tom said hastily. 'I wouldn't dare! She'd rip my dick off and make me eat it. Fancy a beer?'

Devo put down his briefcase. That was another thing: the briefcase. He looked as if he had a headache coming on.

'Sam,' he said, 'it's lovely to see you. I was really glad to get your message. But it took me ages to find this place – will my car be safe outside? – and I've had a long day at work, and you look, frankly, like you should be under heavy sedation — what I'm saying is, is this really the best time for a class reunion?'

Tom put an open bottle of beer in his hand. Devo took a long pull at it, then coughed and choked simultaneously. I had the impression he would have spat if he'd felt more at ease under my roof.

'What *is* this?' he said in disbelief.

'Cruelty-free organic lager,' Tom said, faux-casually. 'We drink it all the time.'

'Well, it's shit. You got any Budvar?'

Tom gave me a long, triumphant glance.

'I got that in specially for you, Devo!' I complained, dismayed. 'I thought you wouldn't drink anything else!'

'A lot's changed since art college,' Devo said. 'And no one's called me Devo for years. I prefer Daniel now.'

'And your suit, your hair—' I said feebly. 'What do you do nowadays?'

'I'm an independent financial consultant,' Devo said with only a trace of embarrassment. I couldn't think of him as Daniel, try as I might.

'Ethical fund management?' Tom suggested.

'Nah. I mean, yeah, sure, I sell it, but it's a package like all the others.' He looked at me. 'I got pretty burnt-out with all the vegan lark. I eat meat now, too.'

'No!' I shrank back against the sofa.

''Fraid so.' He turned to Tom. 'So, what've you got to drink that's not sodding cruelty-free?'

It felt as if all my illusions were shattering. I hadn't realised quite how much I had invested in the image of Devo as a morally perfect person until he jumped down off his pedestal and put on a smart pair of leather shoes. The weird thing was that he hadn't changed in any other way; he was the same person, with the same dry sense of humour. We snapped back into the friendship we had had years ago with barely a trace of awkwardness. Only now he was a financial consultant in a sharp suit, with a tie and a briefcase and a Saab parked outside. No wonder he'd been worried about its safety.

'So what happened, mate?' Tom said, as we settled down to dinner. Since we needed proper beer anyway I had sent him out for an Indian takeaway as well and persuaded Devo to join us. The time while Tom was out we had spent in reminiscences which, though highly amusing to us, would have bored poor Tom to death.

'What happened?' Devo said as he helped himself to onion bhajis. 'What d'you mean, what happened?'

'Well, to you! Sammy described you as some sort of animal avenger. Purer than the driven snow and all that.'

Tom gestured with an eloquent twiddle of his fork to the heap of lamb korma on Devo's plate.

Devo shrugged. I couldn't help staring at him. It was extraordinary how a bit of flesh on the bones changes someone's appearance. It was like those clay reconstructions of the features a naked skull once wore. Devo was less charismatic now: like Richard E. Grant in *Withnail and I*, he had had a peculiar attraction when he was perpetually half-starved. Now it was a nice face, but much more average. Solid. Reliable. Even slightly plump around the cheeks.

'It wasn't some road to Damascus conversion,' he said through a mouthful of food. 'Well, maybe a bit. There was this moment I got clobbered by a copper. Must've been about the hundredth time that happened to me. I was used to it, y'know? Battle scars. I've got a collection of lumps back here –' he touched his skull – 'God knows what a phrenologist'd make of me. Anyway, it wasn't even a bad one, this. Funny. I mean, it wasn't one of the coppers that's always on the warpath, turn his back while four hunters beat the crap out of you. Nothing like that. It was just – I saw the stick coming down, I heard it whistling through the air, and even before it landed I thought: I'm tired of this. Just like that. And then I was on the ground with my face in the mud and a copper hauling me up again to throw me in the van, and I just went to myself: Right, that's it. I've done my time.'

He took a long drink of Tiger beer. I was concentrating on

cutting up my masala dosa pancake with a spoon and didn't respond immediately. Tom, however, seemed fascinated by the whole story.

'So then what?' he said. 'I mean, from hunt sabbing to the Saab—'

Tom had had a good long lust after Devo's car when he went out to get supplies.

'Oh, there was this girl,' Devo said. 'Here, Sam, d'you want me to cut that up for you?'

'Yeah, thanks.'

He started slicing the pancake into bite-size pieces, putting a dollop of sauce onto each one. Devo had always been thoughtful.

'So, there was this girl,' Tom prompted.

'Yeah. It was this big rebound thing from the whole sab scene. I met her at Glastonbury, but she was just slumming it, you know. All these stockbrokers now, they come down and stay in posh hotels nearby and bring picnic baskets in the back of their Cherokees. Completely ruin the atmosphere. Anyway, she lost the rest of them, had a few too many spliffs, fell into this ditch, got covered in mud—'

'Did the traditional Glastonbury thing after all—' I prompted, scooping up some aubergine.

'—I pulled her out of the ditch and we got friendly.'

'You got friendly?' I said suspiciously. 'I distinctly remember you saying to me once that you could kiss a girl who ate meat, but not have sex with her.'

'That's funny,' Tom observed, after having thought this one through. 'I'd have thought it would be the other way round.'

Devo looked a little embarrassed. 'Did I really say that? Jesus, my callow youth . . . Well, yeah, OK, we got friendly, but nothing more. I mean, we were too different. But when I dropped out of sabbing I gave her a ring, and we got together, and . . . I expect I must have been ready for a big life change.' He gestured at his suit.

'You still together?' Tom asked.

'No. But guess what, she's a veggie now. And she's thinking of chucking in stockbroking to do a ceramics course.'

'Big wheel keeps on turning,' Tom said profoundly.

'You can say that again.' Devo burped. This was a good sign; it meant he felt at home here.

'OK, Sam,' he said, turning to me. 'Now I've done the catching-up, it's your turn. And could we start with why you wanted to see me again after all this time – not to mention why you look like you got stamped on by a gorilla?'

CHAPTER FOURTEEN

The screams were like a steam engine, or a kettle boiling: high, loud and insistent, with enough anger behind them to power a train. As I wrestled with whatever was tying me hand and foot, the shrieking cut through my head, sharp as a knife, almost unbearable. And then I realised I wasn't tied up – I was in a bag which had been dropped over me, covering my entire body. The screams were incredibly distracting. I writhed around, trying to wriggle out of the bag. But it seemed to go on for ever, I couldn't find the top, and the more I struggled the more it seemed to tangle itself around me. There was something scrabbling across the floor towards me, clicketing on what sounded like hundreds of tiny feet. Cockroaches, a little motorised army of cockroaches. God, would that woman who was yelling her head off never stop? I had to get the bag off me – I *had* to get it off—

Someone grabbed me by the shoulders. I did my best, disoriented as I was, to head-butt them. The crown of my head landed, jarringly, on their face, but it hurt me worse than it did them. The jolt sent rays of agony up my nose. I shrieked in pain and realised that the screams I had heard before must have been coming from me. They sounded exactly the same.

Finally I got my hands free from the bag and clapped them to my face. This never helps, but at least it makes the injured area feel that somebody cares. Gradually I took stock. It was dark, and, mercifully, it was quiet. I was lying on a futon; I could feel the slats through the mattress. Which meant that I was in my own bed, on my sleeping platform, in my studio, still half-tangled into the mad spirals of duvet and blanket I must have made thrashing around in the throes of my nightmare.

'Sammy?' a voice said tentatively.

I was safe: unless the person I had just head-butted wasn't Tom, but one of the kidnappers. And that was all right, too. Even if I hadn't recognised his voice, I could smell his Aran sweater, that comforting, familiar odour of greasy old wool mixed with curry and beer from this evening. The beer reminded me of Urine-Breath. I started shivering and couldn't stop.

'Sammy? Are you OK? It's me,' Tom was saying, still nervous.

I couldn't answer him; my teeth were chattering like one of those clockwork toy mouths.

'Is it OK if I give you a hug?'

I knew he was asking on grounds of his personal safety; he didn't want me to nut him again. I managed a sort of nod. He shuffled along the bed towards me and enveloped me in a large warm woolly embrace. I could barely move. It felt as if I would break into pieces if I took my hands away from my face and let my shoulders relax.

'You should get Hugo to sleep over with you,' Tom said after a while, his mouth against the crown of my head as he rocked me back and forth. 'I think he's a bit hurt that you haven't.'

'He doesn't like staying here,' I mumbled through my hands into Tom's shoulder. 'He says it's too filthy.'

'Well, it is,' Tom said reasonably, still rocking away. 'Why don't you go and stay at his, then? It'd make more sense. I mean, insisting on climbing up here to sleep is crazy.'

My sleeping platform was built against one side of the studio, accessible only by a wooden ladder. Tom had had to practically throw me up it when I went to bed that evening; my hands were good only for balancing precariously. I couldn't put any weight on them. God, I hated being crippled.

'And it's true you've let this place go,' he said. 'Even the bathroom. I mean, that's usually clean enough, but now there's what looks like amateur attempts to cultivate watercress all over the floor, and a ring round the bath with tufts of stuff sprouting out of it. And don't tell me it's because you're temporarily out of commission. It took more than one day to grow that thing.'

'It took more than one man to change my name to Shanghai Lily,' I muttered, employing a quote from one of Tom's favourite films in a cheap attempt to distract him from the subject under discussion. It didn't work.

'I think you're deliberately living like a slob to keep Hugo at arm's length,' he said.

'I haven't been working for ages,' I protested. 'I've been blocked. I've let everything go.'

'Oh, come on, Sammy, that was your excuse when you were making all those mobiles for your show, before you did the theatre thing! The place was in the same state then and you were working all the hours God sends! Face it,' Tom said in his best shrink voice, 'you're afraid of intimacy.'

'Oh, fuck *off.*' Swearing at him was so familiar it gave me enough confidence to take my hands from my face and sit back on my haunches.

'No, I mean it,' Tom said seriously. 'I think you're very conflicted about the whole Hugo thing.'

'*Conflicted,*' I sneered. 'That's a big word for someone with the emotional age of a baby yak.'

Tom ignored this too. It began to dawn on me that he had been studying communication skills as part of his teacher-training course; that was why he couldn't be sidetracked. This was a worrying development.

'Remember what a state you were in when you snogged that bloke in the toilets and were shitting yourself about Hugo finding out? I mean, in the old days you'd have shagged the guy's brains through the back of his skull and left your knickers on his chest as a souvenir. And you'd probably have told Hugo yourself to stop him getting any ideas. You've changed.'

'*How dare you.*'

I was furious. At least Tom was doing a good job of distracting me from my nightmare.

'You've got to face up to this to move on emotionally, Sammy,' he was saying.

'Tom,' I said coldly. 'I have just been kidnapped, beaten up and nearly raped. My hands are out of commission, I have two broken ribs – *again* – and a broken nose which I've probably just dislocated head-butting you. My entire body right now is a mass of suffering.

And you want me to start dealing with my issues about intimacy.' I spat out these last three words with as much venom as if I were an asp.

'Well, you're not going anywhere for a while,' Tom said, unabashed. 'Maybe this is a good time to take stock.'

I took a deep breath instead.

'Get me my painkillers,' I said firmly.

Tom clicked on the bedside light and fumbled around on the floor till he located the bottle. He put one pill on my tongue, then another, as I chugged them back one by one. We were used to this routine by now: I couldn't open the bottle myself, let alone pick up a pill.

'I'm going back to sleep now,' I announced. 'No matter how scary a nightmare I may have, it can't be as bad as you giving me amateur counselling at three o'clock in the morning.'

'Think over what I've said, though,' Tom said. 'God, you look terrible,' he added in parentheses. 'Your eye's like an explosion in a chartreuse factory.'

It was awful being deprived of my usual range of scathing facial expressions. I couldn't scowl. I couldn't even narrow my eyes at him menacingly without screaming in pain.

'Just for that,' I said crossly, 'you can go and make me a vodka and cassis. It goes really nicely with the painkillers.'

Most forms of alcohol seemed to go well with painkillers, I was discovering. From the cocktail hour onwards I floated around in a happy haze, lightly inebriated and moderately drugged. And the next day I started even earlier. Sunday was the day of liberty for the *Driven* cast and crew, and several of them decided to pay me a visit and see the full range of my picturesque injuries for themselves. It was like having an At Home day, apart from the fact that when Tom opened the door to them no one gave him their card to bring me on a salver. They handed him bottles of champagne instead. And cakes.

'More cake! More cake!' I yelled as the doorbell rang again. It was mid-afternoon and the tea party was in full swing, if one could call it that when no tea had been provided. Everyone had dived straight into the alcohol. I approved of this. Besides, it made good sense for them to get drunk in the afternoon; they could fall into bed early and spend all evening and night sleeping it off. When you had to be on set in Windsor at eight the next morning, these considerations were paramount.

'It's Keith,' Tom announced from the door.

'Come in, Keith!' everyone shouted happily.

'Did he bring cake?' I said hopefully.

'Better,' Keith said, waving a large wrapped packet at us.

'Better than *cake*?' I said dubiously.

'Ice-cream cake!' he proclaimed.

There was a spontaneous round of applause. Keith struck a few muscleman poses, holding the cake in the air above his head as if it were a trophy.

'And pink champagne,' he continued, fishing the bottle out of the plastic bag and handing it to Tom, along with the cake. 'Put it in the fridge, sweetie,' he said.

Tom was already pouring him a glass of champagne. Keith took it, flashing Tom a lovely smile.

'I adore your butler,' he said, joining the group ensconced around what was technically, I suppose, the coffee table. 'Butch but helpful. Very nice.' He looked at me dubiously. 'Are you kissable?'

'Anywhere that isn't bandaged.'

Keith gave me a comprehensive look. 'Mmn, not that much leeway.' He laid a delicate buss on the far side of my cheek, keeping well clear of my nose. 'So how *are* you?' he said. 'Tell me everything.'

There was a collective groan of boredom. Earlier on we had agreed a moratorium on the story of my kidnapping, at least for that day; otherwise I would have had to recount it for every new arrival. I had already done that about four times this afternoon and it was beginning to feel morbid.

'We've heard it over and over already, mate,' Tony explained.

'I would have thought that'd be good for you, Tony,' Keith said, sipping his champagne. 'Tales of dramatic abduction and imprisonment. You could pick up tips.'

'Yeah, well, I may've broken a few bones along the way – my

own, I mean –' Tony hastened to add – 'but thank fuck I've never had a stunt go that wrong. I mean, look at her.'

'I heard you'd done a few others a bit of damage in your time,' Keith said evilly.

Tony shot him a nasty glance.

'Dim and distant past,' he said. 'Sobered up a lot since my wild youth.'

There had been a rumour a while ago, on set, that Tony moonlighted as an enforcer for the kind of people about whom it was best not to ask too many questions. Trust Keith to bring this up. I found it hard to believe myself: Tony seemed so mild-mannered when he wasn't beating people up on camera. Still, the look he had given Keith had not been friendly. Keith limited himself to a murmured:

'Oh, I *see*. Dim and distant past,' before, in a swift return to the previous subject: 'Poor Sam. She looks like a still from a What-Not-To-Do video.'

'She looks like a big insurance claim,' said Karen, who was sitting on the floor, her back to the sofa, working her way through a box of Mr Kipling's Fondant Fancies.

'Jesus, you production lot are scary,' Jimmy the runner said, emboldened by all the champagne. Karen shot him a look which had him blushing up to the roots of his hair.

'You ain't seen nothing yet, boy,' she purred.

Jimmy's blush deepened. Tony wolf-whistled, long and meaning-ful.

'Better watch yourself if Karen's got her eye on you,' he cautioned, leaning over and giving Jimmy a friendly punch on the shoulder. 'She's a real man-eater.'

'Oh yeah?' Jimmy managed to produce a reasonably cool voice, though his cheeks were still pink with embarrassment.

Karen smiled enigmatically and ate another Fondant Fancy.

'Look at the size of her,' Tony went on. 'She takes a liking to you, you're dead meat.'

In her thick rubber-soled trainers, Karen stood more than six foot tall, and her shoulders were as broad as Jimmy's. The latter ducked his head and stared at her bashfully under his eyelashes. How sweet.

'Are there any yellow ones left?' Siobhan said. Karen tossed her one.

'Mmn,' Siobhan said through a mouthful. 'I love these. They take me back to my childhood.'

'Your mum and dad gave you Mr Kipling's when you were little?' Keith said incredulously. 'With all the money you've got? I would've thought it'd have been Patisserie Valerie and Richoux pastries. You disappoint me sorely, darling.'

Siobhan pulled a face at him. As I had previously had occasion to note, she was usually easy-going when teased about her family's wealth.

'*Ec*tually,' she said in an exaggeratedly posh drawl, 'our nanny gave us Mr Kipling's. And we weren't supposed to tell, or Mum would have gone ape. She's got this real thing about additives.'

'Make way, make way,' Tom said, clearing a space on the table for the ice-cream cake. He had found a plate to put it on, something of a minor miracle in this household, and cleaned a palette knife for slicing it.

'Wow,' I said reverently. 'I'm really enjoying this party.'

By the dint of layering practically all my blankets on the sofa, to dull the points of the springs that protruded through the seats, Tom and I had managed to make it relatively comfortable. Perhaps that was an exaggeration; but at least people could sit on it without getting an impromptu acupuncture treatment in the posterior, and by now everyone was too happily tanked up to notice anyway. That was partly due to the champagne, and partly due to the joints that Siobhan's boyfriend was rolling with the regularity of an automated production line.

'Thanks,' Keith said, taking the latest instalment from him. 'I don't think we've been formally introduced, no?'

'Oh, Keith, this is Sanjay,' Siobhan said.

'Sanj,' said the young man in question, giving Keith a friendly nod.

Keith drew on the joint.

'You're working on that film in Studio Two, aren't you?' he said. 'The First World War one.'

'Yeah, that's right. I'm on sound.'

'How's it going?'

'Oh, pretty good,' Sanjay said. 'Hard work, though. I mean, it's not exactly a bundle of laughs, is it? Down in the trenches the whole time. Mud, mud, glorious mud.'

Keith passed the joint along to Jimmy. Tom was handing round slices of ice-cream cake while Karen cracked open another bottle of champagne. It was hard to see how this scene could in any way have been improved upon. Apart, perhaps, from a few young Johnny Depp lookalikes as waiting staff, lithe and oiled and wearing loincloths.

The doorbell rang again. Jimmy jumped up to answer it, so used by now to responding to bells that it must be second nature to him.

'All right, mate,' he said to the new arrival.

'I brought chocolate,' came a voice from the door.

'Lurchie!' everyone chorused.

Lurch looked more than happy with the attention. He was holding one of those monster-size Dairy Milk bars they make especially for bulimics.

'Chocolate,' he repeated, extending it towards me. 'You said you wanted some when I come to see you in 'ospital.'

'Thanks, Lurch,' I said. 'Throw it into the middle and let the vultures have their way with it.'

'Bakewell slice?' offered Karen, holding out the packet to him.

'What happened to the Fondant Fancies?' Sanjay said.

'I finished them,' she boasted proudly.

'Man, have I got the dope munchies. Bung us a Bakewell slice, then,' he said.

The first bite of ice-cream cake slid down my throat. I made a woman-in-ecstasy sound.

'I want some of what she's having,' said Keith, grabbing a plate. 'Oh, God, this is orgasmic. I was at this violently expensive restaurant last night where all the desserts were things like pistachio granita and bay-leaf ice cream and lavender rice pudding with saffron cream, and you know what we did? Paid the bill instead, went down the road and got a Dayvilles. Sheer heaven.'

'Yeah, sometimes you just want to go to a TGI Fridays and stuff yourself with Death by Chocolate,' Sanjay agreed.

'It would be a temptation. But my latest thing has such downmarket tastes anyway that to go somewhere like that would just be encouraging him.'

'You should just've gone to the Ivy,' Siobhan advised. 'Best chips in London. And the puddings are brill.'

This was Siobhan's money showing: she must be the only costume assistant in London who could talk so casually about eating at such an expensive restaurant.

'You're so right,' Keith said. 'And this one's loaded, too. It's his turn to take me out next. I'll book there.'

'What's he do?' said Karen.

'Don't laugh. He owns a photocopier maintenance company. But he's got the best abs in South London to make up for it. Oh, and talking about abs, who was that gorgeous hunk I saw Sarah with yesterday on set?'

'You mean Vince?' Tony said. 'He's an ex of hers. Hanging out to make sure she's, y'know, OK.'

Everyone looked at me for a moment as if to remind themselves of what not being OK would mean in this context.

'I fought she 'ad a copper parked in 'er trailer twenty-four hours a day,' Lurch said through a mouthful of ice-cream cake. 'Like that film, what was it? *Someone To Watch Over Me.*'

'Vince doesn't reckon much to the cops,' Tony said. 'Can't say I blame him neither. I mean, they didn't find Sam, did they? Sarah'll be better off with Vince. Least he can handle himself.'

'He looks like he can handle himself,' Keith said dreamily. 'He's got a rather Russian face, don't you think? Apart from that drop-dead body.'

'God, Keith, you're so blatant,' Karen said.

'You're a fine one to talk, sweetie. Anyway, it's a very good policy to let people know you're hot for them. It often works. When they get horny, they think of you first.'

'Actually, that's true,' Karen said thoughtfully.

'Well, there you go,' Keith said smugly. 'More champagne, anyone?'

'He looks a bit dodgy, dunne?' Lurch said, back on the last topic of conversation but one. 'That Vince, I mean.'

'East End wide boy,' said Sanjay knowledgeably. 'Wouldn't put much past him.'

'Sorry,' Siobhan said to Tom, who was sitting next to her, quietly working his way through a great mound of brownies. 'Must be a bit boring for you, all this shop talk.'

'Go right ahead,' he said with an airy wave of his arm rather spoilt by the half-eaten brownie at its end. 'I always like to hear a good gossip.'

The doorbell rang yet again. Jimmy was on his feet at once.

'God,' Tony said, 'runners and bells. You just can't get enough, can ya?'

'Automatic,' Jimmy said helplessly. 'I keep thinking I'm going to hear someone shouting at me if I don't get up. I'm like that at home when the phone goes, too. I can't bear to hear it ringing.'

'*Jimmy!*' Keith did an uncanny impression of the first AD.

'Please, mate,' Jimmy pleaded, crossing the room to open the door. 'It's my day off, all right?'

'Jimmy! Hi!'

'Hey, Sarah,' he said rather shyly. It was unusual for leading actors and the most lowly of crew members to be mixing socially. Sarah was much more approachable than many stars; the fact that she even knew Jimmy's name was proof of that. And her voice wasn't the over-emphasised, fake-friendly tone she had used for the nurse in the hospital, but genuinely affable. All of which, of course, just made him more bashful.

'All right, mate!' It was Vince. 'Where's the party, then? We brought supplies.'

The box he was carrying appeared through the door first, then Vince himself, wearing a leather jacket which would have cost a fortune if he'd paid full price for it, which I doubted he had.

'Where'll I put this, then?' he said to Jimmy. Tom got up to help.

'We brought six bottles of bubbly and Sarah went and got some posh cakes, too,' Vince announced. 'So, are we sodding welcome or what?'

'Very sodding welcome, sweetie!' Keith said, holding up his glass. I wondered whether Vince had treated Keith yet to some of his more sophisticated metaphors for gays, or whether Keith considered those all part of Vince's rough-edged charm.

'Hi, everyone,' Sarah said, sitting on the arm of Keith's chair. 'I got strawberry and mocha cheesecakes. I thought everyone would like those. Sam, how are you?'

'Stuffed to the gills,' I said complacently.

'Pink champagne!' Tom said, popping the cork. 'I've never had this before. Anyone want a bit?'

He filled my glass and the others outstretched to him.

'That stuff's for poofs and women, mate,' Vince said to him. 'You wanna try the Piper I brought. Now that's a proper drink.'

Glances were exchanged around the circle, but no one said anything to Vince. Sarah was looking uncomfortable enough to carry the guilt for both of them.

'Well,' Keith said, clinking glasses with me and Sarah. 'All the more for us, eh, girls?'

Vince, oblivious to the brick he had dropped, strolled over to us and sat down cross-legged at Sarah's feet. Reaching out one hand he started stroking her ankle.

'That's a nice shirt,' Tony said to him. 'Nice colour.'

'Need more of a tan,' Vince said, fingering the collar of the yellow shirt he was wearing. 'Makes me look a bit pale, dunnit? Look better on you right now, mate. You got all that natural colour. But yeah, it's nice. Ralph. I like me Ralphs.'

'Ralph?' asked Jimmy.

'You need to make a bit more dosh, you do,' Vince said to him amiably. 'Ralph Lauren. No rubbish. Not that I paid full retail, a'course –' he drank some champagne – 'but it's the genuine item. Ralph, Tommy, YSL. Can't go wrong wiv quality, can ya? And you know what, mate? It fits an' all. Not like those strides you're wearing. I mean, what is that about?'

Jimmy looked down at his combat trousers, momentarily abashed. Siobhan chipped in:

'Oh, come on, Vince, army trousers are great. Especially for work.'

'I wear them a lot, Vince,' Sarah pointed out.

'Yeah, you do an' all,' he said affectionately, still caressing her ankle. He was irrepressibly tactile; he always had to have his hands on something, and preferably someone. 'Silly mare.'

'Great for guys,' Sanjay said, patting the big hip pocket on his. 'I can get everything in them – phone, Walkman, wallet – not to mention jumbo-size Rizlas—'

Siobhan laughed. Sanjay licked the spliff he was rolling and sealed it with an expert flick of the thumb.

'Don't think we've had the pleasure,' Vince said to him. 'You ain't on Sarah's TV thing, are ya?'

'No, I'm on the film shooting next door along,' Sanjay said, lighting the joint. 'First World War flick.'

'Hey, I like a good war film,' Vince said with enthusiasm. 'Nice bit of action.'

'It's mainly in the trenches,' Sanjay said. 'Not much action, just everyone getting blown to bits. Guys dying slowly with their guts hanging out, sort of *Saving Private Ryan* without the battle scenes – what?'

Siobhan must have kicked him. But the damage had been done. Tears had sprung to Sarah's eyes.

'Oh, shit,' Sanjay said helplessly. 'I'm sorry.'

It was so easy to forget: especially if you were working fourteen-hour days on a film set. And even with my bandages and chest strapping and bruised face as the reminder of the real violence that had so recently invaded that fictional world, what had happened to Paul seemed unreal. Maybe it was only truly present for Sarah, who had found his body, or me, to a lesser degree, having seen the photographs of what had been done to him.

Vince got up and took Sarah into his arms. She leant against him, still crying.

'It's all right, mate,' he said to Sanjay with surprising gentleness. 'What can't be cured must be endured, me mum used to say. Not your fault. I mean, it wasn't you what did him, was it? There, there, love. You cry it out.' He cradled Sarah's head.

Sanjay looked awful. Siobhan took his hand, but he pulled it away so abruptly that everyone noticed the sharp little movement. Tom, in an attempt to distract us, opened yet another bottle of champagne.

The noise of the cork popping in the silence of the room was strangely sad. It made me think of people drinking at a wake.

'There somewhere I can take 'er for a bit? Be by ourselves?' Vince said in an undertone to me.

'I'll show you the bathroom.' Tom got up.

'Come on, love.' Vince led Sarah off. 'It's all over now, innit? All behind you now.'

'How can he say that?' Siobhan said as they went into the bathroom together. 'I mean, how can he be so sure?'

'There haven't been any more threats or anything,' Karen said, taking the joint. 'That animal rights group's gone dead quiet. The police think they've shot their bolt.'

'Got carried away with Paul and scared themselves,' Tony said wisely. 'Yeah, I'd say it's all over, too. They've done their damage.'

'Set animal rights back twenty years, as well,' Siobhan said with surprising vehemence. 'The stupid bastards. I can't believe they actually killed someone. God, after all we've worked for. People's consciousnesses were really being raised. And now this.'

'Wasn't much fun for Sam being kidnapped, neither,' Lurch contributed. He didn't say much, but when he did it was generally to the point. Siobhan looked abashed. And Sanjay was giving her a filthy look.

'I didn't mean that,' she said. 'You know I didn't, Sam.'

'God, enough already with the apologies!' Keith said. 'We're here to celebrate Sam being OK. Which she is. So could we all cheer up a bit? What about a toast?' He stood up. 'To Sam!'

Everyone clinked glasses.

'You can't drink, Sam,' Lurch cautioned me. 'Bad luck, innit?'

'Oh, all right. Just this once.'

I watched everyone else down their champagne. Lurch grinned at me over the top of his glass. He was such a nice boy. Later on I was going to have to tell him about the conversation I had had with Devo. Damn. I was feeling guilty already, and I hadn't even started.

CHAPTER FIFTEEN

'I'm pretty out of it now,' Devo had explained on Friday night. 'It's been a few years, and lots of things change. If I was still working for the HSL—'

'The what?' Tom interjected.

'The Hunt Saboteurs League,' Devo said. 'Well, that's it. If I was still in place there, it'd be a piece of piss. Ring round a few people, get the word out . . . What you've got to understand,' he said, leaning towards me, his expression very serious, 'is that I can't believe anyone in the AR movement would pull this kind of crap. Not even the extremists.'

'AR?' Tom piped up.

'Animal rights,' Devo sighed.

'Sorry, mate.' Tom sounded offended. 'You should just pass out a list of acronyms at the beginning of the conversation. Save a bit of time.'

He took a long swig of beer and put his feet up on the table, making space for them among the debris of Indian takeaway containers. His whole posture denoted a sulky withdrawal from the subject under discussion. I tried to give Devo a don't-mind-about-him smile but the effort distorted my face so much that, instead of being encouraged to continue, he recoiled and lit a cigarette instead.

'You were saying?' I prompted.

'Oh yeah.' He pulled an empty foil carton towards him to use as an ashtray. Devo might be a suit-wearing independent financial adviser now, but old student habits died harder than one might imagine.

'Everyone in AR is really aware of the public relations side now,' he said. 'There's been a total ban on stuff like letting out minks from farms, for instance. They're monsters, you know. Tiny little teeth like needles. Couple of 'em bit me once and the pain was like nothing on earth. Jesus, they're ferocious.'

I'd always suspected Devo had been involved in action more covert than hunt sabbing.

'Rage through the countryside killing everything they can,' Devo was continuing. 'Terrible PR, quite apart from the bites. They left these bruises, you should've seen them. Extraordinary. Never again. Nah, I can't imagine even your most psycho ALF cell — that's Animal Liberation Front –' he added politely in Tom's direction – 'pulling something like kidnapping people. Especially an actress — young, pretty, everyone fancying her when she was the maid in that Edwardian TV thing—'

'*Park Lane,*' I said.

'Yeah, that's right. That one where she got off with the son of the house. Very pretty.' He looked at me hopefully. 'Any chance of an introduction?'

'Sure, why not?'

'Great!' Devo looked chuffed. 'Anyway,' he went on, 'you see what I'm saying? No matter what shit she'd been saying, no matter how much all those pro-fur statements put people off, as soon as she's kidnapped, public sympathy swings behind her and makes her this total heroine. Nation's sweetheart number one. I can't believe I didn't put two and two together, by the way, Sam. I mean, I was reading all the press, and there was your name, kidnap victim, all that, and I knew you were doing sculpture at college — I can't believe it didn't ring any bells. I was so hung up on the AR side of it, I must've been distracted. And like I say, it's hard to credit this is an AR thing, no matter what they said in their press release.'

He shrugged. 'They'll be giving all the ALF lot in prison a hard time, trying to get them to admit they know this was going down, but none of them'll say a word. That's the real hard-core. Wouldn't talk if you tortured them.'

'Are there many in jail?' Tom asked curiously.

'More than you'd think. They don't do too badly. You'd be surprised how sentimental most lags are. Most people, you see –' I recognised Devo's old didactic mode – 'close their eyes to what's going on in the name of medical research, or cosmetic testing. Or household products. You show someone one photo of a cat cut open with bleach in its guts and – well, let's just say I know one ALF bloke who built up a whole new AR network in the clink. Real hard cases, some of them. There was one bloke I knew, been down for GBH so many times even he had to count 'em up, but his kiddies had a pet bunny he was completely soppy about.'

Tom was fascinated. I felt we were wandering somewhat from the point of the discussion.

'There was something funny about the set-up,' I commented. 'I mean, they gave me vegan food. Vegemite and soya bread. But when I was escaping—'

'You escaped? I didn't realise,' Devo said.

I shrugged. Ow. I must remember how much that hurt my broken ribs.

'For about ten minutes. Then another one of them hit me in the face as I was climbing out of a window. Anyway, I went past the kitchen, and it was full of junk food. Pop Tarts and crisps and chocolate cereal. I.e., not exactly your standard vegan diet.'

Tom made mmm'ing noises, which I ignored.

'And then in my cellar there was this room freshener.'

'They gave you a *room freshener*?' Devo said incredulously.

'Yeah, and it wasn't cruelty-free either.'

'That *is* weird,' he agreed. 'I mean, room freshener! Totally not ALF.'

'Smelly lot, are they?' Tom said unhelpfully. Devo ignored him.

'Besides, you'd think anyone who went to the trouble of kidnapping someone'd be a real fanatic. Purer than pure.' He stared at me. 'Do you mean you think it wasn't an AR action at all?'

'No,' I said slowly, thinking that one through, remembering Thick Boy and his leather-substitute boots. 'At least one of them really looked the part. And talked it, too. That wasn't a pretence.'

'Well then, it's what I thought when I heard about it. Some nutter splinter group. It's the worst-case scenario. No one from my time, though. But mind you, I've been out of it for a few years now.'

Photocopies of the composites of my two kidnappers, drawn for me by a police artist, lay on the table in front of us, half-obscured by plates and food. Devo had already looked at them and denied the ringing of any bells. Now he glanced down at them again, as if to confirm his unfamiliarity with the two faces, and stubbed his cigarette out in the foil carton he was using as an ashtray. The last drops of lamb korma sauce sizzled and died as the burning tip hit them.

'I can ask around a bit,' he offered. 'But I don't know how much good it'll do. I mean, this'll be such a hot topic, everyone might just close down.'

'Even to you? You must be a sort of elder statesman by now.'

I was trying flattery, but it came out wrong.

'Thanks a bunch,' Devo said, slightly offended. 'Besides, everyone knows about my lifestyle change. You really need someone on the inside. Not that that's easy.'

'An infiltrator?' Tom said, coming to life again. 'Sounds like a spy novel.'

Devo laughed. 'If you knew how many coppers we've had coming along, pretending to be activists – one of the best parts of the job, that was, letting them know they'd been sussed. Not that it was hard work spotting them. Jesus. I dunno, you would've thought they could try a bit harder.'

'You got that many?' Tom was really interested now.

'Yeah. But they never got anywhere. It's funny, really. You think about how many of them're trying to infiltrate football gangs, as well – you'd think that'd be a lot easier for them than the AR movement, wouldn't you? But they've never had any luck with that either. Coppers, eh. Only undercover work they're any good at is standing around in public loos waiting for some poor sod to chat them up and then arresting him for soliciting or whatever. Like anyone cared in the first place.'

'And that's not exactly undercover, is it?' Tom said. 'Just waving their dicks at a urinal and looking hopeful.'

Devo snuffled with laughter.

'I mean, it's actually quite flattering when some bloke chats you up in a public toilet,' he said. 'Got to mean your equipment's up to scratch, size-wise, doesn't it?'

'Never happened to me,' Tom said, sounding almost anxious.

'Probably just hanging round the wrong toilets, mate,' Devo said kindly.

'Anyway,' I said firmly, 'what you were saying about having someone on the inside—'

'Be the only way to find out. Not guaranteed, though, by any means. I mean, if it's a rogue ALF cell or something, it's unlikely anyone'd hear about it. Apart from the bigwigs. Besides,' he added, becoming less encouraging the more he thought it through, 'they could be anywhere. The AR community's small, but not that small. If you got kidnapped by some rogue ALF cell from the Midlands, or Scotland—'

'No, hang on,' I interrupted. 'They were definitely Londoners.'

'How d'you know?'

'Not just the accents. They dumped me in Golders Hill Park. Did you hear about that? It's one of the major gay cruising zones in North London. And a lot of guys go there to get beaten up.'

'Each to their own,' Devo said.

'Whatever floats your boat.' This was an expression I'd picked up in New York last year. 'Anyway, my point is that they chose the perfect place to dump me, one of the few in London where two guys chucking another one into the bushes would be guaranteed to have anyone turning a blind eye. You don't know about that kind of thing unless you live here.'

'Or you're gay,' Tom chipped in.

'Trust me,' I assured him. 'These guys are about as gay as Bill Clinton.'

'Well then,' Devo was saying contemplatively, 'if they're Londoners . . . Look, you never know. It might come to nothing. But it'd certainly be worth a try.' He gave me a long hard look. 'Why? You know someone who could have a go?'

'Don't look at me,' Tom said hastily, sitting up straight in such a hurry that he spilt beer all down the front of his sweater.

'But Tom!' I protested. 'You were just saying how much it sounded like a spy novel! I thought you'd be up for it!'

'You must be out of your – you're joking, right? You're joking, aren't you? You cow. You absolute, utter, total cow.'

'He wouldn't do anyway,' Devo said dismissively.

'Why not?' Now Tom was indignant. 'I think I'd do a pretty good job, if I wanted to. Which I don't. At all.'

'Too old,' Devo said frankly. 'No one starts sabbing at thirty-odd. It's for the young. You got to be really dedicated, plus have all that energy—'

'Oh, *I* see. I know exactly who you're thinking about,' Tom said to me with the air of someone who has just cracked a puzzle. 'You think he'd do it?'

'He's very willing,' I pointed out. 'It's one of his most charming traits.'

Hugo never showed up at the party. I knew he was cross with me — he was mortally offended that I had chosen to stay in my revolting studio rather than his exquisitely appointed flat. Still, I had thought he would come. The healing effect of champagne, however, meant that by the time I realised he definitely wasn't coming I was too tipsy to care. Much.

The party broke up at about ten Sunday evening, as I had predicted. Everyone had to get up for work. Vince and Sarah had left much earlier, pretty soon after her fit of tears. Oddly enough, it was the state of my bathroom that did it. Vince had been unable to refrain from a few jovial but pointed comments which had Siobhan and Karen bridling, his gist being that, since women were intended by their biology for domestic tasks, one who couldn't clean her toilet was in a fair way to being a freak of nature. I was a bit embarrassed about the state of the toilet and so let this one slide. Siobhan and Karen didn't, and there was an increasingly barbed exchange between the three antagonists until Sarah said diplomatically that she wanted to go home anyway.

The other men in the party, better trained by years of feminist cannon fire, kept their mouths firmly shut and their eyes on the ground until the door had closed behind Vince and Sarah. Lurch then said he didn't think the bog was in that bad a way, considering; Tom said this would only be true if Lurch were comparing it to a Portaloo at the Oktoberfest; and Keith then said he was over the discussion of any toilets that didn't have George Michael in them, and what about cracking another bottle of Vince's Piper Heidsieck.

'Generous, in't he?' Jimmy said.

'Oh, he's all right,' Tony said tolerantly. 'Just has to shoot his mouth off all the time. And he's doing a good job with Sarah.'

'How long were they together?' Keith said pruriently.

'Oh, a while,' Karen informed him. 'Sarah said she dumped him finally cos she couldn't stand his screwing around. But they stayed friends. She says he's like a big brother to her now.'

'Isn't that nice?' Keith purred. 'A touching story. Now, does anyone want to hear a revolting joke?' he asked, to a general chorus of assent.

'OK. Brace yourselves,' he warned. 'Freddie Mercury and Versace and Princess Di are all in front of the Pearly Gates, waiting to be let into Heaven. St Peter comes out and says: "Sorry, loves, we're all full up. But if one of you can give me a good enough reason, I'll chuck out Mother Teresa – she's getting on everyone's nerves – and one of you can have her place."

'So Freddie Mercury steps forward and says: "St Peter, I have a beautiful voice and I write wonderful songs. If you let me in I'll make the music in Heaven better than it's ever been."

' "Hmm," says St Peter. "OK. Next!"

'Then Versace steps forward and says: "St Peter, I am a superb fashion designer. If you let me in I will make such lovely clothes that everyone in Heaven will look drop-dead gorgeous. I could do you some fabulous robes for special occasions."

' "Interesting," says St Peter noncommittally. "Right. Next!"

'Princess Di steps forward, and without saying anything at all, she pulls out a bottle of Moët, shakes it up, sticks it up her skirt and pops the cork.

' "Right, you're in," says St Peter to her.

' "What!" Freddie Mercury and Versace explode in unison. "With everything we have to offer, you picked her? Why?"

' "Come on, guys," says St Peter, holding the gates open for Di to pass through. "You should know that one royal flush beats a pair of queens." '

Keith's joke was definitely the high point of the party. Or the low one, if you saw things that way. It opened the floodgates for a raft of dirty stories, filthy gossip and bacchanal behaviour. Karen started feeding laden spoonfuls of ice-cream cake to Jimmy; by nine o'clock they were behind the sofa with the remains of the cake, making the kind of noises more usually heard on the soundtrack of soft-porn movies. When they emerged, the front of Jimmy's sweater was dripping with ice-cream, the cue for some extremely ribald and explicit comparisons by Keith. Jimmy blushed yet again. I imagined that a few days with Karen would cure him of that habit for good.

As no one was in any condition to drive, Tom called a slew of minicabs. Karen, taking Jimmy's hand, announced that they would be sharing a car.

'They'll've shared a lot more than that by tomorrow morning,' Siobhan commented after they'd gone, stretching herself full-length on my tatty rug.

She and Sanjay were still waiting for their cab, but by now they were so stoned time had become relatively meaningless to them. Tom, slumped in the armchair grinning happily at the opposite wall, was in much the same condition. Lurch had been puffing away with the best of them, but he seemed much less affected. Skinny as he was, he could certainly put it away. Tom might have the body of an ox, but Lurch had its constitution.

'Lucky Jimmy,' Sanjay said.

'What,' Siobhan said sleepily, 'd'you fancy Karen, then?'

'It's not that so much. Though she's got that look in her eyes, you know, babe, that wey-hey look –' Sanjay tickled Siobhan under the arms, making her squeal and slap him off – 'No, I meant lucky sod having some older woman come along and take him in hand. It's every boy's dream, isn't it?'

'Speak for yourself,' Siobhan said.

'Oh, I am, babe, I am.'

'Oh God,' she muttered after a while, 'work tomorrow. I just feel like passing out on the sofa all day, and I'm behind with my part of the budget again. And I've got Sarah, and she's being so difficult right now. Well, not difficult exactly. She's so *passive*. She just drifts around like a ghost and doesn't notice anything you say to her.'

'Sounds like an easy job,' Sanjay said.

'You'd think so, wouldn't you? But actually it's really annoying. And now Red's hanging round the set all the time, keeping an eye on everything.'

'You can't blame her,' Sanjay said fairly. 'After everything that's happened.'

'Makes it much harder to sneak off for a joint,' Siobhan complained.

The doorbell rang.

'That'll be our cab,' Sanjay said, getting up. He straddled Siobhan and took her outstretched hands, pulling her to her feet.

'Thanks for the party, it's been cool,' he said to me.

'Hey, all I did was sit on the sofa looking like an extra from *Casualty*,' I said.

'I'm so glad you're OK, Sam,' Siobhan said, pushing her hair out of her face. 'We all are. It was really nice to see you. Um, is it OK if I take some chocolate to eat in the cab? I've got the munchies again.'

'Does that guy work on the production too?' Tom said after they had gone.

'No, on a film on the next stage over. Didn't you hear Vince ask him?'

Tom shook his head.

'Talks like he does, though,' Lurch said. 'He's a bit of a skiver if you ask me. Always coming over to ours to hang round the costume trailer. I reckon he's after her dosh.'

'Is she rich?' Tom sat up.

Lurch told him Siobhan's surname.

'Oh, my God! That's the girl you told me about, Sammy! The beer heiress! Why didn't you warn me she was coming?'

'What would you have done, Tom?' I asked. 'Put on aftershave? Washed your sweater?'

Lurch sniggered.

'You can shut up,' Tom said, rounding on him. 'You've got no idea what she's got in store for you.'

'Oh yeah?' Lurch looked at me. 'What's that, then?'

His eyes were bright, his posture alert. If he were a dog he would have been wagging his tail, keen for me to throw him the next stick. I looked down at my hands. It would be a long time till I was throwing anything. Lurch would have to be my eyes and ears for a while to come.

'Lurch,' I said, putting it in a way I thought might appeal to a young male mind, 'how do you fancy being an undercover agent?'

CHAPTER SIXTEEN

Lurch agreed with an alacrity that had even me surprised. I suggested he make us all coffee. It seemed only fair to let him sober up at least by a few degrees before he committed himself irrevocably to any course of action. Not that he seemed drunk.

'Hollow legs,' Tom had said about Lurch once, but it couldn't be that. His were so skinny it would only take a couple of pints each side to fill them.

Now he was bustling around the stove with a sense of purpose and excitement bubbling out of him as if he were a percolator coming to the boil himself.

'What Devo suggested,' I said as Lurch was washing up some of the mugs we had just used as champagne glasses, 'was that you don't pretend to know anything about animal rights. Well, anything more than you do already. You're going to be his nephew, OK? You've just become a veggie and you really want to get involved, but all the AR stuff is new to you. He's going to send you along to a sabbing group he knows. The idea is that you're super-keen to learn all you can. Keep asking loads of questions. You can get away with that without making them suspicious.'

I was remembering Lurch on the set of *Driven*, in the early days before everyone got to know him. He had a thirst for knowledge which was so candid and straightforward that it turned even the grumpiest old focus puller into a fount of information.

'And if it seems appropriate,' I added, 'hint that you're interested in really direct action. But don't overdo it or they'll chuck you straight out. Devo says they'll be paranoid about new people right now, what with me being kidnapped, and Paul killed. They'll think everyone's an undercover copper.'

Lurch, pouring out the coffee, let out a long snigger.

'They won't fink I'm the Old Bill, Sam,' he assured me.

'No, they won't,' I agreed.

'Don't you worry about me,' he said, bringing us over the coffees. He put one down before Tom, but it came too late. Tom was snoring quietly, head tipped to one side. It was a quiet, almost reassuring noise, like the ticking of a black taxi. 'I know just how to play it.'

His confidence was unnerving me a little.

'You'll have to go hunt sabbing with them,' I warned him. 'Build their trust.'

'Be a laugh, won't it?' he said imperturbably. 'Day out in the countryside. Fresh air an' all. So should I take a gander at this Devo bloke before I go along to a meetin'? Build up me cover story. If I'm supposed to be his nephew I should know a bit abaht him.'

I stared at him, taken aback by his initiative. Devo and I had already talked about the necessity for this, but somehow I hadn't been expecting Lurch to pick up on it so quickly.

'Devo said to meet him for a drink tomorrow, if you can,' I said feebly.

'Great. You got his number? I'll give him a bell tomorrow mornin', set it up. You want me to let you know how it went?'

'Yeah, why don't you?' Somehow I felt that my control of the situation was slipping away from me.

Lurch finished his coffee in one long pull, his Adam's apple bobbing crazily in his long skinny throat, and set down the mug on the table with an air of finality.

'Right, I'll be off, then,' he said, getting up. 'I'll bell you tomorrow evenin', Sam. Tom?'

He shook this unfortunate's shoulders to wake him up. Tom let out a mighty, half-strangled snore and jerked into consciousness.

'Whaa?' he said. 'Whaa is it?'

'I'm off now,' Lurch said to him. 'You better bolt the door behind me. We don't want anythin' else happenin' to Sam, do we?'

Tom barred and bolted the door, according to instructions, and came back to his armchair with relief.

'Ooh, coffee,' he said, picking his up and sipping at it. It had to be tepid by now, but he was still too sleepy to notice. 'What's up with you?' he added. 'You look all funny.'

'It's Lurch,' I said. 'He's grown up all of a sudden. I thought I was going to be the one reassuring him, and then before I even realised it, it was him telling me everything was going to be OK and saying he'd better be off. You know what he used to be like, I had to kick him out the door when I wanted to go to bed. He'd hang around here for ever. And he was so cool about the hunt sabbing thing. Just – cool, you know? No stupid heroics, just: Oh, all right, I'll do that then. Like I'd asked him to nip down the chippy for a kebab.'

'Mmn, I could go for a kebab big-time,' Tom said.

'*Tom—*' I said crossly, wanting to be taken seriously. 'It was so weird.'

'Hey,' Tom said, 'your baby's flown the nest. It happens. He's found his wings. You've got to let him test them out. God, this is like some awful parody of Mum and Dad watching the teenager go off to his first rave.'

'Talk about dysfunctional families.'

'I've never really understood that term,' Tom said. 'I mean, what's the definition of a functional family? Urh!' He looked down at the contents of his mug, awake enough by now to realise what he was drinking. 'This coffee's stone-cold! Get that boy back here now to make his old Dad a fresh one, will you, love? I dunno, teenagers these days. Sloppy, slapdash good-for-nothings. And did you see what he was wearing? How's he going to get a girlfriend looking like that? I tell you—'

'Enough, Tom,' I said. 'You're scaring me.'

The most depressing thing about IKEA was the easy confidence of the other shoppers. Wheeling their mega-trollies down the predetermined paths, stopping in front of the Jarlsberg living room with inbuilt Emmenthal spotlights an optional extra on the Edam corner cupboards, they could be heard chatting fluently about their display shelving needs with the cheerful young assistants. Most of them were dressed in nice bright colours and drove giant utility vehicles and people carriers which lined the Brent Cross car park outside. It was like being in a future world from a 1970s film. Of course in that imagined 2020 Tom and I would never have been allowed into an emporium like this. We'd be living in the sewers, being tracked down like dogs by specially designed robots on a mission to exterminate undesirable non-conformists from society.

It didn't help that I was not only in a very stupid mood, but that I had infected Tom too. It was the first time that I had been out in the fresh air since my captivity – unless you counted my brief sojourn in Golders Hill Park – and it had gone straight to my head. I was in a state of thorough-going juvenile delinquency and taking Tom straight down with me.

'I'm frightened,' I wailed dolefully to Tom, raising my voice so that people turned round to stare disapprovingly.

'I know,' he said equally fearfully, taking his cue from me.

'There's so much *stuff*! How can I ever choose!'

'Look, just pick a sofa and we'll get out of here,' Tom said, changing to brisk and upbeat. 'The first sofa you see. Come on. What about that one?'

'It's horrible. And tiny.'

'What about that one over there?'

Tom disengaged his grip on me and headed off across a show kitchen which looked exactly like the kind of place where the modern young mothers of afternoon TV advertising swapped tips on new oven-ready crinkle chips the kids would go crazy for. I didn't even want to set foot in it.

'Isn't that the same one,' I commented, 'only with slipcovers? Oh my God. Did you *hear* what I just said? This place is warping my brain.'

Tom came back across the kitchen floor.

'I need a drink,' I confessed frankly.

'Oh good, you too?'

'Bet there isn't a bar here.'

Tom shook his head. '*But*,' he beamed, 'they do have a shop that sells traditional Swedish products.'

'Reindeer meatballs?' I said blankly.

'Oh, Sam. Do you *mind*? Rudolf!' Tom looked genuinely pained.

'You meat-eaters are such hypocrites,' I said. 'I wouldn't mind so much if you ate dog and cat and horse and Rudolf. But no, you're a bunch of species fascists.'

Tom waved a big hand up and down in front of my face.

'OK, rant over?' he enquired patiently. 'I was about to say that I have the feeling that the typical Swedish products include various kinds of—'

'Alcohol! Clever me! Do I win a prize?'

'You win a bottle of vodka,' Tom said. 'I wonder if they sell traditional Swedish hipflasks?'

It took us about an hour to find the shop, by which time we were both gibbering wrecks. IKEA was laid out on a system of winding paths whose careful planning constrained you to take in the full range of Mr and Mrs Bourgeois 2000 showpiece fitted bedrooms, fitted kitchens, fitted patios . . . everything seemed fitted, even the garden furniture. Following the paths was horribly frustrating, but if we tried to cut across country we got disoriented at once and started panicking.

The discovery that IKEA sold no alcohol of any description in the shop – 'Not even Absolut?' Tom pleaded with the assistant. 'I shall complain to the Swedish Tourist board!' – was a real downer. Until Tom remembered that he had half a bottle of gin in the van. We made a rapid exit to the car park.

Twenty minutes later we staggered back in, temporarily at peace with the world. It was with a fine airy confidence that we set off down the path again, arms linked like Dorothy and the Cowardly Lion.

'Follow the yellow brick road, follow the yellow brick road. Follow the follow the follow the follow the follow the yellow brick road,' Tom sang.

'Aren't there any other words?' I said. 'Oh dear.' I hiccuped.

'We're off to see the wizard, the wonderful wizard of Oz. If ever a wizard of Oz there was, the wizard of Oz is one because—'

'You're spitting.'

'Because of the wonderful things he does! Tralalalalalala.'

'Children are pointing.' I hiccuped again.

'I have a way with children,' Tom said seriously.

'Oh really?'

'Piss off, it's official. They said so in my last assessment.'

'Jesus, Tom, never try to say assessment when you're pissed. Look at your sweater, it's all wet down the front.'

'You're a fine one to talk,' Tom pointed out as I hiccuped yet again.

'Where are we?' I said, looking around.

'We're in IKEA, Sammy. Get a grip.'

'No.' I whacked him with an elbow. 'I mean, are we near the sofas?'

'Fuck knows.'

'Look, that's a sofa.' I headed towards it.

'We've got to stop those hiccups,' Tom said resolutely. 'You can't make a sofa decision with hiccups.'

'What do you think of this one?' It looked like all the others. 'What's it called?' Bending over, I squinted at the label. 'Sigismund. No way am I sitting on a Sigismund. Tom?' He had gone strangely quiet. 'Tom!' I swung round, panicking. 'Tom!'

It was like Red Riding Hood and the wolf. Always stick to the path. Tom had disappeared into thin air. Panic fear derives from the god Pan: the most primitive terror of all, being alone in deep forest. Well, it was nothing to finding yourself in IKEA with a bellyful of cheap gin and your best friend suddenly vanished into nothingness.

'Tom!' I whirled in a circle, trying to spot him. I saw a back which looked like his in the third bedroom suite to my right: but now I was paranoid about leaving the path and being lost too. Basic instinct told me to stay where I was. Revolving back again, I stared hopelessly at the sofa.

'Boo!' Tom popped up from behind it like a jack-in-the-box.

'Aaah!'

'Did it work?'

'Hic.'

'Damn.'

'You really scared me,' I said plaintively. 'Urch.'

I burped and choked down a hiccup simultaneously. It was a

deeply unpleasant experience, but it might have done the trick. I took several slow deep breaths to test out this theory.

'Wey-hey! The hiccups have gone!'

'Let's celebrate!'

We headed across to the far wall, where a series of large leather sofas were slotted in between smoked-glass-fronted shelving units. Clambering onto the sofa, Tom fished the gin bottle out from his pocket.

'My Aunt Louise would have loved these,' I said suddenly, indicating the display cabinets. 'She made my Uncle Harold put up shelves for her ornamental plate collection. But she'd have loved smoked glass and underlighting.'

'I've never heard you mention your Aunt Louise,' Tom said curiously, sitting down next to me. 'Somehow I never think of you as having relatives. I always assumed you were found playing as a baby with a pack of wild dogs in a junkyard.'

'Oh, my Aunt Louise brought me up after the accshident,' I explained, overcome by an unprecedented wave of reminiscence. I felt so convivial I put my head on Tom's shoulder. 'I love you, Tom,' I said. 'You're my best mate.'

'Yeah, yeah.' Tom was determined to get the story out of me. 'What accident? I can't believe you never told me about this, Sammy.'

'The gash main,' I said confidentially. 'It blew up the house with my parents in it. I was the only one who shurvived.'

'Why does that not surprise me?'

'My carrycot was blown out of the window and landed in a bush. My Aunt Louise alwaysh said it was a miracle. Only not in a very happy tone of voice. Poor Aunt Louise.' I stared up at Tom seriously. 'I'm afraid I washn't a very easy niesh to bring up.' I sniffed.

'Poor Aunt Louise,' Tom repeated devoutly.

'Maybe I should ring up Aunt Louishe and apologishe for being a difficult niesh. What d'you think?'

'I think your Aunt Louise would have a heart attack,' Tom said frankly.

'Oh, Tom.' I hit him with my splint. 'Ow, that hurt.'

'Well, come on. Blast from the past. Hello, auntie, it's Damienne Omen, the changeling from hell, sorry about all that devil-worshipping when I was little. Not to mention mutilating the budgie.'

'Can I help you?' came a girl's voice.

We both started, and Tom jogged the bottle, spilling some gin down the side of his sweater.

'Shit,' he said unguardedly.

'Can I help you?' the girl said again, in the tone of voice that suggested that the offer was not as optional as the words indicated. She was dressed in bright primary colours and her blonde hair was drawn back into a ponytail under a red baseball cap. Her smile was bright but artificial, like cubic zirconia, and her gaze was fixed on the bottle which Tom was now failing to fumble back into his trouser pocket. How he'd ever got it in there in the first place was a miracle.

Tom completely misread the situation.

'No, it's can we help *you*!' he said, giving her his best ladykiller smile. 'Sit down, have a drink with us! You look as if you could do with one! Must be hard being on your feet all day, I bet. Oh, and my friend here would like to buy a sofa. Though not this one.' He dabbed at the seat with the hem of his sweater. 'It's got gin on it.'

'I can't believe they have bouncers in IKEA,' I said as we exited into the car park.

'I can't believe that girl was so unfriendly.'

'Well, *I* can't believe you kept calling her Olga.'

'You think she didn't like it? I tried Kristin after a bit.'

'I mean, Olga's not even a Swedish name.'

'Do you think if I'd started with Kristin I'd have been in with a chance?'

'Since her name was Kelly, probably not.'

'How d'you know her name was Kelly?' Tom said, wide-eyed.

'Cos it was written on her name-tag.'

'*Damn.* Damn, damn, damn. I blew it. If I'd just spotted that in time—'

'I really don't think it would have helped, Tom. Not after the mention of Swedish meatballs in the funny accent.'

'I was trying to break the ice,' Tom protested, sounding wounded. 'Wasn't my fault that she had no sense of humour. All that fuss over a little gin on the sofa. You'd have thought it was a sodding antique the way she carried on.'

'Lucky it was leather. Or she'd've made me buy it.'

'Leather doesn't stain much, does it?' Tom said thoughtfully.

I stared at him.

'That,' I said, 'is a bloody brilliant idea.'

CHAPTER SEVENTEEN

Devo rang me that evening after he had met up with Lurch.

'Where did you find him?' he said incredulously. 'He's perfect!'

I smirked. 'I just picked one of my many trained investigators,' I said. 'Someone for every eventuality. I was going to make that my slogan but it sounded rather clumsy, don't you think?'

'You know,' Devo said, sensibly ignoring this, 'I was a bit doubtful about this idea of yours. The whole undercover bit. But Lurch – well, I mean, he might not find out anything, there might not be anything to find out, but no one's going to suspect him, which is the main thing. He's just perfect.'

'Yeah,' I said, 'I told him to stop using his acne medication and washing his hair. Not to mention the lack of deodorant. Add the final touch of verisimilitude.'

'Bugger off,' Devo said. 'You cheeky cow.'

'What was it you used to do, rub crystals under your arms?'

'You must be joking. We thought crystal healing was a decadent Western corruption of the ancient Oriental ways. Besides,' he added more prosaically, 'they're really expensive.'

The doorbell rang. Tom heaved himself out of one of the wings of my spanking-new leatherette corner suite and went to answer it. I found myself so hoping it was Hugo that I couldn't think of anything to say to Devo until I saw who was at the door.

'Come right in, mate,' Tom said.

I assumed from the note of welcome in his voice that it wasn't a balaclavaed kidnapper, and I was right. Though Hugo, in his own way, looked equally forbidding. He was wearing a long, close-fitting charcoal overcoat, a black silk scarf and leather gloves, and, with his fair hair and long haughty nose, he rather resembled the popular conception of a Nazi torturer.

'Devo?' I said. 'Got to go. I'll call you soon.'

We said our goodbyes. By the time I had hung up Tom was pulling on his own coat. Of course I was grateful for this tactful gesture, and, just as naturally, my sense of pride prevented me from acknowledging it.

'Tom?' I said, doing my best to sound baffled. He was already at the door. 'Where are you going?'

'Home,' he said. 'Got to take the van back, remember? See you tomorrow.' And with that he was gone. He didn't remind Hugo to bolt and bar the door. I assumed he thought any potential violence was much more likely to break out on our side of it. Or maybe he thought Hugo might need to make a speedy getaway.

Hugo and I stared at each other in silence. Finally he broke it by saying, almost reluctantly:

'I got your message.'

'You didn't come to tea yesterday,' I said. 'We had a great time.'

'So everyone said. I hear it was a riot.'

'Karen and Jimmy—'

'I know,' Hugo drawled. 'He's covered in love-bites and he's got shadows under his eyes the size of crop circles.'

Another silence fell. Hugo clearly thought it was up to me to introduce a new subject for discussion. I considered this very unfair, when there was such a large and obvious conversation topic to hand in the form of my new corner suite. At the very least, he could have acknowledged its existence.

'Why didn't you come yesterday?' I found myself asking.

He shrugged. 'I couldn't afford the calorie consumption,' he said nonchalantly. 'I heard everyone was bringing cake.'

'We've got a couple of bottles of champagne left,' I offered. 'Vince brought half a case. Do you want some?'

'Maybe a glass,' he said snottily. 'I can't drink too much. I've got a car picking me up at seven tomorrow morning.'

'It's in the fridge,' I said. 'You'll have to open it, I'm afraid. Don't forget I'm injured.' I managed to achieve a snottiness almost equal to his on this last line.

'I haven't forgotten, though you couldn't blame me if I had,' Hugo said with increasing frigidity. 'Since you've made it perfectly clear you don't need me in the slightest.'

'I never said that.'

'No, you just insisted on coming back to this fleapit instead of my flat, where I could have looked after you. And you installed Tom here on twenty-four hour guard. Believe me, I got the message.'

'Hugo—'

'Shall we just forget about the champagne too?' he snapped.

'Maybe you could open it for me before you storm out,' I suggested, my temper rising too. 'Since I'm *injured* and *helpless*.'

'Do you think it was easy for me, all those days not knowing where you were?' Hugo shouted. 'Don't you think I felt helpless too? And then you turn up looking like you've been in a car accident, and I don't know what the hell you've been through, and your bloody ex-boyfriend insists on hanging round the hospital the entire time I'm there—'

'All you did was make stupid cracks about how tough I was! Hawkins was at least sympathetic!'

'Don't try that one, Sam, you hate people being sympathetic! You'd have loathed me if I'd started cooing over you!'

This was so true there was nothing I could say. I wouldn't have been able to get a word in edgeways, anyway. Hugo was working himself up to a fine state of fury.

'Just because you're like one of those cartoon characters who gets hit over the head and pops up again a second later doesn't mean that everyone around you has to behave the same way!' he yelled. 'Look at you! You're strapped up in more bandages than a mummy from a bad horror film, and you're still insisting you don't need anyone or anything!'

'I need Tom,' I muttered sulkily. 'At least he opens bottles of champagne for me on request.'

'If Tom helped you in any way to buy that monstrosity you're sitting on,' Hugo said icily, 'and he must have done, as you couldn't possibly have got that *thing* back here by yourself – my God, smoked glass, I don't *believe* it –' his gaze swept over my new acquisition, pausing on the corner tables with visible disbelief – 'all I can say is that you need Tom like a hole in the head. A true friend would have tied you hand and foot and carried you out of the shop before you committed yourself to purchasing something that grotesque.'

'They delivered!' I said indignantly. 'I didn't make Tom carry it! He'd never have been able to put it together, anyway. The construction,' I explained with pride, 'is surprisingly sophisticated.'

'Oh, I bet they delivered it,' Hugo said sarcastically. 'Jumped at the chance to get it out of the shop, no doubt. It must have been hanging around since 1978 waiting for the only person tasteless enough to fork out for it.'

'Pompous bastard,' I muttered.

The tension in the air had cleared to some degree now that Hugo had let off steam. But his overcoat was still buttoned, his gloved hands shoved into his pockets, and he was poised slightly on the balls of his feet, as if ready to swivel and make a dramatic, door-slamming exit given the slightest provocation. It was clear that he considered himself to have carried out his part of the peace-making process simply by turning up on my doorstep; it was now up to me to mollify his wounded feelings.

'What I really need,' I said firmly, 'is a drink. Why don't you open that bottle and join me on my new sofa suite.' I patted it fondly. 'It's very comfortable.'

Scowling, Hugo stalked over to the fridge and extracted one of Vince's bottles.

'Jesus,' he said, temporarily shocked into a normal tone of voice. 'Piper Heidsieck. He really pushed the boat out.'

'He was very rude about the state of my bathroom,' I said.

'Good,' Hugo retorted unsympathetically. 'He was right. I don't even want to unzip my trousers in there, let alone take anything out of them.'

'Makes a change.'

'I haven't noticed you complaining.'

'How mature we both sound.'

'Shut up.'

He extracted a couple of glasses from the cupboard and brought them over, taking the side wing Tom had just vacated rather than sit on the main sofa next to me. A surprised expression flitted across his face as he sank into it. I was quick to pounce upon my opportunity.

'Snug, isn't it?' I prompted.

Hugo pretended he was too busy peeling off the foil top to answer me.

'Look, you can put the glasses down on the smoked-glass built-in corner table,' I said encouragingly, tapping it. Since Hugo showed no sign of following this suggestion, I reached for them myself. The sight of my splinted and strapped claws coming towards him was too much for his composure. With a muffled oath, he retrieved the glasses from the floor and slapped them down on the glass top.

'It's very convenient,' I said smugly.

'I don't know why you haven't installed a swing from the ceiling with a fake-fur lined conversation pit underneath it,' Hugo said bitingly, filling the glasses.

'That's a brilliant idea!' I said happily. 'God knows I have the space.'

'You are an abomination of nature,' he said, drinking deeply and refilling his glass almost at once. It was amazing what the combination of Piper Heidsieck and me could achieve on someone's expressed resolve not to drink too much. 'The worst part,' he admitted, 'is that this – this *thing* I'm sitting on is actually not at all uncomfortable.'

'It should be. Came from a very posh shop. There were more cows in that place than a film with John Wayne as a maverick rancher.'

'But this is leatherette. *God*, I hate that word.'

'Yeah, its only parents were a string of complex polymers.' I patted the sofa affectionately. 'I was going to get a leather one but then I felt guilty. All that cruelty-free stuff must have got to me a bit.'

'Either that or you were too mean to spend the money,' Hugo said sarcastically.

'How cynical.'

Hugo drank another glass of champagne. He still hadn't taken his overcoat off, nor his leather gloves. The effect was to make him look buttoned-up and unapproachable.

'You look very sexy,' I said hopefully.

'You don't.'

'What if I take my clothes off?' I suggested. 'That might cancel out my face.'

'Or I could put a paper bag over your head,' Hugo said, warming to the idea.

'Why don't *you* take my clothes off?' I said cunningly. 'We could christen the sofa suite.'

For a moment I thought he was going to balk. Using the term 'sofa suite' had not been the best of tactics. He stared at me consideringly over the top of his glass. Then he finished its contents, stood up, and came towards me slowly.

'You haven't got enough to take off,' he said. 'That's not much of a challenge.'

I was wearing my pyjamas under the man's kimono I used as a dressing gown.

'It will be,' I said, 'when you try to unbutton my pyjamas with your gloves still on.'

'I could just rip them off you.'

'As long as you sew the buttons back on later.'

'You've got Tom to skivvy for you,' Hugo said, untying the sash of the kimono. 'Make him do that. I'm just the man who drops round in the evenings to strip you naked on your sofa.'

He took hold of the lapels of my pyjamas and pulled them apart, popping off every single button as he went down.

'Mmn,' he said, bending over me. It was highly exciting being nearly naked on my sofa, the rough fabric of Hugo's overcoat catching on my bare skin. The touch of his leather gloves as he pulled off my pyjama bottoms was almost unbearable. He was kneeling between my legs. I closed my eyes.

'This,' he said, running his hand down my stomach and further south, 'should be the one thing I can do without hurting any parts of your wounded anatomy.'

And he lowered his mouth.

He was wrong, as it turned out. The spasms were hell on my broken ribs. But I wouldn't have stopped him for the world.

★

'Do you know what that felt like?' Hugo said afterwards as we lay on the sofa. It was clearly a rhetorical question, so I didn't bother to answer.

'One of the sex scenes from *Crash*,' he continued.

'Even with all that trying to make sure you didn't have to see my face?'

Hugo had complained that the sight of my bandaged nose and black eye made him feel like a wife-beater committing aggravated assault. I should have been grateful that he wasn't quite twisted enough to find me irresistibly alluring in this condition, but since his fastidiousness made having sex much more difficult, I didn't see the positive side till afterwards. With my hands so damaged I couldn't brace myself; Hugo had to manipulate me like a doll. I had enjoyed that, and so had he, even if he was determined to find something to complain about afterwards.

'This sofa's going to be horribly sticky in summer,' he said drowsily.

'It's wipe-clean,' I pointed out.

I felt his shudder beneath me.

'You're like all my sins come to roost in one compact package,' he observed.

'Makes it much neater that way,' I said consolingly. 'So how's shooting going?'

'Let's just say that it's no bad thing Sarah's playing a tortured junkie who overdoses at the end of the series. I'm not sure she's got much of a sense of the boundaries between life and art at the moment. She's not in a good state. More than understandable, I suppose.'

'Was she serious about Paul?'

'No, not really. I think they were both enjoying the celebrity top-up you get when you're both famous anyway. It's like one plus one equals five.' Hugo sighed, his ribcage rising and sinking. It was like being on a boat in harbour, rocking lightly with the waves.

'Anything else happen on set?'

'What, you mean any more dead foxes? No, that's all gone very quiet. But with a copper permanently in residence, plus the ubiquitous Vince, there's not much opportunity. The question, of course, is whether the dead fox was put there by the same charmers who snatched you. Most unlikely, I should think.'

'God, yes. Those two weren't exactly subtle. They'd have been spotted on set. I mean, they grabbed me at night. During the day they'd have stuck out like sore thumbs.'

'Or broken fingers,' Hugo said, running one hand lightly along my splint to my elbow, and up my arm. 'The theory, for your information, is that they must have parked their own car down the road, then sneaked in through the grounds. That wouldn't be difficult, as long as they were careful. There's plenty of places to get in through the bushes. Then they bundled you into your van and drove out through the gate. The guard lets anyone out; it's just people coming in who need checking. They dumped your van where they'd parked their own vehicle, transferred you from one to the other, and there you go. You were lucky it was a sedate part of Windsor, or someone would have nicked the van. They left the keys in the ignition.'

'Bastards,' I said crossly. 'Who drove it back?'

'I did. Handles quite nicely, doesn't it?'

'It *is* a Golf,' I said with hauteur.

'So who put the fox in Sarah's trailer?' Hugo mused.

'Who do the police think did it?'

'I doubt they have a clue. Red's issued terrifying directives on not talking to them more than one has to. She's battening down the hatches, all hands to the pump – no, this metaphor isn't working, is it? Anyway, we're not supposed to say anything that might upset the production.'

'But doesn't she want to know who it was?' I said innocently.

I was looking forward to meeting Red again and seeing if I could make her crawl. While I was in hospital a lavish and gigantic bouquet had arrived from the production team, but a card whose text was dictated by Karen down the phone to Interflora, no matter how nice it might be, was no substitute for an acknowledgement that Red had been wrong to suspect me of the fox incident.

'No, of course she doesn't. She wants to think it was an isolated episode, nothing at all to do with what happened to you. And I must say, I agree with that part.'

'Hmm.' I pondered the list of possibles. 'Keith?' I suggested. 'He really had it in for Sarah.'

'I don't know,' Hugo said. 'There's something so – so *blatant* about nailing a stuffed fox to a wall and scribbling on a mirror. It doesn't quite seem Keith's style. I see him doing something more subtle. Nastier. Like putting it in her bag and letting her find it. Oh, and that's another thing. I think Keith would set something up so he could be sure of being there when she came across it, don't you? He'd want to see her reaction.'

Knowing Keith, that was very good reasoning.

'I was wondering about Siobhan,' I said. 'She came out with this speech about kidnapping me having set the animal rights cause back by twenty years. I mean, she seemed to take it very seriously.'

'But would she have said something like that if she'd been the fox-nailer?' Hugo objected.

'Sanjay'd been skinning up all afternoon, and we'd put away enough champagne to drown a whole litter of foxes,' I said elegantly. 'We were off our faces. Not the kind of situation where you remember to be discreet.'

'Well, that's a possibility, then,' he agreed. 'And then there's Karen. She's a veggie. And God knows Sarah had been rude enough to her.'

I disagreed. 'Karen's too sensible to do something like that. Apart from anything else, she'd know we'd think of her after that scene Sarah threw in Red's office.'

'She might think that would be a good bluff,' Hugo suggested. 'Karen's a clever girl.'

'I can see that,' I agreed. 'But still, you couldn't control the risk of someone seeing you going in or coming out of Sarah's trailer. If that happened, no bluff would work. And Karen wouldn't really have a good excuse to be visiting Sarah. It'd be much easier for someone in costume or make-up, for instance. Picking up something she'd left in there they needed to wash and iron.'

'Back to Siobhan again,' Hugo said. 'Hmm. You know, I did actually wonder at one point whether Phil was behind it.'

'Phil?' I half-sat up in surprise, clutched at my ribs and relapsed painfully onto Hugo again. He started nibbling at my ear, which had landed close to his mouth. 'Mmmn, nice,' I said in reflex, before wresting my thoughts back on course. 'But Phil's the director! He wouldn't do something like that!'

'Phil has a bit of a history of practical joking,' Hugo informed me, his breath warm on my earlobe. 'Hard-boiled eggs in shoes, things pinned on people's backs. Red told him it wasn't to happen on this production. But, who knows? He might have wanted to take Sarah down a peg. And the way I see it, he'd have got someone else to do the dirty work for him. That wouldn't be hard. Everyone's always sucking up to the director. Little Jimmy, for instance. Promise him a third AD job on his next production and he'd do anything Phil told him to.'

I made disagreeing noises; I couldn't see Jimmy agreeing to that. But maybe I was just being naive. Besides, Hugo was now running his tongue around the inside of my ear. The sounds I was making turned into a moan of pleasure. It occurred to me to wonder whether Red had been so determined to identify me as the trouble-maker because secretly she suspected her own director of it and was desperate to find someone, anyone, to blame rather than Phil himself. It was an interesting theory. But Hugo's tongue was sliding down the side of my neck, and it was too distracting to concentrate on anything else but that. I turned my head to meet his mouth with my own. His hands, which had been executing delicious circles on my stomach, shot up at once, clamping on each side of my skull.

'Keep looking ahead, darling,' he said firmly. 'One sight of your female-boxer-after-a-bad-bout impression and my libido will fade completely.'

I wiggled my hips. 'It's doing fine so far,' I said.

'Exactly. So just – keep – looking – straight – ahead—' Turning me round further, he punctuated each word with a kiss on the back of my neck. 'Pretend you're Orpheus and I'm Eurydice—'

'Ooh, we haven't done that one before.'

'Infinite variety,' Hugo said into the back of my neck. 'Just call me Cleopatra.'

CHAPTER EIGHTEEN

Lurch, on the strength of two days out with the sabs, had become a total convert. He tended to throw himself heart and soul into whatever activity was currently engaging him. Though I approved of this character trait in general, and particularly in this case – there was nothing so likely to make someone seem trust- and confidence-worthy as a willingness to sprint round all day hacking through thick undergrowth being chased by psychotically violent hunt followers – it was becoming increasingly wearisome to spend any length of time in his company.

I had read about hunt bores in Molly Keane and P.G. Wodehouse. What neither of these writers had warned me about was the equal tedium provided by their opposite numbers. Instead of endless rambling anecdotes about drawing coverts at dawn and how Floppy – always been a plucky little bitch – had given tongue just in the nick of time to stop that young fool heading the fox, Lurch regaled me with stories about outwitting the hunt followers, mounting information-gathering raids on local pubs to find out where the hunt was meeting that day, and one triumphant moment where an entire pack of hounds were so confused by the fake scent and whistles that they ran in circles for a good hour or so, practically chasing their tails. I did my best to stay awake and make the right complimentary noises where necessary. He was too modest to boast of his achievements, but, reading between the lines, I gathered that he was doing pretty well.

He was also full of gruesome information. The bit about hunts breeding foxes and throwing the cubs to puppies to spark off a taste for fox meat from the earliest of ages had Hugo declaring that he was swearing off eating fox from that moment on.

'Not to mention hounds of any sort,' he said nobly. 'I cannot be a party to this slaughter any longer.'

Forget sending your teenage son off to a rave. This was like watching him enlist. Lurch was in boot camp – Devo had warned me that he would be given all the toughest tasks for a while, not so much to see if he were up to it as to test him out for possible subversive tendencies – and he was adoring it. The group he had joined went sabbing three times a week; Tuesdays and Thursdays were a reduced party, since many of them worked or had lectures to attend, but Lurch was there every time. There was even talk of letting him drive the van.

'Young men and their testosterone surges. It really is true,' I said to Hugo the next Saturday afternoon. He had had a free day, most of which we had spent in bed. His bed. He had insisted.

'I never really saw Lurch as having all that excess urge for combat,' I continued reflectively. 'He seemed so laid-back. Now all he does is plot strategy and tactics. He'll be reading Sun Tzu's *Art Of War* next.'

'Maybe I could give him a copy as an end–of–shooting present,' Hugo suggested.

'He'd probably love that. God, what have I done?'

'Hey, at least you didn't make him join the paras,' Hugo pointed out. 'This is perfect. He'll get it out of his system after a few years. Probably become a stockbroker or something. Look at your friend Devo.'

'What about the theatre?' I was pursuing my own worries. 'Lurch was supposed to go back to the Cross at the end of shooting. He can't do that if he's sabbing three times a week.'

'He has to follow his own destiny,' Hugo said profoundly.

I kicked him. He was about to retaliate when the phone rang.

'Hello?' he said, lying back on the pillows. 'Lurch, is that you? Hello? . . . Can you speak up, it's a terrible line . . . What? Oh, OK . . . Look, I'll repeat it and you tell me if I've got it right . . . You want us to go back to Sam's? Why, for Christ's sake? . . . Well, can't you bring them round here? . . . No, you're right, it's too elegant to be plausible, Sam's has the right squatty touch . . .' He gave me a limpid smile. 'You're bringing them back when? . . . Eight-ish? OK, we've got lots of time . . . *Move the mobiles*? You must be joking! . . . Oh, fuck it, Lurch . . . All right, all right . . . Yeah, we'll be on the sleeping platform, damn it all . . . probably covered in fleas . . . I said – oh, never mind, see you later. SEE YOU LATER!'

He hung up. I was staring at him inquisitively.

'I think I got most of what he was saying.' Hugo looked very glum. 'He was on someone's mobile, in a bush by the sound of it, whispering so they wouldn't hear.'

'These covert operations.'

'Wait,' he said in a doom-laden tone of voice, 'until you hear. He's got what he calls a "hot lead" on the kidnappers and he wants us to hear what this guy has to say. So he's formed the brilliant plan of bringing him and a few others back to yours this evening. We're to hide on the sleeping platform and listen in.'

'What was that about the mobiles?' I said.

'Oh, he thinks of everything,' Hugo said bitterly. 'They might give the game away. You were in the papers enough for someone to see them and make the connection. So we, or rather I, am to spend the rest of the afternoon padding up your sodding artworks and shoving them away somewhere. Why can't you do tasteful little lithographs instead of gigantic great metal sculptures? You have no consideration.'

'I'm sick of mobiles anyway,' I offered. 'I'm never making another one.'

'You'll never do anything I can put in here, though,' Hugo said, looking around his bedroom. It was papered in wide scarlet and white stripes, with an antique cherry-wood bed and an armchair upholstered in dark navy silk. The floors were parquet and the rugs as good as he could afford. Apart from the fact that it wouldn't have fitted anywhere in the flat, a mobile of mine would have clashed with the Regency decor like a laptop in *Sense and Sensibility*.

'Where are we going to put the mobiles?' I said. 'Thank God there're only a couple hung. Just think if I'd been getting ready for a show.'

'You mean where am *I* going to put the mobiles,' Hugo corrected me crossly. 'I'm the poor sod who's going to be struggling around under those giant pod things you're doing now. Or the ones you were doing before your current artistic crisis. Who are you ringing?'

I was poking at the keys of his mobile with the tip of my splint.

'Tom,' I explained. 'Let's hope he's in. If he brings his house van round, both the mobiles should fit inside. You guys can park it down the street and unload it when Lurch and his lot have gone.'

'Good thinking,' Hugo said appreciatively. 'I don't quite see what's in it for Tom, though, despite the demands of friendship.'

I clicked my tongue at his unusual lack of perception.

'He gets to eavesdrop on Lurch's covert information-gathering session,' I explained. 'He'll definitely go for that. You know men, they all want to feel that they're in a spy novel.'

'We need someone else to play the sultry Eastern European temptress,' Hugo objected. 'You're definitely not looking the part right now.'

'Half of me is. They can just shoot me from behind,' I said firmly. 'Or the neck down.'

'Mmn,' Hugo said. 'Definitely sounds like my kind of film.'

'God, this is all right!'

Lurch's party clomped in through the door of the studio. Their parkas and anoraks rustled like sound effects people in the early days of radio overdoing the brisk northerly wind.

'Cool!' said a girl's voice. The door shut behind them. 'Bit cold, though, isn't it?'

Hugo shot me a triumphant look. He was always complaining about chilblains when he came over.

'What's your mate do again?' asked the first voice. This was a young male. He sounded keyed up, as if the day had been action-packed.

We all waited for Lurch's response.

'Oh, fancies himself as a painter, dunne,' Lurch said, popping open a can of beer. 'He's pretty crap, though.'

I narrowed my eyes.

'Is that his?' the girl asked. A private-school education had trimmed and clipped her speech. She had the clear voice of a prefect trained to read out announcements at assembly. 'The one of the fruit? Because I think that's really nice.'

She must mean Kim's painting, which hung over the fridge. I beamed on my friend's behalf.

'Nah, I dunno who did that one,' Lurch said truthfully enough. 'Yeah, it's all right, innit?'

There was a pause, during which, presumably, they all stared at the painting – which was from Kim's Inappropriately Coloured Fruit sequence – and popped cans of beer.

'Where's all his paints, then?' said a fourth voice which I immediately identified as coming from the kind of person who questions everything on principle. It had that characteristic insistent, nagging tone. Tom, lying beside me on the floor of the sleeping platform, clicked his tongue against the roof of his mouth once to indicate the same observation.

'I *told* ya,' Lurch said, sounding bored and impatient. 'He's up north painting that giant angel they got up there. Fought it would be an inspiration or somefing.'

Hugo, Tom and I all looked at each other, deeply impressed at Lurch's conversance with the Angel of the North.

'Cool,' said the girl again. 'He's got a wicked place, anyway.'

Footsteps on the concrete floor indicated that the visitors were strolling around, checking out the studio.

'Where's the bog?' said the first boy. He was slurring his words a little. It occurred to me that the high in his voice might just as well be from alcohol as action.

'Round the corner there,' Lurch said.

'Nice of him to let you stay here,' the girl said.

'Yeah, he wanted me to keep an eye on it.'

'Where do you sleep?' said the annoying boy.

This was a moment we had anticipated as being potentially tricky. We were all lying behind the futon on a pile of blankets, so that anyone sticking their head up the top of the ladder and giving a cursory glance around would not have seen us. Still, the futon was low, and as soon as someone climbed all the way up our presence would be obvious. Not to mention the fact that all my things scattered around would make the gender of the studio's occupant perfectly obvious. I had the feeling I had left my love eggs on the bed. Well, those could belong to a man, if he was a very considerate lover. Or had a particularly relaxed sphincter.

'I kip on the sofa,' Lurch said. 'He's got a bed and stuff up there but he said he'd kill me if I used it. He's really fussy abaht his bed and that. Best not to get on his wrong side.'

Faintly beneath us I could hear the toilet flush. The bathroom door opened and the first boy's boots emerged.

'Jesus, that loo's filthy,' he commented.

I felt the pointed glances of both Hugo and Tom boring through each of my ears. Staring straight ahead, I refused to acknowledge them. Lurch, aware of me listening in, coughed and muttered the familiar bromide about it not being that bad, considering. Someone hiccuped and giggled. It was a male. I suspected the first boy.

'I feel a bit sick,' he announced. 'Going to sit down for a bit.'

He sank into the leatherette, which sagged under his weight.

'You all right, Pez?' the girl said.

'Yeah, doing fine.' He hiccuped again. 'Good day out, eh?'

'Oh, I dunno,' said the annoying one. 'It wasn't the best I've seen.'

'Come on, Rich, it was pretty successful,' the girl contradicted.

'Don't listen to 'im,' Lurch said. Someone crushed a can of beer. 'You know what he's like. Always sees the downside.'

'Yeah, and you've been sabbing long enough to know,' Rich said nastily.

'Oi, watch it,' Pez chipped in. 'Kev's a natural.'

'Kev?' Hugo and Tom mouthed at me simultaneously.

'Lurch,' I mouthed back.

'*Kev*?' they repeated incredulously.

It was a surprise to me too. I must have heard Lurch's real name only once or twice in our acquaintance. At the theatre where we'd met, everyone called him Lurch. It was like a slave name. And on the set of *Driven*, despite his official presence on the crew list as Kevin Pinder, he was still Lurch. I could see why he hadn't wanted to introduce himself to his new friends as Lurch but I still felt betrayed that the identity he had with me wasn't good enough for them.

I really must watch this maternal shit before it got completely out of hand.

'Yeah, Kev's shit-hot,' said the girl, sounding admiring. I felt my eyebrows raise. 'Did you see that stunt he pulled today? They had us all boxed in and that bastard was coming at us with a chain. And he got the van round that jeep just in time to block him. I'd've sworn there wasn't space for it. You were brilliant,' she said, presumably to Lurch.

'Oh, it wasn't nuffing,' he muttered.

'Yeah, well, I wasn't there, was I? I was taking on the coppers all on my own,' Annoying Rich said petulantly.

'Oh, come off it,' Pez said, sniggering. I had the feeling that Annoying Rich made this kind of boast so frequently that it had become rather discounted currency.

'You needed that bloke you was tellin' me abaht this afternoon, Richie,' Lurch said chattily.

My ears pricked up.

'Which bloke?' said Rich unhelpfully.

'You know, that psycho one what used to go for everyfing that moved. Sounded like a good bloke to have on your side.'

'Oh, fuck. You mean Mass,' said Pez, hiccuping again.

'We're not supposed to talk about Mass,' the girl said, with an edge to her voice.

'Oh, all right,' Lurch said with undiminished cheerfulness. 'I'll skin up then, shall I?'

'Good man,' Pez mumbled.

'I don't see why not,' Rich said. For a moment I thought he was talking about Lurch's suggestion; then he continued: 'I mean, it's been a year now since Mass was kicked out. What's the big deal?'

The girl muttered something I couldn't hear. It only had the effect of putting Rich's back up. He was the type who thrived on opposition.

'After all,' he said sarcastically, 'this is Kev, the hero of the hour.'

'Leave it aht,' Lurch said. He sounded a little distracted. I assumed he was concentrating on the joint. 'Anyway,' he added, 'you guys are like, a different group an' that. Ain't nuffing to do with me.'

I worried that Lurch might be overdoing the nonchalance a bit. But I was wrong. The sofa creaked, an anorak rustled and Pez said confidentially, sounding more out of it by the moment, 'Mass was this fucking psycho, man. He was, like, in it for the violence. I mean, sure it was good to have him on your side and that, but if you tried to stop him he'd turn on you instead. He punched out Andrew once when he grabbed his arm cos he was whaling into some bloke on the ground.'

'He punched out Andrew?' the girl said incredulously. 'I didn't know that.'

'His mate got between them,' chimed in Rich. 'He was the only one he'd listen to. Remember, Pez? Everyone was watching. It was a bit of a laugh, really. Even the sodding hunters standing back to see what'd happen.'

'Lucky his mate was there,' Lurch said casually. 'Here, Di.'

'Oh, Terry was always around,' Rich said. 'He was the one brought Mass along in the first place.'

'He was the committed one,' Pez agreed. 'Mass just wanted to kick some heads in.'

'Can't've been that committed, Terry,' Rich corrected, a certain whine of triumph in his voice. 'Dropped out, didn't he?'

'That was only cos Andrew kicked Mass out.'

'We're really not supposed to talk about people who've been thrown out,' Di said a bit helplessly.

'This Mass guy,' Lurch said thoughtfully. 'He abaht five foot ten, big barrel chest, nose like a potato? Shaved head?'

I'd given Lurch a good physical description of my kidnappers.

'Sounds like him,' Pez agreed. 'How come you know him? I thought you'd only been doing this a couple of weeks.'

'I fink I met him once at Devo's,' Lurch said easily. 'He was kicking up a bit of a fuss.'

'Oh, right.' Pez accepted this explanation.

'Prob'ly complaining about Andrew,' Rich said.

'Well, I bet he didn't get any joy from Devo,' Di said.

'I don't remember,' Lurch said. 'It didn't mean nuffing to me at the time.'

I willed him to leave the subject of Mass and Terry alone now. Any more prompting would raise suspicions. And, beyond a final comment that there were always a few bad apples, he did. The conversation turned to football and then became an impassioned discussion about the student union's inability to procure Red Stripe on draught for the college bar. Pez got drunker and drunker and Rich sounded increasingly stoned. It must have been pretty boring for Lurch; but he was rewarded when Di initiated a conversation about art with him, based on his acquaintance with the Angel of the North.

Our boy did very well, admitting his ignorance with easy grace where necessary and hitting hard on the points on which he was informed. These turned out to be surprisingly numerous. A discussion about Henry Moore versus Anish Kapoor, centring on their use of holes, had us all breathless in admiration. Di sounded genuinely interested in his opinions. I was desperate to see what she looked like, and when one of the boys started snoring I thought this might provide enough cover for me to sneak forward and catch a look. I started easing myself along the floor, using my elbows for leverage. Tom and Hugo immediately tried to follow me, obviously under the same compulsion. I hissed them back. All three of us couldn't be on the move together: it would sound as if there was an elephant up here. And it was my studio. I got to go first.

'God, I'm really impressed with how much you know,' Di was saying to Lurch. 'I'm sorry, does that sound a bit patronising?'

'Not too much,' he said cheerfully.

'Have you ever thought of, I don't know, going to college or something?' she suggested tentatively.

'I'm not that much for books,' he said. 'I like working with me hands.'

'You work in the theatre, don't you? That must be fascinating.'

Tom tugged at the leg of my trousers. I turned round, shooting him a furious glance.

'SHE – FANCIES – HIM!' he mouthed urgently.

'Yeah, it's a laugh,' Lurch was saying. 'Don't want to do it all me life, though.'

A loud snore broke through this little interlude.

'Can't hold his drink, canne?' Lurch said with the air of a sophisticated man of the world.

'Oh, *Pez*,' Di said dismissively. 'He's all right, I suppose.'

There was a pause.

'Rich?' she said. 'You awake?'

Silence answered her. By now I had reached the edge of the platform and was manoeuvring delicately to nudge my head a fraction over it, just enough to catch a glimpse of the situation below. Rich and Pez I saw first; they were both slumped on the sofa suite. Pez was recumbent, his face downwards, his body juddering with the snores, and Rich, though technically sitting up, had his head tilted sideways at an uncomfortable angle. His eyelids were flickering and every so often one hand would twitch hard in reflex.

'Looks as if they're both out for the count,' Lurch said.

'It's just you and me left,' said Di with a certain emphasis.

They were sitting side by side on the rug, their legs under the coffee table in front of them, their thighs brushing lightly against each other. Di's back was to me, which was frustrating in the extreme. She had short mousy hair, streaked thickly with dark red henna, and either she had a plump build or she was wearing four heavy sweaters under her khaki jacket. I caught a glimpse of her cheek, left side on. It was round as an apple. Plump, then.

'You were great today, you really were,' she said, stepping up the pace. 'God, look at all that mud on your trousers!'

'Got that falling in the ditch,' Lurch said shyly.

'It's spattered right up to your knees!'

From the movement of her arm, it looked as if she were tracing the mud stains up the leg of his combats. Poor Lurch, I really felt for him. It was the perfect pulling opportunity, and here the three of us were, listening in from on high like a trio of guardian angels, the downmarket version of *Wings of Desire*. Hugo wiggled up beside me. I pulled back slightly to give him a squint over the edge.

'It's getting a bit late,' Di said. She sounded frustrated. I couldn't blame her.

'Is it?' I hoped devoutly Lurch was looking deeply into her eyes. 'I didn't notice.'

'Oh. That's nice.' Her voice lowered. 'Kev?' she said seductively. 'How about a blowback?'

The girl had a good technique. There was a pause, presumably while she inhaled. I squinched forward pruriently just as she put one hand behind Lurch's head to steady it as she blew the smoke into his parted lips.

'Mmn,' she said, and kissed him. I noticed with delight that the back of Lurch's neck was bright red. One of his hands had come up to her shoulder, and looked for a second as if it was going to push her away; but as it touched, it held. Aaah.

It never occurred to me or Hugo to pull back and leave the young lovers to their stolen moment of passion. We were gripped by the spectacle, a pair of fascinated voyeurs. So it was left to Tom, arriving on my other side, to break up the clinch. In his haste to check out the state of play down below he had moved a little too quickly. Typical Tom. He had the subtlety of a pile-driver.

'What was that?' Di pulled back and, I imagined, looked up at the platform.

There was nothing to see. Hugo and I had been sensible enough to wriggle back as soon as Tom's scuffling became obvious. Lurch cleared his throat noisily.

'Up there?' he said gamely. He must have prepared this one in advance. 'Mice, I shouldn't be surprised. I fink that's why he told me not to sleep there. There'll be droppings or somefing.'

'Oh, right,' Di said flatly. 'Lovely.'

There was a pause.

'Kev . . .' she said again, her tone as seductive as before. I found myself wishing that Lurch hadn't told everyone his real name. I hadn't thought to warn him; he had seemed so sure of himself. But it wasn't exactly good security.

Still, he probably didn't have too much to worry about where Di was concerned. At least if you didn't count her hand moving up his leg. Lurch broke in, desperation in his voice, which sounded higher than normal.

'Can't have those two kipping here,' he said briskly. 'Better wake them up.'

There was the sound of someone, Lurch, I guessed, rising to his feet. Di was silent.

'Come on, you lot,' he said. Moaning ensued from Rich and Pez, the leatherette creaking as they moved. Lurch cleared his throat again.

'Di?' he said.

'Yes?' she snapped, her womanly pride wounded to the quick.

'What I fought was,' Lurch said, 'I've got the keys to Sam's van. I could give you all a lift back home.'

'Oh. OK,' she said coldly. 'Whatever.'

Oh dear, the dreaded 'whatever'.

'I mean,' he said clumsily, 'we'll drop them first.'

'Whichever's easiest.'

Di doubtless thought that Lurch was trying to get rid of her in the nicest way possible. Only we, and he, were able to appreciate his master-stroke. Once he'd got Rich and Pez out of the way he would be free to snog Di much more thoroughly in the van and then angle for an invite for coffee at hers, hopefully this time free of flapping ears.

We waited, hardly daring to move, until the young bloods had vacated the premises. Lurch had turned all the lights off, and it wasn't until we heard the van pull away that we came to life.

'The boy done good!' Tom said jubilantly. 'He shoots, he scores!'

'Nice to know Lurch is reaping some side-benefits from this assignment,' Hugo observed.

'Full-on benefits, more like,' Tom said coarsely. 'She almost had his trousers off down there.'

'She wanted to get a closer look at his mud stains,' I corrected.

'I liked that blowback thing,' Hugo said appreciatively. 'She was very smooth.'

'I wish I'd got a better look at her,' I said.

Tom snorted. 'He's what, nineteen? What's it matter what she looks like? They'd fuck newly dead corpses at that age.'

'Mmn, that's one of my personal favourites,' Hugo said, standing up. 'But I can never get Sam to lie still enough.'

'Or shut up for more than a couple of seconds, I bet,' Tom said.

I would have found this very funny if I didn't have the recent memory of Urine-Breath's hand creeping up inside my clothes as he told me to be a good girl and pretend I was asleep. The memory made me want to retch. I shuddered involuntarily as if shaking his hands off me. Tom and Hugo, oblivious to my reaction, each put a hand under my armpits and hauled me to my feet.

'This calls for a toast,' Hugo was saying.

'To Lurch getting his end away!' Tom agreed, starting down the ladder.

I still wasn't back to normal. I found myself snapping at them like an angry Dobermann.

'You fucking *prats*,' I said contemptuously. 'You're so excited about Lurch getting laid you've completely forgotten the point of this whole exercise. *Men*. Pathetic. You can only concentrate on one thing at a time.'

They both looked genuinely baffled.

'Remember what this was supposed to be about?' I sneered. 'Or was that too far back for you? Mass and Terry. I'll bet you anything Mass was the one who tried to rape me.'

The elation on their faces faded like melting snow, leaving grey-tinged slush behind.

CHAPTER NINETEEN

'What the hell is that?' I said unguardedly as Lurch put his latest plate of food down on the table.

'Black pudding on fried bread,' he beamed, pulling up the yellow plastic chair. Its metal feet screeched across the vinyl floor. 'And I got you your cuppa.'

'Thanks.' It had only been a couple of hours, but already the sight of another polystyrene cup of stewed tea filled me with an awful, sinking familiarity. I had already stuffed myself on fried eggs and mushrooms. There is a limit to how much even I can eat. Lurch beat me there; he was putting it away effortlessly. Still, I imagined that with Di's help he was working up a pretty good appetite. None of us had mentioned her name to him. We were trying to respect his privacy. I gave it another day or so before I cracked and demanded all the gory details.

Lurch was forking up the black pudding with undignified relish. The frying had given it a charred crust. It looked as scorched as burnt toast. I wondered briefly why no vampires in novels ever eat black pudding; you'd think it would be the ideal concentrated pick-me-up. But then, vampires tend to be aristocrats. They don't mind drinking from the working classes, but God forbid they should have to eat their food.

'D'you think I should try ringing the bells again? See if he was sleeping the first time, or somefing?' Lurch suggested.

'No, it's too iffy. I didn't like you doing it before.'

'This is really boring,' Lurch complained good-humouredly. 'I wanna be up and doing.'

'Hey, welcome to the wonderful world of covert surveillance.'

We were speaking quietly, but on this I lowered my voice still further. It was mid-morning, and the caff was nearly empty. Apart from us the only other occupants were some kids bunking school and a couple of old dossers taking a sip of their tea every ten minutes of so, making it last as long as they could. Not that the man behind the counter looked in any hurry to kick them out. He was leaning on it with both elbows, staring blankly ahead of him at the smeared and steamy glass windows. We fit right in here, just another couple with nothing to do and nowhere to do it, getting out of the house to the claustrophobic warmth and orange walls of the caff. Each of us was lost in our own little world.

It was the perfect subject for a modern Hopper, the downmarket version. Sunday Morning at Jack's Café. The plastic wood tables were bolted down in case a maniac with a Seventies fetish should try to steal them. Actually, they were probably highly sought after for the new industrial-look East End restaurants.

Lurch started squashing the sides of the plastic HP Sauce bottle to make the series of whiny, farty noises that kept him entertained for hours. I had a shorter tolerance for them.

'Don't *do* that!' I said, irritated, and felt the gaze of the man behind the counter drawn to our table, hearing my raised voice. He had been sympathetic about the damage to my face earlier.

'You all right, love?' he had enquired. I was so used to my injuries by now it took me a second or two to realise why he was asking.

'Yeah, not too bad,' I said.

He looked hard at Lurch, who returned a sunny smile. The most unlikely people could be wife-beaters, but if anyone looked incapable of it, that man was Lurch. Jack, if Jack he was, looked puzzled as he dished up my fried eggs.

'What happened, then?' he said.

'Walked into a door.'

Jack's wife came in from the storeroom at that moment, plastic bags of white sliced economy loaves dangling from each hand. She made a snorting sound intended to signify disbelief, gave me a long, contemptuous look, slapped the loaves down on the counter as if they were dead fish, and disappeared again. That olde worlde English welcome.

'Take care of yourself,' Jack said, holding out my plate. Then he saw the bandages on my hands. As he took the plate for me Lurch got an even harder stare, to which he remained equally oblivious.

We were staking out the address we had for Mass. It was a council flat down in Wapping, on a large sprawling concrete estate whose rising damp looked like an alternative form of ivy, growing unstoppably up the walls. The only positive thing that could be said for the Walter Raleigh Estate was that it had eschewed tower blocks. Most of the buildings were only a few storeys high. Mass's flat was on the first floor, reached by a concrete walkway with stairs on either side. One of the stairways led up from the parking lot in front of us and was in clear view; the other was hidden in a concrete sheath at the corner of the building, one of those stairwells which might have been specifically designed for the collection of graffiti and urine samples, plus a sprinkling of used condoms and syringes which made squelchy, tinkling noises underfoot. Behind this the walkway ran around the corner and on past the next series of front doors. It was Lurch's task to keep an eye on that side, as if Mass approached from that direction we wouldn't have much time to spot him before he entered his flat.

He wasn't in, as far as we knew. I had tried his number all yesterday but, after six rings or so, a voice always replied which informed me that she was a BT answering service. It spoke with that extraordinarily refined and studied accent which used to characterise BBC presenters and was now almost a historical artefact. Thus there was not even an answering machine message to let me recognise Urine-Breath from his voice. I wondered if this was coincidence, or if he was being very careful.

So Lurch and I were down by the river for the day, this dump of a place where the rich lived within private enclaves – fenced-off and gated blocks of flats with their own newsagents and corner shops and health clubs inside so they wouldn't have to venture out by foot into the wilds of Wapping. Outside those walls it was still rare to find an off-licence that wasn't stacked high with six-packs of beer, offered something more than litre bottles of cheap Algerian wine and wouldn't let kids drink alcohol on the premises. We had been lucky to find the caff, which provided a decent vantage point.

Lurch had insisted, five minutes after we sat down, on doing a dash along Mass's walkway, ringing the bells on every door and then running down the concrete-walled staircase to avoid being seen. I hadn't liked it; I thought we should keep the lowest of profiles. And it didn't prove anything one way or the other. A few people opened their doors and shouted unintelligible insults in Lurch's wake, mouths flapping with anger; those occupants less confrontational, but still curious, twitched their curtains back to peer out; but Mass's door stayed shut and no sign of movement could be seen within.

I was determined to be sure he was the one we were after before I rang the police. I had promised as much to Devo, but I would have done it in any case. Sicking the cops onto someone who might have a tendency to go overboard when hunt sabbing but had never dreamed of kidnapping anyone, let alone chaining them up in a basement, was not my idea of good citizenship.

It had been surprisingly hard to convince Devo to ring Andrew – the guy who headed up the sab group to which Lurch's new friends belonged – and persuade him to come across with Mass's full name and address. I had the feeling that Devo had been hoping that my kidnappers had nothing to do with any organised AR group. The revelation that we had a possible lead on them from that direction came as a nasty surprise. In fact the only tactic that worked was my pointing out that if Devo didn't get in touch with Andrew himself, the police would. He didn't like that one little bit.

'I should never have agreed to this,' he said sullenly. 'Now you've got me over a barrel.'

'God, I'm sorry, Devo,' I said. 'Do you feel used?'

'Yeah. Yeah, I do.'

'Oh, that's terrible,' I said sympathetically. 'Just one thing – do you think you'd feel the same way if it'd been you chained up in a cellar, not knowing if they were going to leave you there for ever, with one of them trying to rape you when he thought you were passed out with the flu? Hmm? Well, would you?'

Devo looked as embarrassed as I had hoped he would. I was genuinely angry.

'One broken nose,' I said, 'two broken ribs, two broken fingers, a sprained wrist, and you should see the bruising. Not to mention the psychological scars. I didn't do this go-karting, you know.'

'All right! Enough! I'm really, really sorry, Sam. I feel a total shit, OK? I just – I was just seeing it from a very narrow, AR perspective.'

'So did they, probably,' I said coldly.

This was the last nail in the coffin. Devo looked awful.

'I'll ring Andrew straight away,' he said. 'What excuse d'you think I should give?'

There wasn't much that would meet the case. Devo settled for saying that he had a mate who needed bouncers for a series of rather dodgy raves and he'd heard there was this bloke who used to be in Finchley Sabs who'd done some of that kind of work. Andrew replied that Mass, if that was the guy Devo was talking about, was a fucking psycho and Devo's mate should stay well away. Devo said that that was up to his mate, who knew what he was doing, and he'd take it as a favour if Andrew gave him Mass's number and address. Andrew had come across, on which Devo had enquired whether Mass hadn't had a friend? Apparently Andrew had become suspicious at this point and said that not even an organiser of geriatric tea-dances would hire Terry as a bouncer, and where had Devo got wind of Mass from anyway? Devo had promptly pleaded a work call on the other line and hung up.

One couldn't say it had gone swimmingly. Still, unless Andrew had deliberately misled Devo, we had Mass's address. We also had increasingly sore bottoms. The formica chairs were about as ergonomic as a bed of nails. At least Lurch could stretch his legs outside every so often; I wanted to keep as low a profile as possible. I had the woolly hat I'd bought in New York pulled down so far over my face that it nearly touched my bandaging, and, in jeans and a couple of huge old sweaters I used for work, I looked as anonymous as possible. Though to blend in round here with total success I should be sporting a designer tracksuit which had never been worn for anything closer to exercise than breaking and entering.

'Sam!' Lurch said, his fork clattering down on the table, his eyes fixed on the view through the window. Reaching sideways, he wiped the steam away with the cuff of his jacket.

I turned my head in time to see a figure in a baggy khaki flying jacket and camouflage trousers appearing round the corner of the walkway. His head was ducked as he reached for something in his pocket, his pace slowing down. Certainly he had Urine-Breath's build, but beyond that I could tell nothing. Then a car honked outside one of the ground-floor flats, and his head turned automatically to look over the edge of the walkway. For a moment I had a clear view of his face. The black eye had faded, but the other one was still swollen and the scar on his cheekbone was livid. Pulling his keys out of his trousers, he opened his front door and went inside.

I drew a deep breath as it closed behind him. The sight of Urine-Breath had stirred up a lot of raw and unpleasant memories.

'Is it 'im? Is it?' Lurch muttered, high with excitement, happily oblivious to my state of mind.

I nodded.

'Right, that's it! You got the cops' number, or've I?' Lurch fished in his jacket pocket, pulling out Hugo's mobile, which we had borrowed for precisely this emergency, and a slip of paper with the number on it. 'Here it is! Give 'em a bell!' He looked at the splint. 'I'll dial it for ya, shall I?'

I walked outside with the phone, finding a quiet spot in front of a boarded-up shop just as the call was answered. DCI Graves, who had been investigating my kidnap and Paul's murder, wasn't there, but the guy who had picked up his phone was on the ball, and when he heard what I had to say he promised a squad car right away. He even sounded like he meant it, which was a first in my experience.

I managed to press the button to end the call and stood there blankly, snapping the cover of the phone shut against the plywood crudely attached to the shopfront. Everything seemed suddenly on hold. I should be triumphant, filled with elation that Urine-Breath was about to get his comeuppance, but somehow I couldn't engage with what was about to happen. It was as if I was watching events through a reversed telescope; they seemed miles away, tiny and insignificant. A sense of emptiness rushed in on me like a deafening wind. I was tired and I ached. The bits of me still in reasonable working order were twitchy and bad-tempered, craving their usual exercise, while the broken and bruised parts were crying out for painkillers, Deep Heat, and bed rest. Ever since I had woken up in hospital this bodily tension had been pulling me in different directions, stilling only, temporarily, as I slept. And I was still having nightmares.

'Sam?' Lurch was standing in the door of the caff. 'Everything OK?'

'Yeah, sure.'

I should walk towards him, go back inside the caff, sit down and wait for the cops to arrive. I couldn't move. Pain was wrapping itself around my skull, sudden and piercing as an ice-cream headache on a warm day. I shut my eyes. When I opened them nothing had changed. In the few panes of glass remaining in the windows of the shop before me I caught a glimpse of myself, the bruising on my face so dark and purple it was impossible to imagine it ever fading again. I wanted to lean my forehead against the glass and close my eyes, shutting out the whole world until I felt myself again. But the sense of total dislocation was so strong I couldn't even remember who I was supposed to be, and I didn't much care.

The shotgun blast behind me sounded like a wake-up call sent to jolt me out of my solipsism. I swung round, staring at the block of flats, but there was nothing to be seen. For a crazy moment I thought the noise had been a car backfire, that I was imagining things – until I saw the shock in Lurch's expression, not to mention the clients and staff of Jack's Café scurrying across the vinyl floor to press their faces against the windows, noses flattened up against the glass in their eagerness to catch the show. There was still no sign of life from the flats. Then the net curtains in the flat next to Mass's flickered and the outline of a head appeared, craning round to the side to get the best perspective possible. This time no doors opened. No one wanted to risk getting caught in cross-fire. It wouldn't be the first armed incident they'd had on this estate.

The silence was eerie. The few people outside had frozen still. Even the kids who had been desultorily bouncing a gaudily logoed football against the concrete staircase had come to a halt. One of them had gathered up the ball and now stood with his arms wrapped around it, pressing it into his chest. Did he want to protect the football or himself? A car pulled into the driveway, coming past the parade of shops. It rounded the corner of the block, heading for a parking place behind it. I found myself wondering whether the driver had noticed the strange motionless people she had passed. We must look like a game of Musical Statues, or the beginning of an old science fiction film, all of us in mysteriously suspended animation, with her still unaware that she was the only one left with the power of movement.

Maybe she had realised something by now. From behind the block of flats an engine revved, tyres squealing as a car shot away. Its roar was subsumed in a much louder noise, the all-too-familiar wail of sirens. And now the statues melted and disappeared with the speed of light. In the blink of an eye, Lurch and I were the only two people left standing outside. Even the spectators had disappeared from the windows of Jack's Café, leaving damp spots on the steamy glass to mark their passage. The inhabitants of the Walter Raleigh Estate responded to certain cues with the swiftness of a lifetime's training.

A police car pulled up outside the flats. I knew one of the officers who got out, though I couldn't remember her name; she was the DI who had been with DCI Graves when he came to see me in hospital. I raised my hand to attract her attention. Walking swiftly, she came over to me, saying sharply:

'We just heard something on the radio. Shots fired, right? What's going on? Is it connected?'

'Just the one shot,' I said. 'And it was more like a blast from a shotgun. There wasn't anything to see, not from here. I don't know if it came from his flat, but it sounded like it.'

'Which one is it?'

'The brown door, first floor.' I pointed.

'Right.' Swinging round she spoke into her radio, her eyes lifted to the walkway. 'Get down,' she said to Lurch and me. 'Take cover inside or behind a wall. Not a car, it's not adequate protection. We've got an armed response team on the way.'

By now my headache was like a vice round my skull, closing so tightly it squeezed out any emotions I might have felt as the situation unfolded in front of us. With the familiar sense of eerie detachment I squatted uncomfortably behind a line of concrete bollards, Lurch by my side, watching the scene. Now that the police had arrived there was no danger in being targeted as witnesses, and people were swarming out to get a good look at the day's excitement. No one from the row of houses on the walkway, though. One guy put his head cautiously out of a window, looked around and pulled it back inside again, not wanting to take any risks. The rest of the inhabitants were mute and invisible. The shot must have sounded like an explosion through those thin walls. Aware how close it had been, they were taking no chances.

The whole procedure went as smoothly as if it had been a training exercise. Shortly a white van arrived, pulling up at the corner of the parade, officers in dark bulletproof vests tumbling out and taking up their stations. Some peeled away round the back of the flats, others chose strategic positions on either side of the walkway. The DI had detailed a couple of constables to hold back the press of people, clearing the area as best she could.

And still nothing happened. What must it be like for the inhabitants of the flats, looking down at our upturned faces, the dark bodies of the armed officers spaced out on the steps, the uniformed constables trying to keep the spectators in a wide, messy semicircle? It was an arena, a stage, cleared for an entrance which refused to happen.

The DI was listening intently to her radio. I sprinted forward across the open space, ignoring a shout from one of the constables, and ducked down next to her behind the main wall. She waved briefly at the officer who had yelled at me, indicating that I could stay beside her. I had been prepared to argue it out, but she seemed not to mind my presence.

'Just keep down,' she said to me, her attention still held by the voice coming through the radio.

'What's going on?' I said.

She held up her palm for a moment, indicating I should wait. When her interlocutor had finished speaking, she said a brief 'OK. Hold the field telephone attempt, then,' and turned to me. 'They think someone's already escaped through the back window of the flat,' she said crisply. 'Reports of a man seen climbing down and driving away. They're going in the back now.'

It couldn't have been more than five minutes, but it felt like twenty before the brown door finally swung open, slowly and evenly. The marksman kneeling on the staircase adjusted his aim by a fraction, a tiny, almost imperceptible movement. Utter silence fell. Then a voice rang out, a deep, gruff bass, sounding forced, as if it were making a concerted effort not to let it rise and betray the pressure it was under.

It wasn't Mass. I knew that at once, even before he formally identified himself for the benefit of the guns trained on the door. Then he came out, his hands empty of any weapons. The padding on the bulletproof vest, ridged and boxy, gave him a barrel chest out of proportion with his long skinny limbs; he was too spindly a figure to carry the weight of collective expectation. Still, at this point only Bruce Willis in a vest, his face singed, blood dripping from a picturesque gash in his arm, carrying an implausibly cute curly-haired child, could have satisfied the expectations of the mob.

A low sigh rolled round the spectators, shoulders sagging as the tension dissolved. Their sense of disappointment was immediately apparent. No dramatic shoot-out, no one gunned down in a hail of bullets. The Walter Raleigh Estate Residents Association had hoped for much more from this morning's entertainment. There was a long series of metallic flicks as a hundred cigarettes were lit, followed by a hundred exhalations, each one long, world-weary, and thoroughly disillusioned.

'Inspector!' the officer from the armed response team was yelling from the walkway. 'We need you in here! We've got a body!'

She looked across at me.

'Safe to bring someone in to ID it?' she called back.

I saw the expression that crossed his face.

'It's not pretty!' he called over.

'You OK? Strong stomach?' the DI said.

'No problem.'

'It could really be nasty. Shotguns do a hell of a lot of damage.'

Clearly she wanted me to come in – it would be much easier to have a positive ID on a potential kidnapper right away – but she was a fair woman and didn't want to push me. I shrugged.

'OK,' she said. 'Let's do it.'

The flat stank of blocked drains. The damp I had already noticed on the concrete outside hung in the air like a miasma, peeling away the wallpaper. That was how long ago this flat had been decorated: it still had wallpaper. Technically. I nearly tripped on the holes in the filthy threadbare carpet in the hall, and the DI caught at my arm to steady me. The living room was even bleaker: no furniture, just the same tatty fitted carpet with a couple of bed pillows on the floor and an enormous TV and video against the wall, standing on plywood boxes, a pool of porn videos strewn across the floor beneath them. The TV screen was so huge and dark it looked as if it had sucked in and eaten the rest of the furnishings, a black hole which had devoured everything around it.

'In here,' another chest-padded officer was saying, indicating the kitchen door. He stood back as we crossed the living room. Junk food cartons were so thick on the kitchen floor it was hard to see the linoleum beneath them. They looked as if they had been scattered there with one quick sweep of the arm to free the surface of the kitchen table, like a parody of a sex scene.

And the body sprawled across the table tied in with that image all too neatly. Its buttocks and thighs were bare, its camouflage trousers pulled down to the knees. Below them were the fourteen-hole DMs I recognised at once. I took a long look at the ruined body and whatever Mass had tried to do to me faded like a magic trick: folded its wings and closed in on itself, disappearing into darkness.

'Is he still alive?' the DI said curtly.

'Just about,' said another armed-response officer standing uncomfortably beside the body. 'Poor bastard. We called the ambulance, but I don't reckon much to his chances.'

'Would you take a look at his face, Sam? You OK with that?'

I nodded. I crossed the kitchen, feeling the cardboard Pop Tart cartons crushing beneath my feet. It was a tiny room, and two short strides took me to the side of the table. Mass's face was lying flat on the table, his arms stretched wide. The officer took a clump of hair in his hand and lifted the head a fraction. It reminded me vividly of that moment in the cellar when I had wrapped my fingers in Mass's greasy hair and wrenched backwards to hurt his throat still further. Now someone else was performing the same gesture for my benefit, and they were as gentle as I had been rough. A gush of blood issued from Mass's mouth as his head came up and the hinge of the lower jaw opened. He was like a broken toy, parts of which still retained their mechanisms. The officer had only tilted the head back a little, and Mass's jaw rested propped on the table. He had been hit on the side of the head. More blood had streamed down into his ear, a few trickles dripping into his eyes, starting to clot. The eyes were open, but that meant nothing. They were dull and empty. Dead already.

'It's him.'

I stepped back. Still I was unable to take my eyes off Mass's body, the great red gaping wound at the base of his spine as if his sphincter had exploded, the singe marks around it where the barrel of the shotgun had been pressed right into the flesh. And the flesh itself was so pale under the heavy sprinkling of hair. There was a particular, poignant nakedness about flesh so white, like fish bellies that never see the light. It looked more exposed, more vulnerable than tanned or darker skin can ever do. And the sheer ugliness of his body, the sagging buttocks, the lumpy thighs, made the sight even more pathetic.

'What's that?' the DI said, pointing at a tube lying on the table, beside the body. No one moved to touch it.

'KY jelly,' one of the officers informed her. 'Must've greased him before he shoved the shotgun up his arse.'

'Christ,' she said devoutly.

Someone behind us in the living room gave a small tense snigger.

'Not even necessary, I wouldn't have thought,' continued the officer. 'Shoving it up, I mean. Wouldn't have made that much difference in the end.'

'Thorough worker,' commented someone else.

'Sick sense of humour,' said the first.

'Knows how to handle a gun.'

'Just the guy we're looking for in B division. Think he needs a job?'

The ambulance siren cut through these uneasy attempts to joke away the horror. Everyone straightened up, looking relieved that in a few more minutes Mass's dying body would no longer be their responsibility. The DI nodded at me, indicating that I should follow her out. We left the flat in silence. The ambulance was parked in front, a couple of paramedics with a folding stretcher trotting up the concrete stairs. The crowd was still there. Despite the let-down it had suffered, it wouldn't leave while there was still some action, however slight.

'In there,' the DI said to the paramedics, nodding at the open door. 'It's a bad one.'

They looked underwhelmed by this warning.

'Now,' she said to me. 'I think it's time you told us how you knew where to find this guy, don't you?'

She pulled a cigarette packet out of her pocket and lit up, offering one to me. I wouldn't have minded, but my hands were so awkwardly bandaged it wasn't worth the trouble.

'Oh,' she added, taking a long, deep draw on the butt, 'and any ideas on how he got himself shot up the arse would be helpful, too, while you're about it.'

CHAPTER TWENTY

'An anonymous phone call,' DCI Graves repeated.

He didn't like it much. Actually, he didn't like it at all. But if I spent much time worrying about the likes and dislikes of the police officers I had encountered in my life, I'd be a babbling wreck by now.

The bandaging on my nose meant I didn't even have to fake my expression. I just went on looking at him.

'Made by a male voice, which you didn't recognise,' he continued, as sceptical as before.

'Nope. He just said that the guys who kidnapped me were called Mass and Terry, and gave me Mass's address.'

'Officially known as Matthew Hooperman and Terence Greene,' said the DI who had brought me back to the station. She tapped the photos lying on the table between us. 'We don't have any record of them being involved in animal rights activity. That's why they weren't among the photographs we showed you before to ID them.'

I remembered what Devo had said about the failure of the police to infiltrate animal rights groups generally. He himself had been in the little collection they showed me, but there hadn't been much and some of the shots had looked suspiciously dated.

'Mass was a thug for hire,' Graves said. 'Very nasty piece of work. Well, you know that, of course.'

He gestured to my nose.

'He didn't do this,' I said, reaching my hand to it. 'That was the third one. The one who got me when I was climbing out the window.'

'The mystery man,' Graves said ruefully.

'Or woman,' I pointed out. 'I never saw who it was.'

'True enough. We're not going to get more than that from the Raleigh,' the DI said.

Graves let out a long sigh. 'Hundreds of people around and no one saw anything. Same old story.'

The DI shrugged. 'No offence, sir, but I didn't expect it. Not when there was a shooter involved. We were lucky to catch that woman before she realised what was going on.'

Graves looked momentarily blank.

'The one who told us she'd seen someone climbing out the back,' the DI clarified. 'We probably wouldn't even have got that if she hadn't just driven in and been taken by surprise.'

I remembered the face of the woman who had passed us in the car just after the shot had been fired; distracted, busy, not taking in the Musical Statues game in progress. She had been parking her car when she had seen a figure climb out of Mass's living-room window and jump onto the roof of a van parked below. The identification wasn't of the best; the figure had, according to her, been wearing a black balaclava and a long overcoat. Taller than average, she had said. It wasn't much to go on.

'Didn't give us anything on the getaway car, did she?' Graves said.

The DI shook her head. 'No joy. Just a general description. Silver, not an estate car, nothing too posh. I didn't push her on it. She'd just have backed down even from that. No leads on our bum-bandit there.'

'Charming,' Graves commented.

The DI didn't even look abashed. 'It's what everyone's calling him, sir. Only to be expected.'

Graves shrugged, as if that kind of thing were far beneath him. 'Well, I don't doubt Terry will be able to help out,' he said. 'When we manage to track him down. Still no joy at his mum's?'

'No sir,' the DI said. 'We've got a couple of officers in there, waiting with her.'

'Is that where he lives?' I said. Somehow it seemed appropriate that Thick Boy should live with his mother.

The DI nodded. 'He'll be the weak link,' she said. 'This Mass's been in and out of the nick ever since he could walk. But we've got practically nothing on Terry apart from a drunk and disorderly with Mass. He'll be in over his head and petrified, I shouldn't wonder.'

DCI Graves looked at me.

'From what you saw of young Terry,' he said, 'd'you think he's capable of shoving a shotgun up someone's posterior?'

'I'd be very surprised.'

'We're looking for someone with a sick sense of humour,' Graves said. 'What about this practical joke that was played on Sarah Fossett? Fox nailed to the wall? You saw that, didn't you?'

I nodded.

'Well, who did you think did that? What's the gossip on the set?'

'Haven't you questioned everyone already?' I said.

Graves sighed. 'I'm willing to bet that producer told them to clam up or they'd get the sack.'

'She couldn't do that. They've got contracts.'

'Then she told 'em they'd never work for her again if they talked to us. We didn't get much that was worth having. Everyone loves each other, it's one big happy family, blah blah fucking blah.' He stared at me. 'You haven't got much of an axe to grind, though. Who did you think did it?'

Names ran through my head. Keith; Karen; Siobhan and Sanjay. And then I thought of Phil, the director. Phil, who had a past history of playing rather vicious practical jokes on people he didn't like. But from that to kidnapping me, disembowelling Paul and killing Mass was a big, big step. And wouldn't he be on set anyway, right now? No, I realised suddenly. It was Sunday. No one would have that alibi.

'Because,' Graves continued, driving it home, 'there is no way anyone's ever going to get me to believe that these incidents aren't connected. No way. Someone does that in Sarah Fossett's trailer. Then you get nicked by mistake for her.'

'You know, I was wondering about that,' I said unhappily. 'I mean, I know it would confuse things. But I was wondering if it was really Sarah I was kidnapped in mistake for.'

'You *what*?' Graves looked as if he thought I had lost my mind.

'Someone on set once mistook me for Siobhan,' I said. 'You know who she is, right? Who her family is?'

He was still staring at me. 'You mean she's one of *them*? Why did no one tell us?'

'Probably thought you knew already. I mean, everyone did. She's incredibly rich. Think of the ransom you could get. And I know what you're saying about the kidnap and the dead fox thing being connected, but I've always had trouble with that. Because when they snatched me, I was right next to my van. I mean, anyone on set would have known that Sarah had a driver to pick her up. All the main actors do. She wouldn't have been in the parking lot at night.'

'But Siobhan would?' said the DI intently.

I nodded. 'And my van was parked next to her jeep. They might have thought I was going for that instead. I look enough like her from behind.'

'Oh Jesus.' Graves and the DI exchanged horrified glances.

'But, you know, by the time I thought of it there didn't seem much point bringing it up,' I said. 'Because no one had tried to kidnap Siobhan when they realised it was me they'd got instead. So I just let it go. Besides, Paul was killed. That seemed to make the connection to Sarah pretty obvious. I wonder if that was Mass? Hard to see Paul letting him into Sarah's flat, though.' I caught Graves's eye. He was looking at me suspiciously. 'Hawkins told me her flat wasn't broken into,' I explained. 'Paul must have let in whoever killed him.'

Graves clearly didn't want to speculate about it with me.

'So how are you mending?' he asked me rather gruffly.

'Slowly,' I said. I was so used to the bandages now that they almost seemed part of me; it was only when someone called attention to them that I felt again the full weight of the splints and padding and the bulky support binding around my ribcage, compressing my breathing. There would be some extraordinary marks on my skin when I finally took that one off. I was betting I'd look like I'd been run over by a tractor.

'Well, don't you worry,' he said. 'One down, two to go. We'll have 'em banged up before you know it.'

'I think I'll get going,' I said. 'Could I ring my friend? He's going to come and pick me up.'

Graves dialled Lurch's number for me. To my surprise, it was answered by a woman's voice.

'Hello?' I said cautiously, wondering whether Graves had dialled the wrong number.

'Hello? Who's that?'

That clipped, public-school pronunciation was very familiar. It took me a moment to work out where I'd heard it before.

'Di!' I said.

'How do you know my name?' she said suspiciously.

Shit. 'Oh God, is your name Di? How weird!' I said, scrabbling around for an explanation. I was sure I wasn't supposed to know who she was. 'What a coincidence!' I exclaimed. 'I thought you were Lur – *Kevin* – putting on a funny voice, I mean, a different voice, haha, and so I said Die! Jokingly, of course. Hi. Um, is he there? Kevin?'

Graves was staring at me in disbelief. I hoped this display of idiocy wouldn't ruin my witness credibility.

'No, he's not.' Di didn't sound very friendly, and I couldn't blame her. 'I'm waiting here for him.'

That was odd. Lurch had peeled off at the estate, taking my van, and agreed to pick me up at the police station when I was done. He had said to ring him at home. And Lurch was always reliable.

'Did he ring you?' I asked.

'No.'

Odder and odder. A girl waiting at home for him, me here – I checked my watch – for over two hours, and he doesn't show up, doesn't even call Di to let her know he'll be late . . . Besides, Lurch lived only ten minutes' drive away from the estate. Even if he had had a puncture, say, he could have walked home and been there ages ago.

I was starting to get worried.

'Look,' I said, thinking fast, 'I'm a friend of a friend of Kevin's, the one whose studio he was looking after. He's driving my friend's van and he was supposed to come and pick me up today. But he hasn't shown up, and—'

'Is that the Golf van?' Di said. 'The green one?'

'Yes, that's right.'

'Well, that's weird. I didn't know he was still driving that. Maybe—'

'What?'

'Oh, nothing. It's just that a while ago – couple of hours or so – I was looking out of the window, just, you know, for something to do—'

Watching to see if Lurch was on his way. How romantic. A modern Mariana in the Moated Grange. Diana in the Peabody Estate. I had a brief sentimental young-love twitch. Funny, I thought that was all burnt out of me by now.

'—and I saw this van pull up in the parking lot,' Di was saying. 'I noticed it because it was like the one Kev, hmmn—' I knew she had been about to say 'gave us a lift in' and stopped at the last minute, unsure about whether I'd like hearing that part – 'was looking after for your friend,' she continued with aplomb. 'So I thought that might be him. Maybe doing an errand for your friend or something.' I approved of this girl. She was covering Lurch's back very smoothly.

'And was it?' I said encouragingly. 'I know he lets him drive it sometimes.' For the life of me I couldn't remember what name Lurch had assigned to the mythical male occupant of my studio.

'Well, that was the funny thing. I thought it was Kev. He was wearing that donkey jacket of his.'

Her voice had gone mushy with affection about Lurch's disgusting old donkey jacket. It must be love.

'But it can't have been, because when he got out of the van this other car pulled up next to him, and he talked to someone in the back for a moment, and then he got in and it drove off. I mean, if it'd been Kev he would at least have run up to see me and told me not to hang around. He's pretty considerate.'

'Did he get in the car straight away?' I was trying to sound casual.

There was a brief pause as she thought about this.

'No,' she said. 'The driver wound down the window, and someone opened the back door for him, and they talked for a moment. Then he got in. Look—'

'Do you remember the make of car?'

'Not really. Silver. Nothing special. Look, what's going on here?' She had reached the end of her tether. 'What's this all about?'

'Just one more question, OK? Can you see the van from the window?'

'Yeah—'

'OK, I lied. Actually it's two questions. Could you read me out the registration?'

Di read back my licence plate, spitting each letter and number out with as much venom as Sid Vicious doing 'God Save The Queen'.

'Shit,' I said. 'Look, I'll ring you back, OK? Soon. Thanks very much.'

She exploded. I hung up and stared at Graves.

'I think my friend's been kidnapped,' I said.

'*What?*'

There was no point messing around with fake stories now.

'He was the one who fingered Mass and Terry,' I said. 'I made up the anonymous phone call story just to cover his back. It sounds like he was picked up outside the flats where he lives.'

And how did they know his address? That wasn't hard to work out. Lurch had given the hunt sabs his real name. Which was also on the crew list for *Driven*. Someone must have put those two facts together, once they had heard that Lurch had been asking about Mass and Terry. And they had panicked and killed Mass. Waited in his flat till he came back, hit him over the head and greased him up for the shotgun barrel.

I found myself wondering whether whoever it was had recognised my van. They would have seen Lurch driving it. Had they recognised it as the same van Mass and Terry had driven out of the studios, with me unconscious in the back? There was something about that picture that struck a chord with me. Something about the van, some association . . .

I put my head in my hands. Graves was asking me questions, but I wanted to block him out till I'd tracked down the vital point, the thing that was still eluding me. It felt, frustratingly, as if I was nearly there. My brain scrabbled around, trying to find the final connecting piece. I stared blankly at the table-top, my mind racing. Directly below me were the photos of Mass and Terry. The former's potato nose had come out very well. Mass looked defiant and Terry nervous. The photographer had captured their personalities very successfully. Matthew Hooperman, Terence Greene. One down, two to go. A long printout for Mass and just a single entry for Terry, one measly little drunk and disorderly, barely a record at all, really—

Graves was shouting at me now. The black and white photographs blurred before my eyes, reminding me of the ones of actors pinned up in Karen's office on set: Hugo and Sarah and Keith, all with their posed smiles or sexy stares. Matthew Hooperman, Terence Greene. Terence Greene. I saw my van in front of me, my lovely prized green Golf van—

'*Jesus!*' I sat up straight. Graves was leaning across the table and his face, red with anger and frustration, was only a few inches away from mine.

'I know who did it!' I said. 'I know who kidnapped me!'

The track was overgrown and rutted, closer to a tractor path than a road. Thick trees on either side pressed close to the side of the car, branches occasionally scraping against metal and drawing a muffled curse from the policeman at the wheel. We were crawling along. I should have been grateful; each bounce and judder of the wheels into a pothole tore at my ribs as if trying to rip the broken bones apart once more. My arms were wrapped around my chest to minimise the pain. But I was twitching with the need to hurry, urgency pounding in my skull. I was trying not to think about what we might find at the end of the track.

It wound round on itself like an ancient stream which had long ago carved out the path of least resistance through a thick bed of rock. And still we could see nothing through the trees. The sky overhead was darkening, dusk falling. It felt as if we would drive on and on through the woods for ever. A particularly nasty pothole on the right side of the car tilted it over and the tyres squealed as the driver dragged over-hard on the steering wheel.

'Could we look where we're going?' Graves, beside me, said irritably.

'Sorry, sir,' the driver said between gritted teeth. 'It's not exactly Le Mans.'

'No excuses,' Graves snapped.

A hairpin bend, the driver taking it so slowly I thought the car was going to stall. A branch whipped across the windshield sharply enough for the DI, in the front passenger seat, to catch her breath in shock. It was like the opening to a horror film, the first inkling that the journey we were on would end in violence. The trees parted a little, giving a prospect of the sky beyond, dark with impending night. The final traces of daylight faded in streaks of greyish orange, the colour of sulphur flares or burnt-out neon. The sky itself was thick with invisible cloud, not a star to be seen.

Lights were blazing through the bushes now. We must be nearly there. The car's headlights scored through the trees, showing a short stretch of stony mud track before we rounded the final bend. I blinked at the scene before us, the police cars parked on the grass in front of the house, headlights trained on its windows, the spinning lights clipped to their roofs throwing regular washes of blue light over the facade. Darkly clad bodies stood around the cars, shadowy figures in the twilight. Two ambulances were parked on the verge, already turned round, ready to make a fast getaway. After the near-silence of the drive all this activity seemed surreal.

It wasn't really a house, now that I looked at it more closely. It was a cottage, a small stone building with painted shutters, cosy and squat, hidden in the heart of the forest like something out of a fairy tale. All it needed was a trail of smoke from its chimney and a little old lady inside, sitting by the fireplace, casting spells.

And there was the silver car – an old-model Ford Fiesta – parked right in front. We had come to the end of the quest. How neat. I was gritting my teeth in tension, and the fact that the bandaging on my hands made me too clumsy to open the latch on my door for a moment assumed the proportions of a grand tragedy. I nearly shoved Graves in my frustration, desperate for him to get out so I could clamber over his side and out through his door.

'Wait here,' he said to me as he got out.

Yeah, right. I followed him straight away, my boots sinking into the muddy grass, churned up by the car wheels which had preceded us.

Graves was talking to someone who must be the officer in charge here, the top dog of the local cops who had got here a couple of hours ago, while we were still on the motorway. They had a brief, urgent conference behind the central police car. The cottage, its facade caught in the explosion of light, looked strangely empty, despite the lights at the windows.

Graves was coming back in our direction.

'Down in the basement,' he said briskly. 'Three of 'em. At least one with a gun. Someone's badly wounded. Haven't been able to talk to whoever's in charge. They just keep shooting at the doorway.'

'What are you going to do?' I said urgently.

'Go down there, try to negotiate,' Graves said impatiently. 'You wait here. Stay well back.'

He looked as if he was regretting ever having brought me.

'No,' I insisted. 'I'm coming down there with you.'

'Look, Miss Jones,' he said, his voice rising with tension, 'I don't think you quite understand your position here—'

With some police officers, increasing politeness is a sign of imminent explosion. I ignored this.

'No, *listen*. I'm the only one who knows any of them. Shit, I know all of them. I can talk to them for you. Set up some friendly dialogue.'

Graves stared at me. The light was in his face and I couldn't read his expression.

'That lot've been trying to negotiate with them for hours now, haven't they?' I said with increasing emphasis. 'And nothing's happened. Someone's badly hurt and they're not even letting them be taken to hospital.' I gestured at the ambulances. 'You need to try something different.'

Graves just went on looking at me. I held up my bandaged claws.

'I'm not in authority,' I said. 'Fuck it, I'm their victim. It'd be a whole other approach.'

He sighed, a long slow sigh.

'You do exactly what I tell you to at all times,' he said.

'Of course.'

The hand with the sprained wrist was recovering reasonably well. If I tried, I could even cross its fingers.

Graves got a pair of bulletproof vests for us and I struggled into mine clumsily. Only when he had checked that it was all fastened up did we cross the lawn and enter the cottage. I followed Graves as dutifully as a pet dog. The front door opened into a narrow hall; on one side was a sitting room, on the other what looked like a study. The rooms were tiny, everything seeming miniaturised. At the far end of the hall was a sash window which I suddenly recognised with a jolt of familiarity that pounded painfully at my ribs. I hadn't even had time to wonder what it would be like, coming back here; my thoughts had been completely taken up with Lurch. And now here I was, confronted with that window and the stone sink directly below it onto which I had clambered. A flash of memory hit me, the weight of the sash under my shoulder, the adrenaline racing round my body, the sound of my breath panting in the silence of the corridor . . .

Graves had already turned and was heading into the larder, through the door at the back, the way indicated for him by a policewoman who was standing mute guard in the hall. I got a grip on myself and followed him, conscious of an enormous lump in my throat. It hurt to breathe. I took the stone steps slowly. More memory flashes were exploding in my head, white light before my eyes. I was feeling again the mixture of panic and exhilaration and fear with which I had run up these stairs only a couple of weeks ago. It felt as if I was acting out a waking nightmare. And, as usual, I had brought this completely on myself. Everyone had tried to stop me coming, but I had insisted, stubborn as always. So here I was, only myself to blame, as I forced my feet to move one step after another, carrying me back down into the basement I had never imagined I would enter again.

Mass was dead. I repeated that to myself firmly, but it didn't help much. It wasn't the person, it was the place whose associations were catching at the back of my throat. The narrow stone passage at the bottom was tightly packed with bodies: more armed police officers, stationed on either side of the door. Only three of them, but they seemed like a whole platoon in this tiny space. Their presence should have given me more comfort than it did.

Graves was squatting down by one of the officers on the near side of the door, looking through a long black tube. After a few moments he gestured to me to come and see for myself. It was a sort of sideways telescope for seeing round corners, a series of mirrors reflecting back the scene inside the basement room.

I knelt down, the stone flags cold under my shins, and bent to put my eye to the telescope. The sight of that basement, even from this perspective, made my gorge rise. My mouth tasted metallic. I felt the urge to hawk, and swallowed hard.

There was someone hanging from the chain which had once held me. But the chain had been pulled back and secured so that his cuffed hands were pulled high above his head, his feet only barely touching the ground. Blood was running down his face, which was a mass of bruises. He had been stripped to the waist. Every bone in his skinny ribcage protruded as if trying to break through the skin. It took me a good few seconds to recognise Lurch. His eyes were closed and it looked as if he had passed out. But he was still breathing. I could see the slow, painful rise and fall of his sharp ribs cutting against the covering flesh.

On the flagstones, a little way from Lurch's suspended body, lay another one, ominously still, its face covered by a black balaclava. There was a gaping wound in its chest and a great stain had spread out beneath it, a motionless, inky pool of blood. And beside this crouched Terry, a gun in his hand, and a couple of shotguns, their barrels sawn off close to the stock, propped against the camp bed by his side. There was a bottle of whisky by his feet and as I watched he lifted it and took another slug.

Graves took the scope back from me and bent to look through it, clearing his throat.

'All right in there?' he said in an unexpectedly gentle tone. 'I'm DCI Graves from the Met, and—'

I couldn't see what happened next. But I heard the shots. Three of them, one after the other, aimed at the open door. Jesus, we were taking a risk being down here at all; the ricochets on the stone wall behind could be lethal, even with our protective clothing. Silence fell once more.

'He hasn't said a word all this time,' one of the officers whispered to Graves.

I nudged him.

'Look,' I muttered, 'let me try, go on!'

Graves held up his hand to silence me.

'No one's going to come in there till you say the word—' he tried again. Another fusillade was the only answer.

He rested the scope on his knees and looked over at me. I could see the indecision in his eyes.

'How's he off for ammo?' Graves whispered to the officer beside him.

'Got enough in there for an army, sir,' was the answer. 'We could be here for days at this rate. And those two in there need to get to a doctor fast. If it's not too late for that one on the ground.'

It was the psychological moment. I went for it.

'Let me try,' I insisted to Graves once more. I pointed at the wall behind the open door, now studded with bullet holes. Graves's head turned, following the line of my hand. I pressed home the advantage.

'After all,' I said, 'what have you got to lose?'

CHAPTER TWENTY-ONE

Graves's assent was unspoken. He handed me the scope and moved backwards, away from the door, allowing me a little space to squeeze as near to the jamb as I could without being in the line of fire.

Keep it simple, I told myself. But don't patronise him either. I grimaced. Easier said than done. I got the scope into position. Eerily, the tableau inside the basement had not altered in any way.

'Terry?' I said. My voice echoed around the stone walls, thin and ghostly. 'You'll never guess who this is. It's Sam. Sam Jones.'

The words sounded fragile, almost banal. And strangely enough the presence of three armed officers and Graves on this side of the door made me feel more pressurised to get it right than the view of Terry down the scope. The slight distortion on the lens shrunk the scene, putting it in invisible quotation marks, as if I were viewing it through Phil's little monitor on the set of *Driven*.

Terry's only reaction to my words was a movement of his head, which came up to stare, I assumed incredulously, at the open door. But there were no shots. A good result, if only in the negative sense. Graves nodded at me, telling me to continue.

'It feels bloody strange being back here, I can tell you.' My voice was gaining strength. 'You in there, me out here. Like old times, eh? Only the other way round.'

Was that laying it on too thick? He hadn't moved; but then, he still wasn't shooting at the door. I paused again.

'Look, Terry.' I was trying for a conversational tone. 'Things're looking a bit rough. Everything's a bit out of control, isn't it? I don't really understand most of what's been going on, but I'm sure you didn't want stuff to get out of hand like this.'

I sounded as banal as a relationship counsellor doling out platitudes like tranquillisers. Care, share, make time to listen to each other. Oh, and what about putting down the gun while you're about it?

'I'd like to help,' I said. 'I really would. You were very nice to me. I'd like to return the favour.'

Terry shifted, pulling the camp bed behind him so that he could perch on it. That had to be a good sign; he wanted to get more comfortable so he could concentrate fully on my words of wisdom. Unless he always reloaded while sitting cross-legged.

Graves, hearing the noise of the camp bed dragging across the flagstones, made a What's Going On? face at me. And from the moment they had heard movement, the armed officers were on extra alert. I held up a hand to show it was fine.

'Do you remember those sandwiches you made me?' I said to Terry. 'The Vegemite ones? And all those carrots? You really looked after me.'

I paused, a thought striking me.

'Are you hungry?' I said. 'We could see if we could find something.'

That had been a mistake. Still, it got him talking.

'*We?*' he said angrily.

I felt Graves's stare boring through the back of my head.

'Hey.' I attempted to sound relaxed, though to my own ears it was working about as well as the Queen trying to show her populist credentials by belting out the latest football chant. 'There are loads of coppers out here, you know that as well as I do. They're just hanging around. Might as well make themselves useful rustling you up some food, if you want it.'

There was a long pause. Then he said:

'I am a bit hungry, I s'pose.'

Graves made a sign to the policewoman in the corridor above, calling her down. He crept up a few stairs and met her halfway, whispering urgently in her ear. I followed him, muttering to her:

'Any food you can find, and make some tea or coffee. One for me too.'

Graves snorted at this, but didn't object.

'Terry?' I said, coming back down the stairs. 'We're just getting some food together. And a hot drink. I thought you might like that. You always made sure I had coffee, didn't you?'

'That was me,' he said. 'The coffee. I fahnd this Thermos, right, and I fought it'd warm you up a bit. Mass said I was being daft . . .'

His voice trailed off at the mention of Mass.

'How is he?' he said, sounding wistful. It was hard to imagine anyone caring whether Mass lived or died. I summoned up a mighty surge of empathy. It sounded like a procedure from the new-look *Star Trek*.

'He's OK,' I lied, refusing to catch Graves's eye.

'Really?' Terry was disbelieving. 'Cos I know what happened to 'im, right. *He* told me.' He gestured to the body on the floor, the one in the balaclava. 'He can't be fucking OK.'

'Well, sure, he's on a life-support,' I said glibly, fighting back the urge to shout: He's dead, dead as a doornail, his colon had so many holes in it one of the doctors is using it as a crochet scarf, OK? 'But they're sure he'll pull through. Might have to wear a colostomy bag, though.'

'You what?'

'One of those bags they put on you when your bowels don't work. The shit comes out through your tummy instead.'

I thought this gave a nice touch of plausibility.

Terry started sniggering. 'I won't half give 'im a hard time abaht that!' he said. 'That'll be well funny, that will!'

'What about you? Are you all right?' I asked. 'Not hurt or anything?'

I was dying to know about Lurch, but it was vital to get Terry reassured first. I just hoped that Lurch, if he was conscious, understood what I was doing.

'No, not too bad.'

Terry's voice was flat, drained of energy. He sounded as if he was running on empty. I wondered whether feeding him was a good idea after all; maybe we should just let him go to sleep, worn out by the day.

'What about the guy in the cuffs? He looks a bit dodgy to me.'

Terry turned his head to look at Lurch.

'He would've died,' he said dully. 'I stopped it. I had to.'

'You did the right thing,' I said, cursing my tone, which had come out as bright as a TV weather-girl congratulating the viewing public for not going out in a snowstorm. 'But he looks a bit uncomfortable, don't you think?'

Meiosis was Greek for understatement. Hugo adored that word.

Terry didn't answer. Nor did he move.

'I mean,' I tried again, 'cuffs are one thing, but being strung up like that looks bloody painful to me. Why don't you undo the chain? I mean, he's not exactly going anywhere, is he!'

God, the vapidities that were coming out of my mouth would make me shiver if I actually listened to them.

'Go on,' I said coaxingly. 'I don't know what he's done, but poor sod, he looks really rough.'

And finally Terry stood up. At this sound, the officer beside me dragged the scope from my fingers before I realised what she was doing. I turned to Graves, furious.

'Why aren't there any more!' I mouthed.

He rubbed the fingers and thumb of one hand together, signifying money, or in this case the lack of it. I narrowed my eyes. No use trying to grab the scope back with my hands in this state. I knocked on her head with my splint just as a chain clinked against itself, running loose across the stone floor. I knocked harder and harder on her head, as if I were trying to crack an egg, till she swore and handed the scope back to me. Being Most Successful Negotiator Of The Evening had its advantages.

Lurch was down on the ground, lying on his back. His hands had fallen in front of him and were resting on his chest, the chain trailing out from the cuffs. I bet Terry hadn't caught him as he came down. I bit my lip, hoping he hadn't hit his head too badly.

Terry was standing in the middle of the room, his posture denoting uncertainty.

'Look,' he said. 'I done what you said.'

But the gun was still in his hand. I didn't think he'd be putting it down any time soon.

'That's great,' I said warmly. 'Why don't you sit down again and I'll see if the food's on its way?'

'Just don't try anythin',' he warned. 'Or I'll do 'im. I said I would and I will.'

The policewoman was coming down the stairs, carrying a bag of Mars bars and another of crisps.

'It was all we could find in the kitchen,' she whispered. But she had a couple of mugs of instant coffee in the other hand.

'Terry?' I said. 'I've got Mars bars here, and crisps, and coffee. You want some?'

'Yeah,' he said. 'I ain't 'alf hungry now.'

'Well, look.' I took a deep breath. 'I'm going to bring them in, OK? But they won't let me unless you say the paramedics can come in and take out that bloke. The one who's chained up.'

There was a long pause. Graves was tapping on my shoulder as urgently as a woodpecker after a juicy worm hiding down a tree trunk. I ignored him.

'What,' Terry said finally, 'like an exchange?'

'Yeah. He needs to see a doctor, Terry. Look at him. He's a mess.'

Terry snorted. 'You haven't seen the worst bit,' he informed me. 'His back's all cut to pieces.'

Blood surged to my head.

'Then why isn't he lying on his front?' I said angrily. 'Are you mad? Look, I'm coming in, and then the paramedics are going to follow me, right? No messing about, Terry. It's important. He could die, and then where would you be?'

'No funny business from you,' Terry said warily. 'I seen what you're like.'

'Terry,' I said wearily, 'I've got my hands strapped up, a broken nose and two broken ribs. The only thing I could hurt in there are those bloody cockroaches.'

Terry snorted with laughter. He was the only one. Graves was violently opposed to the idea. I wasn't jumping for joy myself. But the relief I felt as I saw Lurch carried out on a stretcher was so strong I didn't even care about being back in that damn cellar again with a couple of men in balaclavas. Which demonstrated more than adequately how guilty I had been feeling about involving Lurch in this whole mess.

Terry had already consumed one Mars bar. He was opening a second one, shoving as much of it in his mouth as would fit.

'Cor, sugar,' he said gratefully round the obstacle. 'That hits the spot, that does.' There were great red circles round his eyes and his skin was blotchy with a rash spreading down from his forehead. He looked like an extra from the Masque of the Red Death.

'Why don't you tell me a bit about what's been going on?' I suggested, watching the automatic in his hand. He wasn't pointing it at me, but he wasn't going to put it down, either. I would have to wait till the painkillers started taking effect.

He sighed. 'Fucking cockup,' he said with infinite sadness. 'Everything's just fucking cocked up now, innit?'

Fortunately he didn't seem to need a reassuring answer, since I couldn't for the life of me summon one to mind. Instead I said:

'Can I have a bit of that whisky in my coffee?'

He looked over at the bottle. There was still more than half left.

'Yeah,' he said, reaching for it. 'Fink I will too.'

I tipped out the bottle of painkillers from my jacket pocket.

'Might have a couple of these first,' I said casually. 'Got a bit of a headache coming on. They'll go down nicely with the whisky. Could you open it for me? I can't with my hands like this.'

Terry unscrewed the cap but didn't hand me the bottle straight away. Instead he held it up, reading the chemist's label.

'Bit serious for headache pills,' he said.

'It's since I got hurt. My ribs ache a bit. They're good, those pills. Just take the edge off any aches and pains. Sharpen you up a bit.'

Let him go for it, please. I was trying so hard not to tense up, to look over at him, to say encouragingly, 'Go on, why don't you have a couple too?' that my ribs really were hurting now with the stress of containing myself.

'Might do some myself an' all,' Terry said. 'I'm not feeling so good.'

I shrugged. 'Fine by me.'

Terry tipped his head back. Down the little red lane they went, helped on their way by a generous wash of whisky. I held out my mug and he poured a tot into that, and then a larger one into his own. If I could just keep him drinking, the pills would have him woozy in short order. He capped the bottle of whisky, put it at his feet and took a long pull at the coffee. I took the bottle and pretended to rattle out a couple of pills into my own mouth, then passed the bottle back to him.

'Aah, that's better,' I said with as much camaraderie as I could muster up. I gave him a friendly smile, but he wasn't looking at me, and he didn't speak for a while.

'It was such a simple idea,' he said finally, staring straight ahead. 'Just a few days and then everyfing back to normal and a couple of grand each for our trouble. Easiest money you'll ever make, he said.'

I looked down at the body on the floor. Terry hadn't let the paramedics take it away. God knew why. It was very dead.

'It was Sarah you were after, wasn't it?' I said.

'Well, a'course it was!' He stared at me blankly. 'Who'd'ja fink we were supposed to get?'

At least that knocked the Siobhan theory on the head.

'Can I take his balaclava off too?' I asked.

'Why?' Though Terry must have been hitting the whisky for a while, judging by the fire-hazard strength of his breath – have to be careful he didn't breathe directly on the mattress, it looked like one of those old inflammable ones – he didn't seem drunk. Adrenaline was still buoying him up, counteracting the effects of the drink like a measure of speed in a glass of Coke. Still, it couldn't last for ever. I sipped at my coffee and watched him do the same. His was nearly finished.

'I don't like balaclavas any more,' I said simply. It was true. The sight of the covered face was making me, if possible, even more nervous than the gun in Terry's hand.

'Oh.' He seemed to understand. 'Go on then. But don't forget I got you covered.'

He raised the automatic, pointing it at me as I bent down to pull the balaclava off. The chest wound was the only visible damage to the body; the handsome face was unmarked, the lids closed over those slanted eyes, the fair hair ruffling back from his forehead. I looked down at Vince for a long moment.

'You knew it was him, didn't'ja?' Terry said, his voice wavering. The gun wobbled in his hand. It was still pointing right at me. There was something hypnotic about the little black barrel. Terry covered me with it as I came back to sit down beside him, and I couldn't take my eyes from it, as if it wouldn't fire if I was staring it out. I kept imagining the bullets lying inside, shiny and snug in their little niches, willing them to stay there where it was comfortable and they had company.

'Sure,' I said, hearing the tension in my voice. 'That's how they found you. The cottage is in the name of one of Vince's companies. Once they checked back and found out you were his cousin, it was easy enough.'

I wasn't going to tell Terry how we had found out that he and Vince were cousins. He might resent it having been me who had remembered that Vince's surname was Greene, and connected it with the Terence Greene in the mugshot on Graves's desk.

'Vince said no one would ever find out about the cottage.'

'Vince was a bit optimistic about a lot of things, wasn't he?' I picked up my coffee. 'D'you mind not pointing that at me?'

'Oh, right. Sorry.' He dropped the automatic to his side again, resting it on his thigh, the barrel facing out towards the open door. A long sigh of relief dragged itself out through my lungs. 'Well, you're not wrong there. Y'know, I always fought that idea of his about that bird was fucked. But nah, he was sure it'd work. You'll see, he kept saying, She'll fall into my arms like she did before.'

'Before?' I drank some more coffee. The whisky was very calming, despite being rougher than sandpaper.

'That's 'ow they met.' The camp bed creaked under his weight as he shifted to face me. 'Sarah was really skint. She was living down the Old Kent Road in this crappy little dump and one night she was coming aht of the pub and this bloke grabbed her. She shouldn't of been on her own,' Terry said seriously. 'Asking for trouble, that is, in some of these places. Anyway, this bloke took her round the back of the pub and it was getting really nasty when Vince turned up like sodding James Bond. Pulled him off her and gave him a good kicking. She was well grateful. Fell for him then and there. Course, she didn't know why he was round the back in the first place. He'd come to do over the bloke who ran it cos he weren't paying up.'

'Protection money?'

'More or less. Funny, innit?' Terry grinned at the irony of the situation. 'Vince was well gone on Sarah, anyway. Well, they both was. Major romance and all that. But he couldn't stop playing the field. Some girl offers it on a plate, he's going to pick it up. That's Vince. And Sarah couldn't handle it. It didn't mean nuffing,' Terry said with a worldly-wise air. 'But she didn't like it all the same.'

'So she left him.'

'That's right. He was pretty cut-up, but he wasn't exactly slitting his wrists, know what I mean? And there were always loads of tarts after him. He was doing fine till he started seeing her on the box. That really did his nut. She was in that soap, yeah? And then she got this part in that series in Ibiza and she was never out of the women's mags what his mum had around the house. Vince went mental. He kept saying, That's my ex-girlfriend, and everyone'd take the piss. It got worse and worse. Finally he was like, All right, that's it, I got to get her back. He started ringing and sending flowers and that, but she was going out with this actor – you know, the one what was the vet on that series—'

'The one that got killed?' I prompted.

'Yeah, him. Paul Something.'

'Vince killed him, didn't he, Terry?'

Terry cleared his throat and looked down at Vince's body.

'No harm in telling you now, is there? That was later. I mean, when we'd already snatched you. Vince went round to Sarah's and found Paul there, picking up some of her stuff. He said this Paul bloke got cheeky with him and it all got a bit out of hand.'

I thought of the photos I had seen of Paul.

'Needed teaching a lesson, he said,' Terry continued.

'In what?' I said caustically. 'Advanced Mutilation? How To Get Your Stomach Cut Open? (Only for those who have already completed the beginners' module of this course.)' I took a deep breath, getting a grip on any parts of myself I could reach, and held up my mug. 'Give us a bit more whisky, eh? I seem to need it.'

Terry winced as he refilled my mug and then, automatically, his own. 'Vince doesn't like people cheeking him,' he said, drinking deep. 'Or the word "no". He's big about that – was big about that.

228

Don't like the word no, don't let me hear you say it or there'll be trouble.'

'And Sarah kept on saying no.'

'Well, yeah. So he got this idea. Set it all up again, Vince to the rescue, like before. He knew all about the letters she was getting from the AR lot.'

'How?' I said. The gun was still on Terry's thigh, but now that he had shifted it was pointed at my left hip, which was making me nervous. Steel pins through bone may be a powerful look on the catwalk but for everyday wear they can be rather cumbersome.

'Oh, they always kept in touch. So he fought, right, what if she got kidnapped? Few days in the cellar and then he comes in to save her. How could she resist that?'

'He must have wanted to punish her, too,' I said, 'for turning him down. Otherwise he could just have staged a kidnap and turned up to save her as they were dragging her off.'

'I don't know about that, do I?' Terry had ducked his head, staring at the gun barrel. He might have phrased this in the form of a question but it was one he definitely didn't want answered. I bet that this idea had never occurred to him before. And he didn't seem to like it much.

'And how was he going to explain it being his cottage?' I went on.

Terry knew this one. His head came up again. He was defending himself against the unspoken charge of having agreed to do something for Vince which stank worse than a blocked toilet during an outbreak of stomach flu. Look, his tone said, it wasn't such a stupid idea! Vince'd thought it all through!

'Vince never told no one about this place. I didn't even know till we got here. It was a secret. He said he'd sell it straight after he got Sarah out.' Terry looked away. 'I fink, you know, people he brought here, well, they never come back, know what I mean? One-way ticket to Casa Vince. That's what he told me. So –' Terry took another pull at the contents of his mug, which by now was whisky lightly flavoured with a few drops of cold coffee – 'what he was planning, right, was that after a few days we'd clear out and he'd've charged in. Vince to the rescue. He was gonna say that he'd been pulling strings to find out where she was, right? Vince knew everyone. He was gonna say that he'd had some mates lean on a couple of animal rights geezers in the clink to get them to find out where their mates was hiding Sarah. Then he'd've told them – that'd be us – we had an hour to clear out or else. He'd've got her out pronto and told her to keep it buttoned about how she escaped. He was sure as soon as she saw him she'd melt.'

He yawned without covering his mouth. His teeth looked like a Before photograph in an advertisement for dental reconstruction.

'Well, any bird would, right?' he added, sounding almost cocky. 'What wiv Prince Charming coming in to save ya.'

When I had nicknamed Terry Thick Boy I had done an even better job than I knew. Did he not realise what he was saying? Vince would never have left him and Mass alive, cousin or no cousin. Forget all that stuff about getting them to clear out; Vince would have shot them both and carried Sarah out over their dead bodies. That was the only way it made sense, the only way Vince could have been the real Prince Charming, James Bond surviving a hail of bullets, picking on two targets weaker than cups of tea in a Chinese restaurant. Sarah wouldn't have dared tell anyone about the shoot-out, to protect Vince; and later on, unknown to her, he'd have gone back to the cottage to dispose of the bodies as he did all of the visitors who had one-way tickets to Casa Vince. And that would explain why he had used a pair of incompetents like Mass and Terry, instead of more professional muscle for hire. The latter might have suspected that Vince would be double-crossing them. Terry, his eyes still shining with admiration for his dead cousin, had swallowed the story whole.

'Only you guys got me instead, and then Vince got jealous of Paul and slit him up,' I said. 'Just one little hitch after the other – Terry?'

His head was nodding forward, the mug loose in his hand. I watched the automatic like a rabbit does a snake. His grip on it still seemed firm enough.

He yawned again, rolling back his shoulders. I said:

'And why didn't he kill me when he found out I wasn't Sarah?'

Terry shot me a horrified glance.

'You taking the piss? We'd never've gone for that! You hadn't done nuffing!'

Terry was giving Mass too much credit. The latter would have considered it a positive pleasure to have knocked me over the head and buried me in the woods. But Terry was the conscience of the pair, the one who had salved his own, at least partially, by Sarah's callous attitude about animal rights. If Vince had killed me he'd have had to have taken out Mass and Terry too, as witnesses; and then he would be left without his pair of comparatively untraceable kidnappers. He probably hadn't wanted to sacrifice them for such a poor result; maybe he had still been planning a possible kidnap of Sarah, if she proved unmalleable, and wanted them in reserve.

'Well, not till you tried to escape,' Terry admitted. 'Mass wanted to – well, never mind. But Vince said if you disappeared for ever there'd be too much of a hoo-hah.' He coughed. 'We put our balaclavas back on while he was knocking you out,' he explained. 'I fought if he knew you'd seen our faces we'd all be in big trouble.'

'We'd all have been dead,' I said frankly. Terry had saved my life along with his. 'So what about that bloke you had chained up?'

'Oh. He was asking round this sabbing group I used to be wiv. Bloke who ran it gave me a bell, said I might want to watch me step. It was more Mass, really. He's the psycho,' Terry said affectionately. 'Got the both of us kicked out, he did. So I told Vince this bloke Kevin was sniffing around and he did his nut, said there was a Kevin looked just like that on the TV thing Sarah was doing. He was –' Terry looked at me, his eyelids heavy – 'he was . . .'

'So Vince picked him up?' I said quickly, before Terry could make the connection between Lurch and me.

'We went round to his. I drove, Vince sat in the back. Showed him this, made him get in . . .' Terry waved the gun, pointing it at me more by accident than design. Still, I flinched back. He squinted down the barrel for a moment and then, seeming to find it increasingly heavy, let it fall back to his thigh. It slid backwards onto the camp bed, taking his hand with it. Now it was not only between him and me, but pointing to the floor. I breathed again.

'Then Vince started doing him over,' Terry was saying. 'It was bad, it was really bad . . . cut his back like somefing out of some torture scene from a film . . .' His head was nodding down to his chest, the words increasingly slurred. 'I couldn't take it, he was gonna kill him . . . he'd've definitely've killed him . . . and when I told him to stop he just laughed, and then he told me how he done Mass . . . and there was the shooter right there, what he'd done Mass with, and before I knew it I'd picked it up . . . it was like a bomb going off, the noise . . . and then I didn't know what to do. It was me or him. Cos he'd have done me an' all, you know?'

Terry's head was as far down as it would go. The mug was tilting in his hand, the angle more and more extreme, till finally the few drops of whisky still left inside began to trickle out, dripping onto his trousers. Terry didn't notice. I sat, paralysed with indecision, wondering whether to make a dash for it. But it would take me a good few strides to reach the door, and if he realised what I was doing he would shoot me. I was sure of it. He wouldn't fire while I was sitting next to him, but to shoot me in the back in his drunken, drugged state would be a reflex, done before he had time to think. I didn't move. I just watched the mug as his fingers finally loosened their hold on the handle and it fell to the ground, shattering on the flagstones.

Then it happened very fast. The noise of breaking crockery startled Terry; his head jerked up, his feet shot out and the gun went off. He was right. Even a handgun firing in the cellar made an almighty row. For a moment everything went black.

When I opened my eyes again I was behind the camp bed, clutching onto the mattress as if it would protect me from a bullet. Terry must have got his finger stuck against the trigger; ricochets pinged around the cellar like a flight of crazed screaming bees rebounding off the walls. What seemed like an endless pause followed. And then the basement exploded to life again. Suddenly it was full of people. Someone was bending over me, asking if I was hurt, helping me to my feet. Frantically I checked myself for damage. I was so hyped-up by now there could be a hole in my back that came out through my windpipe and I wouldn't notice.

I could stand; I seemed to have all the limbs with which I had started the day; my ribs hurt to buggery but that was nothing new. Bloody Terry still had my painkillers. I looked over to him, hanging between two officers, still screaming. There was the smell of cordite in the air and for some reason tiny flakes of material and what looked like foam were falling lightly to the ground around him.

'My foot!' he was yelling. 'My *foot!*'

When the gun had gone off, it had been pointing through the mattress at his right foot. Where once had been a fourteen-hole boot was a bloody stump of flesh, ragged with black leather-substitute, torn up as if a wild animal had been chewing on it. Terry's foot had taken the whole charge of a fully loaded automatic at close range.

CHAPTER TWENTY-TWO

'You left me no choice,' Gav said. He held the knife almost casually. Which only intensified its menace. 'You realise that? You left me no bleeding choice, you cunt. You think I like having to do this?'

'No, Gav – Gav, *please*—' Chaz tried to back away but was held too securely by the man behind him to be able to move. He was sweating again, great drops on his forehead like glycerine tears.

'No, I don't like it. Right. Good boy, Chaz. Got it in one.'

And with that Gav lunged forward, sinking the knife into Chaz's belly and jerking it upward with one short brutal stroke, his other hand on Chaz's shoulder for leverage, his face pressed up against his victim's.

'*Aaah!* What the—' Gav exclaimed, just as the knife sank in. He jumped back, looking down at his hand in disbelief.

'I'm all *wet!*' he complained, in the most Hugo of tones. 'What on *earth*—'

Everyone else on set was doubled up with laughter.

'I am completely fucking soaked!' Hugo was still in shock. 'What – God, Keith, I thought you'd pissed yourself!'

Keith was crying with laughter.

'You should see your *face*,' he gulped out. 'That was *hysterical*.'

'This is you, Phil, isn't it?' Hugo waved the trick knife menacingly at the director, who was laughing harder than anyone.

'Careful, Hugo,' Phil managed. 'You could really wet yourself with that—'

He gave a great roar of laughter which set the rest of the crew off again.

'I really thought Keith had pissed his boxers,' Hugo admitted.

'It's because you're always complaining about how much I sweat, darling,' Keith explained. 'Phil thought it would be funny.'

'Well, I can see that it was a riot of laughter for everybody else,' Hugo said rather aloofly. 'And you do sweat like a lager lout on the beach at Torremolinos.'

'Hey, you try *holding* him,' said the actor who had been pinning Keith's arms behind his back. He had already let him go; now he wiped his hands down on his trousers.

'Sorry, loves,' Keith said flirtatiously. 'I always get over-excited when I'm under restraint.'

'Now that I can understand,' Hugo said. 'But must you perspire as well?'

'Phil?' said the first AD. 'Now everyone's had their fun, maybe we should get in those close-ups before lunch?'

Phil sighed.

'All right, all right,' he said wearily. 'OK, boys, we've had our five minutes of play, back to hard reality.'

'OK, close-up of Keith, can we hurry it along, please?' The first AD was on the other side of the studio, but her stentorian tones cut across the set as if they'd been a blowtorch.

'Come off to the trailer,' the costume designer said to Hugo. 'I'll get you dried off.'

'You could have seen me half-clothed at any time!' Hugo complained, following her away. 'All you had to do was ask! There was absolutely no need to stage this elaborate set-up just so you could get my trousers off.' He dabbed at them fastidiously. 'How come it didn't wet me the first time?' he said to Phil as he passed him.

'Switch in the handle turns it into a backwards water pistol when the blade starts to retract,' said Phil with admirable concision. 'Good one, isn't it? First time I've used it but it won't be the last. Talk about a result.'

Joanne was picking her way through the tangle of wires and past the camera set-up.

'At least you're sup*posed* to be sweating,' she said to Keith, dabbing at his forehead. 'We just want to take it down a little.'

Joanne, I thought, wasn't looking at her best. And, aware of that as a make-up artist must be, she was over-compensating. Her flirtatious manner was brittle and exaggerated and her own make-up was executed with a frightening competence which only made it look more artificial. It had been a long shoot, and there was still a way to go. Six days out of seven with no natural light was turning everyone into grey-skinned moles. I just didn't think that lipstick the colour of a Caribbean sunset helped, no matter how carefully it was applied.

I wandered off, hugging the wall to avoid being trampled by the art department, thundering past en masse like a herd of elephants who had to turn a watering hole round a hundred and eighty degrees by teatime. I was feeling spacey and detached.

The rehearsal bell went. It was unusual for Phil to take that trouble for a close-up. But after playing a practical joke maybe he felt the need to restore some seriousness to the proceedings. As I reached the far door Jimmy came up behind me to station himself there, barring the way. He too looked rough, and not from an excess of late nights with Karen. I had heard that she had transferred her attentions to a producer based in the main building.

'All right, Jimmy,' I said, going past.

'Nice to know someone is,' he said gloomily.

The drizzle outside seemed as constant a feature of the studios as the stages themselves. I scampered around the honey wagon, heading for Hugo's trailer, fishing out the keys from my pocket as I went. I planned to settle in on his couch, prop myself up with pillows and read some trashy magazines.

Foiled again. Almost as soon as the door closed behind me, someone was knocking on it.

'Yeah?' I called ungraciously.

Sarah put her head through. 'I heard you come in,' she said. 'I knew it couldn't be Hugo, he's tied to the set— My God! Your bandages are off!'

'Only the nose.'

'But still! God, I can actually see your face! Come through next door for a moment, I've got the kettle on.'

'I was going to have a bit of a lie-down,' I temporised.

Sarah dismissed this. 'You've got loads of time for that! You're going back with Hugo, right? We won't be finished till seven. Come on.'

Her unusual authority, not to mention high spirits, were too much for my weakened mind to resist. Five minutes later we were ensconced in Sarah's cosy trailer, curled up on the sofa with comforting mugs of tea. Sarah had taken to burning those violently expensive single-scent candles in minimally designed square glass holders which supermodels always rank highest on their Must-Haves For Travel lists, along with cashmere throws and Evian water. Mmn, right. Those lists would have a touch more credibility if they ran: 1. Drug dealer's mobile number in city of arrival. 2. Drug dealer's home number, ditto. 3. Laxatives.

The latest candle smelt pleasant, though I couldn't identify the perfume.

'What's this?' I asked, sniffing the air.

'Tobacco leaves,' Sarah said. 'It's nice, isn't it?'

'I preferred the fresh grass.'

She pulled a face. 'Made me sneeze. So!' She raised her mug. 'To your nose! Back to normal!'

We clinked mugs. 'Do you really think it's back to normal?' I said, depressed. 'I was hoping it was a bit straighter.'

'It was always straight,' Sarah said.

'No it wasn't. It came out bumpy in photographs.'

'Oh, did it?' She was immediately serious, as only an actor could be about that kind of flaw.

'Mmn. Well, we'll see. It's still a little swollen. I'll wait for that to go down.'

'It was Vince, wasn't it, who broke your nose?' Sarah said. 'That was when you were escaping, and the other two were chained up in the cellar. Hugo told me.'

'Yeah, it was.'

I was surprised that she had mentioned Vince's name; I would have thought the whole subject might have been too painful for her. Especially in the context of the damage he had done to me. But she didn't seem to have any inhibitions about discussing him.

'I can tell *you* this,' Sarah said intently. 'You'll understand.'

She looked wonderful, I realised. It was the first time I'd seen her since my return to the cottage. After Paul's murder she had been little more than a giant set of tear ducts in full flow, a washed-out, boneless waif; now she was so lit up that all she needed was a single-note scent and you could have stuck her on the coffee table in a square glass holder.

'I feel – released,' she was saying, her pale eyes shining. 'Liberated. Ever since I heard about Vince being killed, it's been like someone let me out of a cage. Do you remember what I was like after Paul was killed?'

I grimaced. 'You looked like a wet dishcloth Vince had thrown round his neck.'

'Exactly. There was something about him that drained me. That's what he wanted. Well, not a dishcloth, exactly, but an accessory, you know? Something hanging on his arm. He never really left me alone after we broke up. Every so often he'd send flowers or a note or a present. You know, checking in, reminding me he was still out there. It stopped me getting serious with anyone else. I never realised that till now, but it's true. There was always Vince, hovering in the background. I think subconsciously I knew what would happen if I settled down with a guy, what Vince would do to him. He'd started ringing me, too. Asking to meet up. He'd seen the articles about the whole animal rights thing and he said he thought I needed someone to keep an eye on me. It really wound me up. All very well being over-protective, but that didn't mean he wasn't going to be eyeing up all the pretty girls wherever we went.'

'So didn't you suspect him?'

'It never occurred to me he had anything to do with the kidnap. I mean, now I know I can see it was typical Vince. He thought he could do anything, that the normal rules didn't apply to him. But it never entered my mind at the time.'

She shrugged.

'I really meant when Paul was killed,' I said. 'The way he died. That was a revenge kill, wasn't it?'

Sarah looked horribly uncomfortable.

'I did suspect,' she admitted in a small voice. 'That's partly why I was such a dishcloth. But what could I have done? I was so scared by that time, everything had beaten me down. And, I mean, I might have suspected he'd had something to do with Paul being killed, but not kidnapping you. I was still petrified something would happen to you. Or that they'd come back for me. And Vince was keeping me safe. Or so I thought. I told everyone there was nothing going on with us, and in a way there wasn't. I mean, I wouldn't sleep with him yet. I was too upset. And scared, I guess.' She pulled an expressive face. 'For a while I managed to convince myself that if I just got back together properly with Vince, everything would be OK. God, you realise how easy it is to get into this battered-wife mentality, you know? Just as long as I can keep him from exploding, it'll be all right. And I still loved him, in a way. I always did. He was so charismatic.'

She shivered, but not in remembered fear. It was as if she was shaking something off her shoulders.

'I loved him *so much*,' she said wistfully. 'It was amazing. The way we met, too. Do you know what happened? It was down in this really seedy part of the Old Kent Road, I was coming out of a pub and this guy put his hand over my mouth and pulled me into a back alley. It was horrible. He was trying to pull my skirt up, he was going to rape me, I was completely terrified – and then suddenly he was pulled off me. Like a giant hand coming down from the sky. I staggered back and the next thing I knew he was on the ground, bleeding, and Vince was standing over his body, holding out his hand to me. Looking like something out of a film. We just fell in love then and there. It was irresistible.'

'And then he started screwing around?' I prompted.

Sarah didn't ask how I knew. She snorted in anger, putting her empty mug down hard on the table.

'*Started*? He never stopped. That was Vince. You know how physical he was, he couldn't stop touching you. I'd look round at one of the parties we went to and he'd always have his hands on some girl. At first I told myself that was just Vince's way, he was really tactile. Then I caught him at a party with some snooker player's tarted-up girlfriend, and he had the nerve to tell me it was my fault for not dressing up more. He said he'd take me out and buy me anything I wanted if I'd just make more of an effort. You can imagine. Dresses slit up to the waist and lots of jewellery. It just wasn't my thing.'

Sarah gestured to the baggy jeans and fleece jacket she was wearing.

'The only thing I wanted him to buy me was trainers,' she confided. 'They're so expensive. But he wouldn't, not even for a birthday present.' She stuck her feet out and contemplated the swollen, bulbous, luridly striped monstrosities on her feet with a smug smile. 'At least now I can afford my own. I've got fifteen pairs.'

I averted my eyes. They had more plastic inserts than a porn star, but the effect was considerably less pleasing. I was with Vince, at least on this one.

'How's Lurch doing?' Sarah asked. 'I haven't been able to visit him for the last couple of days.'

'Oh, not too bad. He gets out of hospital tomorrow.'

'Already?' Sarah looked incredulous. 'God, the NHS chucks you out faster than the speed of light.'

'He's going to go and stay at his new girlfriend's,' I said. 'She's already dosing him with Bach flower remedies and calendula cream and God knows what.'

Di hadn't forgiven me, either for hanging up on her or for getting Lurch involved with Mass and Terry in the first place. Still, as I had pointed out to her yesterday over Lurch's hospital bed, if I hadn't been guilty of the latter she would never have met him. I was leaving her to ponder that one at leisure. And she had done Lurch a world of good. Even the nurses had admitted that the arnica cream seemed to be working for the scars on his back. I had the feeling that Lurch was secretly quite proud of them. It was like some awful tribal male rite of passage. He had already referred to *A Man Called Horse* twice, with more than a hint of self-conscious pride.

Someone knocked on the door of the trailer.

'Sarah?' Siobhan called. 'You're wanted in costume.' She opened the door. 'Only I thought you might want a drag on this first,' she said conspiratorially, lowering her voice as she displayed the joint she was holding. 'Just got it off Sanj.'

'Just a couple of puffs,' Sarah said. 'I don't want to be too out of it.'

Leaning against the bathroom door, Siobhan lit up. In a couple of seconds the delicate aroma of tobacco leaves was a distant memory.

'OK, that's my lot,' Sarah said, handing it back to Siobhan reluctantly. 'God, what I wouldn't give to stay in here and get stoned all afternoon . . . You two wait here and finish it if you want. Just snub the door locked behind you when you're done.'

'Ooh, luxury,' Siobhan said, settling herself on the part of sofa that Sarah had just vacated. 'Better make sure I don't get too cosy, though, or I'll pass out. The one thing about smoking a joint behind the honey wagon is the drizzle keeps you awake.'

She passed it to me. I took a drag to be companionable and handed it back to her.

'How's Sanjay?' I asked.

'Oh, cool! He's moving in with me!' Siobhan looked very happy. 'And it looks like we're both on this ITV film they're shooting in Cornwall the month after next. We want to learn to surf.' She blew out a gust of smoke. 'No, it's all going really well. What about you?'

'Splint comes off next week.'

'Great.' Siobhan seemed rather deflated by this, all the good news I could muster. 'Well, Sarah looks gorgeous, doesn't she?' Whether it was the dope or the success of her relationship, Siobhan was clearly determined to think positive. It was like being trapped in a small room with Julie Andrews in *The Sound Of Music*. At least Siobhan didn't have a guitar or a floral skirt.

'Yeah, she looks great,' I agreed. 'I just wonder when she's going to realise that no one's found out yet who put the fox in her bathroom. At the moment she's all keyed up about Vince being off her back for good, but when she stops and thinks about it she's bound to fathom that he couldn't have done that. Nor could Mass or Terry. They barely knew how this place worked.'

Siobhan started giggling. I waited patiently, but the laughter just went on and on. Finally I took the joint out of her hand. It was about to fall on the sofa anyway; she was so relaxed that her fingers were as floppy as old carrots.

'Did you do it?' I said suspiciously.

'No,' she said, still giggling, 'but I know who did! Give me that back!'

'Not till you tell me.'

'Cow. OK, it was Joanne. Gimme, gimme . . .' Siobhan reached out her hand.

'How do you know?'

'God, you're a hardarse.' She caught her breath. 'Me and Sanj saw her down Portobello Market about a month ago, buying the fox at a stall. Sanj said it'd look better in that awful lipstick she wears than she does – you know how bright it is, I always think it'd go fluorescent in a power cut . . . go on, Sam, pass it over, a joke's a joke . . .'

I handed over the joint. Siobhan relit it and drew on it as hard as if she were an asthmatic puffing at her inhaler.

'I never even thought Joanne had it in for Sarah,' I said, baffled.

'No, me neither. But it was definitely the same fox. And I could tell she was really enjoying it when Sarah was all upset, you know? I mean, I wouldn't have noticed if I hadn't been keeping an eye on her. But she looked dead smug.'

She took another long drag.

'Right, that's it. I should get back. Jem'll be screaming for me.'

We left Sarah's suite together. Siobhan dashed away in the direction of the costume trailer and I followed more slowly, hugging the sheltered side where there was little rain. The make-up trailer was the next one over to Hugo and Sarah's. I found myself ascending the steps. As always there was a little double-take as I entered, a sense of disorientation before I remembered that the make-up trailer was set on chocks and didn't sway gently like the others. No sea legs needed.

Joanne was inside, working on a blonde wig for Maria. She looked up as I came in, seeing me in the mirror in front of her.

'You've got your bandage off,' she observed. 'Looks like most of the swelling's gone down. They did a nice job of resetting it.'

'Professional approval,' I said cheerfully. 'How nice.'

Joanne went back to the rollers she was setting into the wig, her movements precise and unhurried. Everyone on a TV set was so used to working with an audience that they had no self-consciousness about it.

'I just remembered that you worked on *Country Vets*,' I said, perching on one of the make-up stools, a little way along from the wig Joanne was now spraying with setting lotion. The starchy chemical smell was not unpleasant. 'First series, right?'

'Right,' Joanne said shortly.

'So you knew Paul.'

'Of course.'

'How well did you know him?'

'What is this,' she said crossly, 'the Spanish Inquisition?'

'Just little me,' I said affably, looking at her in the mirror. 'Idle curiosity. I was wondering whether you had something going with Paul then. It would explain why you were pissed off enough with Sarah to put that fox in her dressing room.'

Joanne's head jerked up, the bottle of lotion falling from her hand and rolling along the floor till it hit the opposite wall. Whoever had put the chocks under the trailer wheels hadn't got them quite level.

'How do—' she started. 'I mean, *why* do you think it was me?' She was trying for casually surprised, and failing dismally.

'I saw you buying the fox in Portobello Market,' I lied.

'I don't know what you're talking about,' Joanne said unconvincingly. She had rested both her hands on the counter in front of her; looking down at them to avoid meeting my gaze, she realised that they were shaking and pulled them sharply away.

'Come on,' I said. 'I won't tell anyone else, I promise. I'm just curious. Was it because of Paul?'

'I haven't got the time to stand around here listening to this rubbish,' Joanne snapped. Whipping past me, she practically ran out of the trailer.

I kept staring at myself in the mirror, tilting my head from side to side to see if that bump on my nose was still there. A few seconds later I heard someone coming up the steps and turned to see if it was Joanne, having worked out a story and wanting to try it out on me.

'Sam?'

Julie, Joanne's assistant, was such a quiet thing I didn't think I'd exchanged more than two words with her the entire shoot. She put down what she and Joanne called their toolbags and stood looking at me, her head tilted slightly to one side. The blonde curls were carefully pinned and sprayed into place, her eyes outlined with dark blue liner, her round cheeks blushed and shaded to give them more contours; and yet Julie was such a shy retiring type that she was always the last person to be noticed in a crowd. It was her stance, the ducked head, the human equivalent of a dog scraping its belly along the ground to signify submissiveness.

'I heard what you and Jo were saying,' she informed me, her voice as light and faint as a puff of air. 'Don't give her a hard time about it, please. She won't do it again. Honestly. She got such a scare when you were kidnapped in mistake for Sarah, she was terrified they'd come after her. I had to follow her round tidying people up. She was sending them out looking like freaks.' Putting out a hand, Julie closed the door. 'Don't want anyone else hearing, do we?' she said. 'These things are terrible for eavesdropping.'

She walked over and stood behind me, turning my head to face the mirror once more with a touch so delicate her fingertips hardly brushed my skin. We stared at each other, her face above mine.

'I could cover up the rest of that bruising for you,' she offered. 'I haven't got anything to do for an hour or so – it's just Keith and Hugo for a bit, and Joanne does them. Want me to try?'

'Sure, why not?'

Julie looked pleased. 'Great,' she said. 'It's good practice for me, you know. I mean, you're doing me a favour. Swing round, then.'

She started mixing up a base colour for my skin, her eyes flicking back and forward to my face as if I were a canvas which needed retouching. The brush strokes were as light as her own fingertips, a gentle dabbing of my skin which was strangely pleasurable.

'Does it hurt?' she said after a while.

'Doesn't even tickle.'

'Oh good. Because that's part of it too. I mean, you could do the best job in the world but if you're poking at someone's bruises they're not exactly going to ask for you back, are they?'

Julie narrowed her blue-rimmed eyes. I noticed that her mascara was dark blue as well, and reflected on the oddness of her own make-up being so out of date. 'Mmn, lots of yellowing round that eye,' she said to herself, dipping the brush into the mauve once more.

'Jo just got a bit carried away,' she said after a while, as if there had been no break in the conversation. 'And Sarah was being a real cow,

244

there's no denying it. You remember how she was carrying on, before? She got up everyone's noses. Even Karen couldn't stand her, and she's usually the first one to calm things down.'

I didn't say anything. It was very restful for me. Clearly, Julie knew exactly what she wished to say; all I had to do was sit up straight and keep my head still, and she would tell me what I wanted to know as her brush flickered like a butterfly across my skin. Maybe she found it easier to talk when her hands were busy; maybe, shy as she was in company, she preferred a captive audience of one, so that she couldn't be rushed.

'Close your eyes,' she said, her breath on my right cheek scented with mint. The ability to cover up bruises without inflicting pain might be important for a make-up artist, but lack of halitosis was crucial.

Julie dabbed so lightly on my eyelid that I could feel every individual tiny bristle in the brush, soft as human hair.

'Jo did have a thing with Paul on *Country Vets*,' she said. 'You were right about that. I don't think she was that mad about him, but she did like him, and they went on seeing each other afterwards.'

'Till he met Sarah?' My voice sounded very loud after Julie's tranquil half-whisper. I regretted having spoken; it was as if I had broken a spell. 'Sorry,' I found myself saying.

Julie went on working, but there was a long pause before she finally volunteered:

'There were lots of girls before Sarah. Nothing as serious, though. But Jo was basically over him, I think. What got her was that Sarah was so casual about him. He didn't really mean anything to her. Jo was really annoyed by that. And when all the trouble started with those animal rights letters Sarah got so *snappy*.'

Julie said this as if it was the worst thing imaginable, which probably for her it was.

'Jo should just have told her off when she started playing up. It wasn't like her, really. Sarah, I mean. It was all nerves. If Jo had been firm from the start I think she'd have calmed down. But she wouldn't say anything, and Sarah got worse, and Jo finally said to me, "She needs teaching a lesson."'

Julie took a step back, considered me critically, reached for a sponge, dipped it in powder and started rocking it back and forth over my face to set the make-up.

'I think she was almost looking for an excuse, actually,' she observed, her mouth an inch away from mine. 'Mmn. Right. Do you want me to make you up as well?'

I nodded, not wanting to speak.

'I'll do some eyeliner. You'll hardly feel that going on. I don't want to drag at your eyelids with a pencil, they still look sore. Close your eyes again.'

The eyeliner brush, needle-fine, swept along the roots of my lashes. Julie's touch was sure as a surgeon's.

'She didn't actually tell me what she was going to do,' Julie said. 'But I guessed. I mean, I'd have guessed anyway, but I definitely did when I heard the writing on the mirror was done in pink lipstick. The way I saw it was, anyone who'd bothered to get a stuffed fox would have bought some red lipstick too. So if they didn't, that meant it was Jo, because she'd worry that they'd see bright red lipstick and think of her. It's like her signature.'

I had ruled out Joanne for precisely that reason. Julie was cleverer than I was.

'Pull your lips back across your teeth,' she instructed. I felt the stiff tip of a lip brush outlining my mouth and then filling it in.

'Just a little colour in the cheeks . . .' she murmured. 'This stuff's brilliant. It's the biggest thing on my budget.'

She squeezed a lurid red gel out of a silver tube and dabbed it onto the apples of my cheeks.

'I know it looks bright, but you'll hardly notice it,' she reassured. 'It blends in really well. OK, here you go.'

She swung round the chair. I couldn't believe what I saw in the mirror.

'Is it OK?' she said, sounding hesitant.

'It's a miracle. I look better than ever. You're a genius.'

My skin was smooth and flawless, tinged with a hint of colour, the black liner flicking my eyes up at the corners, accentuating their slight slant. Julie had done my lips a lightly transparent cherry red which made my skin look paler and my eyes even darker than usual. Not content with simply covering the bruising, she had dotted every one of those tiny red marks everyone has on their faces with concealer. It looked as if I had been airbrushed to perfection. My mole was even darker and more striking against the unreality of this ideal background.

'Will you come and live with me for ever?' I said hopefully.

She smiled, pleased. 'I'm glad you like it. You can hardly see the bruising, anyway.'

'Hardly see it? It's completely vanished!' I touched my face in awe. 'You are a fucking genius!'

'Thanks.'

'Can I ask you something?'

She nodded, shy again now that we were on even terms.

'Are you seeing anyone right now?'

'No, not really.'

'Well, what kind of man do you go for? What's your type?'

'Oh, big,' she said seriously. 'Tall and chunky and nice-looking. Kind-looking. Not trendy or anything. I like them to be – comfortable.'

'Like an old sofa.'

'Exactly.'

'Why don't you come out for a drink with me and Hugo tonight?' I suggested. 'We're meeting up with a friend of mine. I think you two would get on really well.'

'OK,' she said.

Tom would owe me big-time for this. It sounded as if he and Julie were made for each other.

I showed off my new improved face around the tea urn, to a chorus of oohs and aahs that was very flattering. But I was too worried about it being washed off by the rain to stay for long. I retreated to Hugo's suite to wait for him, wanting him to get the full effect of my temporary perfection. And his reaction did not disappoint.

'My God,' he said as he caught sight of me. I had turned on all the lights for the full effect. 'My *God*. It's the Sam prototype doll. Do you look like that all over? I mean, did they paint out your nipples and your appendix scar?'

'No, I'm human from the neck down.'

'Glad to hear it. You look rather frightening all flawless. It's so unlike you. What happened?'

'Julie used me for bruise cover practice. Oh, she's coming out for a drink with us tonight.'

Hugo pulled a face. 'Did you really have to go that far to thank her? I mean, I can see she's done a meisterwork on you, but the thought of making conversation with that shy little snip of a thing for hours—'

'She's not that bad,' I said loyally. 'You just have to let her do the talking. At her own pace.'

Hugo nearly choked.

'How you must have suffered! My poor sweet!'

'Anyway, she's for Tom.'

'Julie?' Hugo looked thoughtful. 'Blonde – tick. Thin – tick. Quiet – tick. Air of fragility – tick. You may be onto something there. But what about her?'

'She likes men who look like old sofas,' I said triumphantly.

'Say no more. It's a done deal. God, I need a drink.'

He bent down to open the little fridge.

'Don't tell me you finished all the Chablis – no, there's a bit left. Lucky for you, my girl.'

He swivelled round, glass in hand, and eyed me suspiciously.

'What's up? Beyond your beauty makeover. You're strangely quiet. If this is the effect Julie has on you I shall ban you from seeing her and Tom when they get married.'

'I've had a brilliant idea,' I said smugly. 'And you'll never guess where it came from. The cellar. Where they had me when I was kidnapped.'

Hugo still looked baffled. 'Don't tell me you're going to do some ghastly torture dungeon installation.'

'Nope. Cockroaches,' I said happily. 'Giant motorised cockroaches. Whizzing all over the floor. You go into this darkened room and there are these giant motorised cockroaches making that clickety cockroach-on-the-move noise—'

'Forgive me if I don't nod knowingly at that reference—'

'—only they react to the heat in your body so they never actually bump into you. When they get within a foot of you they turn at a right angle. But you don't know that till you work it out.'

'Do they bump into each other?'

I hadn't thought this one through.

'I don't know,' I admitted. 'I want them to look quite realistic, though, so probably not. Or they'd get their legs stuck together and fall over. What do you think?'

'Can you actually do that heat-reacting thing?'

'Oh sure. I mean, I can't, but I know people who can.'

'Well, you know perfectly well what I'm going to say. It's a revolting idea, it's thoroughly exploitative of your recent horrendous experience and it bears only a faint resemblance to what most people would consider art.'

'You really think it's that good?'

'Better. It'll be a roaring success.'

We clinked glasses.

'And when it is,' Hugo said, 'the Chablis is on you. Which,' he added sternly, indicating the empty bottle, 'will make a long-overdue change.'